# *NEXT BIG THING*

## A Novel by Terry Kitchen

urban campfire press
pob 133
boston ma 02131
www.terrykitchen.com

All Shadowland lyrics © 2013 Terry Kitchen, urban campfire music, BMI.

Jules Shear lyrics used by permission:

"Lovers by Rote" by Jules Shear © 1978 Unichappell Music Inc., BMI.

"Convict" by Jules Shear © 1978 Unichappell Music Inc., BMI.

Cover design by Francisco Gonzalez.

Author photo by Tim Casey.

ISBN-13: 978-1491096895

ISBN-10: 1491096896

*For Dennis Brennan and Rick Berlin,*

*the two truest believers I know.*

"If you're gonna spend your life beating your head against a wall, you should at least pick a wall you like."

–Billy Zoom, *X*

# 0. *REWIND:* Harding, Ohio, August 198*1*

*Killing time.*
*Just killing time.*
*Just killing time 'til time runs out.*
*Just killing time 'til time kills us.*

I put down my pencil, strum a minor chord and sing. Not quite. Needs more irony, a twist. I keep strumming, trying variations: *'til their time comes, 'til there's no more time to kill, 'til it's d-e-a-d dead.* I shake my head, try another chord. I take off my glasses, rub away the droplets of moisture that have collected in the stuffy August heat.

Maybe I should take a break, call Chas, go swimming, see if Will's girlfriend Jackie is sunning herself at the town pool in her bikini again. With the top untied. Jesus, lucky Will.

*No.* I want to get the song done, by rehearsal, so I can hear it with the band. I slip the wire frames back around my ears, pick up my pencil again. *Focus, Zodzniak.* I write a line, scratch it out, try another. I sense movement, watch a fly walk across the screen of my attic bedroom window, looking for a way out. I know the feeling. I lean forward, slide the screen up half an inch, but the fly buzzes back inside and alights on the upturned edge of a dusty Mott the Hoople poster I'd thumbtacked to the low angled ceiling back in high school.

Great, now I've got weird compound fly eyes staring down at me as well as every rock star in the pantheon, all wondering what I'm going to come up with. David, Lou, Jules: *Whatcha got, kid? Come on, we're waiting.* I see John, arms folded across his New York City sleeveless. What would he say if he saw me slaving? *Don't force it, Mark. Let it come to you. Look around, round, round.*

I take Lennon's advice, stare out at the church steeple poking up through the canopy of maple trees. I notice half of the leaves are downside up, like a summer storm's coming. I picture Jackie's untethered bikini top, dancing in the breeze. *Focus, Zodzniak!* Down on the ground, catching a sliver of sun, is a rectangle of white amidst the green. I realize it's a headstone, and I feel an involuntary pang. It doesn't jolt like it used to, but it gives me an idea. *Grave stone, grave plot, same spot.* I scribble a couple more lines, roll my guitar over and strum.

*Maybe.*


## 1. *FAST FORWARD:* I-84, Connecticut, December 1985

*Fuck Will. Fuckin' Will. Fuckin' fuck-face Will.*

That's what I've been muttering, like a karmic death mantra, for the past eight hours. Our record release party is *tonight*, in Boston, and I'm somewhere near Danbury, Connecticut, speeding back in the world's ugliest rent-a-car from the pressing plant on Long Island, where our record was just assembled – *this morning.* I've got the pedal maxed, and I'm bobbing and weaving between cargo trucks in a valiant effort to get the vinyl – and me – back in time for the show.

Of course the radio's broken, and it's also drizzling, so add the intermittent metallic rasp of worn-out wipers etching twin colorless rainbows into pock-marked glass:

*Fuck Will.* SCREECH. Repeat.

I wouldn't mind the Hero's Quest if it wasn't all so completely *unnecessary.* The album should have been – would have been – done months ago, but every step of the way, from choosing the songs to whether to multitrack the handclaps to what exact fraction of an inch high to make the lettering, the aforementioned Willard – our prima pretty donna boy bass player – had to put in his three cents. And then scream like a bad haircut if he didn't get his way.

Okay, in a democracy everyone's entitled to their own wrong opinion, even Will, but more and more his opinion seems entirely based on negating *mine.* If I wanted to open side two with "Risking Your Life to Rescue a Dead Man," he'd say it works anywhere *except* side two, cut one. Then we'd have to line up the swing votes, Boone and Chas, bribing or blackmailing them into our corner. If we didn't have Wayne, our producer, as tiebreaker we'd still be recording the first track.

Will's recalcitrance would just be a pain – a royal, bucktoothed bite-in-the-shorts pain, but just a pain nonetheless – if

I didn't sometimes get outvoted about important stuff. Like the drums on "Dogtown Rain." Chas is a *great* drummer, subtle even, so why make him sound like a robot, and make us sound like fucking Duran Duran Duran? "Because they sell a lot of records" is not a valid response. And the constant bickering's also cost us *time*, and in the pop world timing is everything. (Just ask the Amplifiers, whom you've never heard of, because their record label went bust – the week their album was released.)

It didn't used to be this way. Back in high school, in Ohio, it seemed like Will and I agreed about everything – Bowie, Python, *National Lampoon*, a hazy Marxist utopianism, Vicki Shehovic as the epitome of womanhood. We'd started Shadowland in the spring of tenth grade, as much out of self-defense as anything, two literate, paranoid glams stranded and exposed in a school, and town, ruled by jocks and Young Republicans and Lynyrd Skynyrd fanatics. I was also from out of state, and therefore suspect, and Will had the added liability of being the son of the school janitor. The band wasn't just an escape, but a way to spread our world view, a way to search out fellow travelers also dying of boredom and neglect in the hollow heart of the heartland.

It hadn't gone particularly well, since nobody who came to teen centers or DeMolay dances in, say, Bucyrus or Elyria expected or wanted to hear original songs, especially mine, and even our choice of covers (Mott's "Death May Be Your Santa Claus," Gil Scott Heron's "Winter in America") was too obscure for the average teenage headbanger. But then Will would do a spot-on version of, say, David Essex's "Rock On," and Chas would nail the drum break in "Train Kept A Rollin'" and we'd at least avoid getting lynched. We'd made a few fans, mostly depressed teenage girl poets who wrote me long letters about their cute but insensitive jock boyfriends, or manic drama club types who would call Will incessantly for a week, and the occasional guy in a trenchcoat who wouldn't talk to anyone all night but then would stick around to help us load out and ask what drugs we'd tried. (Me, none; Will, a few; our drummer Chas, whaddya got?)

Chas, though not on the same Bowie/Python wavelength, upped our overall musical prowess considerably and inspired Will and me to at least try to learn how to play our instruments. We kept at it through college, jamming and practicing every vacation, and the summer after graduating we loaded up Chas's van and my little Datsun and got the hell out of Harding. Will and Chas might have settled for Cleveland or Detroit but I'd held out for Boston's punk/Nu Wave scene, and after a weekend scouting trip of seeing club after club packed for bands we'd never even heard of, we made the move.

That was four and a half *years* ago. If you'd told me it would take this long just to get a record out, no way I would've believed you. Not that I ever pictured us selling out stadiums and cavorting backstage with Bob Geldof and Princess Di, but I at least thought we'd be a cult band by now, like X or Squeeze or Jules and the Polar Bears, with a small but rabid national following and four-star write-ups in *Rolling Stone* and *Rock & Roll Confidential*. We'll be lucky to even get reviewed, since our album's not out on a major – yet – it's on our producer's vanity label, A Hole in the Middle Records. But still. Even with the round trip to Long Island, today's unquestionably a ten on the Mark Zodzniak Richter scale, equal with the day I first met Maggie, my major ex-sex-fiend/co-conspirator/soul mate, on the dorm stairwell at Antioch, or the day I first heard Will singing "Life on Mars" in the choir room at Harding High.

Talk about ancient history. Now everything's changing: punk and ska are dead, Nu Wave's old news, and I'm racing through the winter-brown Connecticut countryside to get our records back to town before they, and we, go completely out of style. The rental's heater's not working either, so I'm shivering like the last in line at a South End methadone clinic while I try and keep my calories up with stale Pringles and cold rest stop coffee. At least there's no traffic aside from the eighteen-wheelers, each hulking gray ammo box form big enough to create its own wind tunnel as I shoot past:

Whoosh! *Fuck Will.* SCREECH. *Et cetera.*

I want to get back to town, take a shower, do some vocal warm ups, change my strings. We better be fuckin' great tonight – Wayne's invited half the local music scene out for the show, including all the jocks from WROB, the major rock station in town, and we've invited everyone we've met since we hit Boston. Maybe Kat will even come. Wouldn't that be nice – then today would be a ten and a half. Even Boone, our hired-gun lead player, is excited, since his last band didn't get this far. And Will should be on good behavior since there'll be a crowd.

I pass another eighteen-wheeler, this one with an overflowing cornucopia painted on its side, the symbolic opposite of our last four years. But I glance over my shoulder, see the stacked boxes of Shadowland LPs behind me which despite Will's best efforts *will* be at our concert tonight. *Good work, Z-man. Have another potato chip.*

That's when I look up and slam on the brakes.

## 2. *REWIND:* Rockport, Mass., September 198*1*

BAM!

My eyes pop open. It's totally dark, darker than my room in Harding, and the bed feels harder. There's also background noise: steady, driving rain.

BAM!

Right. Rockport. Shadowland's new World HQ.

BAM! "Mark! Let me the fuck in!"

Chas. I feel for a light switch, then run to the front door and swing it open.

"Nice weather," he says. Water's rolling off him like he's in a car wash.

"Yeah but no tornados."

We're in a dingy off-season vacation rental an hour north of Boston, as close as we could afford in the city's jacked-up real estate market. No matter: we're here, with even Will going along after I'd basically promised we'd get rich and famous. In a year. Well, maybe two. Will's mother cried – her baby leaving home. Chas said his mother cried too, which surprised me, since he's been mostly living out of his van or Will's basement since she got remarried to a bruiser a few years ago. My parents hadn't cried. About that, anyway.

Chas peels off his slicker, claims a bedroom and crashes. I head back to bed, but I can't sleep: tomorrow's day one of The Plan: *Shadowland, unleashed*. I lie awake, listening to the constant Unknown Soldier drum roll on the slanted shingle roof, picturing

11

how it's gonna happen. Not if, but how. When. *If* we're as good as I think we are. If *I'm* as good, or at least my songs are. I'd won a couple poetry prizes at Antioch, and we'd gotten a couple nice reviews in the Harding paper, including an "off to make it big" interview, complete with photo, just before the move. So what. My sister had a shelf full of ribbons and award cups by junior high. That memory, plus the rain and the black-on-gray shadows in the unfamiliar room, gets me thinking about ghosts, might-have-beens. I'd spent last night at my aunt's in Morristown, New Jersey, where my family used to live before Ohio, and I'd driven by the cemetery on my way out of town. I'd been in a rush to get going and hadn't stopped. Now, in the middle of the night, adrenaline dissipated, that feels pretty shitty.

I roll over, try to change the subject. *Maggie*. I wonder what time it is in California, if I'd wake up her mom if I called. I'd called a few weeks ago to ask Maggie what she thought about me, the band, moving to Boston. It hadn't gone as well as I'd hoped. In fact it hadn't gone well at all.

I lie there another minute, just listening, feeling lonely as the rain. What the fuck. I click on the light and dial.

"Hi Mrs. Preston. Is Maggie home?"

"I'll see." She doesn't bother with "Hello, Mark, how are you?" though in her clipped tone it wouldn't matter. I hear a talk show nattering so at least the TV was up. In a minute I hear the receiver lifting.

"Hey..."

One word and I immediately feel myself swelling. Whatever's complex about Maggie's and my relationship isn't the sex, which has always been stellar. Not that I have much to compare it to, just a couple Antioch flings and an adolescence of stolen moments with the Mark Eden "enhance your bust" ads in the back of my mom's *Cosmo*.

"We're in Massachusetts," I say. "Well, me and Chas anyway. There's plenty of room if you change your mind." Boston had been Maggie's idea first, when she'd applied to the Museum School last spring. Then she'd faked me out by deferring her acceptance and moving back home to Redondo.

"Can't. I got a job."

"You're a painter, Mags. *That's* your job."

"Tell my mother. She's charging me rent."

"See, capitalism sucks," I say. We'd been prominent radicals on campus, the John and Yoko of Nowhere Springs, Ohio. "What's the job?"

She says it's at the senior center, helping the polyester set with their Social Security and Medicare forms. "But it might not last. The budget's getting cut."

"Sorry. Appeal to the White House."

"Ha."

"So move to Boston."

"And be your girlfriend again?" She says it like a joke, but her voice has a steely edge to it. I don't have a clever comeback, and a minute later we hang up. Despite the tension there's still a half-mast bulge down below.

Have to work on my pauses, I think, as I listen to the downpour, think about Maggie three thousand miles away 'til I fall asleep.

Morning is sunny, no trace of last night's deluge, and Chas and I sit on the balcony spooning Coco Puffs and (Chas) polluting the cool salt air with Marlboros. We can see the ocean shimmering silver blue a block away, more than making up for the washed-out drabness of the house itself: wooden clapboard siding weathered gray on the outside, and threadbare carpets worn gray from years of tracked sand on the inside.

After breakfast we unload the van, carrying amplifiers and drum cases down into the basement, empty except for a hot water heater perched in one corner of the smooth concrete floor. It's a one-eighty from the musty claustrophobia of Will's parents' house, with its stacks of old furniture and constantly-accumulating piles of *True Detective* and *Readers Digest* leaning up against our speaker cabinets. Not to mention the wasps that had started coming in through a crack in the plaster last summer, necessitating us rehearsing with a can of Raid at the ready. Maybe that's how Sting got his name.

Chas hits his snare drum and it rings like a rifle shot. "Man, this place could use some egg cartons."

"No wasps, though," I say, balancing my Boogie on a stack of plastic milk crates. You can argue Gretsch versus Gibson, but it's duct tape, milk crates and egg cartons that make rock 'n' roll possible.

"Hel-lo-o," we hear from the door in a bad French accent. It's either John Cleese or Will. My money would be on Cleese except we're done unloading.

"Typical, shows up the second we're finished," Chas notes.

"We waited down the block 'til you were done." In the three days since I've seen him, Will, who's shorter than Chas and me and dimpled, has started growing a moustache, possibly to remind us he's hit puberty.

"Nice face, ass-wi–…hey, Jackie," I say to the girl stepping through the door behind him. While Maggie is slim, like a half-starved alley cat, and exudes a California waif's sexuality, Peggy Lipton with a rat tail, Jackie has the deep, smooth bends of a Spanish guitar, beneath a river of luminous chestnut hair. Plus she's *here*. Both Chas and I stand up a little straighter. "Welcome to rock 'n' roll heaven."

Jackie whispers something to Will, who laughs. "She said, it's like I died and went to Rockport."

Will shows her around the house, and we hear them shoving beds together in the room we'd saved them. Hope the walls are thick. We help them carry in suitcases from the Chevy Impala Will inherited from one of his older brothers, then make mustard and cheese sandwiches out of leftover road food. Jackie pours warm Vernor's ginger ale into some *Empire Strikes Back* glasses she finds in a kitchen cabinet.

"To Shadowland," I say, lifting Luke Skywalker skyward.

"To world…domination!" Will exhales, sticking his new lip fuzz over the rim of his glass for some James Earl Jones resonance.

"Beats workin' at the fuckin' Whirlpool factory," Chas says, draining his Wookie.

That night we make our first noise in the basement. I don't want to do any of our old Ohio songs, so we just play: Chas starts a doubletime ska beat, each hit reverberating off the bare concrete, DOM dom dom dom DOM dom dom dom, then Will adds some octave jumps on the Hofner Beatle bass his mom had bought him back in high school, behind his father's back. I start noodling some seventh chords on my nicked-up Gretsch 'til I find something I like. The rhythm's different, but the chords remind me of an old bubblegum hit *circa* third grade, and I dig down through my AM radio brain for the lyrics: *And I don't know if I'm ever coming home.* We keep it going and Will joins in on the "do do do do do do" part. We make it to the end, then crack up, but it feels good. It feels *new.* Five minutes into Shadowland's new career, and it feels like it's all gonna work.


## 3. *FAST FORWARD:* I-84, Waterbury, Connecticut, December 1985

*Shit.*

The rental's jammed up against a concrete embankment, its rear wheels a foot off the ground. Everything's thrown around inside, glove compartment open, maps and coins and potato chips everywhere, windshield dripping with spilled coffee. My left wrist stings from where it must have hit the armrest, and my neck is sore from where the seat belt caught it. My heart is beating through my chest and I'm doing tantric breathing exercises to keep from hyperventilating.

I hear the whoop of an approaching siren. It clicks off mid-cycle.

"You okay in there?" a gruff voice asks. The voice is connected to about six feet two of cop, in a Connecticut State Police windbreaker and a Mounties-style wide brim hat.

I feel like hell, especially my wrist, but I need to get back to Boston for the concert, so I tell Officer Do-Right I'm fine.

"Wanna tell me what happened?" Lights are still flashing atop his cruiser, and I can feel passing drivers slowing to look at us, scanning the roadside for mangled bodies.

I think back, try to place the split seconds in sequence. "Car pulled out, right in front of me." I flick my chin at an entrance ramp fifty feet back, then immediately regret the neck motion. "Some gas guzzler. Maybe a Pontiac. Or a Ford." I'd tried to change lanes so I wouldn't hit him, but the cornucopia-logo produce truck I'd passed was now barreling down the hill in the passing lane. I could either slam into the gas-guzzler or get squashed by the truck. Instead I'd jammed the worn brakes, skidded on the wet pavement and steered into the concrete divider. Bad move. I'd bounced off the divider, shot back across the highway like a pinball and rear-ended the embankment on the other side, just missing another eighteen-wheeler in the process. The car and trucks hadn't even slowed down. Thanks for the help, guys.

"Pontiac or a Ford, huh. That narrows it down." The trooper looks behind me. "What's in all the boxes?"

I consider lying, don't want him to impound the rental looking for drugs if I say I'm a musician. Good thing my hair's shorter these days. "Records."

Maybe he thinks medical records, because he lets it go by. He asks for my license and the car's registration, which I find in the debris beneath the passenger seat. Sit tight and he'll call it in. I roll up my window with my good hand, then sit shaking from cold and traumatic shock. Maybe I should be thanking whomever that it wasn't worse, that I'm not splayed out on the pavement, fresh warm blood commingling with the cold rain. But instead I'm wondering if they arrest people for brake failure, or worse, if they'll think the car's stolen since it's not rented in my name. And how the fuck am I gonna get the records, and me, to the show on time? Tell the trooper who I am and see if he'll give me a ride? Ask him to radio for a helicopter?

After ten minutes or so a tow truck comes. The driver looks over the damage, then rigs up the tow and pulls me off the wall while his dog looks on impassively from the passenger seat. The trooper strolls over, hands me a hundred-dollar ticket for reckless driving, then peels out without a word.

Of course the dickhead who cut me off is getting away scot-free. And if only *Will* had given in on one detail, one fight, none of this ever would have happened, and I'd be home right now, dripping from a hot shower, sipping tea and humming vocal warm-ups while I chose what stage clothes to wear. Instead I'm wedged in next to a wet Springer spaniel in a tow truck full of fast food wrappers, ash trays that haven't been emptied since Nixon resigned, and a Hulk Hogan-proportioned driver wearing camo pants and a T-shirt that says *Kill 'Em All and Let God Decide.*

16

"Want one?" He's offering me a toxic-orange peanut butter cracker from a small cellophane pack.

"Sure, thanks."

"I meant Elvis." The dog snatches it out of his hand.

*Fuck Will. And Connecticut.*

Four hours later I pull up to the Tam. Miraculously the rental was drivable, barely, once the mechanic pried off a drooping fender and hammered a flap of wheel well away from a tire. I'd limped home at half speed like a single-headlighted Cyclops, my forearm getting more swollen every mile. I'd finally stopped at McDonald's to get a baggie of ice to wrap around it, but it hadn't helped much.

Will comes out to inspect the damage and whistles. "Nice driving, Z-Man. We missed you at load out."

Fuck you, Will. The one time in five years *he* makes it and I don't.... I hold up my wrist. "I wouldn't have been much help anyway."

"Ouch. Can you play? Not that you ever could."

I let the jab go by. "Guess I'll find out."

"Come on, there's a crowd." We each take a box of records and go inside. Will's right — there's a good-sized mob, about half of whom I recognize at first glance, friends, other musicians, habitual club-goers. I see my guitar up on its stand and make my way to the stage. I try to finger a bar chord, but I can't press down, and it hurts like hell when I try. Fuck. I think for a minute. No way we're cancelling tonight, not even if I'd been in the Beechcraft with Buddy Holly. I find Boone, ask him to cover my guitar parts. I change into the purple-and-black striped pullover Chas brought me, then borrow a scarf from Jackie and wrap it tight around my wrist. I down a handful of Tylenol from the bartender's stash and splash some water on my face. Showtime.

Tommey, the hobbit-like editor of the punk mag *SCREAM!,* introduces us. He says he usually hates pop bands but kind of likes us; I guess that's better than saying he loves pop bands but hates us. Our producer Wayne says he tried to get Peter Wolf, ex of the Geils band, to do the intro, but who knows.

"So here they are – Shadowland!" Tommey barks, ducking from the stage.

Chas starts a thumping pulse on his kick drum. The

spotlight Wayne's rented for the evening is focused in tight on the drum, so you can see its skin flex with each beat. Chas counts four and Boone and Will hit the opening chords as the spot widens and the fill lights come up. It's a small room as clubs go, without the oversize hanging video screens that seem to be everywhere these days, and waves of sound come bouncing back off the plaster walls and plate glass windows. We're not so much in stereo as in Sensurround.

I'm still staring at Chas's bass drum, my back to the audience. My black Gretsch Duo Jet is sitting in its guitar stand – no sense wearing it if I can't play it. Instead of John Lennon tonight I guess I'm Johnny Rotten, or maybe Iggy Pop, except I'm not, and I feel naked, exposed without my instrument to hide behind. Fuck it, no matter. I take a breath, throw back my shoulders, wait for the downbeat, then twirl around:

*Those diamond dreams they sell you well they're made of glass*
*And tick tock baby midnight's coming fast*

The crowd is a sea of bobbing heads in the dim offstage light. I take a step towards them, grab the mic stand with my good hand:

*So let's forget the future and ignore the past*
*Just love it love it love it baby while it lasts*

I lean forward as we hit the chorus, Will and Boone in high thirds above me: *You say you want to be the next big thing – ooh, next big thing....* I know I'm singing to myself, to us, at least as much as to all the other bands out there. But tonight, for almost the first time, it feels like we're in the game. *We* have a record. We, Shadowland, exist.

Chas crashes a cymbal and Boone starts his solo. It sounds pretty good, even without my guitar, drums solid, Will's bass pulsing, Boone bending strings high up the neck of his Fender Jaguar. I slap my leg with my good hand in time to Chas's downbeats and shake my hips a little, feeling silly. The real Iggy Pop would be diving into the crowd, but that's way beyond my introvert's comfort zone, especially with a possible forearm

18

fracture, not to mention my wire rim glasses. And our crowd would be so stunned they'd probably forget to catch me.

As the band hits the last chord I conduct the cut-off like Casey Jones pulling on his steam whistle. I've certainly seen enough rock stars strut their stuff over the years, from sneaking downstairs to watch *In Concert* and *The Midnight Special* back in Harding to being force-fed MTV in every club in town, so I should be able to fake it for an hour. Boone switches to twelve-string for "Garden of Eden" and Chas splashes his cymbals behind me as Will nails the high harmony. It's a little empty without my rhythm part, but people don't seem to mind, and I can feel the energy build as they sway in place.

Will, wearing a shiny new Rickenbacker strapped over Chas's old marching band jacket, and hair coiffed straight up for the occasion, comes center stage to sing "Second Glance," his vocal on the record. Now what do I do? Go see a movie? In addition to his drums Chas had added a shaker part to the rhythm track, so I find his Schlitz can full of two penny nails and rattle along to the groove. When we hit the double time, Maggie and Simon, Jackie, Chas's girlfriend Deedee and a few of Boone's female admirers start dancing for real and pretty soon it's *American Bandstand*, with the whole dance floor packed. My shaker's not adding much, so I jump down off the stage and start dancing with the audience, holding my bad arm in against my body. They make room for me, and the spotlight operator notices me as well and catches me bumping with a female fan. I glance up at the stage and see Will's pink, cherub-cheeked face glaring down at me. Oops. Stealing focus. But the audience is having fun and I've got to do something.

Will's still pissed as Chas starts pounding out "Risking Your Life to Rescue a Dead Man," but it's the angriest song on the record so it kind of works. I make it onstage in time for my vocal, and Boone takes an amazing solo where he uses his microphone stand for a slide. Will's attitude and my swollen forearm aside, tonight definitely feels like an event, some long-delayed gratification coming our way. *About fucking time.* But belated or not, it feels good so many people have come out to cheer us on, including a fair smattering from other bands – The Corvettes, Talon, Park Street, Boone's old band Rock Paper Scissors,

Genevieve from Moon Over Jupiter, even Alexis from Red October. Boone seems happy and relatively under control, no spontaneous key changes, and even Chas, who usually grimaces like a Soviet weightlifter when he's playing, is all smiles, tossing his blonde curls from side to side. Wonder if he realizes all of Wayne's guests got in for free. Will's got his fake stage smile back on, so at least we'll look like a united front if anyone from a record label is watching.

I take a gulp of water, out of breath from the double time lyrics in "Dead Man." As Boone starts a slow arpeggio I notice a tall woman towards the back of the club with coppery hair. Like Kat's. If it is her, I hope she takes the next song with a grain of salt, since it's basically about what a lying sack of shit I can be. Even so it's my favorite track on the record, because it *sounds* like us: Chas's drums aren't beefed up beyond recognition, Will's bass tone is warm and round, and you can hear the breaths in my vocal track. We'd even added a horn section, for a rootsy, *Exile on Main Street* vibe. Will thought it was too slow, didn't even want to put it on the album, but I'd snagged Chas's vote by pointing out I could tell his girlfriend Deedee about the one-afternoon-stand he'd had – on the day of *their* first date.

It's a blues, one of the last songs I'd written for Maggie, and some couples slow dance despite, or maybe because of, the warning in the lyric: *Hold your finger over a candle, there's a good chance that you'll get burned....* I'm feeling a little more comfortable *sans* guitar, and as I sing I start prowling the lip of the stage, like Otis Redding at Monterey. The spotlight stays with me, and I can feel people's eyes following, watching me more intently than at a usual gig when I'm just one more guy with a guitar. Forty minutes ago the extra attention made me want to hide, but it's starting to feel good, like the crowd's really with us, with *me*. I hold out some notes, play with the phrasing, and it's almost sexual, like I'm teasing them. This must be how it's supposed to feel. It's only happened briefly, in fleeting snatches, before tonight. It's exactly what's been missing from our shows.

I take a deep breath and hold out the last note as long as I can: *Don't let him break the same heart twiiiice.* I snap the mic chord like a whip, hear a gasp from the front row. As the spotlight fades we get our best ovation of the night. I shoot Will a glance, like *check this out*, and in the between-songs dark he looks doubly pissed. So much for Camelot.

Chas clicks his sticks four times for "Car Keys," the one that Wayne and Padric, the studio engineer, are calling the single, the song will make us famous. Will had also sensed something in the studio and had insisted on trying the lead vocal, but despite him bribing Boone and Chas with their choice of illicit substance it's my rawer version that made the record. It's the straightest rock 'n' roll tune on the disc, almost old fashioned, maybe the least "Shadowland" song on the disc. But the dance floor's packed, and soon I'll get to scarf another handful of Tylenol and ice my wrist again. This time I reach down with my good arm and pull a couple women onstage to dance with during Boone's solo. Will, glued-on smile back in place, comes front to join us, and we sing the last chorus on the same mic, Mick and Keith style, then wave goodnight.

Four hours later I'm still wide awake, at the three-way intersection of post-gig adrenaline, ten kilohertz ear buzz, and swollen throbbing hand. I've got the ice pack back on, and Nigel All Nite playing in the background for company. Ever since Chas moved in with Deedee I've had the whole apartment to myself, and at four AM it can be a little creepy, especially now that the building's going condo, like about half of Brighton, and is almost empty. The developer has also stopped doing any maintenance, to drive out the last of us tenants, and you can sometimes hear rats burrowing in the walls. Now *that's* a chick magnet.

Tonight I don't care, though. *The concert.* Not our best show technically, since Boone was covering my parts on the fly, but it was our best *received* show, ever. *Two* encores. And it was wild how differently the audience related to me as lead singer. Usually I'm happy at gigs if we play the songs in the right order and a few people dance. Tonight I felt like I could shoot lightning out of my fingertips. And, more importantly, it felt like people *got* the songs. *Finally.*

Despite my high, I need sleep. I turn down the radio, close my eyes, but it's not the cheering crowd at the Tam that I see. It's a slow motion movie: the highway, the rain, the asshole cutting in front me, the concrete retaining wall. *Screech, BAM, crunch.*

I could have easily missed the concert, who knows what else. *I'm too young to die*, I think, *especially now that we have a record out.* As if any of that matters.

### 4. *REWIND:* Rockport, Mass., October 198*1*

"Who's got the bitch, who's got the bitch?"

We're sitting around the cracked Formica kitchen table, eating mac and cheese and playing hearts like we did during lunches back at Harding High. All that's missing are the limp green beans and the cafeteria jukebox blaring "Sweet Home Alabama" for the umpteenth time. In a row.

Cards are cheap entertainment, which we need since we're short on cash: we've been in Rockport a month, and instead of doing bullshit cover gigs like we did in Ohio, we've all gotten starvation-wage day jobs to pay the rent. I'm activities coordinator/dodge ball target for aspiring juvenile delinquents at an after school program in Gloucester, the next harbor over. Chas makes custom Little League jerseys at a shirt factory in Ipswich, a few clam shacks to the north. Better, Will's a clerk at a record store/head shop halfway down Route 1, so he gets the occasional free LP or concert ticket, as well as getting Chas a deal on his rolling papers. Best, Jackie's working at a women's gym in Gloucester, so I get to leer at her leotards if I give her a ride home – the most action I've gotten since Maggie flew back to California last spring.

"Who's got the bitch?" Will taunts again.

Chas throws the queen of spades down on the pile. "You got her now."

"Chas, he's gonna run," I warn. The trouble with us playing as a foursome is how predictable we are: Chas and Jackie almost never make a run, Will and I almost always do, or at least decoy like we're going for it. I can either let Will take the hand, or eat the queen myself and end up with more points than anybody, which is bad since low score wins. Fuck it. I throw down the king.

"Now who's going for it," says Will. I shrug noncommittally, then lead a seven. If Will wants to stop me he'll

22

have to pay. While he thinks about it we can hear the soft explosions of waves crashing on Back Beach – *boosshh, boosshh.* What a great sound; maybe we can use it on an album someday. Shadowland: *Broke Rockport Blues.*

"Play a card, Englebert," I say. At Jackie's insistence Will's lost the moustache, but in retaliation is growing Vegas-lounge-singer sideburns. He ignores me and stares at his cards.

Chas flips a page – since Will and I take so long he's been reading the *Bosstown Bean* as we play, checking out club ads and occasionally calling out band names for comparison. We'd known the famous groups – The Cars, J. Geils, Aerosmith, The Modern Lovers – but it seems there's a never-ending supply of bands further down the food chain.

"Kinsey and the Reporters. Houdini Museum."

"Good one," Will says.

"You're not supposed to be listening," I say. "You're supposed to be picking a card."

"I can do both."

"No way," Chas snorts, then wipes away the beer foam trickling out his nose with his shirt sleeve. He slides the paper across to Will and points.

Will stifles a laugh mid-bite while Jackie makes a face.

"What's so funny?" I ask, piqued at being the last to know. Will swivels the paper so I can see. I scroll down the column of ads – the Bad Motor Scooters at the Rat, the Rocking Icons at the Western Front, Beezelbub at the Beachcomber. Halfway down I see it – one of the bands playing at Mavericks tonight is named The Muff Divers. It's funny, but I don't want to give them the satisfaction, so I keep on my after-school teacher face. "Very droll."

Chas shakes his head again. "You can't call your band...." Ohio bands have names like Topaz and Rockestra. And Shadowland, for that matter.

"Reminds me of that dog," says Will. "At the rest stop." On our scouting trip we'd seen a Hollywood-pretty blonde exercising a black, curly-haired puppy, and it had repeatedly and enthusiastically thrust its nose up into her crotch. Lucky dog.

Jackie whispers something into Will's ear, and he cracks up. "The Muff Diving *Poodles.* Now *that's* a band name. The

MDPs for short."

This time I do laugh, since it's Jackie's joke. She points to another ad.

"Hey," Will says, "Khartoum's at Jonathan's tonight."

Khartoum's been getting tons of press, even being hailed "best band in Boston," and I want to check out the competition. "Let's go," I say, tossing down my cards.

"First things first," Will counters, laying an eight over my seven. "So much for that run."

Jonathan's, in Salem, is the closest place to Rockport that has original bands, and their cover's about half of what the clubs downtown charge. I pull the heavy door open and there's a bomb blast of escaping sound, a wall of guitar noise so dense it takes physical effort to walk through. The doorman doesn't even try to talk, just holds up five fingers and I slip him a five-dollar bill. He doesn't check my license, but he checks Will's, and checks out Jackie in general. Will and I both hang back to make sure he doesn't try patting her down.

I turn a corner and *whoa*: Khartoum's jumping around the stage like they're killing cockroaches, sweat pouring off their faces. I'd seen a few punk bands at Antioch, and even we have our rough, New York Dolls side, but nothing like this: snare drum blast on every beat, guitars buzzing like hornets, vocalist screaming at the top of his lungs, all loud enough to melt glass. I only catch tiny snatches of the lyrics, which seem to be about AK-47s ("Ratta-tat-tat!"), mental hospitals ("Guest of McLean's, I'm a guest at McLean's!") and sewer rats ("gnaw his leg, gnaw his leg, gnaw his leg!"), but it's enough to grok their *Apocalypse Now* world view. And Khartoum's look fits their sound – shoe-polish-black flat top hair and work clothes like Will's dad wears. They look like striking auto workers about to burn the factory down. My ex Maggie was into English punk – The Clash, The Jam – but this is all-American, no-wave hardcore.

The crowd seems in as much culture shock as we are. This isn't the Channel, some giant converted warehouse deep in the concrete jungle, full of jaded urban hipsters. This is the 'burbs, graffiti-less walls and plush padded seats, and the audience is mostly big haired girls and guys out to pick them up. Aside from a

24

few spike-haired kids pogoing by the stage, they seem mostly mystified as they cover their ears and then applaud politely after each song. I flash Will a concerned look – we're not even the Monkees compared to Khartoum, we're more like the Archies, and if this is what the *Bean*'s gushing about, maybe this isn't our town – but Will seems to be into it. Chas tries talking to a few of the local fauna but can't make much headway against all the noise, so he just chain smokes Marlboros and bobs his head in time. I ask the bartender for a napkin, rip it in half and shove the pieces into my ear canals. It still hurts.

As the band plays on I notice people start drifting toward the exits, and by the end of the set it's just us, the bartender and the kids who were pogoing – everyone else has given up and gone bowling. Khartoum looks like they think it's funny, like it was their *goal* to drive everyone out. I wonder if they'll still get paid. I debate going up to say hi, but what would I say? *Way to clear the room, guys.* Will does goes introduce himself, and comes back speckled with second-hand Khartoum sweat. Maybe Jackie should sleep in with me tonight.

"They were so fuckin' *loud*," I say on the way home. "Drowned out their own lyrics." Between the van's engine hum and the ringing in my ears, my voice sounds disembodied, like the words are just floating in the air.

"Think one was about rats," Chas says, wrinkling his nose.

"I liked that one," Will says. "Made me hungry."

"And that baseball song: *Denny McLain! Denny McLain!*" Chas beats the rhythm on the steering wheel.

"Um, Chas, I don't think–"

"Doesn't matter," Will interrupts. "It's the whole…*gestalt.*"

"*Gesundheit.* Of course it matt-"

"*Gestapo,*" Will interrupts. "No it doesn't."

"*Gazpacho,*" I counter. "Yes it does."

"*Gethsemane.* Nobody but you listens–"

Jackie pulls Will over, whispers in his ear, and he cracks up. "*Gethsemane Sam.*"

"*Gethsemane Salmonella.*"

"*Gethsemane Salmonella Fitzgerald.*"

"*Gethsemane Sam and F. Scott…*"

Chas leans over and cranks the radio to drown us out, since he knows we'd keep going all the way back to Rockport. I reach up and click it back off. "As I was saying, fuck anyone who says the words don't matter. Do you have any idea how hard it is to write decent…"

Will rolls his eyes at Chas, so I don't bother finishing the sentence. But I'm still worked up.

"No, of course you don't. But don't you at least want to know what a song's *about* before you applaud for it? What if it's, like, racist propaganda for some Reagan Youth movement?" I remember seeing a *Life Magazine* photo – taken in Boston – of some black guy getting poked with an American flag by a white street mob. In Harding there weren't any actual blacks, so any minority was fair game. Say Czech, for instance.

"They seem like nice enough guys," Will shrugs. Jackie leans over and whispers in his ear again, and he laughs. "Besides, Mark, this is Massachusetts. They only burn witches."

Next rehearsal Chas tries out the Khartoum four-on-the-floor beat. Will matches the groove on bass, and I start doing some staccato off-beat hits to try to make it more interesting, less assaultive. It still feels primal, but a little disjointed too, like Ike & Tina Turner on the bottom with early Talking Heads on top. The tension makes me think of conflict, duality, feeling versus thinking, head versus body. I flash on how complex things had gotten with Maggie back at Antioch. If only we could turn off our brains and keep it simple, animal to animal. I start chanting, or maybe yelling, "animal to animal" every other measure, and Chas starts filling in the spaces with drum hits and cymbal crashes:

*Animal to animal!* (ticka ticka ticka ticka ticka boom CRASH)
*Animal to animal!* (ticka boom ticka ticka ticka boom CRASH)

I lead Will through a twelve-bar chord pattern, and start talking stream of consciousness until I have something that mostly rhymes:

> *Two panthers move through the heart of the city*
> *So strong and silent, so sleek and pretty*

We climb to the IV chord, and I raise the melody accordingly.

> *Steam rising up off the ground*
> *Circle each other without a sound*

Will slides down the neck of his Hofner to the tonic, then we both land on the V,

> *One pounces but he doesn't bite*
> *Just licks her fur all through the night*

then back home:

> *Animal to animal* (ticka ticka ticka ticka ticka boom CRASH)

Chas keeps the rhythm going, and next time through Will joins in on the *animal to animal*s. I take a solo and aim the pickups in my Duo Jet right at the amp, so it starts squealing in a feedback loop. Will and Chas get wilder too, and the effect is somewhere between mating panthers and a subway crash. This is about the point Hendrix would light his guitar on fire, or the Who would smash their equipment, but since we can barely afford new strings I settle for knocking over a milk crate. Never mind the bollocks, here's…Gethsemane Sam & the MDPs!

## 5. *FAST FORWARD:* **Brighton, Mass., December 1985**

Phone ringing. Daylight. I pull the blanket back with my good hand, squint my way to the hall. Since Chas moved out and took our little Goodwill entry table, the phone's sitting on a year-old pile of *Bosstown Beans* I should recycle before the developer uses them to torch the building. I grab the receiver mid-ring.

"How's the wrist?" Will.

I glance down; it's thick as a Nerf football. "Still fucked up. I should probably walk over to Saint E's." Maybe I should check myself in for some R&R; aside from the swollen wrist I have a dull headache, a stiff neck and a scratchy throat from a hundred second-hand cigarettes. A few years ago I could leap out of bed the morning after a gig, go for a five-mile run, and then pick up my guitar again. Now I want Tylenol, hot tea and a long shower.

"I just got a call from a not-very-happy rent-a-guy."

It was inevitable. Boone and I had dropped off the severely dented Plymouth under cover of darkness after the gig. It would look even worse in the morning. "Yeah, I figured."

"They're gonna have their insurance adjuster look at it, then call me back."

"Okay."

"It's not going to be pretty."

"Yeah, okay."

"Just so you're prepared."

"I'm prepared. Just let me know." I'm starting to hang up but he's not done. Having expressed his concern, he's free to be sanctimonious.

"Maybe you should have driven slower."

Uck-fay ou-yay, Will. "Yeah, that's just what I was thinking as I was careening off the concrete." This time I hang up.

They called Will because officially *he* rented the car. I've never had a charge card – and now probably never will – so we went to the office together and both signed on as drivers. One might ask why Will didn't just get the records himself, or at least come with. Right, he was closing a sale and couldn't miss work. And Boston was my idea anyway.

The phone rings again as I'm getting out of the shower, half-soaped because my left hand is useless.

"For all they know, *you* were driving…" I begin, caustic as I can muster this early in the AM.

"Hello? Mark?"

Female voice, tentative but friendly. Kat? Kat!

"Hey," I say breathily, surgically removing any trace of bile from my tone. "Thanks for calling."

"This an okay time?"

28

"Yeah, sorry. Thought you were a guy from my band."

"Oh, how was the show? Sorry I couldn't make it."

"It was great, really fun." Not counting almost passing out when somebody grabbed my bad wrist to congratulate me after the set. But we'd sold our first fifty records, and Wayne had given away another fifty copies to various influential scenesters who'd made the show. Half of the freebies will be in used record stores by the end of the day, but what can you do.

"So I talked with Trav and Jan. We all thought you seemed pretty nice for a rock and roll star."

"Well maybe not 'star.' But if I bite the head off a pigeon or two...."

Kat laughs. "Don't let Jan hear you. She fundraises for PETA."

"Thanks for the warning."

"So...," she pauses, taking a breath, "we'd like to invite you. To live with us." I can hear her smiling with the good news.

"That's great, thanks." I mean it, since this rock 'n' roll star's butt is out on the street in a couple weeks. It would be even greater if I knew the deal between her and Travis, who looks like a *Lonely Planet* version of JFK Jr., all chiseled Ivy League features and Guatemalan peasant pants. I'd instinctively disliked him at the interview, and had to resist calling him Trav-Trav. Kat and I discuss the details, and she apologizes again for missing the show, she was getting some project ready for her class. She'd told me at the interview she teaches special ed, and I'd said it might come in handy dealing with the band. She'd laughed, and I felt a little flutter I haven't felt in a while. Since Maggie, really, which makes it quite a while.

In a pause I can hear her lips smacking, but unfortunately I don't think it's because she wants me uncontrollably. "Pistachios?"

"Yes, sorry, bad habit." She'd gone through half a bag full at my interview, but they hadn't shown on her long, coltish body, or at least what I could see of it beneath the thick wool sweater she was wearing.

"Not compared to some people's. Make that *most* people's." I could tell her about Boone's history with hallucinogens, or the box of truly disgusting truck stop pornography Chas had left behind in his closet. Or, more to the point, I could say that since Maggie I've had the habit of acting more interested in women than I really am, just to stave off loneliness, or that I've never *not* cheated in a relationship. I settle for saying I'm addicted to Tastycakes, my early-childhood junk food of choice back in New Jersey. "Can't get 'em up here, so it's cold turkey. Not very pretty."

"So you bite the heads off birds?" she says, laughing. There's that flutter again.

## 6. *REWIND:* Rockport, Mass., November 198*1*

"Hey, I get to sing one."

The band's set up in my bedroom: Will's bass amp is in my closet, my amp is on the dresser, and Chas's trap kit is spread over half the floor – he has to climb over the bed to get behind it. We tried recording in the basement, but the bare walls were so boomy it sounded like a Phil Spector outtake, and since we're just renting we can't egg carton like we did in Harding. Jackie vetoed us taking over the living room, so I shoved my furniture against the wall and here we are. Now Will, fresh from being the prodigal son at Thanksgiving – and having six older brothers and sisters ask if we've made a record yet – is asserting himself.

"At *least* one."

"Soitainly!" I say, *a la* Curly Howard. Chas and I had stayed in Rockport for the holiday, scarfing more mac and cheese and watching Channel 38's twenty-four-hour Moe-athon, even blasting Iggy Pop's *Raw Power* during commercials for the complete Stooges experience. I'd eventually burned out on the nyuck-nyuck jokes but Chas had stayed up for the whole thing, putting away a case of Rolling Rock in the process. The next morning I'd found him face down on the couch, delicate spider thread of saliva hanging from his open mouth, surrounded by empties. Of course I'd gone through a half-gallon of butter pecan before I crashed, so to each their own. But back to mollifying Will. "You sing on just about everything. Sound great, too. Wish I had those notes"

"I mean *lead*, ass-wipe."

"Will, we're an original band now. We need to record our originals."

Will slides his hand up the neck of his bass for a "vroom" sound, like a race car starting. "It's a demo tape, to demonstrate our talents, one of which is my singing. *Ergo*, I should sing one."

Moe himself would respond to the debate team logic by shoving two fingers up Will's nose and yanking forward, but I just shake my head vehemently. "No covers. That's why we left Ohio."

"Fine. So let me sing one of yours."

I sigh. As a singer Will is a great *imitator* – he can do "Wild Is the Wind" just like Bowie and "Crazy Little Thing Called Love" just like Freddie Mercury. But Will imitating me when I'm standing two feet away doesn't gain us very much. In fact I'd say it *loses* us a step, because it makes it like a cover version instead of the real thing. I might not be the smoothest singer – back in Little League I took a ground ball to the throat, and ever since my voice has had a ragged, barbed wire quality to it – but at least I don't sound like I'm pretending to be somebody *else*. And when Will sings my songs in his choir-boy tenor, they wilt, lose their power. So why bother?

"That ska thing's cool," Chas says from his drum throne. We've jammed on "Last Train to Clarksville" a few times now.

"Yeah, but Mark sings it. I just go 'do do do do.'" Will flicks his lips with his finger so it sounds like baby talk. "How about 'Waiting for the Man?'"

"That's still a cov–"

"I don't give a flying fuck," Chas interrupts, "let's just *play* it. Otherwise I'm going for a smoke." He starts climbing back out over the bed.

"Okay, okay," I say, holding up my hands. "Waiting" is an old Velvets tune we learned back in Ohio off a live Bowie bootleg. Will sings it *exactly* like Bowie, who's singing it exactly like Lou Reed, but at least it was never a hit. We also record "Animal to Animal" and a new song, "So Didn't You," North Shore speak for "so did you," all live, right onto cassette. The room's painted Pepto-Bismol pink, so our demo becomes *Shadowland Live from the Pink Room*. We add a quick bio and ask Jackie to take a picture of the three of us looking moody on Back Beach: tall, bony blonde Chas peering off into the distance; me in the middle, my half bangs and wire rim specs looking down at the sand; babyfaced Will a couple inches shorter and a few pounds heavier, giving his best Bobby Sherman teen idol gaze right to the camera. If we were smart, we'd enclose a picture of Jackie in her leotards, then we'd definitely get the gig. I'd seen her coming out of the bathroom that morning wrapped in a towel, the tops of her breasts glistening, her bare thighs perfectly smooth, and had to lock myself in my room until the swelling went down. Maybe I should fly Maggie out from California just for self-defense.

I wait a week, then call Jonathan's. They say they haven't listened yet, call back in another week. I call, they say they haven't seen it, maybe it was lost in the mail. I say I dropped it off. Jonathan or whoever it is puts the phone down, and I hear rustling sounds, then a conversation about a beer delivery, then a door slam, then silence. A minute goes by, then another. Should I call back? I'm just about to hang up when someone else picks up the phone. "Yeah?"

I start over. This guy finds our package. "Nice picture. Are you guys from Salem?"

"Rockport."

"Close enough. How's a week from Thursday, opening for Drive Train? One set, seventy-five bucks."

We made twelve hundred bucks playing a week at the SOP in Bowling Green over Christmas vacation last year, but at Jonathan's we won't have to slog through "Baby Hold On to Me" or "Takin' Care of Business." Will and Chas won't like it, but I say fine. We have our first Massachusetts gig. Our first *original band* gig. Don't tell Jonathan's, or Will and Chas, but I'd do it for free.


## 7. *FAST FORWARD:* Chestnut Hill, Mass., January 1986

*Strange Days. Wild Gift. Ziggy Stardust. Let It Be.*

It's New Year's Day, but I'm skipping the Southie Polar Bear swim to unpack my record collection. It's going slow because I'm rereading all the album notes as I go. Also because my wrist is elbow-to-knuckle in plaster.

"You hot for the Flying Nun?" Chas brings in a couple

more boxes. Since I'm crippled – the x-ray had shown a hairline fracture in my left ulna – he's doing the grunt work. Will and Jackie are still on their way back from Ohio, no surprise, and Boone's at his folks' on the Cape.

"Yeah, I saw that," I respond. Kat – Katherine – has a cross over her bed. I've been a devout atheist since about eighth grade so this could be interesting.

"I've never done a sister," Chas says, popping one of the beers I'm paying him with. "Let me know how it goes."

I nod. They probably take their vow of chastity the morning after sleeping with him. I'm more worried about Travis, though. I have to walk through his room to get to mine, like in a New Orleans shotgun shack, and when I'd frowned at the layout Kat had said not worry, Trav-Trav doesn't sleep in his room. She didn't elaborate so I'd assumed the worst.

Not that I should care. We've had two quick phone conversations, and one short interview. But still. Something about her just seems…friendly. Warm, like a seventies acoustic album in a world full of industrial noise-rock. My love life has been more like the latter recently. Not that I haven't deserved it: my last girlfriend, if that's even the right word, was burned out on the city and defined me as part of the problem, not part of the solution. She moved to New Hampshire and broke off all contact with everything in her previous life, especially me. I hadn't helped matters by sleeping with Maggie again when Maggie was going through one of her periodic pre-Simon nose dives. Since then I've just been sort of drifting, meet a woman, take what's offered, move on, but no one's gotten to me, made me feel any less lonely. 'Til now. Maybe.

Chas takes off, beer in tow. I'm going through the booty that came with the Who's *Live at Leeds* LP when there's a knock behind me. My neck is still so stiff I have to swivel my whole body, like a crab.

"What's so funny?" Kat asks through the open door. She's as tall as I remember, a head taller than Maggie, and her wavy reddish-brown hair is tucked inside the neck of her sweater.

I hold up a piece of EMI stationary. "This rejection letter, for the High Numbers' demo tape. Shows you what record companies know."

"The who?" she asks.

"Exactly," I nod. "The Who. Sorry about all the boxes in the hall."

"No problem. Jan and Trav don't get back 'til tomorrow."

*That's interesting.* I'm about to ask if they're a couple when she sees my cast.

"What happened to your arm?"

I tell her.

She puts her hand to her throat. "That's awful. You might have been killed."

The thought's occurred to me, but it sounds much worse when she says it. Maybe she does like me.

"Can you play guitar?"

"Not for a while." I motion to the bed. "Have a seat if you want."

She shakes her head. "I need to turn up the heat. And I want tea. You want some?"

I say thanks and she disappears.

I'm straightening out my mixed-up imports – Siouxie and the Bunnymen, Echo and the Banshees –when Kat comes back with two mugs and hands me one.

"Thanks." It feels warm, a nice change since the apartment, the whole first floor of an unkempt late-eighteen-hundreds Victorian, seems to have Arctic breezes blowing through it. Kat sits down on the bed and pops her first pistachio while she waits for her tea to cool. She offers me one but I shake my head, since I'd have to shell it one-handed.

"That's a lot of records. Are they alphabetical?"

"Nope. I like having to dig through them, reminds me what I have."

"Do you have a favorite?"

"Do you have a favorite kid in your class?"

She laughs. "I know I'm not supposed to, but I do."

"Me too. A couple, actually." One is an old Stones LP I'd discovered when it was on a list of records our church youth minister had banned. The other's a Velvet Underground album that's probably even less wholesome. "Um, a Rolling Stones album from '68. It's mostly acoustic, lots of blues." I pull it out and hand it to her. "*Beggars Banquet*."

"Don't know it."

I could put it on, but since one side starts with "Sympathy for the Devil" and the other side has a song about statutory rape I figure we'll work up to it. "Do you have a favorite? Record, I mean."

"Sort of, but I don't even own it. It's a live Springsteen bootleg somebody in college had. *Winterland '78*. His records are okay, but he's so much better live."

Now that our album's out I wonder if people will say that about us. At my interview she'd mentioned being into Bruce. Not that I'm a fan, but I'd made sure to tell her I was born in Jersey. I hand her a record. "I hear these guys are pretty good."

"Oh it's you! How exciting! But you look so mean."

The cover shot, by a professional this time, is us standing in a field, with long shadows trailing behind us and storm clouds roiling overhead. We have our version of the blank cold rock star expression on our faces, with Boone in aviator shades and Will with his arms crossed. "We're not that mean, I promise."

"Do you want to play it?"

"Maybe later." We'll work up to that, too – I want to get a feel for what she likes beyond Springsteen. I flip through my collection. "Ever hear of Jules and the Polar Bears?"

For the next few hours we chat and listen to records as I unpack. It's comfortable; she tells me about her college friends and her classroom, I tell her about being a DJ at Antioch, and before that moving to Ohio, meeting Will and Chas, then moving here and adding Boone to the mix. I'm thinking about moving up on the bed and asking her to rub my neck when the phone rings. Kat frowns, then says she'll get it.

She's still talking an hour later when I go to bed.

## 8. *REWIND:* **Salem, Mass., December 198***1*

"Move the drums or we walk, that's what we *should* say."

We're huddled on the dance floor at Jonathan's, trying to salvage our big debut. Drive Train's just finished their soundcheck and won't move their drums, meaning Chas will have to set up at the front of the stage or, worse, all the way down on the dance floor, and I'm pissed.

Will is appalled. "You want us to walk out on our first gig?"

"And turn down all this cash?" Chas snorts, creating an instant cloud of Marlboro.

"No, I want them to move their fucking drums." It's not just a respect thing: if Chas sets up his kit dead center, Will and I will barely have room to play, let alone move around.

"Let me talk to the soundman," says Will, Mr. Suave Diplomat.

"Bet we get all their brown M&Ms, too," Chas snorts again. An Ohio band we know had opened for Van Halen in Dayton, and found a small rabbit-shit sized pile of M&Ms, all brown, in their dressing room. Evidently David Lee Roth and Company like playing with a sugar buzz but are superstitious about color. *I'll* settle for a goddamn stage we can play on.

Will comes back, shaking his head. "Their drums stay. He said we're lucky to get a soundcheck at all. Most openers don't."

I look at the stage. "What if Chas just plays their drums? They're already miked."

Will shakes his head again. "I asked that too."

"Why not just play their guitars," Chas says. "Leave all our shit home."

"Good point," I say. I start putting my Duo Jet back in its case.

"Hold on." Will looks at the stage a minute, frowning. "What if Chas sets up to one side? That would give us some room."

I look at Chas. It would be different than every other band, but why not? "Make us unique."

Chas shrugs. "As long as the beer's free."

I start to wheel my amp centerstage, but Will shakes his head. "*I* need to be next to Chas," he says. "So we can play in sync."

As if I don't. But it's already eight-thirty, so I push my amp stage right, leaving Will, who's singing lead on exactly two songs, the middle. *Grrr.* Maybe I should sing my vocals on his mic, standing right in front of him. Then *he'll* break out the platform heels he wore in our Roxy Roller teen center days. Then *I'll*...

We soundcheck the mics, Chas chanting *tickle test, tickle test, tickle test* like he's done at every gig since tenth grade. Don't tell Will, but it's actually kind of nice playing without Chas's ride cymbal six inches from my ear. Will might end up like his dad, who's mostly deaf from some weird viral infection he got when Will was a kid. His father would still complain about the bass, though – Will's instrument – rumbling the walls as he tried to lip read *Kojak* or *Police Woman* overhead in the living room. Will's way of getting attention.

We change in the opening band's dressing room, probably the office I'd called because the only furniture is a desk, a phone, and a filing cabinet piled high with press kits and demo tapes. I glance through the stack; some of the kits look pretty slick, with bright color photos and pages of reviews and hype. But that doesn't mean the bands can *play*, or that their songs are any good. A surprising number look like straight hard rock bands, with skin-tight pants and layered hair, like they want to be the next Loverboy or Def Leppard. Maybe they should move to Ohio. Or build a time machine. Same dif. We're more interesting, I hope, a little punk, a little ska, a little British Invasion, all mixed together and sleeked down into something cool, artful and original – *Shadowland*. And it starts tonight. Even if I am shoved half offstage.

Chas puts on a gold Clam Box bowling team shirt over newly pressed jeans. Will goes for a vintage leather bomber jacket he found at a second-hand shop in Gloucester. I put on a black turtleneck, black cargo pants, and a black and white checked vest to go with new white Chuck Taylors and my black guitar. Collectively we're somewhere between the random retro look of the power pop revival and the skinny tie dress up look of the Cars. Casual genius. Intense but fun. *Not* from Ohio. I write out copies of the set list as Chas chugs his second pint and Will teases his hair.

"Which one's that again?" Chas points to a song I'd written for Maggie, towards the end, called "Why Don't You Show Me Your Wrists." I clap out the drum pattern for him. "Oh yeah."

I do some scales on my Duo Jet to warm up my fingers, and I can tell I'm nervous. Will, hair in place, gets out some guitar polish and a rag and shines his Hofner. Chas idly flips his drumsticks, marching band style. He'd be more nervous if they were paying us more.

Jackie arrives with a couple of her *Shape It!* co-workers who also look like they'd be killer in leotards. Lissa immediately catches my eye, dark curly hair with a serious, wary expression that's kind of like Maggie's. She catches Chas's eye too. May the best man win.

Nine o'clock comes, but no busloads of big haired girls. The soundman comes in and says five minutes. I ask about the crowd. He says Salem State's in finals, so everybody's either studying or already home for Christmas. Great. Shadowland's Massachusetts debut will be witnessed by a soundman, a bartender, three aerobics instructors, a couple of drunks at the bar, and another band who probably won't even come out of their dressing room. Even so, this is it, the first babystep in the dream, and I feel keyed up, stomach tight, like waiting for the starting gun at a track meet.

We take the stage and check our tuning as the soundman gives us a half-hearted intro. There's a smattering of applause as Chas, stage left, counts four and starts a taut martial beat, boom THWACK boom boom THWACK, and Will comes in on the root. I play my intro riff, take a breath and start "Killing Time," the last song I'd written before leaving Harding, about all the kids who never will:

> *Never see never know never taste never touch*
> *Never dream never go never ask for too much*

I look out at the audience. It's what, ten people? We've probably played proms back in Ohio with close to five hundred. But this isn't Will singing about some Puerto Rican girls just dyin' to meetchu, this is *my* song. *Our* music. It may be ten people, but they're *listening*, even the bartender. Babysteps. I glance over at Will and Chas, laying down the groove as I dig power chords out of my Gretsch. They've put their trust in me, and I know it's my job to make it happen. But whatever happens, at least we're not stuck in aspic back in Harding:

*Every week bow their heads while they wait for the Savior*
*But they're just killing time 'til time returns the...*

Chas fills the pause with a cymbal crash just as I sing

*favor.*

Liftoff.


## 9. *FAST FORWARD:* Brookline, Mass., January 1986

I'm lying face down, shirt off, cast dangling from a leather-padded examining table. There's a groove in the top section so I breathe without turning my head, but the room's overheated so now my cheeks are stuck to the leather. I'm trying not to flinch as a silver-haired man in a white coat and a red yarmulke pokes up and down my spine.

Turns out my arm wasn't the only accident casualty: since the smash up, rigor mortis has been setting in from my shoulder blades up, and I'm at Brookline Chiropractic taking the cure. Dr. Weiser showed me my x-ray, all of the vertebrae sitting nicely on top of each other except one rebel halfway up my neck that's cocked at a thirty-degree angle, the Marlon Brando of neckbones. Dr. Weiser's attempting to coax Marlon back into position before I go completely rigid. At least the x-ray didn't reveal something worse, a dark area that's not supposed to be dark, but even without a broken wrist I could barely strum my axe.

"So why so tense?" he asks, popping some neck cartilage like it was bubble wrap. "I see the whiplash, and one shoulder's an inch lower from all the guitar playing. But the whole region's tight, knotted, muscles fighting against each other. So I ask again, so why so tense?"

*Moi?* Tense? Maybe it's because it's been over a month and WROB still hasn't added our record yet, despite our producer Wayne schmoozing everybody from the station manager to the guy who gives the astrology reports. Or maybe it's that half my day job paycheck is going to the Ghost of Autobodies Past, paying off a rental that was a wreck to begin with. Or I could say I've got a thing for a girl who does in fact have a boyfriend.

Kat's beau is not Travis. Trav-Trav, when he's around, is an item with our fourth housemate Jan, who's attractive enough in a lefty, no-animal-tested-cosmetics kind of way, with frizzy hair and Earth-mother breasts. She and Trav both have tempers, though, and they break up and make up more than Sean and Madonna. Kat's calmer, more like the dorm RA, and since that first evening she and I have had an ongoing series of great late night conversations. I'll come back from rehearsal, say hello, make tea. We'll start chatting, and pretty soon we're deep into some subject – favorite obscure movies, religion, best and worst relationships – and hours will go by. Then, at the stroke of midnight, the phone rings.

They met in college. He's a couple years older, and is now halfway through med school back in St. Louis, Kat's hometown. So if she plays her cards right, she'll be married to a doctor. And not just someday, but soon – he's already asked her, twice. Maybe just as well since my post-Maggie relationship lifespan seems to be about six months, and anyway now that the record's out we'll be gigging more than ever.

But yet. Last night Kat and I were lying on the living room floor, talking late as usual, our bodies splayed out in opposite directions but faces just inches away on the same pillow. The lights were down, and she was telling me about her class. Her kids are all autistic to varying degrees, and each one of them is unique: the boy who has to straighten all the chairs before he can leave the room, the boy who knows what day of the week every world event happened on, the boy who loves marching bands and comes every Halloween dressed as John Phillip Sousa, complete with conductor's baton. There's even a girl down the hall who takes off all her clothes whenever she gets upset.

I was half listening and half just watching Kat's lips move, trying to resist the urge to lean over and kiss them. I was losing the fight, and pretty sure she was losing the same fight. Our voices had gotten hushed to the point of silence, our lips almost touching, when...        BBBRRRIIINNNGGG!!!

And that, Dr. Weiser, is why I'm so tense.

After my appointment I step into the cold and gingerly hop the subway to Pegasus, my latest day gig. They design music software, so your computer can tell your synthesizer and drum machine what to play, thereby eliminating the need for you altogether – I'd probably be doing the musicians of the world a favor if I blew up the factory. But with our still-negative band earnings I need the paycheck, and I was using up my voice yelling at kids all day. On the plus side, some of the more techno-geek rock stars – Greg Hawkes of the Cars, Jerry Harrison of Talking Heads – have stopped by Pegasus for prototypes, so I've got a stack of Shadowland albums by my work area just in case.

Since the accident, Daryl, my boss, has been giving me desk work I can do one-handed. As he hands me another stack of packing slips to invoice, the Scorpions' "Rock You Like a Hurricane" comes on over the warehouse speakers. Daryl strongly prefers Mozart, but he's been letting me monitor WROB to confirm they're not playing us yet. He sticks his index finger down his throat during the endless guitar solo and staggers back into the warehouse. "That's not a comment," he says over his shoulder.

"Ah, the deft touch of a German metal band," Will intones from the warehouse door. He earns commission upstairs, where it's warm and carpeted.

"Save me, brave knight," Daryl calls from the packing table. Will tunes the dial to something with French horns and Daryl pats his heart with relief. With their blown-dry hair, clipped facial adornments and meticulous clothing, they could be brothers. Or possibly more, since Daryl leans that way. Maybe Jackie's a front, and all those nights behind closed doors in Rockport she'd just been moaning with an upset stomach.

Will points in my direction. "To Bee or not to Bee?"

"Gimme a second." I click off the dot matrix and grab my jacket. Two minutes later we're in our favorite booth at the Bee, and five minutes after that we're halfway through a cheese-and-mushroom omelet (me) and baked ziti (Will), both of which come with side orders of translucent French fries.

Will raises his pebbled plastic tumbler and rattles the ice cubes. The waitress, who's somewhere between thirty and sixty-five, with orthopedic nurse's shoes, flesh-colored stockings over varicose veins and hair tinted the shade of Lucille Ball's in 1967, appears carrying a full pitcher of Dr. Pepper. Being waited on makes me feel vaguely uncomfortable, like I'm part of the ruling class, but Will takes it in stride.

"Thanks, Doreen," I say, then try to steal a French fry as Will takes a drink. He jabs toward my good hand with his fork, just missing. I tell him about the chiropractor wanting me to get a hollow-body guitar. I can see the doc's point, since my Duo Jets weighs about the same as a Les Paul, which weighs about the same as the Statue of Liberty. "Jimmy Page was probably six-four when they started Led Zeppelin."

"Ha. You still owe me a fifty, by the way." Back in high school we were offered a prom gig, two hundred bucks for four musicians, but I refused to learn "Stairway" and they took their business elsewhere. "So when can you start playing again?"

I hold up my cast. "I suppose I could use this as a slide." I gingerly lay my wrist back down on the Formica, the same oyster gray we'd had in Rockport but with less cracks. "I'm plastered for six more weeks, then physical therapy." I take one of my own fries, dip it in the half ketchup, half Worcestershire puddle on my plate, try my best to sound casual. "But I don't know. It went pretty well at the Tam with just Boone."

Will shakes his head dismissively. "One time deal, Mark. Special event. Don't go thinking you're the next Jim Morrison."

"*That's* who I reminded myself of. Maybe I should get leather pants."

"I'm serious, Zodzniak."

I know he is. I am too but I don't press it. Instead I laugh. "Hey, I just thought of this. What do the Doors have in common with Jules and the Polar Bears?"

"They're both completely irrelevant to making music in the decade *we're* trying to get a record contract in?"

"No. No bass player."

Will takes his last bite of ziti, stalling for time while he thinks of something clever to come back with. He makes a sucking sound as the straw drains the last of his Dr. Pepper. Finally:

"Doesn't it ever bother you that no one's even heard of your favorite band?"

"No."

"Well it scares the shit out of me."

## 10. *REWIND:* **Morristown, New Jersey, December 198***1*

"Merry Christmas Mrs. Preston, is Maggie there?"

It's our first Christmas in Massachusetts, but none of us are actually *in* Massachusetts: Will, Jackie and Chas are all back in Ohio, and I'm calling Maggie from my aunt's in New Jersey, a few blocks from where I grew up. My mother's here too, acutely noticing that I'm her last hope for grandchildren as my cousins' kids tear into their vast piles of loot. *Don't hold your breath, mom.* Nowhere Man's still in Ohio, supposedly for work but probably counting down the minutes until Dillon's Happy Hour opens. Not that he's ever actually happy, so maybe it should be Dillon's Misery Loves Company.

Over the phone Mrs. Preston doesn't wish me Merry Christmas back, just says "I'll check" as if Maggie would have the good sense to pretend to be out at nine a.m., California time, on Christmas morning. After a minute of sleigh bell-laden background music, she picks up.

"Hey..."

I feel my usual physical reaction. Luckily I'm on the extension in a back bedroom. "Merry Orgy of Capitalist Consumerism."

"Back atcha," she says. "Where are you?"

"Morristown. You wouldn't believe the piles of presents these kids get."

"That's America. More is more."

"And less is less," I respond. I'd just gotten a few boxes of Tastycakes and a Hot Dog Johnny's T-shirt, plus a small guilt check from Nowhere Man. "Should've given the boys Sandinista action figures to blow up Malibu Barbie's Dreamhouse."

"Sexist pig. How come girls never get to blow shit up?"

"Hey, I don't make the rules." The Perry Como arrangement of "Frosty the Snowman" comes over the line, just the thing for Christmas in LA. "Nice Muzak your mom's listening to."

"Yeah, I have to work on her."

"And speaking of music..."

"You really didn't have to, Mark."

"I know. But I thought it would remind you of me." I'd sent her, as a joke, an EP by an Italian spaghetti-punk band, I Peni

Equini, that I'd found at Will's record store, plus, as a peace offering, John and Yoko's "Happy Xmas (War is Over)."

"I listened to the Lennon three times already. Poor Yoko."

"Yeah, it still sucks." We'd been in our tiny off-campus apartment in Yellow Springs when Will had called with the news. Maggie and I had taken a long walk, holding hands, not saying much. Then I'd gotten out all my scratched Beatles 45s, and we'd had a wake, lighting a scented candle and slow dancing to "Don't Let Me Down," then just holding each other as the needle scraped.

Maggie breaks the moment with a sardonic laugh. "Of course now I feel shitty I only sent a card. Probably your plan all along."

"No plan, Maggie," I say quickly. "And the card was beautiful." She'd done a folded, rough-papered miniature with a crooked, Picasso-esque guitar painted on it, the first work of hers I've seen since Antioch. "Probably be worth millions someday."

"Ha. Don't tell my Mom, she'll up my rent. So how's my city?"

I tell her about the impromptu Christmas party we'd had, when I brought a van load of my after-school thugs to our Rockport house and we'd played them a punked-up "Feliz Navidad" and a surf-rock "God Rest Ye Merry Gentlemen" and then made mutant gingerbread men. It was going fine until somebody stepped on somebody's foot, somebody else shoved back, and then our spindly Charlie Brown Christmas tree was lying on its side, one kid pinned beneath it while another sat on top shoving a tinsel Star of Bethlehem down the first kid's throat. Jackie had stopped the riot by sticking her chest between the boys, giving them something else to think about while I herded everyone back into the van.

Maggie laughs, a good sign, so I ask how painting's going. Her last canvasses at school had been images of blood dripping from a dove impaled on an arrow, called *Stigmatas 1-13*. I'm pretty sure I was the arrow.

She says okay, but that her job at the senior center sucks because all Reagan's budget cuts are kicking in. "It's heartbreaking. These are the people eating cat food."

"So what do their cats eat?"

"It's not funny, Mark."

44

"I know, Mags. But maybe you should do something more cheerful. You know how sad you can get."

Mistake. "That's your answer for everything, isn't it. Don't get involved." She exhales, a three-thousand-mile sigh. "Shadowland notwithstanding."

"Maggie, I'm just saying. Save something for yourself."

"You sound like that fucking shrink at Antioch." Then her voice softens, Christmas truce. "How's your mom?"

"*Media y media.* We went to the cemetery this morning."

"Must be rough."

"I think that's why my dad stays in Ohio."

"How about you, Mark? How are you?"

"Fine." It comes out terse, too fast. I called her, I remind myself. "Maybe a little lonely." I look out the window, see a dusting of new snow on the lawn. I flash on me and my grade school mates speeding down the hill at Villa Walsh, then hitting a bump and rolling over and over in the snow, laughing 'til our sides hurt, not minding the cold. "It's weird being back in Morristown; it looks like home but I probably wouldn't recognize Rob and Eddie if I walked by them on the street. If they even still live here."

"You've been gone a long time, Mark. Don't expect so much."

But I *do* expect so much, I want to tell her. "Guess we need to get famous, so they'll all come backstage and visit."

"You've got Will and Chas. And Jackie."

"I know." Though I notice she didn't add "And me." I change the subject. "Hey, any good bands coming to town?"

She says on New Year's Eve she and her friend Nance are going to see the Tubes at Perkins Palace. She asks me what I'm doing. I say I don't know, but next Orgy of Capitalist Consumerism I plan to give her a Shadowland record.

"Can't wait."

Neither can I.

I'm the first one back to Rockport, and in the early dusk the whole town seems deserted. Some Saturday night. I turn on all the lights in our freezing bungalow, grab my guitar for company as the rinky electric heaters tick on. As the charcoal sky beyond our balcony gradually deepens to blue-black, I idly strum, feeling alone, holed up, like I'm back in my bedroom, not in Morristown, but that first lonely winter after we moved to Harding. My Anne Frank year, when I wrote my first god-awful songs in lieu of keeping a diary, when I wouldn't leave the house from after school Friday 'til school Monday morning. Maybe part of me's still there, still in hiding, warily watching the world through a keyhole. I think about how out of sync my mom and I both felt at my aunt's house, the party going on around us, but not really being a part of it. I think about Nowhere Man, back in Harding, even less connected to life. I start noodling a descending riff, playing off the distant breaking waves. I think about my after-school kids, already labeled losers, misfits, with parents who drink and drug too much and think about them too little. I flash on Maggie and her cat-food-eating seniors, who society's given up on as irrelevant. More misfits. *Merry Christmas, gang. Have some more Little Friskies.*

The riff coalesces as I stare out the sliding glass door at the last shred of twilight: empty street, empty town, then turbid inky water stretching on to infinity. They call it Cape Ann, but you have to drive over a causeway to get here, so it's really an island. *Hmmm.* That rings a bell. I start humming along with the riff as the final darkness falls, feel words start to fall into place:

*Another Saturday night on the island of misfit toys.*

Guess that covers just about of all of us.

### 11. *FAST FORWARD:* Worcester, Mass., January 1986

"Are you sure the Rolling Stones played here?"

Chas is standing on the empty stage at Sir Morgan's Cove in Worcester, our first gig since the release concert. If I assumed having a record out meant we'd automatically be granted respect, creature comforts, and the adoration of the masses, apparently I was mistaken. That's the downside of having our album out on A Hole in the Middle, or A-Hole Records, as Will's taken to calling Wayne's label: it's a record company in name only, no advertising budget, no tour support, no payola or arm twisting to get our single on the radio. If the Tam had been an adrenaline high, give or take me needing my arm in a sling, Sir Morgan's is the equivalent of the morning after: dark, grungy, not much of a crowd, aside from a few carloads who've made the hour's drive from Boston.

"Hell yes the Stones played here!" shouts a burly guy at the bar with a graying ponytail and a black leather Hell's Angels jacket with the sleeves ripped off. "Three hundred and fifty people packed inside, another ten thousand in the street trying to get in."

Just like tonight.

"Were you here?" Boone asks.

The Angel takes a drag on his cigarette like it's a joint. "I could bullshit you and say I carried Keith's guitar," he smiles, "but I think it was Ronnie Woods'."

I remember reading about it in *Rolling Stone*; it was a warm up date for their '81 tour, the month before we moved here, It's almost worth the trip to play on the same stage, even if it wasn't the Brian Jones *Beggars Banquet*-era Stones.

We start our set. Chas looks bored, and Will's smile looks especially pasted on. Worse, there are big video screens on either side of the stage, which the club hasn't bothered shutting off, so while I sing I'm flanked by close-ups of Wham! and Bryan Adams lip-synching their latest hits. It's really bugging me, and finally as Boone starts the intro to "Same Heart Twice" I hold up my cast-free hand.

"Could somebody *please* shut those off?" I say over the mic as Wang Chung's giant dueling haircuts fill the screens. I wait a few seconds, squinting through the stage lights to see if anyone from the club is paying attention. Evidently not, because the video's irritating jump cuts proceed without interruption.

"I'm serious," I say. "We're not playing 'til it's off."

The few people on the dance floor start drifting back to their tables.

"Mark," Will hisses out of the side of his mouth, "we're losing them. Let's just finish the fucking set."

I look back at the band; Chas is rolling his eyes and Boone looks like he could go either way. But I don't want the distraction, and we need to be great tonight: Kat's here, her first time seeing us.

I'm about to give the club another ultimatum when I make

out a sizable figure approaching the stage. Finally. Then I realize it's the Hell's Angel, looking about as wide as your average refrigerator.

"Give you twenty bucks to pull his pony-tail," Will says under his breath.

I'm flashing on Altamont – where Marty Balin of the Jefferson Airplane got knocked unconscious by an Angel before the Stones even took the stage. Then halfway across the dance floor the Angel pivots and heads for the sound table. I can only see his back, but the winged motorcycle helmet logo seems to swell and levitate as he raises his muscle-and-fatbound arms and rests his knuckles on size-forty-eight hips.

Wang Chung's poofy 'doos abruptly vanish as the screens go dark.

There's a ripple of applause as I nod to Boone, who resumes the intro. Even in the half-empty club I can feel people gravitating towards me, like now that I've got their attention they're expecting something big. I try to move around a little more, feel the lyric, project to the back wall. It's hard work, much harder than at the Tam, the dark space of Sir Morgan's just sucking our energy. But I do my best, kneeling James Brown-style for the last chorus, and we're rewarded with a pretty decent ovation.

I'm still not playing guitar, but I'm borrowing a synthesizer from Pegasus, and as Will and Chas start the groove for "Second Glance" I add some one-handed keyboard. Jackie and few others come back to dance, and during the break I climb down and join them, taking care not to swivel my neck too fast. My eyes find Kat sitting at a side table, and I nod my head towards the dance floor, but by the time she gets up the song is ending and I have to climb back onstage. She dances with Jackie, though, and we trade smiles the rest of the set.

After the show I find Kat and Jackie talking with some of the other Boston faithful. I want to ask Kat what she thought, but with the sparse crowd I know our performance wasn't exactly *Winterland '78*.

"You're gonna miss your phone call," I say, and she shrugs. "Thanks for coming out on a school night."

"Sure. It was fun. You're good, all of you."

"Thanks." I feel like there's a "but" coming, but if there is she's too polite to say it. We still have to load out, so Kat volunteers to give Jackie a ride back to Boston.

Will appears and gives Jackie a perfunctory kiss on the cheek. "Way to almost get us killed up there," he says when they're gone. "It was like Poe Ditch all over again."

I laugh. Poe Ditch – "Ohio's Woodstock" – happened the summer after tenth grade, our first year as a band, and we'd tagged along with one of Will's older brothers. It was heavily advertised as "rain or shine," and we'd suffered through some middling Midwest acts before a storm blew through. The headliners never even took the stage, the crowd rioted, and we'd had to flee through a hail of beer and soda cans. On the plus side, we'd gotten to gaze at a suntanned Vicki Shehovic in her white cut-offs, and Chas smoked his first joint. "Hey, this guy was on our side," I say.

"*Your* side."

Right, Will, like you would have wanted to sing while…

Will nudges me. "Speak of the Angel."

The club's clearing out, but the Hell's Angel is still on his bar stool, holding court with Boone and Chas, a mostly-empty tequila bottle in front of them. Guess it's Will or me driving home.

"Think I owe you a drink," I say, approaching the Angel. "You saved our butts up there."

"Nah," he says, "we're good. Pisses me off you guys don't get treated better." He nods to the screens, both blazing again, as he lights another cigarette. "That MTV crap is killing real rock 'n' roll."

I nod. I've never cared for videos, at least the lip-synched fake-mini-movie kind. Will of course loves them and thinks we should do one ASAP.

"Drinking age ain't helping neither. Club's just tryin' to stay in business." The Angel's proud he's never set foot in the Centrum, the glitzy new arena a few blocks away. Foreigner's there tonight, which might explain the lack of groupies here. Or maybe they're home watching MTV, since thanks to Beacon Hill no one under twenty-one can go clubbing anymore. One more reason we should have gotten our record out ages ago.

Boone and Chas drain their shot glasses, then we pack up our gear and get paid. As we're saying goodnight damn if the

Hell's Angel doesn't get up and carry Boone's guitar for him. When we get to the truck we give him a Shadowland album, which he makes us autograph. It's not a hundred buxom screaming women all throwing their bras at us, but it's better than nothing.

"Keep your asses rockin'," he says. I say we will.

Kat's asleep when I finally get back home. There's a note under my door, though. It just says "Great show!" with a smiley face, and it's signed K. It works: I smile.

## 12. *REWIND:* Kenmore Square, Boston, January 1982

New band night at the Rat. Our first real Boston gig. It's a mid-winter Monday, seventeen degrees, crusted snow on the pavement and Arctic wind whipping off the Charles. Anybody sane is home, Chas says, but, as I point out, sane people are boring. The Rat is neither. Seedy-but-legendary music club downstairs, seedy beer joint/hang out spot upstairs, it's the hub of the Hub's music scene, Boston's answer to the Cavern Club. Lots of black leather and mascara on the patrons, years of unfiltered Camels and spilled Budweiser in the air, and a jukebox full of local bands' singles: "When Things Go Wrong" by Robin Lane and the Chartbusters, "Don't Look Back" by Barry and the Remains, and dozens of songs, and bands, I've never heard of. No REO Speedwagon here. We load in through the back, the whirr of the Mass. Pike behind us, giant CITGO sign flashing red overhead. We're on second on a three-band night.

I asked the guy who booked us how to get a weekend gig. "Bring a crowd." So we thought of people we know in Boston. A lefty friend of Maggie's who's here working for MASSPIRG on the bottle bill. The little sister of a summer camp friend of mine who's going to B.U. A lesbian professor of Will and Jackie's who's now teaching at a women's college somewhere west of town. Chas doesn't know anybody outside of us, the health club girls and the shirt factory stitchers, two of whom he's now bedded. Jackie's invited her *Shape It!* gang again but Boston's a trek from Cape Ann, especially on a Monday, *aka* laundry night. But we're *here.*

We soundcheck, stow our gear, then head upstairs where it's warm. It's early, but the tables are full of people, all of whom look like musicians, drinking, talking, smoking. Which is good, since downstairs is empty as a graffiti-coated tomb. Maybe I should shout "air raid!" just before our set. We find some space at end of the bar as the organ riff from Jonathan Richman's "Roadrunner" fills the room.

"Think they're all here for the show?" Will asks.

"Let's find out."

There's a guy in a leather jacket paging through a copy of *SCREAM!* a few feet away. "You in a band?" I ask him. He nods. "What one?"

"We don't have a name yet."

"I'm in Shadowland. We're playing downstairs tonight, around ten."

"Mondays suck," he says, and walks back to his table. *Punk Rocker Perishes in Air Raid.*

I take a *SCREAM!* back to the bar. Its logo is the Edward Munch lightbulb figure, mouth open wide and hands over ears, but wearing a crudely-drawn, three-stringed guitar and yelling into a microphone. Which pretty accurately describes the music they champion. "Khartoum won their reader's poll," I say, pointing to the headline above a shot of the band standing in a dumpster.

"Well I didn't vote for them," Will says in peasant falsetto *à la* Terry Jones in *Holy Grail.*

"Maybe we should take out an ad."

"What, *band seeks fans*?" Chas laughs. He slides a cigarette out of its pack, since our corner of the room still has a few oxygen molecules.

"Why not? Like a fake personal ad. *Intelligent Midwestern power pop group, recently relocated, seeks fans. Apply next Wednesday at the Channel, you won't be disappointed. Signed, Shadowland.*"

"*Seeks groupies,* maybe," Chas says, striking the match with his thumbnail.

"No really."

"Interesting marketing idea," says Will, hand on his chin. Jackie had also nixed his sideburns, so there's a nascent goatee sprouting beneath his fingers. "But is it brilliant or stupid?"

Jackie whispers in Will's ear. He smiles and nods. "Ah, the eternal question."

"It's stupid," Chas says, shaking his head through a cloud of his own second-hand smoke.

"Can't it be both?" I say, waving my hand reflexively. "Look, if we were playing in Harding, you'd tell everybody in the drum line, Will would tell his brothers and sisters and the drama club, and I'd tell the track team and we'd have a decent crowd."

"Considering there's not a fuck lot else to *do* in Harding," Chas shrugs.

"Yeah but you know what I mean. Since we don't have people to come see us, we have to *do* something to get noticed."

"Like be good?" Chas asks.

I shake my head. "*Aside* from that."

"We could play naked," says Will helpfully. "Change our name to the Mooners."

Jackie whispers something else to Will. "I'm not touching that one," he says.

We head downstairs to hear the first band. When we go in the dressing room, the third band, who were heading out for a pizza when we soundchecked, is back, adding their name to the wall. For every name I know – The Police, Joan Jett – there are a hundred I've never heard of. Not very good odds when you think about it.

"Hey, you guys sounded great. Was that a Monkees tune?"

We'd soundchecked with "Clarksville." Asking is a perky-looking blonde in a Lt. Uhura-length mini-skirt.

I say it's actually an anti-war song about a guy getting drafted. "And it was a hit right at the height of Vietnam. Pretty subversive."

"He means yes," Chas says, eyeing her up and down.

"Cool, I'm into bubblegum," she says. "Music should be fun."

"Leaves yours out," Will says in my direction.

"I'm Mark," I say, holding out my hand. "We're Shadowland."

She takes it, bouncing it energetically. "We're Rock Paper Scissors. I'm Annie."

"Chas," says Chas, casually flipping his dirty blonde locks. Flaunt it if you got it.

"Shadowland like the Peter Straub horror story?" asks an extremely tall, lanky guy wearing a sixties Fender Jaguar with the sunburst finish.

"Well, we're from Ohio, so the horror part's right," Will says.

"You all moved here together?" When I nod, Annie says she and Boone, the guitar player, met at Berklee, the music school in town. They seem like us, basically regular people who happen to be in a band, as opposed to the crowd upstairs, which looks like a Ramones theme park.

They open their pizza box and offer us a slice. I'm about to take one when Annie lets out a scream that would make Edward Munch proud.

"Jesus H. fuck, what?" Boone asks.

Annie points. I start, too: there, on a ceiling pipe, is an actual rat, his gross twitching nose extended down towards the pizza. I've never really seen one up close before, and it's big, much bigger than a mouse. It looks like a dirty sneaker with paws and a long thin tail.

"Shoo!" Boone yells, waving his hand. I shut the pizza box in case it was planning on jumping, but it scampers off back up the pipes, and we all let our breaths out.

"Shit," Chas says after a minute, shaking out a cigarette with an unsteady hand. "Now we know why they call it the Rat."

We hear the first band starting. It's actually just one guy with a stack of synthesizers, who calls himself Death Takes a Holiday. He sounds moody and electronic, like Kraftwerk, but with tortured operatic screeching instead of hypnotic chanting, and any hope I had of the scenesters upstairs paying three bucks to check out the show is now dead. I sip my lukewarm ginger ale and try to block him out by humming vocal exercises.

Mr. Death introduces his last song and we go to the dressing room to get ready: guitar scales (me), hair fluff (Will), drum rolls (Chas). When I told Maggie about being nervous before our Jonathan's set she suggested I get try getting high before shows.

"Like Hendrix at Woodstock," I'd said. "I can talk about going to Saturn between songs."

"You're so all-or-nothing," she sighed. "There's a middle path." The Tao of Maggie. I'd reminded her that her first party at Antioch she'd ended up passed out under the dorm piano, and had to ask me the next day if we'd had sex. Luckily we hadn't.

Death finishes unplugging his stack o' synths and we wheel our gear into place. The soundman says over the house mic, "Please welcome, all the way from Indiana, Shadowland!"

Chas starts the drumbeat, boom boom BAM BAM boom boom BAM, heavy on the toms. We're opening with "Misfit Toys," which I'd finished while watching Dick Clark and his cavalcade of also-rans ring in the New Year. *Our year.* Will and I play the riff in tandem, locking in with the drums. The sound, bouncing off the brick walls, is huge, with a natural echo that's better than any cheesy effect. We've played eight measures in Boston proper and already we sound better than we ever have. We sound like a real band. A real *Boston* band.

As I approach my mic the soundman brings up the front row of stage lights, hanging from a rack a few feet in front of my face. *Double whoa*: they're bright as lasers and they're hot, even in the cold club. Next time, sunglasses. Not to mention sunscreen. When my pupils have adjusted to the point where I can make out the crowd, I sing the last few lines towards Annie:

> *I'm tired of waiting to not be chosen*
> *Don't waste your life staring at the frozen sea*
> *Come on, it takes a misfit toy to love a misfit boy like me*

We get some real applause despite the small crowd, and launch into the rest of the set. When we do "Clarksville" Jackie and Annie get up to dance, making it worth the trip. By the time we finish the set I'm drenched with sweat and my voice is shot, but I'm psyched as we carry off our gear.

"Great show!" I say, flicking a sweaty towel at Chas.

"Yeah, too bad it was wasted," he says, nodding at the less than full house, basically each bands' handful of friends plus some college students they'd probably let in for free.

"Hey, they liked us. One fan at a time."

"Yeah," says Will, "at that rate we'll sell our first million records in only, what, three thousand years?"

"Way less," I say. "Don't forget Leap Year."

We go out and watch Rock Paper Scissors since they sat and listened to us. We say hello to our few friends, then pull up stools at the bar. Annie and RPS are interesting, sort of a prog rock band with a pop/Nu Wave singer, like Belinda Carlisle fronting King Crimson. Boone's a hell of a guitar player, with a full array of distortion and delay boxes spread around his feet, and the other players are good too, but on the whole I think we're a little funkier and grittier (the Harding, Ohio Players?). Annie and Boone appear to be an item, so I mentally add her to the list of women I'll never sleep with, alongside Ursula Andress, Emma Peel, Cherie Currie, and Suzy Cowsill. Not to mention Jackie. I wonder if Chas even has a list.

"Hey, want to go to IHOP with us?" Annie asks as we're loading out. It's after midnight and we have an hour's drive back to Rockport but what the hell.

"Sure, thanks, we're starving." Our take from the door should just about cover the check. Chas follows their station wagon along the river to Soldier's Field Road, and we sprint inside and gorge on pancakes with fake maple syrup and bottomless cups of overbrewed coffee and talk about life, music, and Boston while Chas and I scope out eligible waitresses. Now *this* is how rock bands party.

Annie tells me she really likes my songs.

"Thanks. Yours too."

Then she tells Will he has a great voice. "You should sing more."

"You think?" he says, and kicks me under the table.

"Absolutely. And you've got fabulous hair. The little girls'll go wild."

Thank *you*, Annie. Maybe I should take Jackie off that list.

## 13. *FAST FORWARD:* Chestnut Hill, Mass., February 1986

"Lindsay Buckingham's at the Paradise on Friday. The whole band's going, wanna come?"

Kat and I are in our kitchen at 1941 Comm. Ave. We're trying to make dinner, but all the pans are dirty. Our housemate Jan is a walking metaphor for why revolutions fail: a devout socialist who never does her own dishes. Trav-Trav is even worse; he always wears hemp sandals and leaves a trail of clipped toenails wherever he happens to be sitting. I'm not exactly neat by nature, but I'm making an effort to impress Kat, so I grab a pan and start scrubbing with my good hand.

"The Fleetwood Mac guy?" Kat asks. I figure a group date is less threatening and easier for her to explain to Dr. Kildare. Besides, per Will via Jackie, all is not well in the house of love: Kat spent the whole trip home from Worcester complaining about how David – Dr. Kildare – was pressuring her to get formally engaged.

"Buckingham's a lot more fun solo," I say. He's also a rarity, playing guitar with just his fingers, no pick, so maybe I'll learn something.

"Okay, why not," she says. "I should live a little."

Speaking of living, we're having steamed Co-op cauliflower with grilled American cheese, served on unmatched plastic plates. Very posh. Kind of interesting to be living with somebody before you've even kissed. I know what she looks like in the morning without mascara on. She knows what I look like in the morning without mascara on.

"Great, pick you up at eight."

"I'll be right across the hall."

The Paradise is packed, way beyond any sane fire code limit. I see Boone's head sticking above the crowd and we make our way toward him. Will and Jackie are there – Will with a white silk scarf draped over his brown bomber jacket for a rock-star-as-WWI-flying-ace effect, and Jackie in a plunging V-neck that more than one guy sneaks a peek at. Chas is here with his new girlfriend Deedee, who could be his twin: she's tall for a girl and just as slender, with sandy blonde curls the length of his. Deedee's frowning as usual, unhappy about the cramped quarters, and Chas goes off to get her a drink. She hadn't made our Worcester show so I introduce her to Kat, and Kat starts telling her about some of the Springsteen crowds she's endured.

There's no opening act, so the stage is already set for Buckingham. There are amplifiers and drums, so it's not Lindsay solo *per se*, but it won't be F. Mac's greatest hits. A Stevie Nicks video comes on while we wait and half the crowd boos and hisses.

"Mark!" I hear behind me. I turn around and it's a woman I know I know. Right. Halloween party. The *polar bear*.

"Hey, how's it going?" Linda? Lisa? Livia?

"Good, how about you?" She'd been dressed in white thermal underwear that fit her extremely well, with white bear ears and a little fluffy white tail. She'd never heard of the group, so I'd spent half an hour explaining why the Jules and Polar Bears, who I'd only discovered by accident while combing the stacks at Radio Free Antioch, were the best American band since the Velvet Underground: quirky cool music and lyrics that are funny and tragic at the same time, which is exactly how life feels – *The one nice thing about true hopelessness is you don't have to try again. Stupid questions about love are the stupidest questions of them all. You gotta make your mind your own before you find your mind a match.* Plus you can dance to them. Linda/Lisa/Livia had been intrigued, and I would have invited her over to check out my record collection, but I was still with Ms. New Hampshire, so I just got her number for future reference. Then I'd met Kat and never called.

Tonight Linda/Lisa/Livia's not in her white thermals, but in tight black jeans that are almost as revealing. Officially, Kat's still with David. Hmmm. What to do, what to do. I glance back at Kat, see her chatting away with Jackie and Deedee like she's known them for years. She looks up and flashes me a quick smile. Okay, busted. I start to head back, but then Linda/Lisa/Livia notices my cast and asks what happened. I tell her about the accident, but she's more impressed with the fact we have a record out. "Hey, I'm doing multi-media this semester at school, maybe I could film you," she says, giving my good hand a little squeeze. "Call me sometime."

I say I will. The house lights start to come down so I nod

goodbye, then push my way back to Kat's side. "Sorry, I should have offered to get you a drink."

"Don't worry, Boone's getting me one." That gets my attention – after what happened with Maggie, maybe I should do a better job of protecting my turf. When Boone gets back I make a point of paying him for Kat's beer.

The crowd quiets to a murmur, and in the glow of the exit lights we can make out Buckingham's band filing onstage. A police whistle blows, and all at once a cacophony of drumming starts, like a band of all Chasses. As the lights come up, every musician onstage is hitting a different sized drum, all pounding away in unison: DOM DOM dom dom dom DOM DOM dom dom dom. After a long minute the bass player puts down his mallet and begins plucking a riff in counter rhythm, DOM dom dom DOM. It's "Tusk," one of the weirder Mac tunes. Lindsay, who seems to be wearing brown eye shadow to match his guitar, walks to the mic, looks uneasily out over the crowd and starts to sing in a paranoid whisper: *Why don't you tell me what's going on…* It's still loud, and I tap Kat on the shoulder and offer her a couple of foam earplugs. She mouths "thank you!" and we both put them in. It's still loud, and after the song I take her hand and push my way towards the balcony, where the pressure per square inch is slightly kinder.

We find a sliver of an opening and claim it, settle in for the show. To my surprise Kat doesn't pull her hand back. *Hmmm.*

"Pretty."

It's hours later and we're still holding hands. We're looking out on the lights of Boston – the Pru with its red radio beacon, the glass-walled Hancock, the cluster of skyscrapers further downtown – all slightly out of focus in the damp midnight mist. We're standing and shivering in a tiny park at the top of a hill somewhere near the Brighton/Brookline border, but neither of us is in a rush to go. We'd begged off IHOP, hopped the Green Line and got off a few stops early, then climbed in a zig zag pattern until we ran out of up and found the park. The cold feels good after the body-heated, claustrophobic Paradise, and David or no David there's definitely some electricity flowing between our fingers.

We've been keeping the conversation neutral as we

climbed, nonchalantly ignoring our hand-holding as we exhale our little clouds of steam. Kat, who's been living at 1941 Comm. Ave. for a year, has been giving a history of the house, telling which piece of furniture was left by which former roommate. She doesn't know about the easy chair, which by its worn braided burgundy upholstery looks like it could have been left by John and Abigail Adams. I tell her I inherited my current bed from an Antioch friend who was here for grad school. "I did get a brand new mattress, though."

"You know that wooden table in my room?" Kat says.

"With all the names carved into it?"

"It's from my dorm. In St. Louis"

"You *stole* it?" Kat's such a goody-goody, it's like hearing Marie Osmond say she pulled the Brinks job.

"They were getting rid of it. I would have taken the couch too but I couldn't fit it in the U-haul." She says the couch, along the dorm wall just outside her bedroom, was the hangout spot for the whole floor, so she felt like she knew everything about everybody, and that they always went everywhere, dances, meals, Cardinals' games, as a mob. "Half my friends are still there." She gives a little laugh. "Married to the other half."

I reflexively start to let go of her hand, but then change my mind, since she's not even my girlfriend yet. "Never had a mob," I say, thinking all the way back to grade school. "And Antioch was more like this loose collection of rebels, scattering to the ends of the earth day after graduation." Maggie hadn't even waited to get her diploma. And *nobody*, I don't say, even the few in committed relationships, was getting married. "So why leave?"

Kat shakes her head, and a lock of her copper hair comes forward. I'd brush it back with my free hand, but it's still in its cast and I don't want to knock her out. She leaves it hang, thinking. "I guess I didn't want St. Louis to be the only place I ever knew. I wanted…I *want*…I don't know…an adventure." In her wool pea coat looking out at the fog she looks like a red-haired sailor. I'm in my surplus Army field jacket, so it feels like we're on shore leave.

"You could have hopped a river boat down the Mississippi."

She laughs. "That's *Huck Finn.* I was always more *Johnny Tremain.*" Kat reads constantly, like my sister used to, and her

59

room has more books than mine has records. Kat purses her lip, smile disappearing. "The hard part was telling David."

Her hand pulls away, breaking the connection, and disappears into her coat pocket. Mine, still extended, feels cold and incomplete, and slinks its way to the lining of my jacket.

Kat produces a couple pistachios, offers me one. "You see *Desperately Seeking Susan?*"

I nod yes to the movie, no to the pistachio.

"That's what I felt like there," she says, "like I was Rosanna Arquette, and David's the hot tub salesman, and we were going to have this very nice, very boring life while somewhere people were actually *living*, actually having fun."

My date had identified with Madonna, then promptly moved to New Hampshire to have fun. She may be the first. "Sounds like Harding," I say. I turn in to face Kat, blocking her view of the city, trying to reassert our connection without being too obvious about it. "So are you going back someday?" She's an inch or two taller than me, and up close I can see the bump on her nose, the fine capillary lines in her cheeks, her earnest green eyes.

"Are you?" she asks, a little puff of vapor escaping with each word.

"Not even in a box."

She laughs again, but doesn't draw back. "I didn't hate it that much. St. Louis is fine. David's fine. He's a decent person." She shivers, and her voice gets more plaintive. "But he wants this country-club bridge-playing life. He knows what neighborhood he wants to live in, has our house all picked out. Has the *furniture* all picked out." She sighs another mini-cloud of vapor, and I'm close enough that the moisture fogs my glasses. "And a carved-up table from my dorm wouldn't fit. *I* wouldn't fit."

I reach out, put a consoling hand on her hip. "Fits in okay at our house."

"Thanks." She lets her head droop forward, halving the distance between us. "So do all your bricks and boards."

"Thanks. Picked 'em out myself at Grossman's." I reach in her pocket, tug her towards me, then slide my fingers through hers. "So you ready for that adventure?"

She laughs, but quieter, shyer this time. "Lose my memory and meet Aidan Quinn?"

"Or somebody."

She tilts her head some more, so we're almost touching. "I *think* so." She closes her eyes, and I move in for the kill. Then her eyes pop open again, and I freeze, a millimeter away from her lips. "But…"

"But *what*?"

She lets her forehead rest on mine, closes her eyes again. "But it would feel…I don't know…dishonest." She straightens up, breaking contact, and looks out at the fog. "What if right now *David's* kissing somebody esle? How would that make me feel?"

"But you don't love him," I say.

"I don't *know*." She shakes her head. "And he *thinks* I love him. So it would be pretty scummy to fall in love with somebody else."

Fuck – it feels like being back in high school, back in the bourgeois, pre-sexual-revolution Midwest. Which I moved here to get away from. "Okay, no problem," I say, trying to sound casual. Linda/Lisa/Livia and I would probably be in bed by now. I let go of Kat's hand, feel something small and hard at the bottom of her coat pocket. "Maybe I'll take that pistachio."

My impatience must have shown through, because Kat draws back, a quick shadow of hurt, or disappointment, across her face. Our first less-than-perfect moment. Just the same, she shells it for me and slips it into my mouth with her fingers. I bite down and catch her fingertip, and we stand that way in the mist.


## 14. *REWIND:* Chinatown, Boston, February 1982

"Nuts!" says Chas.

"In a vise!" adds Will, as a car the size of my Datsun darts ahead of the van and slides into the fifth parking spot in a row we've had our eyes on. We've been looping the same canyon-esque block of Ping On Street for an almost hour, after crawling for miles through an ever-tightening Venus fly trap of one-way downtown traffic. Rock Paper Scissors invited us to play at their bass player's loft party in Chinatown tonight, but it's looking like we should have taken the train down from Rockport and just wheeled the equipment from North Station.

"There's one!" Will yells again from the shotgun seat. A sedan's starting to pull out, but there's a red light between us and him. I slide back the side door, jump out and sprint my way to the spot before anyone else can pull in, then wave away the pissed-off competition 'til Chas arrives.

Luckily the building has a freight elevator, and we unload and ride to the top. The loft is huge, covering the whole floor, and instead of rooms, areas are curtained off, the whole space dimly lit by glow globes. The bass player, Jay, who goes to MIT, has a bunk bed with a motorcycle parked where the lower bunk would be, and a picture of Albert Einstein sticking his tongue out safety-pinned to the curtain. There are lots of people milling around already, and I'm expecting the sweet burnt odor of pot smoke, but instead they're gathered around oxygen canisters. Actually, nitrous oxide. Evidently the drug of choice at MIT is laughing gas.

At least people should be in a good mood, and hopefully like us. Annie's offered to introduce me to a Berklee friend who's coming who could possibly record us – for free – at the school's studio, so even though it's just a party I want us to be good. And it's just the sort of weird artsy happening Talking Heads used to play at before they got signed, so you never know. Maybe the Cars or Jonathan Richman will stop by.

Rock Paper Scissors are set up in an open space with a large picture window behind them. Between two sleek glass skyscrapers I can see a clock on an old stone tower, then miles of twinkling lights curling around Boston Harbor. I flash on Maggie, three thousand miles away in LA, and get a pang of what feels like homesickness. Maybe she'll still move to Boston. Then what?

We stash our gear beside the stage area. Annie is talking to a *zaftig* girl dressed up as a sixties go-go dancer à la *Shindig*, with white knee-high boots and a matching leather cap, and waves me over. Meredith, the girl, is the one taking the production class at Berklee. I'm a little surprised – quick, name a female record producer – but free studio time is free studio time. I flag Will and Chas and introduce them. Will says we'll try not to suck. Chas asks what she's drinking, then follows Meredith to the makeshift bar.

RPS are fun, much looser than they'd been at the Rat. Nobody actually dances, but people sway in place and hoot after songs. Boone takes an amazing solo on an instrumental, "The Martian Boogie," and then they out-square us by covering Norman Greenbaum's "Spirit in the Sky," complete with cheesy echo effects.

Then it's our turn. We do most of our normal set, but in deference to Annie toss in a couple obscure covers that Will sings. We still get our biggest ovation for "Last Train to Clarksville," with Annie, Jackie and Meredith all dancing up front, and we extend it and throw in bits of "Gloria" and "Twist and Crawl." After the set I want to ask Meredith what she thought, but Chas beats me to her and they head back to the bar.

Jay, our host, sees me and waves me over to the nearest nitrous canister, where he and Boone are deep in conversation.

"Guitar tone," Boone is saying. "Unless you hand-wire the pick-ups the other way."

"Would magnetic tape still work? Or would we have to go back to cylinders?"

I gradually get that they're talking about the effect of reversing the Earth's magnetic poles. Who knows, maybe MIT is about to do it. Jay holds out the nitrous nozzle. "Yes, no, maybe?"

"Um," I say. My dentist only used Novocaine.

"It's safe." Jay holds it up to his nose and inhales, then hands the tube to Boone, who does the same.

Part of me wonders if I should loosen up, like Maggie says. But then I picture all the Harding High stoners killing time behind the school gym everyday while I ran my laps. They'd take turns tossing pebbles at the metal drum trash can, *ping, ping, ping.* Then they'd gather up more pebbles and do it again. And again. "I don't think so," I say. I need my brain cells intact, since unlike Will I'm never gonna make it on my fabulous hair.

"I'm in," Chas says, wandering up with Meredith in hand. They each take hits and start giggling almost immediately. Then Chas hands the tube to Will, but Jackie frowns and Will passes, at least for now. Chas pulls me aside, hands me the keys to the van and says he'll catch a train tomorrow.

Actually it's Sunday before he gets back. He says Meredith thinks we're cool and is willing to record us. Will says "good work" and I have two thoughts: great, they'll break up before our session's over and she'll burn the tape, or, they won't break up and the drums will be louder than the vocal.

The next Saturday Meredith catches the train to Rockport. Our basement is unheated so we're still set up in my bedroom, and we play through our half dozen or so best originals and, at Will's insistence, a couple of the covers she'd heard at the loft. Today Meredith's dressed like a typical college student, in jeans and a sweater vest, but with her throat scarf and sturdy frame she looks more like a Bohemian opera singer. Hope Chas's bed is up to it.

Meredith likes "Killing Time" and thinks it could be an anthem like "London Calling" or "My Generation." She wants something to contrast that, so I play her a love song, "Just like Where the River Meets the Sea," that I'd written for Maggie early on, after she'd told me about camping with her family on the beach when she was a little girl. A creek flowed down from San Onofre Mountain, and they'd stayed up 'til midnight to watch the grunion run – thousands of little minnows flopping on the sand, flashing silver in the moonlight. When I'd played it for Maggie the next day she'd told me there was now a nuclear power plant standing there. Fuckin' progress.

Will argues for one he sings instead, but Meredith likes "River" and since Chas is hoping to get back in her pants he doesn't protest. And besides, I remind Will, no covers. Meredith says we'll need to pay the tape costs, but the studio time's free (or rather, is already figured into her tuition). We can take her out to dinner and stick her on the guest list.

Two weeks later Meredith walks us into Berklee's Studio A.

"Wow," says Chas, a second before I would have. The so-called studio at Radio Free Antioch was a glorified broom closet, with a microphone, a stool and a turntable, and miles of wires running in every direction. This is like a mini-cathedral, spacious and open with high ceilings and beautiful wooden floors, with every mic cord neatly wound on a wall rack. Behind a glass partition is a control room with the largest tape recorder I've ever seen. Bet the reels would fit my Datsun.

Meredith has Chas set up his drums in the center of the room and puts Will and me in little cubicles lined with foam baffling. I've got new Ernie Balls on my Duo Jet, and Will's boiled his bass strings for extra pop. She sets up mics and gives us all headphones, then disappears into the booth. I wonder if this is how the Beatles felt their first time at Abbey Road, if they knew it was the start of something big. I glance over the baffling at Chas, who nods, then over at Will, who gives me a thumbs up. We're poised, psyched, ready.

I'm expecting to hear "Take one!" over the phones, but instead Meredith matter-of-factly says, "Kick drum."

Chas obediently thumps his bass drum.

"Again."

Thump.

"Again. Keep it going."

An hour and forty-five minutes later, after checking every drum, cymbal, amplifier and microphone, Meredith says *she's* ready. My initial adrenaline rush is long gone, replaced by a jittery almost-boredom, like I've had too much IHOP coffee. I run in place to rouse myself, and Will and I recheck our tuning for the umpteenth time.

"Rolling."

Chas counts off "Killing Time" and I play my little intro riff. He and Will come in on the downbeat, and it's immediately too fast, like a pent-up tiger escaping from a cage. I stop and wave my arms.

"Guys, we're not the Minutemen." Now that the moment's here, the adrenaline's back, feeding more jitters.

"Okay, take two," Meredith says, rewinding the tape. "Rolling." Chas counts us off again.

"Fuck," yells Will a few measures in. "Dropped my pick."

"Take a deep breath," Meredith says, and we hear her exaggerated inhale over the phones, like Brenda Vaccaro doing squat thrusts. "Okay, here we go."

Take three's better, we make it through the first verse, then I lose my place and play the wrong chord. Shit. We're just doing the rhythm track, without vocals, and it's disorienting. "Sorry," I say.

"Thought we had it," Will says.

Meredith tells me to mime my vocal so we know where we are, and Will makes a big show of mouthing his harmonies. It takes a few more tries to get all the way through, but she finally calls us into the booth.

She presses a button on the console and the giant spools begin turning. *Wow*. It had sounded pretty shitty in the headphones – drums too loud, guitar too thin, bass too flabby – but the playback's a hundred percent better. She's added some flanging on my guitar, so it seems to oscillate back and forth like a fan, and some reverb to the drums so they jump out of the speakers. Maybe all that knob fiddling was worth it. I want to sing the vocal right then so we can hear it finished, but the mics are set up for the band so it's more efficient to move on.

"River" takes us even longer since it's a slow one, but we finally get a decent take. In the booth Will's bass sounds huge, and Chas's echoed cymbal splashes sound liquid and dreamy.

We have the studio 'til eight, and it's now seven-thirty. We've killed the *whole day* just doing two rhythm tracks. Meredith says don't worry about it, we can do overdubs tomorrow, as she starts unplugging mics. But we still have half an hour. I ask her if Will and I can get vocal mics. She asks what we're doing, and I tell Chas to count off "Clarksville."

"You said no covers," Will says, hands on hips, Superman-style.

"The arrangement's totally different," I respond. "It's nothing like the original." It's also, cover or not, the best received song at the three gigs we've done so far.

"Fuck you. You mean it's okay because *you* sing it."

"Will, the clock is ticking. We can have this argument, and then not record *anything*. Humor me, okay?" I nod to Chas to start his intro. Will huffs but comes in on cue.

We sing it live, one take, just like at a gig. It's a little fast, but we make it through, and it's a relief not having to concentrate on where we are in the song. The Monkees fade out on their version, but I give a nod for the last chord. Either accidentally or on purpose Will plays the wrong note, but it sounds kind of cool. We're so punchy Chas and I start cracking up, but Will's still pissed.

"Thank you," I say. "Was that so hard?"

He doesn't bother responding, just lays his Hofner in its case and locks himself in the men's room until everything's loaded.

We take Meredith to the No Name Restaurant for dinner down on the waterfront before dropping her and Chas off at her apartment in the Fenway. Will's still sulking on the drive back to Rockport – no bad puns or running commentary about what's on the radio.

"Remember Jonathan Swift?" I say to break the ice. We'd read *A Modest Proposal* back in Honors English.

Will, who's driving, ignores me.

"I said –"

"I heard you."

"Well, do you?"

"Sure. Pinch runner for the Indians."

"Seriously."

He blows a puff of air, and, sounding bored, says, "*Soylent Green* meets the Age of Enlightenment. Any other College Bowl questions?"

"Exactly. 'A foolish consistency is the hobgoblin of little minds.'"

"That's Emerson, you asshole."

"Of course. 'Karn Evil Nine.' *Brain Salad Surgery.*"

He doesn't crack a smile.

"Will, I'm apologizing. You can sing something next time. Promise."

"If there is a next time."

"What does *that* mean?"

"We're supposed to be a *band,* fuckhead, not the Mark Zodniak Experience. Chas and I aren't going to stick around just to be abused."

"This is being hit on the head lessons. Abuse is down the hall."

"Same dif." He takes a long pull on his milkshake. We'd set aside the animosity long enough to stop at Steve's Ice Cream. "One consolation, though."

"What's that?"

"Of the three of us, *you're* the one who's not getting laid tonight."

There is that.

Later, Will and Jackie are extra loud, probably in my honor. I fall asleep with the pillow over my head.

Will and I are back at noon for overdubs, but no happy couple. The studio's locked so we kill time reading the lobby bulletin board: Zappa-inspired guitarist looking for rhythm section to jam, GB band seeks attractive female vox for wedding gigs, art-punk band seeks exhibitionist front man, Oedipal complex a plus. Fifteen minutes later they appear, Meredith in front. She's all business, barely says hi. Chas rolls his eyes. *They've had a fight.*

While she's setting up the mics I whisper, "What happened?"

"Was it your deviant sexual practices?" Will asks, eyebrows raised.

"Fuck no, she liked my deviant sexual practices."

"So?"

He rolls his eyes again and sighs. "So last night she was playing me her demo tape."

"You didn't say it sucked," Will says.

"Of course not, I said it was great."

"How was it really?" I ask.

"Yeah, did it suck?"

"It was okay, kind of funky, but she's no Chaka Khan."

"So?"

Chas glances through the glass to make sure Meredith's still out of range. "She said she's trying to get a manager to get her a record contract. So I said she might want to take off a few pounds, so she'd look sexier on the album cover."

"Oh, Chas," Will says, shaking his head.

"Well you saw her mauling that lobster." She'd gotten every bit of flesh, sucking out each claw like it was a Bob Marley spliff.

"That's not the point."

"I told her about Jackie and her friends working out, and how buff they are—"

"Chas, for a sexaholic you know nothing about women." Even Maggie, who's borderline anorexic, had stood on our bed every morning to see how her jeans looked in the dresser mirror.

"All I meant—"

Meredith walks back in so we shut up. Maybe she *will* burn the tape, or at least wipe the drum tracks. I would.

I go into the live room to sing "Killing Time," the rhythm

track blasting in the phones as I sing along. Will gives me feedback after each take, encouraging me to sing harder ("More Graham Parker! Less Ian Hunter!"), until I'm almost shouting at the microphone. Once again it sounds tinny in the headphones, but better in the booth, and the raw quality in my voice makes the song feel real. Meredith has Will add his harmony, then I go back out to overdub a guitar solo. It takes me a few tries, but it's fun playing along with myself, and the extra guitar and vocal make it sound like a real record. Will this be our "Space Oddity"? Or at least our "Just What I Needed"?

I go back to the mic to sing "Just Like Where River Meets the Sea," but my voice is ragged from "Killing Time." Fuck, maybe we should have done them in reverse order. I drink some tea and try again, but it's still pretty rough, even by my standards.

"Okay, come on back in," Meredith says. As I walk in the control room, Will strolls out into the studio and puts on my headphones. Now it's my turn to say, what are we doing? "I just want to try something," she says. She starts the rhythm track, and *Will* begins singing.

"Hey, that's my song," I say. I tell her I can come back tomorrow, or next week.

"No time, I have to turn this in for class. He was singing along in here, I think he'll be fine."

"Yeah, but –" *I wrote it for Maggie,* I want say. *Will wasn't anywhere around.*

Meredith cuts me off. "Mark, *I'm* the producer. We only have the studio 'til four. You had your chance."

Maybe that's why Will had me screaming my head off. As I listen to him running down *my* song I feel like I'm six years old again, in the backseat of our Mercury Comet. My mom asks me a question, but while I'm thinking of the words, my big sister leans over and answers for me. My mom answers back, like she doesn't even notice it's the wrong kid, and she and my sister go on talking the rest of the trip like I'm not even there. I want to punch her – my sister, Meredith, my mother, Will, take your pick – but considering it's basically a free recording session and we don't have the tape yet, I hold my tongue.

It's not just that it's Will singing my song. It's that he sounds so…*mechanical,* like he's reading it off the lyric sheet.

Which in fact he is. I shake my head, start stalking out of the control room.

Will starts another verse: *You're tired, I'll enfold you and rock you to rest....* I stop in the doorway, head down, listening. It's a late night love song, a lullaby, and he's selling it like it's a show tune. I can either keep going, wash my hands of it, or turn around. I listen to one more line, then take a step back toward the mixing board. "Can I talk to him a minute?"

"Sure." Meredith stops the tape.

"How's it sound in there?" Will asks on mic.

"Sucks like a thirsty hooker," I say, pressing the talkback button.

"I was *asking* our producer."

"It does sound a little stiff," Meredith admits.

I lean in again. "Sing it like you'd say it. Not so melodramatic."

"I'm doing Bowie. 'Rock and Roll Suicide.'"

Ah, that explains the faux-Mayfair accent. "It's not a fucking *Bowie* song." I can't very well tell him to visualize Maggie's face, how wistful she looked talking about her dad giving her a piggyback ride on the sand. "Think about Jackie. Sing it to her. It's two AM and she's crying and it's her favorite song and you're rocking her to sleep."

"Jesus, Mark, am I wearing pajamas or in the nude?"

Chas reaches for the button. "Definitely PJs. But *Jackie –*"

Meredith cuts him off. "Rolling."

Will takes a breath and starts another verse. It's better, but still too formal. Hmmm.

"Hey, can I sing it *with* him?" I ask Meredith. "So he hears me in the phones?"

Meredith holds her hands up. "Mark, we're only doing this because you couldn't sing it in the first place."

I shake my head. "Not to record me, but just so I can lead him."

"If it were me I'd be insulted," she says. "Any real singer would."

"It's my song," I say. Chas rolls *his* eyes; we'd spent an hour last rehearsal with me and Will calling out random drum patterns for Chas to try: now the kick, now the snare, now the tom.

70

He got fed up with us, but we ended up with a cool groove. I look back at Meredith.

"Fine, let's just do it," she says, shaking her head. "We're running out of time." She tells Will the deal.

It helps. I still think I sing it better, but it's more human than it was, and even I have to admit Will *does* have a nice voice, if a little Vegas smooth. Meredith adds too much echo, but by now I don't even bother complaining. When Will's out of earshot I ask for an instrumental mix, so I can do a vocal for Maggie sometime.

There isn't much to mix on "Clarksville," but it sounds fun, with some nice call-and response fills between my guitar and Chas's drums during the outro. She makes us a reel copy of each song, plus a cassette for the car. We thank her and pack up. Chas whispers something to her on the way out but she shrugs him off. At least she didn't burn the tape.

On the way home we blast it. It's not perfect, but it's us, and the louder we crank it the better it sounds.

"Which one do you think they'll play?" Will shouts.

"'Killing Time,'" I say. The rhythm track could be Generation X, with its guitar crunch and insistent snare hits.

"I don't know," says Will. "'River Meets the Sea' sounds pretty nice."

"Might be confusing with a different singer."

"That's why the Beatles never made it."

"Maybe they'll play both of them. Maybe they'll play all three." I have a fleeting vision of us sweeping WROB's local chart.

"Right," says Chas.


## 15. *FAST FORWARD:* Allston, Mass., February 1986

"*What* next record?"

It's three weeks after the Lindsay Buckingham concert, and we're in the Batcave – our damp, dark rehearsal space beneath Allston Realty Associates – waiting for Boone as usual. I've just played Will and Chas a clunky, one-handed piano version of a new song, "Wolf in Wolf's Clothing," which I think might be good for our next record, but Will doesn't want to work on it.

"We just spent a fortune on this one," he continues. "And even if we sell them all we'll still lose money."

"This pressing," I say, waving my white plaster cast for emphasis. "You have to think bigger."

"Yeah," says Chas from his drum throne. "So we can lose *more* money."

Will nods to Chas, *good one*, as I shake my head.

"Besides," Will says dismissively, "if you haven't noticed, protest songs went out with Kent State."

"The Clash? The Pistols?"

"Old fucking news, Zodzniak. Plus they're *English*. If we wanna get signed, we have to give the people what they want."

"Now *you* sound like the Gipper."

"Hey, he's a great salesman."

I make a choking sound. I could keep arguing, but what's the point? I flash on Will thirty years from now: graying temples, Brooks Brothers suit, toasting the locals at the Erie Pub in his elevator shoes while the campaign bus idles outside. *Vote for me and I'll net the fee.* The scary thing is, he'd be perfect – great hair and flexible principles. Even just coming to rehearsal he's all about image: paisley button-down shirt, thick weave corduroys, vintage Dead Puppies desert boots. Our first retro-hip president.

"And anyway," Will says, laying his arms across his shiny-new, commission-paid Rickenbacker, "if we spend another penny, it should be on a video."

Sure, Will. It was pulling teeth – and stretching every non-existent dollar – just to get the damn album done. I can't imagine navigating a video on top of it. And aside from that, ninety-nine percent of the clips I've seen have absolutely nothing to do with the song. I'm about to say something cutting about style over substance when we hear size thirteen loafers clomping down the wooden stairs two at a time.

"Hey guys!" says Boone, ducking his head under the beam. "Guess what I just heard!"

"What?" says Will, dropping the combativeness.

"'Second Glance'!"

"What station?" I ask.

"W fuckin' ROB!"

"Yes!" Will yells, throwing a punch in the air.

Of course it's the one Will sings. Now he's running for the White House for sure. But it's ROB, the Rock of Boston, the break we've been waiting for. For years, really. I sigh, two months of stress releasing like a dam being blown up. "*Now* can we try 'Wolf in Wolf's Clothing'?"

Chas is looking over at Boone, lowering one eyebrow skeptically. "Really? 'Second Glance'? ROB? Just now?"

"No, not really," says Boone, totally deadpan. "New song?"

When I get back home, I want to tell Kat about Boone's stunt, which had actually been pretty funny once my heart started again, watching *Will's* face crash, but Kat's on the phone as usual. Even with our almost-kiss after Lindsey Buckingham, she's been keeping up the late night calls to St. Louis before tiptoeing to my room. We've been talking as much ever, sometimes rubbing each other's shoulders, even crawling under the covers to stay warm while we talk. But nothing blatantly sexual, nothing we could call each other on as out-and-out romantic. The tension's still there, though, more pent-up than ever.

To distract myself I pick up a book on the Beatles' trips to America, which an Antioch friend had helped research. The bookmark is a scrap of paper with a name and telephone number on it. Liz! The art student/polar bear with the extremely cute butt. I'd said at the Paradise I would call her. Maybe I should, if Kat's still on the fence about Dr. Kildare. Besides, maybe Liz can do a cheap video for us and get Will off my back.

Of course I can't call Liz at the moment because my almost-girlfriend is on the phone with her almost-fiancé. Wouldn't stop John Lennon, who per the book had sex with seven starlets in the same evening at a party in Hollywood in 1966. Bet he was trying to beat Paul.

I'm imagining myself in John's place, explaining to Liz and the other starlets that I'm saving myself for Cynthia, when there's a soft tap at my door. It swings open an inch, and I can see Kat's profile in the shadows.

"You still up?" she whispers.

"Um, sure, come on in."

Kat enters, in her winter flannel nightgown and knee-high

slipper socks. "Guess I'm not marrying a doctor."

"Wow." I slide over to make room. "What did you say? What did he say?"

She sits on the edge of the mattress. The nightgown is covered with pink roses and has a little bow at the collar. Not exactly a negligee, or even white longjohns, but she still manages to look cute in a *Heidi* kind of way. "I could have said all that stuff about not wanting to be just a society wife, doing charity bazaars the rest of my life."

"You didn't have to say anything." It wouldn't be the first time I've been somebody's secret. And so far there hasn't been much to be secret about.

"Yes I did. I owe that to David."

"So what did you tell him?"

"I told him…" She looks down, picks at the thread of one of the embroidered roses. "That I met somebody."

"Wow," I say again. In my experience, most guys, myself included, wouldn't burn their bridge like that, at least until the last possible moment: *P.S. Sorry you can't make it to my wedding. Maybe we can get together afterwards.*

Kat's not done. "And…that I might be falling in love."

I start to say "with who?" but it comes out "me too."

Now it's Kat's turn to say wow. Her and me both.

"Really?" she says, looking up, eyes wide as spotlights.

Fuck. It just popped out. I take another breath, examine it. It doesn't *feel* like I'm lying. I've actually been very careful to *not* say it when I don't feel it, even in bed. Especially in bed. That had been high on the list of Ms. New Hampshire's complaints about me. *Won't lie to me in bed.* "Really."

"You're not just saying it because I did."

Um, well, probably, make that definitely, but too late to start backpedaling now. I shake my head. "I don't know that I would have said it so soon. But I've been feeling it. Feeling something."

I have, actually, this weird kind of relaxed glow I get when we hang out. Very different from the heat Maggie and I generated, fanned through constant banter about art and revolutionary politics, and lots and lots of sex. Kat and I haven't even *kissed* yet. But still.

"Well good," she says, sounding relieved. "I was scared

you'd laugh at me."

"Kat." I move my good hand under the covers 'til it finds hers, interlocking fingers. "Of course I wouldn't."

"Not on the outside, you're too polite. But on the *inside*." She looks down into her lap. "I'm just this…school teacher. You're like this rock 'n' roll guy." She shrugs half-heartedly. "Maybe I'm just another groupie."

Now I do laugh. "The myth of groupiedom is highly overrated." Not that it's never happened, but John Lennon did better at that one Hollywood party than I've done in a decade of being in Shadowland. I could also say that if I *were* looking for a groupie, I probably wouldn't pick the one wearing slipper socks and a *Heidi* nightgown. But instead I just say, "You're not a groupie, okay?" Our shoulders are touching, and I reach over and turn her chin so we're eye to eye.

"Promise?" she whispers back.

"Promise."

I brush her hair back, move in slowly to kiss her. She reaches out and clicks off the light. *She is a shy girl,* I think. Might be a good first line for a song.

"Oh," she says later, as we're coming up for air. "I forgot, you asked me what David said."

"That's okay," I say, my voice husky with more immediate concerns. "Tell me later."

"He wants to come meet you."

*Fuck-ola.*

## 16. *REWIND:* Lansdowne Street, Boston, March 1982

*Havana to Heartland* reads the headline. We didn't know it at the time, but there was a critic from the *Bosstown Bean* at our Jack's show last week, our first gig after recording at Berklee with Meredith. He was actually there for the headliner, Guy Havana and the Lipstikz, but he liked us enough to give us a couple paragraphs. After leading with a description of Havana's punk-camp feather-boa-waving stage antics, the writer says nice things about Chas's drumming and Will's bass tone but busts my singing and inadvertently shortens my name from Zodzniak to Zodiac. Will of course thinks I should keep it, and immediately starts brainstorming stage names for himself: *Will Sagittarius. No, Will Apollo. Will Adonis! Will Napoleon! Will Plutonium! Will B. Free!*

The best thing about the gig was that on the way over we'd heard one of the college stations play "Last Train to Clarksville" and then announce the show. It sounded just like we'd played it, sloppy and too fast, but it was a definite buzz hearing it on the air, even if the signal didn't penetrate past Cambridge Common. We cranked it up, rolled down the windows and shouted "Tonight at Jack's!" to passersby. We weren't even going to do "Clarksville" at the show, but Will of all people said we should add it, and it got our best ovation of the night. Great, our debut hit *is* going to be a cover. And a bubblegum cover at that. But better than no hit at all. Maybe.

The *Bean* review is the first piece of actual press for our press kit, good timing since WROB is sponsoring a "Rock 'n' Roll Symposium" at Metro, a huge disco complex nestled between the Turnpike and Fenway Park. Through a rear doorway is a much smaller, darker and hipper club called Spit. I can't imagine a club called "Spit" in Ohio in a million years. Possibly "Spittoon."

Will B. Fabulous and I are sitting in folding chairs a few rows back from Metro's stage, a shopping bag full of Shadowland press kits between us. We'd come early, and good thing: the place is now bursting with bleary, translucent-skinned rock 'n' rollers, decked out mostly in black, squinting like vampires in the brightly lit club.

Despite the early hour there's a buzz in the crowd that's half caffeine, half ambition. Everybody, us included, is looking around the room to see who's here, and trading business cards and gig posters with the people next to them. It feels like a high school assembly, if the auditorium smelled like coffee, cigarettes, and last night's spilled drinks instead of dust motes, chewing gum, and teenage B.O. A few minutes after ten a.m. we're called to order, and the panelists, looking at least as bleary as the audience, come onstage from behind a curtain.

"It's Ric!" I whisper as Ric Ocasek of the Cars, looking impossibly tall and skinny, picks his way across the stage like a sunglassed and gold-earringed stork. I finger the cassette in my pocket.

"And Steve and Joe!" answers Will, as Steven Tyler and Joe Perry from Aerosmith, hair unkempt and looking like they'd had a rough night, or possibly a month of rough nights, take their places beside him. They might look like sleepy, bloated rock stars now, but we'd seen them blow away a gymnasium full of half-stoned Bowling Green State University students on their *Toys in the Attic* tour, and Will had sung "Dream On" about a thousand times in our cover band days.

We don't recognize the next panelist by sight, but he gets a big ovation so it's somebody famous. The moderator introduces him as Tom Scholz, from the band Boston. Not one of my faves; we'd made fun of them at Antioch for being an instant dinosaur band when music was slimming down to the sounds of Blondie, the Police and Dire Straits. I duck my head towards Will and make a gagging sound.

He elbows me, hard, whispering, "*You* sell five million records, jerk-off. Then we can barf all the way to the bank."

Will fits right in with the other thousand rockers in attendance, with his black jeans, black Al Capone dress shirt, and thick brown pop star hair, now offset by a caterpillar-like soul patch under his lip. I'm in a red T-shirt and green combat pants, virtually the only color in the place, and my hair, lighter and finer that Will's, is in its usual middle part above my wire rims. But I'm aware the clock is ticking, genetically speaking. One more reason to get signed in a hurry.

As Ocasek talks about the Cars' new studio, I imagine us on the other side of the glass, playing "Killing Time" or "Animal to Animal" as he cocks his head, listening, eyes closed behind his shades, unconsciously nodding along with Chas's beat. Would he dig us? Would we have enough *attitude* for him? Bet we would. I imagine him dialing Elektra Records, holding the phone out into the studio so they can hear us at their padded leather conference table, tapping their pencils in time as they decide whether to give us a three- or a five-album deal. Or would Chas get stoned and hit on Ocasek's girlfriend, getting us tossed butt-first out onto Newbury Street? In any case, "Produced by Ric Ocasek" would look a lot more impressive on the back cover than "Produced, in a huff of petulant indignation, by Meredith Miller."

Steve and Joe talk about life on the road, deftly avoiding any mention of rampant cocaine use, or of Joe's quitting and rejoining the band. I wonder, as a ballpark figure, how many groupies each of them has slept with, despite not being exactly pretty themselves. There's my first question for the Q & A – *how do ugly fuckers like you…*. Scholz describes having to invent and build his own equipment to get the sounds he wants, and he mentions growing up in Toledo, so he gets a few bonus sympathy points.

I look around at the large crowd – pierced punks, metalheads, Berklee progressives, Nu Wave peacocks. The Boston rock scene, all in one place. If a bomb hit it would be just two guys with banjos in Harvard Square. Of course they're all trying to get record contracts too. May the best band win.

The moderator opens it up for questions and hands shoot up around the room. Nobody asks Joe how many groupies he's had, but somebody asks him about being lead singer for Journey. (That's *Steve* Perry, the moderator replies.) After the panel I move forward, tape in hand, to try to meet Ocasek, but other Type A personalities elbow me out of the way and I can't get near him. Fuck. Will manages to shake Steven Tyler's hand, but a platinum blonde Amazon in a Judy Jetson jumpsuit gets Tyler's attention before Will gets to say anything. We do manage to meet some other local bands and trade press kits: Red October, Moon Over Jupiter, Park Street. The only band we actually know – Rock Paper Scissors – have a weekend gig in New Hampshire, but if one of these other bands gets famous before we do maybe we can open their tour.

Next up are radio and A&R. Marlowe, the program director at WROB, talks about the Beanpot, the battle of the bands they sponsor each summer, and Nigel All Nite, the local music director, talks about how many tapes they get and how few they actually can air. An A&R guy from Epic says everybody focuses on the A – artist – but that the R – repertoire – is just as important, and tells the cautionary tale of a local band who didn't record a song he suggested – "Pop Muzik," a catchy but vacuous tune that later became a global hit by M (just M) – and the band's record didn't sell and they got dropped.

"Good for them," I whisper. "Pop Muzik" was a terrible

song and gimmicky record, like sanitized Devo without the humor.

"What's good? They got dropped," Will whispers back.

"They made a stand. They didn't sell out."

"You're not at Holy Hand Grenade anymore," Will hisses. H.H.G. is Will's name for Antioch, another *Grail*-ism. "It's a business. Like selling carpeting." Jackie's dad is the Wall to Wall Wazoo of the Maumee Valley, and Will left a promising career as a rug jockey to make the move.

"Yeah, well I need a break from the business." I take a walk and find my way to Spit's upstairs lounge, painted blood red to contrast with the black decor downstairs. Would I possibly record a song as bad as "Pop Muzik" to get a record deal? I certainly hope not. And what would Maggie think of me if I did? What would *I* think of me?

I see a short, tense-looking guy who vaguely resembles Lou Reed getting a drink at the bar. Marlowe from WROB. I introduce myself and say the Beanpot sounds fun, we might be interested. He nods and backs away from me like my T-shirt has "Ohio" stenciled across the front it, then mumbles something about the roster being full this year. Maybe next year. *Next year?* I'm planning for us to be famous by next year, Ocasek or not.

When I head back downstairs a lawyer is onstage explaining why every band needs one. I stop listening when he says how much he charges.

"Wash off the filthy stench of capitalism?" Will asks.

"Not enough soap," I shrug. "You know, I was just picturing Jackie and Chas, all alone back in Rockport... Think that was such a good idea?"

"Never happen," he whispers. "Rhythm section solidarity."

"That's what I mean. All for one...."

Will shakes his chin dismissively. "Jackie's a one-man girl. And besides, even if it did happen, which it won't..." He tilts head forward and picks at his soul patch, like a pirate plucking flies out of his beard. "Better him than you, mate. Better him than you."

## 17. *FAST FORWARD:* Park Square, Boston, March 1986

"Of course. I'm –*ahem* – here to help."

We're sitting with our producer Wayne in his lawyer's office, on an upper floor of the Park Plaza building downtown. The whole floor has the feel of a nineteen-forties Humphrey Bogart movie: footsteps echoing down darkened hallways, etched frosted glass on the office doors. All that's missing is Trixie, the blonde bombshell receptionist huffing over her just-painted nails.

Instead we get Michael Hayek, Esq. Rather than die holding our breaths waiting for WROB to add us for real, I've asked Wayne to start shopping us to the majors, and he thinks our package will look more professional coming from an attorney. It feels a little like selling out just being here, but as far as I know Cesar Chavez doesn't do record contracts.

Hayek is small and wiry and speaks in a halting half whisper. He's explaining the service agreement he's just presented us with, which entitles him to a percentage of any deal he negotiates on our behalf, above what we've already agreed to give Wayne. As he talks, Hayek's dark, squinting eyes dart around the room, never meeting ours directly. When he steps out to let us discuss the contract, Will immediately dubs him Morocco Mole.

"So this clown's gonna own a piece of us forever?" Chas says, shaking his head.

"If this *clown*," Wayne answers, "can get you a record deal, then you'll be worth owning."

"What's the alternative?" Boone asks, elbow leaning on a filing cabinet.

"Pay his hourly rate," Wayne says. "Then you're free and clear."

Fat chance, since his hourly rate would keep Keith Richards in coke for a year, and our gig fee hasn't exactly climbed through the roof.

"Or don't hire him," Chas says.

"And don't get signed," Wayne shrugs. "Your call."

I glance through the papers one more time, clicking Hayek's retractable pen as I try to parse the fine print.

"You're stalling, Mark," Will says, enjoying my discomfiture. "Give me the pen."

I sign my name. "When you've got 'em by the balls...."

Chas laughs. "What was his name? Gambini?"

"Gamboli," I correct. "Ninth grade civics student teacher. Quoting Nixon: their hearts and minds..."

"...will follow," Chas finishes.

"Nice," Wayne says. He holds out the pen. "Anybody else?"

Will signs, then the others reluctantly follow suit, Chas grabbing his crotch. I'm not thrilled either, but like Wayne said, it's worth it if it gets us a deal.

When Hayek comes back he asks if we've ever played New York. We haven't so far, but Wayne says we can set something up when the time comes. Boone mentions that Talon and some other local bands have bussed fans down from Boston for label showcases.

"Great idea," says Wayne. "A&R people love screaming fans. That way they don't have to decide for themselves if you're any good."

"But we *are* good," I say.

"It's just a little insurance. Like salting the mine."

"Maybe we should release mice," Will says. "Like they did at Fabian concerts."

"I can see the headline," says Boone, holding up his forefingers and thumbs like he's framing a newspaper. "*Mice Signed to Multi-Album Deal.*"

Hayek says we should also think about doing a video. "So the label guys can see how you look without leaving their office."

Will shoots me his "told you so" look. But I'd met Liz Polar Bear for coffee and she'd said even a decent black and white clip wouldn't come cheap. And god forbid label execs should have to go out and hear live music.

Wayne says it's on our list. Hayek shakes our hands goodbye and for the first time it dawns on people my cast is off. My left wrist looks pale and skinny compared to the right, and I've been warned not to strain it. Wayne asks if I've played guitar yet and I shake my head no. I tried, but reaching all the way around the neck and then pressing down really did hurt. I know I wanted to be lead singer, but maybe I should be careful what I wish for.

In the elevator Will does a dead-on impersonation of

Hayek. "Hello, Arista?" He glances quickly from side to side, even though he's talking to an imaginary phone. "This Mr. Mole calling. Mr. –*ahem* – Morocco Mole?"

I suddenly get why the voice sounds familiar, and why I was thinking of Bogart movies. Excellent. We're being represented to the gatekeepers of the music industry by *ahem* Peter Lorre, the obsequious weasel from *The Maltese Falcon* and *Casablanca*. Now I *really* feel confident.

Back home Kat kisses me hello, a lingering kiss that feels like it could lead right back to my bedroom. *The secret lives of schoolteachers.* "Your mother called."

Erection gone. "Any message?"

"She asked me if I knew you'd been in a car accident."

Fuck. "What did you say?"

"I said yes, you had the cast on when you moved in."

"Damn." I blow a puff of air.

"You didn't *tell* them?"

"I don't *tell them* anything."

She looks hurt, and I realize my tone might be brusquer than it needs to be. Kat calls her parents every Sunday, so my quasi-estrangement from mine might be hard to fathom. She's even told her folks about breaking up with Dr. Kildare – and meeting me – thrilling them, I'm sure, on both counts. At least she's talked David out of jumping on the first jet to come beat me up. If he still misses her in a month or two, then they'll talk.

"Sorry," I say, gently brushing back Kat's hair. "I just didn't want them to worry." My wrist had been in its cast when I saw my mom at Christmas, but I'd just told her I sprained it playing hoops. "So how –"

"She said she saw –"

"*Will's mother,*" we say together. Of course. Will still talks to his mom almost every day, and probably tells her how many orgasms he and Jackie have had since their last conversation.

"Down at Elmer's Pantry," Kat continues, "and she asked your mom how your broken arm was doing. Sorry. How *is* it doing?"

I take a rubber handball out of my pocket and give it a squeeze. "Hurts."

"Sorry," she says again. "Can I get you your ice pack?"

I nod. It's not *just* that I don't want my parents to worry. Now I'm going to get non-stop letters from Nowhere Man reminding me to buckle up, with cut out *Toledo Blade* articles about fatal car crashes. He's still got high blood pressure from when Will casually mentioned that Maggie and I had gotten arrested at a peace demonstration outside Wright-Patterson Air Force Base senior year. Maybe I should kill myself now and get it over with. And Will's next.

## 18. *REWIND:* Rockport, April 1982

"Hi Mrs. Preston, is Maggie home? Okay, well please tell her I called."

It's a gray Saturday in early spring. We've been in Rockport six months, with just a couple to go before the rent goes up and we get kicked out of town. And despite our *Bean* review and "Clarksville" making some college playlists, we're still not famous. So I'm feeling down, and more than a little lonely.

Will and I hadn't come home from the symposium to find Chas and Jackie in bed together, in fact Jackie had been making brownies and Chas had been helping. And not just stirring in cannabis leaves. Now the three of them are down at the Danvers mall seeing *Airplane II – The Sequel.* I could have tagged along, but for once I wasn't in the mood for bad puns and stupid sight gags. It's funny, the same ocean that gives Rockport its great scenery and tony property values can also make it melancholy as hell. I'm theoretically staying home to practice guitar, but I'm too pent up; it's been a long winter and I'm restless. I grab my coat and go walking, turning inland from the water to the abandoned quarries behind town.

It's barren here too since the leaves aren't out yet, but from the tops of the rock formations I can see all the way to the horizon, an infinity of roiling blue-gray ocean and low hanging sky. I keep going and notice some old cellar holes beneath the sticker bushes. Dogtown. I don't know the details, just that it used to be a village in colonial times, and for whatever reason the people left. It begins to drizzle as I walk through the ruins, and I start humming to keep my throat warm. I'm thinking about Maggie, who I haven't seen now for almost a year, and eventually words start to come:

> *Walking through the Dogtown rain*
> *Wondering could it be the same*
> *Wishing I had listened instead*
> *To her heart and not my head*

After I get back home and towel off, I grab my guitar and search for chords to fit the brooding melody floating around inside my head:

> *Watching the sky fall down*
> *Nobody for miles around*
> *Just a fool and his pain*
> *In the Dogtown rain*

It's the opposite of "Pop Muzik," bleak and pensive and moody. I'm sure the A&R guy would hate it.

The phone rings, late.
　　"Hey…"
　　Part of me is instantly awake. "Hey back." I can hear Maggie breathe out over the long distance line. I hope she's not chain smoking again. It's like a Maggie mood ring – the more she smokes the more turmoil she's in. Our last semester at Antioch she'd smoked constantly, pot and cigarettes both, and then gotten bulimic and worse. But rather than ask point blank I try to keep it light. "Were you out seeing the Sweeties?" Geoff, an Antioch friend who's into the Beatles like I'm into the Polar Bears, is now living in LA and always after Maggie to come hear his band. Somebody at Antioch had pulled some strings and gotten him an internship at *Rolling Stone*, but then he got mono and couldn't go. Too bad, maybe he could have gotten our tape reviewed.
　　"Nope, at the Nuart. Cary Grant double feature with Nance."
　　"Is that who I remind you of?"
　　"Nance isn't counting the days until her hairline recedes."

84

"Ouch, brutal." I change the subject. "Hey, guess what, we're official. The *Bean's* annual Boston band guide is out, and we're in it."

"Congratulations. Did they say more nice things?" I'd told her about our write-up.

"This is more like phone book, a directory of bands so people can call us up for gigs."

"So are they?"

"Not yet. But they could. They will." I lower my voice, pull the phone cord into my bedroom. "I'm almost scared to show it to Will and Chas."

"Why?"

"I counted the bands."

"So?"

"Guess how many."

She exhales. "No idea."

"Guess."

She exhales again, a little exasperated. She generally doesn't like it when I make her guess. "A hundred."

"More."

"Two hundred." I don't say anything. "And fifty."

"More."

"Mark, I'm not going to run up my mom's phone bill –"

"Two *thousand*."

"Wow." She's quiet for a second. "That's like LA and actresses. You're gonna have to be good."

"I know. We're practicing a lot. Every night."

"And lucky."

"Luck is what happens when preparedness meets opportunity." Seneca notwithstanding, we're gonna have to be *really* good. And if there are two thousand bands just in Boston, how many in New York and LA and Philly, all vying for the same record contracts? It's too much to face without having sex. "Hey, I have an idea. Why don't you come visit?" The Lennon Christmas record seems to have helped my status; each time we've chatted Maggie's been a little friendlier.

She's quiet, thinking about it. "When?"

"Whenever. Sooner the better." I picture her, us, in the throes of action. Maggie may have a skinny tomboy body, but she's got nerve endings bundled in all the right places, and her restlessness carries over into her sex drive. In fact she generates so much electricity that she shakes for minutes afterward, like the aftershocks following an earthquake. "We're having an Easter party, come then."

"*You're* having an –?"

"I know, I know. But we have to move out anyway, so we may as well get kicked out. Think vernal Druidic fertility rites. Nymphs and satyrs humping on the lawn."

"Sounds like Spring Carnival at Antioch."

"Ha. We can even sing 'Jump for Jesus.'"

She exhales, almost a laugh this time. The song, which predates our time on campus, was probably made up by some cynical philosophy major who'd been asked one too times if he'd been saved. It basically says that since Jesus gave his life for you, why not repay him by taking a flying leap off the spires of Antioch Hall?

"It wouldn't mean anything, Mark. If I came, it would just be a visit."

"Fine, Maggie, just come. I miss you."

She exhales again, then says she'll check airfares. I say I'll buy eggs.


## 19. *FAST FORWARD:* Beverly, Mass., March 1986

"The laddie doth protest too much, methinks."

We're in the truck heading north on 93, and Will's invoking the Bard in regard to me not playing guitar yet. My wrist is still tender, but I can make a few chords, probably enough to get through our set tonight. But I don't *want* to play guitar tonight. It's a Friday, Grover's will be packed, and I want to get the crowd excited, get *us* excited, make us break on through to the other side. Which seems a lot more doable without a guitar hanging around my neck. "What do you want, a note from my surgeon?"

"Just gimme some truth, Zodiac." He's quiet for a minute, holding on as Chas takes the narrow curve onto 128. "I know. I'll ask Kat. *She's* not a lying fuck head." He sinks back in the shotgun seat, looking smug.

In fact Kat's heard me, tentatively strumming as I try to get my fingers to move in concert again. Part of it's psychological; I think if I press down too hard my ulna will re-snap and my hand will drop like a boneless chicken. "Boone can handle it," I say, rubbing my wrist.

At the moment Boone's lying face down on Will's bass cabinet, apparently unconscious. His day job is computer programming but he prefers working at night, so his circadian rhythm's always in flux. He also minored in recreational pharmaceuticals before getting kicked out of U. Mass., and his alcohol intake seems to be rising, so it may be a chemically induced coma. We'll splash some cold water on his face when we get to the club.

"What Boone can handle," Will retorts, flicking his head towards the corpse, "is not the point."

Don't I know it. Which is why I left my guitar at the rehearsal space.

The show, in my humble opinion, goes great. Boone wakes up and wails, Kat, Jackie, and Deedee start dancing right away and by the second song the dance floor's packed. I play my synth part on "Second Glance," then jump down into the audience during Boone's solo. I hold the mic out to the crowd and get them shouting along on "Car Keys," then right before it ends I call out "Rebel Rebel" and we do an impromptu medley. I can see Will glaring – this had been one of his big Bowie show stoppers in our cover band days – so I nod for him to take the second verse. I grab Chas's cowbell for some extra percussion, then join Will for the last chorus, and we even nail the *David Live* ending perfectly until out of instinct Boone blasts the first chord of "Moonage Daydream." Oh well.

We've brought a box of records and people line up for us to autograph them. A few friends had asked us to sign their copies at our release concert, but these are strangers, so it feels like a big deal to be made a fuss over as I scrawl "M. Zodiac" – *Shadowland conquers Beverly! Now onto Danvers!* Deedee chaperones Chas, warding off potential competition, and Boone has a little entourage that's half women batting shadowed eyelids at him and half aspiring guitarists asking what string gauges he uses. Only Will seems less than pleased, slinking off to the far corner of the bar with Jackie and stewing over his tepid white wine.

At the end of the night Will and Jackie beg off IHOP so after unloading we all just go home.

"That Will," Kat says, keeping me company as I stand in front of the fridge scarfing leftover veggie lasagna. "He makes me so mad."

I swallow a chunk of cold zucchini. "Why does Will make *you* mad? Not that I don't occasionally want to strangle him with one of his own bass strings." Like last summer when our producer Wayne casually mentioned that if we were ever thinking about changing our name, we should do it now, before the record comes out. We weren't, but Will ran with it and made us all brainstorm band names for two solid weeks – *The Buddha Babies! Brides of Christ! Schrodinger's Cat Box! Howard the Duck!* The one the rest of us actually liked – Mark and the Stance – Will vetoed because he didn't want my name out front. By the time everybody knew we were sticking with Shadowland, our graphic artist was off on vacation, making the artwork a full month late. The delay cost us any chance of getting on the *Bean's* end-of-year "best of" list, and In Your Face wouldn't even stock us until after the holidays. And oh yeah, the records weren't ready 'til the day of the show and I *broke my fucking wrist* getting them. I'm still paying off the stupid rent-a-wreck, though at Jackie's insistence everyone else is also kicking in some gig and album sales money.

Kat frowns, a rare occurrence. "Because he doesn't appreciate you. The show was wonderful, you sold a bunch of records, and all he does is sulk." She glances down at the pan. "You know I could heat that up for you."

I shrug, take another mouthful.

"Doesn't he see how hard you work?"

I nod at the table and we sit down, the lasagna pan between us. "You know Will was a theater geek? All through high school. College too."

"I'm not surprised, with all his costumes." Kat's noticed how Will keeps his stage outfits hermetically sealed in zippered garment bags – and then goes to change just when it's time to move equipment. My stage clothes, if they're not already on, are rolled up in a gym bag with my guitar cables.

"Tenth grade he got a big part in the musical. He was so short and baby-faced he was like the mascot, like a puppy, older girls flocking around and petting him, doing his makeup for him while he stared down their blouses. It was disgusting." I hold the fork out towards Kat but she makes a face, so I stab it into the cold crusty cheese. "Chas and I were jamming with this guy Jerry, a year ahead of us, who played bass, but nobody sang."

"Not you?"

"Not then. I was still learning to play guitar." I finger an F scale on my forearm, like I used to do in chemistry class when I should have been sketching molecules. "Plus I was shy, new to Harding. And being named Zodzniak didn't help. I only started singing to write my own songs." I slide my F up to a G, the entire progression of the first tune I ever wrote, an instrumental called "Cumulus." "So we needed a singer."

"Will," Kat says, and I nod.

"I'd heard him messing around in the choir room, and invited him over to Chas's garage. He sang us 'All the Way from Memphis' and 'Suffragette City' just like the records and the rest is history. Or will be. At least that's the plan."

"It will," Kat says, touching my arm. Nice that *somebody* believes in us. We hear the front door, then arguing – Jan and Trav-Trav coming in from a party – but they go into Jan's room without saying hi. While Kat's head is turned I start to swig some milk, but she turns back around so I pour it into a glass instead.

"Anyway, when Will took the gig it was like he was doing *us* a favor – we got a bunch of pool parties right away because people knew his older brothers and sisters. It wasn't until Jerry graduated that Will even started playing bass. *He* was the singer, roaming the stage, working the crowd, getting the girls. Like I'm doing now."

"Getting the girls," Kat repeats, extending her lower lip. "Hmm."

"Just one." I lean forward, bite down gently, then pull her into a kiss. "But it drives Will crazy, watching me have *his* fun."

"But that was high school. He's been playing bass for years. And he's good."

I nod. "He's okay." He's actually more that okay,

especially considering the only lessons he had were with a Bowling Green drop-out who insisted on being paid in pot. "But that's beside the point." I point my fork at myself. "*I* was always playing guitar. Ego-librium, I guess you could say."

I thought it was a pretty good line, but she lets it pass. "But you're *injured*, Mark. Will's being childish. As soon as you start playing guitar again…"

I shrug. "I don't know that I really need to. Boone's got it covered."

Her eyes widen. "Ohhh," she says, doing the mental math, like if I'm *choosing* to not play guitar, then I'm the one fucking Will over, not the other way around. "Will's *really* not going to like that."

She looks troubled, and I can feel myself slipping down a notch from rock-star-in-shining-armor. "Kat," I say, sitting down across from her again. "Here's the thing." I lean forward. "You've only seen us since *this*." I touch my wrist. "We were okay before, just as good in a lot of ways. I'm a decent guitarist. But people never seemed to *get* us." I turn my fork so I'm gripping it like one of Chas's drumsticks. "But *now*," (*tap*) "ever since I stopped wearing my axe, people are paying *attention*. I can *feel* it." (*tap*) "It's exactly what I've – what *we've* (*tap, tap*) – been waiting for (*tap, tap, tap*). I can't give that up."

Kat wrests the fork out of my hand, lays it on the table. "But what about Will? You can tell he's mad, even onstage. He's just going to get more and more upset."

"He's a big boy."

"Aren't you worried he might quit?"

I reach for my fork again but Kat gets there first, moves it out of range. "No way. Will's invested five years of his life just since we moved here. He's not going to quit when it finally starts paying off."

"But if it's not paying off for…" Kat breaks off, then leans forward, lowering her voice like she's sharing a secret. "Jackie told me her dad wants them to move back to Ohio. Make Will a *partner* in his carpeting business."

I laugh. "Trust me, Kat, Ohio is like St. Louis with no Arch and no Cardinals. And Will's ego needs him to get at least a little bit famous. Which he can't do in Ohio."

"I don't know, Mark, it sounds risky." She sounds wistful, sad almost.

"Kat," I say, taking her hand. "This keeps the band *together*. If we don't get a break soon we're not going to last long anyway. I'm more worried about Chas and Deedee. And Boone's never been exactly the Rock of Gibraltar."

"Okay," she says, pursing her lips. "I hope you're right." She lowers her eyes, a lock of copper hair falling across her forehead. "I just wish you and Will could be...*friends*. Like you used to be."

"We *are* friends," I tell her, brushing the strand back behind her ear. "This is nothing – ask Chas to tell you about the Vicki Shehovic wars sometime."

"God, what I missed at St. Cecelia's."

"Hey, I've heard about those girls' schools." I stand and give her arm a tug. "Let's go to bed."

There's going to bed and then there's going to bed. That first night when Kat told me she'd broken up with Dr. Kildare, we'd talked late and she'd eventually slipped under the covers with me. But her nightgown had stayed on. She's been crawling in ever since, and slowly, timidly, letting me explore more of her body, but the *Heidi* flannel chastity belt's stayed more or less in place. It's frustrating, in a cold shower sense, but it's also kind of sweet, going slow for a change. It's like once you fuck, you forget how to make out. Maybe if Maggie and I had fucked less and talked more, things might have ended better.

Kat and I kiss for a while, and I tentatively add another inch to the territory I'm allowed to caress. Forget what I just said about going slow being sweet. At least with my cast off I can use both hands. I'm regrouping for another reconnaissance mission when Kat rolls on her side to face me in the dark.

"How about as a kid?" she asks.

"Girls? I guess summer camp. Which *was* co-ed, by the way."

"No, music. You told me about high school, but what about before? I sang in our youth choir back in St. Louis, but I'd never do a solo, I'd be scared to death."

I pause to think, letting go of my next-base aspirations. I

almost never think back that far, so it takes a minute. "I guess playing Ed Sullivan," I finally say.

"The TV show? You would have been a baby."

"Almost. My sister would set up chairs in the dining room, invite our parents and the neighbors and we'd put on little shows. Charge everybody a nickel."

"Did you sing?"

"Sort of. We'd play records, sing and dance along with them: 'It's a Small World After All,' 'Let the Sun Shine In.' I had a little plastic guitar I'd put on for 'I Want to Hold Your Hand.'"

"God, I bet you were adorable." She reaches for my good hand under the covers and squeezes.

I shake my head, even though it's dark. "It was mostly my sister, I was just the sidekick. You know we even did a couple songs she made up." A sing-song melody comes into my head that I haven't thought of in decades, and a rhyme about our cat Lollipop.

"Must have rubbed off," Kat says. "Did your dad ever make home movies? My dad filmed everything."

"Nah. He tried once, got a camera and everything, but he pressed the wrong button and nothing came out." I say, shaking my head. "One more thing my mom can't forgive him for."

"Poor guy."

"Yeah well."

"He's still got you."

"Yeah well," I repeat. "You should go to sleep. You've got school tomorrow." I lean over and kiss her forehead.

"I love you, Mark," she says, and snuggles down against my shoulder.

"I know." Then, because I don't want be an asshole like Shaft and Harrison Ford, I say I love her too.

Her eyes close, but a minute later, so softly can I hardly hear, she whispers, "Don't forget, Mark. He's still in there."

I don't know who she means. "Nowhere Man?" Still knockin' 'em back at Dillon's Happy Hour?

"No. The little boy with the plastic guitar. That's who I'm rooting for. *That's* who I'm in love with." She nuzzles my neck again, then falls back asleep on my pillow.

Poor Kat, if she expects me to be my six-year-old self. That boy is long gone. And poor me if that's what she's really in love with.

But maybe she's right about me and Will. Maybe I am pushing him too hard, too far. And I hadn't been completely honest with Kat earlier. Not that I'd lied, but I'd left out some details in the Mark and Will saga, like Will teaching me to how sing. Well not sing, exactly, but how to sing *onstage*. How to pick a spot, a light switch on the wall or whatever, focus on that so you don't get distracted. How people can't tell the difference between someone *pretending* to be confident and actually being confident, so you may as well go for it. How I was so shy that Will even sang *my* songs for me our first couple years. How since Will did all the talking for the band, both onstage and off, any girls I did get were mostly thanks to him. It wasn't until I got to Antioch that I came out of my shell, and I did it by doing a *Will* thing: I picked a character – John Lennon, early solo period – and I played him as best I could. Eventually I grew into the character, found my Yoko – Maggie – and became myself, found my voice. And didn't need Will as much anymore, at least in the same way. So maybe all Will's bullshit is my fault – I changed the rules. Of course he'd found his Linda – Jackie   so he didn't need me the same way either. But John and Paul had conquered the world by the time they grew apart, and Will and I have barely conquered Allston/Brighton. So we *do* still need each other, if we're gonna make it. And it's got to happen *fast* – Chas's new girlfriend is already dropping hints about wanting him to quit, and when sex is involved he's got the backbone of a planarian. WROB has to add us, *now*, so labels will take our phone calls, take us seriously. Nigel All Nite needs to see us live, *now*, before my wrist heals and Will gives me a real ultimatum. But how to make it happen? DJs gets passes for every show in town, so why come see us when he could hang backstage with U2 or Depeche Mode? Lure him with cocaine, like record promoters do? Set up under his condo's bedroom window? Kidnap him? I'm still working on a plan when I finally drift off at first light.

## 20. *REWIND:* Inman Square, Cambridge, April 1982

*Thump, thump, thump.*

We're soundchecking at the Inn-Square, week after Easter. Maggie couldn't get a cheap plane ticket in time, so she hadn't made our party, meaning I now haven't had sex for longer than any time since I first *had* sex. And it's the first nice night of the year, almost balmy, so long-dormant hormones are waking up in bloodstreams all over town. While loading in it seemed like every Cantabrigian under the age of thirty-five was out on the street groping and French kissing the person nearest them. And not always of the opposite sex.

*Thwack, thwack, thwack.*

Inside the bar, however, it's the diametric opposite of sex – a bunch of paunchy, middle-aged butcher-and-baker types stopping off for a beer or six on their way home from work, whose primary entertainment is yelling sarcastic comments as they watch an early Sox game on TV. Don't let *us* disturb you. The air smells heavy, like yeast and cigarettes, and I wish they'd prop the door open, but they can't, or so we're told, because the city will revoke the club's liquor license if they get any more noise complaints. Maybe I should chew some oxygum, like Marine Boy.

*Thump, thwack, thump. Crash.*

On the plus side, we're opening for Moon Over Jupiter, who have a pixie-like lead singer who's the first songwriter I've really liked since we hit town. They had a mini-hit called "The Young and the Restless" which got them sued by CBS, and they're now more famous for the lawsuit than the song. Too bad, because Genevieve's songs have actual melodies instead of just the usual pentatonic riffs and pounding percussion. She's also cute, in a spacey Kate Bush kind of way, with thick dark hair and a long, form-fitting blouse bisected by a pirate's belt. She's an item with their drummer, though, thus ensuring my streak continues.

Will's turn: *plunk, plunk, plunk.*

The Maggie-less Easter party had been low key, just a few of our Massachusetts friends joining us in Rockport for food (Chas's killer chili), drink (Budweiser, Yoo-hoo, and a bottle of Jack Daniels, also courtesy of Chas) and dessert (Jackie's congo bars, plus a few pounds of Easter candy from the A&P). The weather had still been crappy, so we'd mostly hung around inside and then had a jam session. Rock Paper Scissors had caught the train up from Boston, and we met them in the parking lot behind Gray's Hardware. While walking up our driveway in his size thirteen docksiders, their guitar player Boone had surprised me by pulling a little square of paper out of his jeans jacket. Had I ever tried acid? I shook my head no. Maybe in '67 in the flower power-ness of it all, but at Antioch drugs had seemed more about just getting fucked up than any deep quest for self-discovery. And I knew from my sister that even good drugs couldn't save you. Boone had shrugged and slipped the square back into his pocket. He didn't seem to act any differently but I kept my eye on him, especially whenever he got near our balcony, and I was glad the jam session was in the basement. Boone's playing was as fluid as ever, a mixture of Jeff Beck, Mick Ronson and Carlos Santana, and we did everything from Beck's "Freeway Jam" to Kiss's "Christine Sixteen" to Smith's "Baby, It's You," with Annie nailing the giant "BAY-BEE!" in the last stanza perfectly. We'd also tried "Animal to Animal" with everybody joining in, and with all the extra percussion it had sounded unnervingly like the theme from *George of the Jungle*.

My turn, finally: *strum, strum, strum* (feedback squeal). The soundman asks for a song, so I start making up lyrics about Jackie's aerobics friend Lissa. She'd come to the party, and Chas and I had taken turns trying to snag her in conversation (me) or getting her drunk (Chas). We both mostly struck out, but Chas succeeded on his own behalf, or maybe took the tab I'd declined, because he started staring intently at the records going around on the turntable and mumbling Styx lyrics to himself. He also made a pass, more of a stagger, at Annie, but we got him to bed before he did any permanent damage. Later, after RPS left, I overheard Jackie and Lissa talking about Lissa's divorce proceedings. With my luck she'll be ready for a fling just as Maggie finally does visit, hopefully over Memorial Day. In the meantime, six more weeks of celibacy, of stealing glances at Jackie in her leotards and listening to Will describe their last nights' exploits.

All together now: *Tickle test, tickle test, tickle test. Thump, plunk, strum. Crash.*

By the time we start our set the Inn-Square's clientele has diversified, with hip-but-crunchy twentysomethings counterbalancing the after-workaholics. The stage is tiny, and the small, packed room makes it feel like a real event. We open with a new song, "All for Glory," a comment on the Falklands Islands fiasco set to a rapid one-two march:

> *Capture the flag, kick the can*
> *Turn that boy into a man*
> *Put a rifle in his hand*
> *All for glory*
> *Margaret Thatcher let it go*
> *The world doesn't have to know*
> *How tough you are, how far you'll go*
> *All for glory*

The Red Sox fans at the bar don't seem to give a shit about the Falklands, but Moon Over Jupiter's fans like us, and we do a decent set despite me breaking a string and playing our encore without my high E. Genevieve makes a point of saying how much she likes my songs, a nice change from Will scanning every new lyric sheet I hand him for typos and mixed metaphors. She also tells Chas he looks sexy when he plays, so maybe she just has a thing for drummers.

Moon Over Jupiter's set is interesting, because it's obvious it's Genevieve's band, and the other players are just there to make her sound good. She plays guitar, barely, on a couple tunes, piano on a couple others and sometimes just sings, and not everybody in the band plays on every song. It's more like a cabaret act than a normal rock show, and the different textures – keyboards, sax, flute – really make the songs come alive. We didn't even do "Dogtown Rain" because Will and Chas didn't want to slow down the set with a ballad. Genevieve had sung two ballads, and they'd both been beautiful. Even the bar crowd had been quiet. Their wider sound gets me thinking about expanding the band, or at least changing the bylaws so I can't get outvoted.

As Moon Over Jupiter finishes up I wipe my forehead. It's hot in the club, and still warm outside as we load our equipment. *Summer is a comin' in.* Time to start thinking about our next move.

## 21. *FAST FORWARD:* **Kenmore Square, Boston, April 1986**

*Look over here! Over here! Over HERE, you asshole!*

We're halfway through our set at *SCREAM!*'s annual birthday bash and Nigel All Nite – WROB's local music director – is less than twenty feet away. But he's ignoring us. He's got his back to the stage, and he's talking with *SCREAM!*'s editor Tommey and a woman in a powder blue body stocking. Unless she's actually naked, and the blue sky, complete with clouds, is just painted on. Either way, she's got their attention, not us. I'd only gotten us on the bill by offering to bring our sound system and mix all the other bands for free, but it's going to be wasted effort if Nigel's oblivious.

And he's not the only one. The party's in the new balcony at the Rat, and two hundred or so of Boston's rowdiest scene-makers are all crammed on the narrow deck, talking, laughing and yelling for beers as if we're not even there. It would serve them all right if the balcony came crashing down, except we'd go down with it. So what can I do? We've tried full-on aggression – Boone's raving slide solo on "Risking Your Life to Rescue a Dead Man" – and camp – Will singing a punked-up "Stop in the Name of Love." If I try a split on the tiny stage I'll take out three mic stands and the snare drum as well as give myself a hernia. We're so packed together, it's like one of those cemeteries in Italy where you're buried standing up.

That gives me an idea. Can I? I glance around the stage, re-arrange a couple mic stands, stealing the one from inside Chas's bass drum. I peel off my wire rims, lay them inside the bass drum for safekeeping. I call out "Same Heart Twice" to Boone, then kneel down on the stage, butt to the audience, place the mic between my knees. As he plays the intro I lean forward, lowering the top of my head and putting my palms down flat. I get a twinge in my wrist but keep going, putting more weight on my skull. A cheerleader at the summer camp in the Poconos I'd gone to had taught me; hope I can still do this. I lift my right leg in the air, then the left. I rock forward but catch myself, then slowly straighten out my legs so they're pointing at the ceiling. It takes a few seconds to feel my balance, so Boone vamps on the V chord until I'm ready. I can see people upside down in front of me, it's a low stage so I'm staring at knees and crotches. I take a breath, start singing.

At first there's no discernible difference, and I feel like an idiot. But by the second verse the crowd noise drops. I lower my gaze, or rather raise it, so I can blurrily make out people's faces, and they're pointing and staring at me, nudging their friends. Now if I can just make it to the end of the song before I pass out from all the blood rushing to my head. Or Will tips me over.

I hit the last note and let myself collapse down. People clap and cheer and cat call. I turn back to the band and call out "'Sympathy'!"

Will flashes me his "what the fuck?" look – it's not on our set list, and we haven't played it in public since Ohio. But Boone's got to know it, and it seems like the perfect moment.

Boone yells "In E?" and I nod. He starts the chunky chords, heavy on the upstrokes, like Keith on the live version from *Ya-Yas*, and Chas fits the African rhythms of the *Beggars Banquet* version in underneath: DOM DOM dom dom dom dom, dom DOM dom dom. Will comes in high up the neck, popping the suspensions on his Rickenbacker. I sing this one standing up, *Please allow me to introduce myself....*

After the first chorus I mouth "'Rock 'n' Roll'!" to Will, and he nods. We'd noticed back in high school both that the Stones' tune and the Velvet's tune had the same chord changes, so we'd done them as a medley. He turns to his mic: *Janie said when she was just five years old....* Now for the fun part.

I stand at my mic and wait for downbeat, glance over at Will. As I sing Mick's verse about the cop, Will sings Lou's verse about the TV sets. We keep it going, and it's kind of cool in a mindfuck kind of way, and I see Nigel and Tommey now both staring intently at the stage. Then we get to the chorus and it's a total trainwreck: Boone plays the Stones' changes while Will plays the Velvet's bass line. Chas doesn't know what to play, then does an out-of-time fill that ends on a cymbal crash. I wave my hand to cut everyone off, then yell "'Car Keys'! One two three *four!*"

After the set people who would normally ignore us for not being hip enough make a point of congratulating me, though for what I'm not exactly sure. *Best headstand by an unsigned band.* But our fifteen minutes of fame are cut short when Tommey and the woman in the bodystocking take the stage and play a duo version of Michael Jackson's "Billie Jean" – on bugle and accordion, no less. Now *that's* entertainment. I don't see Nigel in the crowd anymore – time for his radio show – but he definitely heard us, and saw us. *Good work, Zodzniak. Have another ginger ale.* Now if Wayne comes though with that pound of cocaine for Marlowe we should be all set.

## 22. *REWIND:* East Boston, May 1982

I'm pacing the lower concourse of Logan's Terminal C, watching the arriving passengers descend from their gates. Each planeload gets my hopes up, but so far every female form has either pushed on to baggage claim or jumped into other waiting arms. To distract myself I'm also halfheartedly glancing through *SCREAM!*'s Beanpot preview, which has Khartoum as the heavy favorite over Ipso Facto. Maybe we should get tattoos and gig in steel-capped work boots, too. Not that it matters, since we're not even *in* the Beanpot. The commercial stations haven't exactly been jumping all over our Berklee tape, so maybe next year's more realistic. I just hate to wait.

There's a wiry female figure with light feathery hair eschewing the escalator and taking the stairs. My groin recognizes her before I do: rattail braid bouncing off one shoulder, thin sleeveless top clearly showing the points of her nipples, ripped jeans riding low on bony hips. As her waif's eyes restlessly scan the crowd I can sense her energy. She spots me and sprints across the lobby into my embrace. Maggie. In Massa-fucking-chusetts.

"God you feel good," I half moan. I've got one arm wrapped around her back and one hand sliding down her ass and I can feel the pressure of her breasts against my chest. I want to undo our zippers right here, right now. But considering the parade of passengers, airline employees and Massport security guards passing by, I restrain myself. For the moment.

Maggie feels skinny, even by her standards, and she's added a cobalt streak to her unkempt bangs, but otherwise she seems the same. I'm a head taller, so as we grapple I can see people leering at us as they walk by, but it's been a long time so fuck them. We get her bag and decide to wait for rush hour to subside before driving back to Rockport. We find a little park along the water and stand in another embrace as the planes fly overhead:

> *It's so nice to* (whoosh).
> *I really missed* (whoosh).
> *I* (whoosh) *too.*
> *I think your mom* (whoosh).
> *She can be a real* (whoosh).

We watch the sun setting orange through the back-lit chess pieces of the downtown skyline, and see the pale face of the moon levitating over the Deer Island landfill. We hold hands on the ride home, and are seriously groping by the time we hit the Gloucester rotaries. Aside from steering the car I'm barely in control of my own actions. I'm also praying Will, Jackie, and Chas have gone to see a movie, preferably a triple feature.

The lights are ablaze, and of course everybody's home. Maggie exchanges hugs with Jackie – the band women, together again – then Will, then even Chas as I check his hand placement. Jackie's made something green and tofu-y in Maggie's honor, and we sit down to a late dinner, W/J/C asking Maggie about California and the scene there and Maggie asking about Boston and the band. I suggest a walk down to the beach and Will says "great" 'til Jackie kicks him.

Back Beach is deserted, moonlit and beautiful. We find a rock, sit, and immediately begin necking. Maggie has an excellent neck. She tastes of salt and a little musky perfume, not that I need the encouragement. I can't tell if waves are crashing or it's just my blood pressure.

"My whole body is happy to see you," I say, nuzzling her ear.

"I can tell," she says.

I start over. "I mean, I'm relieved. I missed you. You feel like…home."

"You feel like home too, Mark." There's an edge of wistfulness in her voice. My limbic system is so high on her pheromones I barely have a mind, but I manage to ask if she wants to talk.

"Later. This is nice."

I slide an arm around her, and we look out at the ocean a while. There's a breeze off the water and I feel her getting goosebumps. "Want to head back?"

She nods. I take Maggie's hand and lead her straight to my bedroom. Will and Jackie and Chas can listen to *us* for a change.

"Mark Lindsay?"

We're standing on the red brick trail in front of Old North Church, and our colonial-clad guide has just asked if we can name the other rider who set out with Paul Revere. The guide, a local college student who was probably eight years old when Lindsay sang Paul & the Raiders' last hit, just shakes his head blankly and says William Dawes. Why do I even bother?

"Revere must have had a better agent," Will says over his shoulder as Maggie pinches me under my shirt. It's Maggie's first time in Boston, so we're showing her the sights. The church itself yells classic New England, with its white wooden steeple and wrought iron-railed garden, now in early summer bloom. Inside there's a wedding going on, and Will and Jackie reach for each other's hands. She's taller, so their profile isn't so much young lovers as a still-shapely mother and her teen-age son. Who happens to have a goatee. Maggie and I, on the other hand, who have been holding hands all day, disengage. Chas hangs back and shares a Marlboro with Paul Revere's horse.

We blow off the rest of the tour and hop the subway to Steve's Ice Cream. It's around the corner from the Cars' new studio, so we contemplate wandering over to say hi and accidentally spilling hot fudge all over their new forty-eight channel mixing board. ("They'd remember us," says Will.)

We walk by the art school where Maggie applied, and look at the students' work in the windows: abstract drip paintings on Plexiglas, pen-and-ink drawings that look like blown-up *Millie the Model* comic book panels, complete with melodramatic dialog ("Blake, I'm…pregnant"), a row of fifteen or so right-footed shoes, with the caption "Where's the Left?" Clever, but nothing as good as Maggie's best paintings, so maybe she made the right decision opting out.

We show Maggie our future accommodations: Will and Jackie are renting a big apartment in Brookline they'll share with a couple extra housemates, and Chas and I are renting a cramped one bedroom off Ringer Park in Brighton, with me taking over the living room. The best feature is a small balcony directly over a dumpster we can drop our trash into. Maggie asks why we don't get an apartment all together, but after eight months of waiting for Will to blow each individual hair dry every time he takes a shower it's time to move on. It's exciting, though; we'll be a short subway hop away from the Rat and the Channel instead of the hour's drive, and after gigs we'll be hitting the same parties as Ocasek and Peter Wolf and Nigel and the WROB jocks. I tell Maggie there's room at our place if she wants to stay, even though there isn't. She says she'll think about it.

Rock Paper Scissors have a gig tonight at the Paradise, opening for Marshall Crenshaw, a rockabilly guy who got discovered playing John in *Beatlemania*. Kind of ironic, since the real Lennon hated having to wear the same collarless monkey suit to play the identical set night after night. It's a plum gig, though, and I'm jealous; Annie's day job is at the management firm that handles Aerosmith, so that may have helped. It's still daylight on Comm. Ave. when we get there, the Green Line trains full of graduating college students bisecting the traffic, the rows of low-storied fast food joints and auto supply stores letting in more sun than the skyscrapers downtown. Jackie's cleavage gets us backstage, and we find Rock Paper Scissors' dressing room, which is just unpainted drywall, cigarette-burned carpet, and a couple of folding chairs. Not even any brown M&Ms.

"What's the word, guys?" Jay says, looking up from his bass tuner. I immediately say "aardvark" as Will says "Zimbabwe." Jay laughs and I introduce Maggie around. Jay has a rattail himself and is significantly awed by Maggie's, which she's been growing since high school. Aside from the band there's their drummer Stevo's girlfriend and a guy we haven't met yet with a kind of old fashioned, Clark Kent look. Annie, smiling, introduces him as Boone's college roommate, back from his first year at law school.

We go out for the show. The place is packed, and the sound

is awesome: Stevo's drums are huge, Jay's bass is taut and Boone is wailing. But usually when Annie steps to the mic, the band backs off. Tonight whenever she opens her mouth, Boone seems to get louder, throwing bullet clusters of notes at her. Something's wrong in Scissorville.

Even Maggie, who's never seen them, says, "What's the deal with the guitar player?" Annie's a trouper and keeps going, but I catch her looking at Boone whenever she isn't singing. Boone won't return her gaze, but whenever she's turned toward the audience he bores holes in her back. It's so crowded there isn't really room to dance, so we just stand there witnessing. They finish their set and then reappear *sans* Annie to move their equipment. Will and I duck backstage and see Annie keep walking right out the exit, followed by Boone's college roommate.

In their dressing room I say "wild set" and ask Boone if he's okay. He says sure, like everything's fine. I go back out to find Maggie, and get the scoop from Jackie, who got it from Stevo's girlfriend: Boone's pissed because Annie and his ex-roommate are falling for each other, big time. After he introduced them. Leave it to the L word to fuck up a band.

"Poor Boone," says Maggie.

"Let's rock!" says Marshall Crenshaw.

## 23. *FAST FORWARD:* Central Square, Cambridge, April 1986

"Hold on a sec."

Kat and I are strolling down Mass. Ave. after seeing *The Adventures of Buckaroo Banzai* at the Orson Welles. We've been holding hands as we stroll, partially to keep warm in the late afternoon shadows and partially because I'm trying to be more attentive in public. Kat had noticed at our annual Easter bash that I'd introduced her around as my housemate and not as my girlfriend. Maggie had hated the word "girlfriend" because it was so pre-feminist *Happy Days*, but that wasn't it.

Liz Polar Bear was it. She'd been there, in her tight black jeans and Dead Kennedys *Frankenchrist* T-shirt, looking like the jaded Boston art school post-punk sophisticate she was. (The night we met, at the Halloween party, Wham! had come on the stereo and she'd leaned over and whispered, in rhythm, "Take it off, before I blow-blow, my brains out on the sofa." I'd been so impressed I almost fucked her on the spot.) She'd phoned me up with some more ideas for a video, and it had seemed rude not to invite her to the party. Kat had immediately picked up on the vibe between us, and after everyone had gone, in her shy way she'd called me on it. We hadn't fought exactly, since I'd mostly plead guilty, but we'd had this intense discussion about attraction, love versus lust, sex versus making love, monogamy versus reality. Then we'd made up, in the best possible way, going slow, slow, slow, but finally getting there. Afterwards Kat had asked me if she walked different.

Now as we walk down Mass. Ave. I suddenly disengage my hand. Liz Polar Bear is nowhere around, but in the window of the pawn shop we're passing is Will's worst nightmare. "Just a minute," I say.

Inside the shop is an overweight clerk watching candlepin bowling on a portable black and white TV. I point towards the window, ask if I can see it.

"Ah, the Green Monster," he nods knowingly. He takes it down, wipes it off with a dusty rag and hands it to me. It's huge, about twice the size of my Duo Jet, but it's a hollow body, so it's lighter, with violin-like f-holes, and a country-style Bigsby wang bar. Another Gretsch. And it's all the slightly nauseating color of key lime pie. The strings are so old they're crusty, but the neck has a nice smooth feel. They have an old Fender amp so I borrow a cord and plug in. The basic tone sounds like early George Harrison, or maybe Chet Atkins. I play a few licks, check the intonation.

"That's subtle," Kat says, taking it in as she steps through the door.

"Will wants me to play guitar." In fact he's threatened to try out for a local production of *Jesus Christ Superstar* if I don't start playing again at gigs. Judas, I assume.

She shakes her head. "Were you two *always* so competitive?"

One time on a trip for a weekend gig in Michigan, Will and I had played backgammon for seventeen hours straight. He'd also found Jackie, who's pretty but isn't my type, after I'd gotten farther with Vicki Shehovic than he had. (Moot point, since we found out later that Chas had gotten farther than either of us.) Of course Will was the one who always got free French fries at Frisch's because the waitress thought he was cute, and who got asked to the Winter Formal by his *Brigadoon* co-star while Chas and I ran sound for the band. I had better grades, but Will started driving first. He had better hair, but I was taller. He was stocky, but I wore glasses. I can write songs, but he's got a three-octave range. "What do you mean?" I say.

I put some money down to hold the guitar 'til I can come back and trade in my Duo Jet. I can't wait to see Will's face at rehearsal.

## 24. *REWIND:* Kenmore Square, June 1982

*Thud, thud, thud, thud.*

The room's tiny, maybe ten feet long by eight feet wide, which doesn't sound that tiny until you put a drum set, bass amp, guitar amp, rehearsal PA, mic and music stands, and three musicians into it. And there's no closet, so add cases for all of the above. And, we're actually *sharing* the space with another band, so multiply everything I said by two. It's even more crowded than Will's basement in Harding, where his dad once piled thirty-two ripped auditorium seat cushions that he'd rescued from the trash at Harding High, just in case. Too bad they're not here now, maybe they'd soak up the sound.

*Thud, thud, thud, thud.*

The constant thudding is the band next door, and whenever they stop we can hear other bands thudding down the hall. We're in our new lair at the Kenmore Complex, a fifty-years-past-its-prime ex-hotel that overlooks the square like a thick wedge of brick-and-mortar pie, where about half of Boston's bands rehearse on a nightly basis. Just being here makes us edgier – if we tried a ballad, the band next door would be louder than we are.

*Thud, thud, thud, thud.*

On the plus side, our one window has excellent view of the

square, dwarfed by the green steel girders of Fenway Park looming just behind it. On the minus side, the window's painted shut, and every time Chas lights up the hot, stale air triggers my gag reflex. *And* the Complex's lone elevator's broken, so we had to hump all our gear up the narrow stairway, almost worth it to see Will hefting his own bass amp for a change. But if that's the price of being an official Boston band, then so be it.

We'd packed up the Rockport bungalow and moved to town the previous weekend. Despite my hangdog face Maggie had used her return ticket and gone back to LA, so I'm feeling forlorn despite our new digs. It had been a nice visit, though, no major fights, and we'd fallen back into our Antioch rhythm of sex / sleep / sex / anything else. We'd never gotten around to talking very much, so I'm not sure if her visit was the first step towards some kind of reconciliation or just a week's worth of r & r, but either way I'll take it.

The one down moment wasn't Maggie's fault – blame Nowhere Man. The day after our sightseeing trek the top of my head felt sunburned, so I'd leaned over and asked Maggie to check it. She looked, then without a word went and got a hand mirror and angled it so I could see. *Fuck.* There, dead center on the top my head, was a patch of bare pink skin, as big and round as a nickel. *Double fuck.*

Vanity is one thing, but quick, try thinking of a bald rock star. I felt around, and sure enough my temples were starting to go, too. *Fuck, fuck, fuck.* Maggie had been sympathetic, but had pointed out the obvious: half the world is hungry, with no plumbing or electricity or medicine, and the half that are women are even more oppressed, so in the scheme of things…. But *they're* not rock musicians, I didn't say. And I'll *never* hear the end of it from Will and Chas. If they even stick around to be in a band with the next Mr. Clean. We better get signed, and quick, before it's too late. Maybe I should get a porkpie hat, like the ska bands wear. Nah, it would feel fake, like a costume. Plus I'd probably look like a Cuban insurance salesman.

We do one more song at rehearsal and stretch it out into a jam. As we trade solos I notice Chas is in perfect sync with the drummer next door. Maybe if we got a few more bands to join in we could bring down the building.

After we unplug, Jackie joins us for a celebratory feta cheese pizza at the Greek place across the square. Through our booth window we watch the city's nightlife, just heating up at eleven p.m. – the cabs clogging the intersection trying to beat the stoplight, the summer term BU students heading for Lansdowne Street or Narcissus in their designer jeans, the punked-out kids loitering and sneaking joints in front of the Rat. It's Times Square compared to Harding, where we'd be playing mini-golf or possibly parking with our dates at the reservoir. The city feels *alive*, electric, makes *me* feel alive, despite missing Maggie, despite my new bald spot. Right here, right now is the place to be.

"We're lucky," says Will, arm around Jackie's bare shoulders, fingers toying with the edge of her bulging tube top. *Maggie, where are you?* Will's already got his new urbanized look going: hair buzzed close on the sides and piled high on top, like the British New Romantic groups are wearing, and one fingernail painted black. The rebel of Back Bay.

"Speak for yourself," Chas says, eyeing Jackie's top from across the table.

"No, I'm glad you think so," I say, agreeing with Will. "Our progress has been slower than I hoped, but it's still Year Zero. And now that we're in town things should happen faster."

Will shakes his head. "I meant the Sox, Gunga Dim." He flicks his chin toward Fenway. "If they were home tonight, this place would be mobbed."

A few days later I'm biking up Newbury, just a few blocks over from Kenmore, on the rusty ten-speed I'd brought from Ohio. Good thing, too, since the bike's gotten me employed, unlike my multi-thousand-dollar Antioch degree. It's my first day messengering for Pedal Pushers, and I should be rushing contracts downtown so some corporate law firm can make yet another fortune squeezing the proletariat. But I'm pretty sure I just saw Elliott Easton of the Cars walk down from Boylston and I'm tracking him, weaving slowly between the double- and triple-parked delivery vans. In my shoulder bag alongside the contracts is a cassette of our Berklee demo, and this could be the perfect opportunity to slip it to him. I don't have a clear plan, but I'm hoping he'll, say, stop for take-out and I'll ditch my bike and maneuver myself next to him at the counter and we'll strike up a conversation about favorite surf-rock guitarists. He'll invite me back to the studio to hang out, and we'll eat crab Rangoon in the lounge while our tape blasts over their ten-thousand-dollar Jensen studio monitors. Ric Ocasek will rush in, breathless, saying "Who the fuck *are* those guys?" and the next thing you know it'll be *our* gold record on the wall.

Elliott, however, turns off Newbury towards Commonwealth, heading away from their studio. Damn. Maybe it's not Elliott at all, maybe it's just some other skinny mod with a *Rubber Soul* haircut; I never did really get a good look at his face. Oh well, next time.

While I'm here I stop by Will's new job, at a record store called In Your Face, to tell him to keep a lookout for Easton and the other Cars. I scan the store, see racks of Clash and Sex Pistols T-shirts and posters along the walls, and long rows of punk and Nu Wave imports down the aisles. What I don't see, however, is Will.

"Check your bag?"

The Jam's "Town Called Malice" is on the stereo at a discrete hundred-and-ten decibels, so it's a little hard to place the voice. I turn behind me, and pointing at my knapsack is a blonde chick with serious cheekbones.

I shake my head no. "Will around?" I shout.

"The new guy? I think he's at lunch."

I lean closer, so I don't have to yell. "Could you tell him Mark stopped by? I play in a band with him."

"Okay."

"You play with the Ocelots, right?" I've seen her picture in *SCREAM!*

"Used to. We broke up."

"Sorry."

"No biggie. I'm getting a new band together."

"Staying in the feline realm?"

She looks at me like I'm an idiot and goes back to pricing LPs. I take that as a no and go jump on my ten-speed. Maybe it was the bald spot.

Our show tonight is at Jumbo's, in Somerville. I must be getting acclimated to Massachusetts because I can tell the locals'

Somervillese (more nasal, sharper consonants) from the broader Southie you hear at the Channel, or the dropped r's you get north of the city. Not that western Ohio's flat-as-dirt vowels are anything to write home about.

We're supposed to be splitting the night with Rock Paper Scissors, but when we arrive there's another band we don't recognize soundchecking. The bartender tells us RPS cancelled, and that these are the Clever Dicks, a band of Tufts students playing their first gig. "Not good," Will says. Not that Jumbo's is the Fillmore, or even the Rat, but it's a big deal to cancel a gig, or at least it should be. I've sung on sore throats, played through fevers so we wouldn't cancel. Maybe Annie had never stopped walking after their Paradise gig.

The show goes okay, as long as we keep it loud the locals and the Tufties like us, and nobody notices my extra forehead. We get our biggest ovation for a new song, "Visibly Shook," that I'd written about a campus suicide pact that had shaken the city, myself included. It had made me want to call Maggie, just to hear her voice, make sure she was okay. Nice the Jumbo's crowd appreciated the guitar noise, but I wonder if they even caught what the song's about. At least they got the *gestalt*, as Will would say.

With Maggie gone I check out the natives. They favor leopard and zebra print tops, have 'dos even bigger than the chicks at Jonathan's did, and hold their long-necked beer bottles like weapons-in-waiting. Even Chas doesn't put the moves on them, and I'm content to watch Jackie dance for the evening. As we're loading out a shouting match erupts between two (drunk) women who evidently have the hots for the same (drunk) guy, and when the bartender tries to break it up they both turn on *him*: "I'll shove this bee-uh up yuh mothuh's fuckin' ass, asshole! So min' yuh own mothuh fuckin' bizness!" Hope Jumbo's has insurance.

After we escape, we don't have the hour's drive to Rockport, but the elevator's still broken at the Kenmore Complex so I guess it all evens out.

I call Rock Paper Scissors' house the next day, and their drummer Stevo answers:

"Yo?"

"Hey, missed you guys last night. We could have used the

protection."

"Yeah, sorry about that. It's been pretty weird over here. Boone's locked himself in his room."

"Really?"

"Really. We know he's in there because whenever anybody tries to talk to him he turns up his stereo. We assume he comes out to go to the bathroom when nobody's around."

"I hope so. Do you think he's tripping?"

"Dunno." Luckily they're on the first floor, so even if Boone jumps out the window he'll just land in a hedge.

"How's Annie?"

"She's kind of a wreck, which is probably the point."

"College roomie still around?"

"'Til August. He said Boone did the same thing at school, and to just hide the liquor and wait him out."

"Well let us know if we can do anything."

"Maybe bring a pizza over. With mushrooms on it."

"Boone's favorite?" That would make sense.

"No, mine."

A couple days later I have to make a bike delivery to Harvard Square. I pass Annie's day job so I stop in to say hi. It's a trip; the walls are painted purple and black and decorated with framed, autographed LP covers – *Get Your Wings*, *Rocks*, *Draw the Line* – and there's a cardboard cut-out of a scarved Steven Tyler lifting his mic stand in one corner. Annie looks a little haggard by her standards, and she's without the extra dose of eyeliner she wears onstage. She's robotically sticking labels on hundreds of postcards announcing the agency's new signing, which per the card are going to be – ta-da – "America's NEXT BIG THING!"

"Neon Tiger? Never heard of them."

"No one has."

"Any good?"

"Awful. But don't take my word for it." She flips me a cassette. The cover is a picture of four guys with bleached blonde hair wearing orange and black tiger-stripe suits.

"I thought we were going to be America's next big thing. Or you."

Annie shakes her head. "Not us. I think we're breaking up."

"Sorry. How's Boone?"

"He's out of his room."

"That's progress."

"He's still not talking to me though."

"Stevo said you and his old roommate might be getting together."

"Paul. Boone's best friend."

"Ooh, that's a little awkward."

She tilts her head and looks up at me. "That's the thing. Boone's all upset now, but he's never once, in the two years I've known him, said a word about the future, or even called me his girlfriend. We just started making out after band practice one night. Paul talks about how he wants to get married, start a family. Did you know he's a big brother? I mean like in the Big Brother program. He's cramming through law school, and he spends four hours a week visiting some poor fatherless kid."

No wonder Boone locked himself in his room. I'd jump out the window if I were competing with that. I wonder if that's what every woman wants, even if they don't know it yet. Hard to picture Maggie changing a diaper, though. And I've never even *held* a baby. Whereas Will's been an uncle since he was ten years old. And who knows how many kids out there look like Chas. *Drummer Moves to Massachusetts to Escape Multiple Paternity Suits.*

"But even if we break up I want to do one more show."

"Won't Boone freak out again?"

"Only one way to find out," Annie laughs, a little ruefully. She says if they do it she'd like us on the bill.

I say fine. Annie seems mostly okay, but I feel bad for her, and for them. Being in a band is more than just playing notes together, you have to be inside each other's heads, and lives, to know where the music comes from. So breaking up a band must be like a four-way divorce. I also feel bad for us; it's like Shadowland is losing its collective best friend.

That evening I'm sitting on our little balcony, looking out on the scrub oaks and broken glass of Ringer Park, and in my pocket I find the cassette Annie had tossed me. I start thinking about all the Next Big Things that have come and gone, from the Bay City

Rollers to the Knack to the New York Dolls. Most crash and burn spectacularly after a record or two, but even the ones who make it show the strain. I guess too much success can kill a band as easily as too little. Which will we be? I get my guitar and find a rhythm that's somewhere between "Hollywood Nights" and "Viva Las Vegas," and picture James Dean with a gold top Les Paul:

> *You got the look and you got the style*
> *You got the voice and you got the smile*
> *You've got a manager to take your calls*
> *You've got a lawyer, yeah, you've got it all*

I think about Annie losing her band, Dean and his car wreck, Elvis and his pills. Maybe Neon Tiger should watch out.


## 25. *FAST FORWARD:* Brookline, April 1986

"Maybe a five-string hot pink Flying V with running lights up and down the neck."

"Maybe you can spit blood like Gene Simmons."

Will and I are in our booth at the Bee, halfway through grilled-cheese-and-pickle sandwiches. I brought the Green Monster to rehearsal for the first time last night and Will was suitably appalled, so now he's brainstorming outrageous basses. But he's actually in a good mood for once, since he considers it a victory that I'm playing guitar at all. Good thing I brought it too, since Boone didn't bother to show up. Chas thought maybe he'd locked himself in his room again, but considering Boone now lives alone that seems like a futile gesture. We'd called both his work and home numbers but got no answer; I felt like one of Boone's girlfriends trying to track him down. Generally he doesn't bother telling them he's broken up with them; they have to discover for themselves that he's moved onto someone else. But at least Boone's amp was still in place, so he wasn't out two-timing Shadowland.

My boss Daryl walks up to our booth and I slide over on the striped vinyl seat cover.

"Slumming?" Will says.

"I'm not eating," Daryl says, making a face at our sandwiches. "Gotta stay in shape if I don't want to join the 4H Club."

He doesn't mean the one in Harding that gave ribbons out at the county fair. Some of Daryl's friends are starting to get sick – AIDS, it's called, and it's primarily hitting homosexuals, Haitians, hemophiliacs and heroin users. And it's almost always fatal, though it's never mentioned by name in the obits. There's even a rumor that Guy Havana, the drag queen singer we first opened for in town, was recently diagnosed. Reagan says it's God's revenge. What an asshole. Maybe Reagan is God's revenge. In which case I guess God's the asshole.

Daryl nods his head at me. "Phone message."

"Sorry," I say. "It could have waited."

"From Wayne. Two words: tune in."

He's got to mean WROB. We scarf our food, leave Doreen a handful of change and hurry back. I turn up the warehouse radio as they're finishing the national Friday countdown. Will stays in the warehouse, pacing the aisle.

The first local song isn't us, it's by a new band called the L Street Hammers. The hook is that they're Irish, and their song sounds like a pub brawl set to a thromping bass drum beat left over from the St. Paddy's Day parade. We pace through a Ford and a malt liquor commercial, then freeze as the DJ says, "And here, from their brand new eponymous EP, is Shadowland."

"Awright!" I yell. *This* time it's really happening. W fuckin' R O B. Never underestimate the power of a good headstand.

"Eponymous," Daryl says. "Impressive." He holds up his hand and I high-five him as Boone plays the opening riff of "Car Keys." I go to high-five Will, but he ignores me and starts pacing again. He's probably pissed they're playing "Keys" instead of "Second Glance," the one he sings. Will, Will, Will. Pretty tacky being so solipsistic in *our* big moment. Maybe's Boone's fake-out got his hopes up. I'm about to say something consoling yet pointed when the first verse starts.

I freeze again, listening. The lyric's right, but it's *not* right. I mean the words are, but it's *not* the record. It's *Will* singing. Holy fuck. Somehow ROB got a hold of a bootleg mix of the version Will sang in the studio. The version Wayne and the rest of us voted down, voted *off* the record. I whirl around and stare. Will's nodding to himself, lips pursed, but I can sense a major shit-eating grin dying to get out.

"What the fuck!" I yell.

"Don't look at me," he shrugs.

"What the fuck do you mean, don't look at you?"

"Talk to Wayne."

"Wayne?" What did *he* pull?

"Hey, aren't we supposed to call in and vote? I can get the sales office to call." Will starts trotting out the door.

"Will, this isn't funny. This is like…*mutiny*."

Will shakes his head dismissively. "We're not the fucking *Bounty*. And you're the one who keeps saying it doesn't matter who's singing. All for one, right?" He pivots and walks out the warehouse door.

I follow, my head still spinning. Will waves to get sales guys' attention, then tells them the deal and gives them WROB's number. I haven't seen him so gung ho since he won the Harding High talent contest, singing "Only Women Bleed" in full Alice Cooper regalia. And me in the shadows playing guitar for him. Jack, one of Pegasus' owners, comes out of his office to see what's going on, and I realize he might not want his software company used as our personal phone bank. But Will tells him about ROB and he says, okay, let's see if we can get it to number one.

Will and Jack and the other sales guys start calling. I'd rather call Wayne and find out what the fuck is going on, but we only have a few minutes to vote so I head back to the warehouse and pick up the phone. It takes a few tries to get through, and I hope they don't say, hey, I know that voice, you're in the band! But it's just some receptionist or intern, sounding bored:

"Rock of Boston. Who you voting for?"

"Shadowland."

Click.

I get Daryl to call in too. Counting the sales staff, that's nine votes. Won't exactly jam their switchboard, but it's better than nothing. We hear them announce that voting's over, then wait through another round of commercials for the results.

Out of the three local finalists, we're third. But we've made the countdown. And *that* means we've made the playlist. And *that* means we might finally make the Beanpot. But it *doesn't* explain what the hell happened. This time I dial Wayne. He doesn't answer, but I let it keep ringing. Forever, if necessary.


## 26. *REWIND:* Downtown Boston, June 1982

Cantone's, in the heart of downtown, is close to capacity for Rock Paper Scissors' goodbye show, our biggest Massachusetts crowd so far. Annie's hired a photographer for the occasion, so flash bulbs are popping as we take the stage, and she's also invited a DJ from a local college station to MC. He's called Knife, though not, I suspect, by his parents, and he's got an antenna-spiked 'do that would make Sid Vicious proud. "Please welcome Sha...dow...land!"

Chas counts off "Next Big Thing," which I want Annie to hear since it started with our conversation. I hope it's dark enough for the DJ, who's wearing a ripped T-shirt with *No Future!* stenciled on it:

> *Oh 'til you've been up you don't know how far down can be*
> *Just wait and see, wait and see...*

Will responds to all the attention with his best McCartney soulful gazes and falsetto screams. Chas plays so hard he breaks a drum head on "Animal to Animal" and has to finish the set on Stevo's snare. I make some extra loud space noise in "Visibly Shook," and we invite Annie up for the "do do do's" on "Clarksville."

We keep our set short since it's Rock Paper Scissors' night, and when we're done I wander around the club, which is in even worse shape than the Rat, if that's possible, with broken chairs and fist-sized holes in the walls. It's supposedly a restaurant by day, but who would eat here? *Free tetanus shot with every meal!*

Maybe a week's worth of wild sex with Maggie has removed the scent of animal desperation, because on my way to the bar two girls stop me to say how great we were. They're

115

young, probably college students, and both reasonably cute – one's in fishnets and black lipstick, the other in embroidered jeans and a muslin peasant blouse that she fills out nicely. Chas, doing the math, comes over, making a wide circle around our ex-producer Meredith's table, and we chat up the girls and invite them to IHOP after the show.

RPS sounds okay, and Boone keeps his guitar in check during Annie's vocals, but there's a tinge of melancholy to the set. Then they do an extended "Martian Boogie," with Boone, Jay and Stevo all taking solos, and the band starts to catch fire, like they realize it's now or never. They get their best ovation of the night, and Annie says, "We'd like to invite our friends Shadowland to help us say goodbye."

We grab percussion toys out of Stevo's bag and stand around an extra microphone, and Boone starts a descending scale. It's an old Motown tune, "Signed Sealed Delivered," Annie sings the first verse and we all join in on the chorus. Then she looks over at me. I slip the mic out of its clip, and sing an approximation of the second verse, drifting centerstage so I'm standing right next to her. We alternate lines on the bridge, dipping in like Marvin Gaye and Tammy Terrell, or maybe Sonny and Cher, then hit the chorus again, with Will, in dark glasses, adding ad libs and swaying his head from side to side just like the boy Wonder. Boone takes a solo and a cacophonous jam ensues, with all of us shake, rattle and rolling our noisemakers and Chas getting a nice Latin counter-rhythm going on cowbell. Boone and Stevo gradually bring down the volume while Jay slips in a I, bIII, IV bassline. Off mic, Stevo starts chanting, *na na na na, na na na na,* and we all pick it up: *hey hey hey, goodbye.* The audience joins in too, and everybody, offstage and on, is dancing and clapping in time, stomping and pounding ashtrays along with Stevo's beat. If they can get a crowd going like this, *why* are they breaking up?

Actually I know why: Annie's moving to DC to be with Paul while he sweats law school. And Stevo's announced he's moving to Providence because his girlfriend got a teaching gig there. And Jay, in his last year at MIT, will be in the computer lab night and day. That leaves Boone. Hmmm.

Boone lifts the neck of his Jaguar and cues the cut off, Stevo knocking over his cymbals for effect. I get a hug from Annie on my way offstage, as Knife the DJ yells, "How 'bout one more from Rock Paper Scissors?"

It's daylight before I get to bed. The two girls, Jill and Cindy, had hung around on the condition we give them a ride home to Melrose, somewhere in the north 'burbs. We'd talked late at IHOP, about bands and clubs and who we'd grown up listening to, Chas gradually honing in on punkette Cindy and me focusing in on love child Jill, whose parents were first generation hippies and whose mother still teaches yoga. Then we'd stopped at Revere Beach, just as dawn was breaking. Chas and Cindy locked themselves in the van for some horizontal bopping while Jill and I sat on a picnic table and watched the miniature, harbor-sized ripples lap the sand. I'd put my arm around her, and we'd leaned on each other and kissed as the first rays of pink penetrated the endless gray horizon. I had a fleeting thought of Maggie, now three thousand miles away again, but she could have stayed in Boston if she'd wanted to. When Jill and I got back to the van its windows were completely fogged in, and I'd rapped on the sliding door and yelled, "Open up! Police!" A minute later the door had slid back, a flush-faced Cindy adjusting her top as Chas, cigarette dangling, resumed tying his shoes. Drummers. We'd dropped off the girls, getting their numbers and promising to let them know next time we're gigging.

Now, in my dream, Jill, who's petit but voluptuous, with long dark hair and almost Indian coloration, is teaching me the secrets of the *Kama Sutra*. We're halfway through Backwards Purring Cheetah when my subconscious hears an engine starting. It sounds like Chas's van, coughing and sputtering a few times before roaring to life. I open my eyes, hear Chas jump out of bed and run to the balcony.

"Holy fuck, somebody's stealing my wheels!" He pounds on my door and says to call the cops, then races out of the apartment.

I call 911, tell them what's happening, pull on shorts and run outside. Chas is sprinting down the middle of the street watching his truck make the tight turn onto Comm. Ave. half a block away. "My van! My...my...pussy wagon!"

I turn around to get my car keys, but halfway up the stairs I have second thoughts. Not only will they be long gone by the time we can give chase, but what would we do if we actually caught them? Block the road? Use the Vulcan death grip? *Future Rock Stars Flattened In Daring but Stupid Econoline Rescue.*

I trot back downstairs, find Chas wheezing at the end of the block. That's what he gets for being a Marlboro man. "This really sucks," he says between gasps for air, hands on thighs like he's just run the marathon. He eventually straightens up and kicks an empty soda can that's lying by the curb. The clatter reverberates like a gunshot in the Sunday morning hush.

"Yeah," I agree. The van is one of two possessions he gives a shit about. And he's never had sex on his drums. That I know of. "Cops'll get it back."

"Right," he says.

In a few minutes the police cruiser comes, and Chas gives them the description and license plate number. Chas's van is, or was, reasonably well decked out, with shag carpeting and a nice stereo, maybe why the thieves wanted it. One of the officers looks up from his pad.

"Get a lotta action in it?"

Chas shrugs noncommittally.

"You should try a Harley."

I say we're a band, and we need the van for gigs.

"Christ," the other cop says. "Another one. Let me guess, and you just moved here." The cops could be twins, white over-the-hill jock bodies bursting through their dark blue uniforms, close-cropped hair, *Simon and Simon* handlebar moustaches.

I nod. "How'd you know?"

"'Cause anybody from here with half a brain knows enough to get a steering wheel lock. Or better yet, not to drive a pimpmobile in the first place. May as well leave the key in the ignition."

Little late for a lecture now. I ask if he thinks they'll find it. He says it's probably already in somebody's chop shop, getting a new paint job. They give Chas a form to fill out, and a number to call to see if it's turned up.

"You're better off than that other band," the first cop says. "Their van was full of gear."

Chas whistles.

"Yeah," moustache #2 laughs. "Thief watched them load

up after a gig, then drove away all their rich kid equipment when they went back in to take a piss."

I feel sick to my stomach. Losing the van is bad enough, but fuck. What would we even do? Become an *a cappella* group? Borrow Rock Paper Scissors' gear every time we have a show? Move back to Harding with our limp penises dangling between our legs? Un-huh.

Chas and I take a ride around Allston/Brighton in my tiny Datsun, searching for vans with wet paint. Good luck getting Chas's drums to fit in *here*. I tell Chas if it doesn't turn up we'll chip in and buy a used one; in the meantime I guess we'll have to rent something for gigs. Or take a very big cab. After winding through the derelict triple-deckers of the Allston floodplain and the maze of empty parking lots around Harvard Stadium we circle back to Twin Donuts. I treat Chas to a coffee and a couple chocolate cremes, then we head back to the apartment. I fall back into bed and try conjuring up Jill and the *Kama Sutra* again, but I keep thinking about all our equipment getting stolen, and in my dream I'm singing "I Wanna Be Sedated" in the subway for quarters while plucking a cigar box strung with rubber bands.

That afternoon Will and Jackie come over to shoot baskets in the park, and we tell them what happened.

"That really sucks," Will says, for once not being a wiseass. Jackie whispers something in his ear. "Welcome to the big city."

"Yeah, welcome the fuck to Boston," Chas agrees, bouncing the ball dejectedly. "Back home my mom doesn't even lock her door."

"Hey, what about gigs?" Will asks. "My speaker cabinet won't fit in the Impala." He's wearing tennis shorts and a shirt with an alligator on the pocket, like he's still trying to sneak into the Harding Country Club. The game on the next court is mostly shirtless and headband-wearing Hispanics, so he fits right in.

Chas, in his usual ripped jeans, shrugs. "Cancel. Stay the fuck home. We never make any money anyway."

I steal the ball. "Hey, cops'll find it. Or we'll get a new one." I take a shot, which rolls off the netless rim.

"With *what*?" Chas asks, shaking out a cigarette, his

workout over.

Will grabs the rebound. "We could take some Top Forty gigs. They pay." He fakes a shot, which I move to block, so he passes the ball to Jackie.

"No way," I say, as Jackie banks one in. "Be the next Duck Band." They were the reigning Ohio cover band when we were starting out, phenomenal musicians, played everything as good or better than the original recording. Then they finally did their own demo – one song sounded like Genesis, one song sounded like Hendrix, one song sounded like The Eagles. They had no identity, and zero chance at a deal. Last I heard the lead player was giving lessons in a music store in Ashtabula, probably wondering what the hell happened. I grab the ball, put up a layup, which also rolls out.

"At least they still have their fucking *van*," Chas says, blowing out smoke. Jackie puts her hand on his arm, gives a consoling squeeze. She's gotten transferred to a *Shape It!* in Newton, and today is in pink hot pants and a sky-blue V neck that Chas, depressed or not, is staring down for all he's worth.

"Yo! Eye check!" Will bounces the ball, hard, at Chas's crotch, but Chas jumps out of the way just in time.

Jackie whispers in Will's ear again.

"Jackie just reminded me. Guy beneath us needs a driver."

"What kind of driving?" Chas asks. Since we moved to town he's been getting up at dawn to reverse commute to his shirt factory job. Probably another reason he's cranky.

"Easy," Will says. "Slow."

"Huh?" Chas asks as Jackie trots to retrieve the ball. The game on the next court stops to watch her pass, but then so do we.

"And your passengers never complain," Will says, continuing. "And people get out of your way when you go by."

"What the fuck are you talking about –"

Will starts whistling, *the worms crawl in, the worms crawl out.*

"No fucking way. I'm not being Herman fuckin' Munster."

Jackie returns with the ball, flips it to Will.

"Chas, chill out," I say. "Will's shitting you." I look at Jackie for confirmation, and she gives me a tiny flicker of a nod. Will shrugs and tries a hook shot.

Kidding or not, I can feel a shiver rippling down my back, as I picture the black squareback Cadillac slowly making its way through Morristown, me and my parents following in the over-air-conditioned limo. I shake my head to clear the image.

"Your loss," Will says, grabbing his own rebound. Then he says Daniel, the neighbor, makes deliveries for a bunch of Jewish bakeries. "Lucky Chucky's circumcised, yes?"

"None of your damn business," Chas says.

"Think Daniel would let us borrow his truck?" I ask.

"Why not? It just sits there all night. We'd pay him, make it worth his while."

"Get one of those steering wheel locks," I say, too little too late. But at least we won't have to learn "Jessie's Girl" and "Let's Get Physical."

Jackie whispers to Will again. He nods. "Yes my dear." He takes another shot, which slowly rolls around the rim and in. "He really named it Lucky Chucky."

One of the shirtless headband guys comes over and asks if we want to play four-on-four. We accept. We lose.

Our next night at the Kenmore Complex I casually say, "You know, Boone's a *really* good guitar player."

"No shit, Sherlock," says Chas. He got the delivery job but still has to get up at dawn, so he's even more cranky.

"Real hair, too," Will says in my direction. Jackie had noticed my bald spot when we'd gone swimming at Walden after playing basketball, and, as predicted, Will's added it to his arsenal of digs. I'm tempted to shoot back that with his stubby fingers Will's not exactly Jaco Pastorius, but since I want something I let it go.

"You know what might be fun?" I say instead, still casual.

"Having your shag mobile stolen?" Chas shoots back from his stool. I'd taken him to a Clint Eastwood movie for some revenge therapy, but the real cops haven't done squat.

"Letting me sing lead?" Will says.

I ignore them both. "I meant inviting Boone over to jam sometime."

"Hmmm, interesting concept," Will says, stroking his upper lip. At least that's not a "no."

"Think he'd want to play with us?" Chas asks. Chas tried a moustache once, but with his blonde curls and perennially red eyes it made him look like rabid, like Ted Nugent on the cover of *Cat Scratch Fever*, and scared all the girls.

"Why wouldn't he?" I say, stroking my upper lip in sync with Will. I may have a few days of between-gigs stubble, but I'd never sculpt my face the way he does. "We're good."

"Well," Will frowns, pulling his hand away, "if he joined that *would* kind of commit us to staying."

I'm perched on a narrow stool, and jerk so hard I almost tip over. "Now *you* wanna go back?" I've been so worried about Chas losing heart, I feel blindsided. "We *just* moved to town. You and Jackie just got new jobs. So did me and Chas."

Will shakes his head. "I'm just saying, it would be unfair to invite Boone to join, and then leave. The goal was to move here to get signed."

I stand up, bumping my amplifier and setting off a nuclear detonation of reverb springs. "You want to move back to Ohio *after* we get signed?" *That* thought's never occurred to me. "Put a studio in your parents' basement next to the sump pump?"

"No! But Jackie and I have plans. *I* have plans." He looks down at his Hofner dismissively. "I don't want to be just some anonymous four-string plunker my whole damn life."

"Could be worse. Could be a drummer."

Chas doesn't bother responding, just reaches for his beer can and takes a swig, forgetting that's where he's just put out his last cigarette. He makes a face, then spits the butt out on the floor.

Show over, I turn back to Will. "You'll sing more, I promise. I can write something –" lightweight, schlocky poppy, impossible to fuck up, I don't say.

"I want to *act*," Will says, cutting me off. "Like Bowie."

"You've been acting like Bowie since high school."

"Ha ha. You know I mean."

I *do* know what he means. Shadowland getting famous isn't the end of Will's rainbow, it's just the beginning.

"You said a year. Maybe two. Right, Chas?"

Chas, done choking, manages a nod.

"Hey, we're getting there. We're getting our name around town, and we've got half a dozen new songs, maybe more, good enough to put on an album."

"Great, Mark. So where the hell's Capitol Records?"

"In Hollywood. Where *you* didn't want to move, remember?" I'd floated the idea of LA, but despite his acting pretensions Will had thought it was too far from home. Chas too. Pure coincidence, of course, that Maggie's there. But LA or Boston, I need Will and Chas to stick it out. Boone too, maybe, if it works. I change tack. "Will, we just have to keep gigging, record some more demos. Get people's attention. Play New York." We'd talked about moving there too, but then Maggie had applied to the Museum School, and I'd read an article in *Rolling Stone* about the Cars building their studio, and Boston had seemed like fate. But that was nine months ago.

"Fine," Will says, popping another bass note. "But let's do it *quick*. I don't want to keep splitting shitty fifty dollar gigs with Bernie Boom Boom and the Scumbags."

Actually it was the Clever Dicks but I let it go. "Okay. And I think Boone could help us get a record deal."

"He *is* kind of spacey," Chas says from his drum throne. "I mean, locking yourself in your room is kind of weird."

I shrug. "The more talented you are, the weirder you get to be."

"But boy could he play guitar," Will says. I take that as a yes.

## 27. *FAST FORWARD:* Bay Village, April 1986

Wayne's in the booth with Padric, the studio engineer who probably took a year off our lives with all his second-hand pipe smoke. A cloud of Borkum Riff, just what you want in your lungs while recording vocals on a hot summer night. Today there's a band set up in the main room, and the red light's on, but I barge in anyway. Wayne sees me coming full bore and jogs out of the booth to head me off.

"What the fuck –" I begin.

"In the lounge," he says, cutting me off. He walks me away from his new charges. Little do they know.

Once we're in the lounge he shuts the padded door. "What the fuck –" I begin again.

"Want a Jolt?" He takes two cans from the mini-fridge.

"No!"

He hands me one anyway. "Nice to see you too, Mark."

"Wayne, this is serious. How the fuck –"

"Mark, I did you a *favor*."

"I don't see how, without even telling –"

"Take a breath. Sit down if you want." He pops the top on his can, takes a swig, then leans an elbow on the broken *circa* '75 Elton John-in-giant-platforms pinball machine.

I don't want to sit. I want my bullshit detector on high. I shake my head, cross my arms Sitting Bull-style.

"Okay. After that *SCREAM!* anniversary thing you did, I stopped by ROB to remind Nigel about your record, and pushed 'Car Keys' as the single, just like we talked about. He found the album in the pile, and we listened to it, right then. He liked it, said it had a good hook, even with your burry vocal."

I almost snarl. If my vocal was burrier than usual, it's because Wayne had me record a hundred takes, sometimes just redoing the same line over and over. It had taken me a full month of herbal teas plus a half-dozen expensive voice lessons to recover. "So great. But that doesn't explain how –"

"Just listen. ROB also just added the L Street Hammers. Guy sounds like the Southie Joe Cocker." He looks me in the eyes. "*Burry vocal*. Just like you. Nigel said they wouldn't have a slot for 'Car Keys' for maybe three months, longer if the Hammers stay hot. And by then the record's six months old, and who knows what's come in in the meantime. We were dead in the water. Dead in the fucking water."

I'm gripping the soda can, tight. The guy from the Hammers does kind of sound like me, so maybe Wayne isn't completely full of shit. My long-lost Irish twin. But still. "That doesn't explain –"

"I'm getting to that. So we listened to rest of the record. Nigel played a few seconds of each cut. Anything with your vocal, same deal."

"What about 'Second Glance'?"

"He thought it was okay, but not a home run. I tell you,

'Car Keys' is the one. But not with the Hammers already on the playlist."

"*So?*" I ask impatiently.

"So I told Nigel, what about the same song with a different vocal? He said he'd take a listen."

"And you didn't think that was worth even *telling* me, let alone *asking*?"

"Hey, I didn't know what he'd say. And pardon me for caring, but I figured if I just told you and everybody that ROB had passed on the record, morale would go to shit."

"But you told *Will*." He'd obviously known something was up, the way he was pacing the aisle at Pegasus.

"Will had the tape. Nigel even called him to make sure it was okay."

Fuckin' Will. "Well Nigel should have called *me*."

"He did. Said your number was disconnected."

Oh, shit. When we sent the promo copies out, I was still on Ringer Park, in the place I'd shared with Chas. Then between breaking my wrist and moving I'd never given Ma Bell Kat's number.

"Look, Mark, forget Nigel. Blame me. *I'm* the one who got you your record added. To the biggest station in town, I might add." He tilts his head back, takes another swig.

Now I am confused – maybe Wayne *had* done us a favor, sort of. I know behind the scenes shit like this happens all the time, like when Phil Spector added strings to "The Long and Winding Road" without McCartney's consent – and then it went to number one. Or when John Cougar didn't even know they'd changed his name from Mellencamp until his first single came out. I take another breath, hold the chilled soda can against the veins throbbing in my forehead.

*No.* This is different. Taking *my* voice off *my* song. So what if we're on ROB, if it's not really us. "Still, Will should have known. You should have known. Nigel should have known."

"So sue him, Mark. Sue me. Sue us all. Explain to the judge how having a hit record is going to destroy your career."

"Fine. So tell ROB to pull it."

"Absolutely. Just as soon as we take a vote on it, like we did on every fucking other little thing making the record."

Fuck. I'm screwed. After five years of pushing a boulder up a hill like fucking Sisyphus, we're now going to be known by Boston, and maybe the world, by our most generic song, sung by our most generic singer. Maybe we should change our name to the Generics. Just have a giant bar code for the record cover. And we can cover "Pop Muzik" for the flipside. Thank you Will. Thank you Wayne. Thank you WROB.

Two weeks later we're in Pizzeria Uno in Allston, having dinner before our gig across the street at Great Scott. Everyone else is celebrating the Will-vocal "Car Keys" making number one on WROB's local chart. And (sound of out-of-tune trumpet fanfare) our invitation to play in this year's Beanpot. Finally. Wayne's here too, showing his face since there's good news, and he's telling us how he's pushing ahead on all fronts.

"Know what Double's Eagle's first question was?"

We look up from our half-chewed slices expectantly. Double Eagle is the booking agency that has a hammerlock on the local scene, not just the headlining club slots, but all the college mixers, and even the upper-end high school dances. In short, all the gigs that pay. I'd contacted them when we first hit town and they wouldn't even give us an audition.

"What?" I ask Wayne impatiently. I want him to know all is not forgiven.

"If the bass player is available for promo appearances?" Luckily all the airplay hasn't gone to Will's air-blown head.

"Close, actually," Wayne says. "It was, do they have a video?"

Fuck, this again. We *finally* get our single on the biggest station in town, and now they want a *video*?

"Told you six *months* ago we needed one," Will says caustically.

I ignore him. "What did you say?"

"I said not yet," answers Wayne. "They said call us back when you do, or when you win the Beanpot. Preferably both."

"So let's do one," says Will. "We've got the single."

"With *what*?" Chas asks, meaning scratch. We've just about paid off the rent-a-wreck, but as a corporate entity we're still in the hole.

"I know how we can do one cheap," I say. Since Kat and I breeched the final citadel, I haven't wanted to push it by calling Liz Polar Bear. But if duty calls...

Will immediately shakes his head. "Not some weird out of focus Super Eight shit by that art student you're hot for," he groans. "I mean a real video."

"Name one MTV video that actually enhances the meaning of a song."

"That's so beside the point, Mark, and you know it." He bites into a giant crust bubble and it pops like a flour balloon. "It's about marketing. Branding the band."

"Like toothpaste," I say dismissively.

"Four out of five dentists prefer Shadowland," Boone says, reaching a long spider arm forward for another slice. "Do you ever wonder about that fifth dentist? What was his problem?"

"Forget MTV," Wayne says, the first thing he's said I agree with. "Double Eagle says it's M77 that counts."

M77's a local UHF channel that switched to music programming last year. It's cheesy, with low production values, but unlike MTV it's broadcast, not cable, so anybody can watch it for free. "Some group with a killer video gets on the air," Wayne continues, "that's who the kids in the suburbs know, who they want to play at their dance. Look good on M77, double your price. And with the new drinking age killing the clubs, schools are where the money's at."

Fuck, I think. I'm living in the Age of Will. Pretty soon it's going to be just me and the Hell's Angel from Sir Morgan's Cove holed up in a cave with some Grand Funk Railroad albums and the last Marshall stack. And I don't even *like* Grand Funk.

"So what are we waiting for?" Will asks, ignoring the money question as usual.

"Why not just win the Beanpot?" Boone says from across the table. "Somebody has to."

Good man. I slide a basket of breadsticks towards him.

"Fine," answers Wayne. "That's a one-in-twenty-four shot, depending on the judges, the sound mix, not breaking a string during your solo."

"Hmmm," says Boone. It's the hmmm of defeat, of me being outvoted. Again.

Wayne offers to call a producer he knows at a local TV station, and everybody else nods in agreement. There's one slice of pizza left. I reach for it, but Will gets there first. If I still had my cast I'd whack him with it.

The check comes, and Wayne grabs it. "For going number one. Good work, guys."

Yeah, good work, Dr. Frankenstein. You've created a monster.

Kat doesn't make the show – first one she's missed in a while – so I skip IHOP to make sure she's okay. When I get home our housemate Jan is sitting on Kat's bed, eyes red and a pile of damp tissues beside her. Kat has her arm around her protectively, like my sister used to do when I'd trip and fall while roller skating down our driveway. I guess we're out of Kleenex because now Jan's wiping her eyes with one of Kat's Laplander-pattern knee socks. When I put my guitar in my room I notice all of Travis's stuff is missing from the walk-through. *Uh-oh.* I come to Kat's door and she motions me in.

Clutching the sock like a rosary, Jan says Trav-Trav's left in a big way: he's moving to Colorado, where some college friends have a llama farm. He'd mentioned it in passing a few months ago, but he only just told her he'd decided to join them, virtually on his way out the door.

"And now he's gone," she quivers, burying her head in Kat's shoulder again.

"Wow," I say, "that fast." Maggie and I went through months of back-and-forth break-ups and make-ups before the Boone episode finally drove a silver stake through our romance. Maybe quicker is better. Even so, I tell Jan I'm sorry.

She leans forward and hugs me, hard, her face hot and wet against my neck. I've probably never touched her before, other than shaking hands at our housemate interview and maybe brushing by her in the kitchen. Now I can feel her pressing her loose, full breasts against me as she trembles in my arms. There's something about a crying woman that gets to me, makes me feel protective and turned on at the same time. But Kat's two feet away so I break contact and slide in on the other side of the bed. As Jan talks on about her love life, it feels almost like we're Ozzie and

Harriet and she's our well-endowed teenage daughter, jilted on prom night. I want to say, *You've got your whole life ahead of you...and maybe now you can do some dishes for chrissake.* Well maybe not.

When Jan's finally talked out, Kat gives her long hug. They've both lived here more than a year, so Kat's a connoisseur of the Jan and Trav saga.

"I feel so bad for her," Kat says when she's gone, taking Kat's damp sock with her like a security blanket.

"Yeah, but they fought more than anything," I say. "It was probably inevitable."

"Still, to suddenly be so alone." She draws her knees up, wraps her arms around her shins.

"You're not. Alone." I lean in to kiss her.

She starts toward me but then pulls back. "And for Travis to just leave her like that."

"Pretty scummy," I say. *Thanks a lot, Trav-Trav.*

"He's such..." She lowers her voice to a whisper. "...a selfish *jerkhole.*"

It sounds so incongruous coming from Kat that I have to laugh.

"It's not funny. I don't know how Jan put up with him. She even covered his rent when he was off climbing mountains in Peru or snorkeling in Costa Rica."

I'm sad for Jan, but half of me's jealous that Travis has done all that stuff. "Yeah, he seemed like a prick," I agree. But maybe you *need* to be a prick to do all that. John Lennon, Woody Guthrie, even the Buddha left a wife and kid behind to go find enlightenment. Not much fun for Mrs. Buddha. "So maybe she's better off."

"Maybe," she says doubtfully. "But you know what Jan said hurts the worst?" Kat leans forward over the pillow on her lap. "Three years together, and he didn't even ask her to come along. He just *left*." She looks at me questioningly, like how could he, or anyone, do that?

"Yeah, that's awful," I quickly agree. I hadn't exactly invited my ex Maggie back to Harding with me after we graduated from Antioch. Not that she would have wanted to spend her summer painting landscapes of barns with Mail Pouch tobacco ads on them while Shadowland rehearsed all day, but I didn't give her the option. I just went ahead and made my plans, just like Trav-Trav, no consultation allowed. Sorry, Mags, he says five years too late. Hope Simon doesn't turn out to be a selfish jerkhole.

I change the subject. "Jan might have seen it coming. She was checking out Boone at the Easter party."

"What do you think?" Kat asks.

"Jan and Boone? I don't know that he's a step up. He tends to disappear." Various of his girlfriends have called me looking for him, or shown up in tears at our rehearsal space.

"And he drinks a lot." Kat's dad is in the military, which seems to be synonymous with "alcoholic," so Kat has good radar.

"Among other things. But somehow, he's always got women waiting in line."

"Maybe that's why he takes them for granted," Kat says, nodding. "Jealous?"

I kiss her nose. "Not anymore."

"Good. Who knows," she shrugs, "maybe they'd be good for each other."

"You're such an optimist."

She squeezes her pillow. "I just want people to be happy. Hey, how was the show? Sorry I missed it."

"Don't be." It was a Thursday, which used to be a strong night, everybody feeling the weekend coming. But Wayne wasn't kidding about crowds being down. Great Scott is halfway between BU and Boston College, and through the windows we could see scores of students parading up and down Comm. Ave. But now, if you're not twenty-one… Will and I had started sneaking into clubs at sixteen courtesy of his brothers' driver's licenses; maybe we should forget music and go into the fake ID biz. Wayne had stuck around for the show and had loved my new green guitar, but he'd insisted Will sing "Car Keys" since it's him on the single. I expect a consolation hug from Kat, but it doesn't come.

"Mark, your band's on the radio. You're in the Beanpot. You should be grateful."

Through the wall we can hear Jan sobbing into her sock. All things considered, maybe Kat's right.

*Nah.* Will must die.

## 28. *REWIND:* Back Bay, July 1982

"You're listening to Remote Control, and we're talking to Shadowland. It says here in your press kit you're from Ohio."

"Yeah, it's a better place to be from than to actually be," I quip.

"It's a rock 'n' roll exchange program," says Will. "Some poor Boston band had to move there."

"Do you have to go back at the end of the year?"

"NO!" we all yell in unison.

"Do you guys know Devo and Chrissie Hynde?" In the bright lights of the studio Knife the DJ looks even younger than he did onstage at Cantone's. And while his hair isn't spiked as high tonight, it's freshly dyed jet black. You can tell because his scalp is dyed black too.

"They're from Akron," I say, "the exciting, tire-making part of the state."

"We're from the boring, cornfield part," Will adds. "Harding."

"Never heard of it," Knife says.

"Neither have we," I say.

"Not a lot of action," confirms Chas.

"Except the occasional twister," says Will. "Remember the Great Cow Drop?"

"Cow drop?" Knife repeats, like he isn't sure he heard correctly.

Fuck, Will, let's just stamp "hick" on our forehead. But he's off and running: year before we graduated, a twister had touched down a few miles south of town, lifting – and subsequently un-lifting – a small herd of cattle, in a kind of mass meat tenderizing experiment. But I'd rather talk about our music.

"On a good night, I think we're pretty exciting."

"There's your slogan," Knife says. "Shadowland – more fun than a dozen dead heifers. But you can decide at home."

"We won't steer you wrong," Will says. Maybe I should tape his mouth shut.

"And on that note," Knife groans, "ready to play us a few tunes?"

We say sure and he cuts to a station ID. Finally. Actually,

I'm a little nervous, and not just because we're on the radio. Boone came over to jam last week and now we're asking him to sit in, after one quasi-rehearsal. The red light goes on, and Chas counts off "Visibly Shook."

Will and Boone enter in tandem on the riff, sounding muffled in the sound-insulated studio. I attempt to make my usual guitar noise, pick-ups aimed at my amp for controlled feedback, but it's not loud enough to really catch fire. But when I start singing, Boone takes over and makes sounds I can only dream of, coaxing multiple repeats from his Echoplex that time perfectly with Chas's hi hat. *Whoa.* When we finish, there's a small round of enthusiastic applause – Jill and Cindy, the girls from Rock Paper Scissors' goodbye show, are perched next to Jackie on top of an old upright piano, and Knife is conducting them to sound like a crowd. We do "Animal to Animal," which I dedicate to Jill since she's three thousand miles closer than Maggie, then close with "Dancing in the Streets," with Boone doing the horn lines on his Jaguar while Will lists Boston neighborhoods – *Medfa! Southie!* – instead of Philadelphia and D.C. It's a thicker sound with Boone, and half the time my own guitar seems superfluous. So why bother playing it?

After the set Knife asks if we have anything new coming out. We say not yet, and he tells us a local label's doing a compilation of new bands, maybe we should be on it. He's right, we need a record – the Berklee tape was okay, but WROB never played it, not even after we got Jackie to call up and request us. And only bands that ROB's played on the air are eligible for the Beanpot.

Since Chas's van still hasn't turned up, we're using one of Daniel's delivery trucks. It doesn't have a shag rug though, so Chas is going to have improvise. We do IHOP, *sans* Boone, who says he has to do some computer work, and I mention our thicker sound. "You know," I say, as casually as I can, "Boone's so good a second guitar is kind of beside the point."

"I agree," Chas says. "You're out of the band."

Chas is kidding, but Will's on it like a hawk. "So *that's* what this is about. What a slimeball. Boy, Mark, those *na na na*'s the other night really went to your head."

Chas looks one step behind, so Will clarifies.

"Fucking Zodiac here is staging a coup. He wants to take over as frontman."

I shrug noncommittally. "Might be a better show with someone to work the crowds."

"What crowds?" Chas says, motioning to the girls, and Cindy giggles. She's wearing bright red lipstick tonight, so thick that the rim of her coffee cup looks like a *Rocky Horror* poster.

"Frontman meaning *you*," Will says, pointing a hunk of waffle at me.

I hold out my palms. "Just an idea."

"Well you're not Michael Phillip Fucking Jagger. And I didn't move to Boston just to be in *your* backing band." He gobbles the waffle like a snapping turtle.

"Okay."

"Plus," he adds, spraying a little syrup for good measure, "you're going *bald*." He turns to Chas. "Just what we need, Yul fucking Brynner for our frontman."

"That's why we need to get signed *soon*," I say, but Will just shakes his head.

Jill leans over and puts her lips against my ear consolingly. "*I* think bald men are sexy." She digs her fingernails into my thigh. "My dad's bald."

I have no idea what to say to *that*, so I just ask for the check.

We drop off Will and Jackie, park the bread truck at Daniel's garage, then walk the few blocks back to the apartment. Chas and Cindy disappear into his bedroom and shut the door.

"I've been thinking about you," Jill says, her back against the hallway wall. She's wearing stonewashed jeans and a loose madras shirt, but even so I can make out her rounded, voluptuous curves, with maybe twice as much girl flesh as Maggie.

"I've been thinking about you, too," I manage to say despite my suddenly dry mouth. "Want a drink?"

"I'm okay."

I get some water, gulp it down, and she follows me into my room. There's really no place to sit but the bed. "Have a seat. Want some music?"

"Sure." She strolls over, shakes off her sandals, then climbs up on the mattress and lies on her side, watching me.

I flip through some albums, looking for something mellow but sensual. "Van Morrison okay?"

"Fine. My mom's into him."

I nix Van and put on Al Green. I know we made out on the beach, and I'm the one who's older, but I feel a little nervous, especially after the dad comment. Does she want me to put her over my knee and spank her? Jill seems pretty relaxed, though, twirling the bedspread with her finger. I guess we just start kissing and go from there. Al starts singing *I'm so tired of being alone* and I slide in next to her.

"Light's too bright," she says, shielding her eyes. "Give me your shirt."

"Um, okay." I'm still wearing my Stiff Little Fingers T from the broadcast. I peel it off, and Jill drapes it over the lampshade. The room gets fifty percent dimmer, and I can see our soft outlines on the wall.

"Much better," she says, as she pushes me down and straddles me. "Almost perfect." Then she pulls off her own top and lays it across mine, so the lamp is just a faint glow. "There."

I'd unhook her bra but she's not wearing one. Her breasts *are* perfect, full and ripe with thick brown nipples. As she leans down to kiss me we hear mattress springs and animal noises from Chas's bedroom. I turn up Al Green.

During a lull in the action I ask her when classes start.

"Middle of August. There's a week of freshmen orientation, then they start for real."

Oh shit. "You're just starting?"

"Yeah. I'll be a freshman, or freshwoman. Freshperson."

Fuck, is this even legal? "And your parents are okay with you being out all night?" I'm up on my elbows, in the jet stream of the Goodwill fan.

"Don't worry, they think I'm at Cindy's."

"And Cindy's...?"

"Her folks think she's at my place. We do it all the time. Besides, she's a sophomore. She can do what she wants."

So at least Chas won't go to jail. Hopefully Jill's old man isn't a cop. Or a DA.

"You okay?" she asks.

"Yeah, I just...you know, maybe we should have gone

slower."

"I'm not a virgin."

"Not anymore."

She laughs. "I mean before tonight. And you like me, right?"

I can make out the curves of her body in the ambient darkness. "Very much."

"And you like, you know... doing it with me?"

"Very, very much."

"Okay then."

"Okay, then."

She rubs her foot up and down my calf. "Tired?'

"Not a bit." I lean over, kiss the back of her neck, start working my way down. I stop thinking so much.

## 29. *FAST FORWARD:* Copley Square, May 1986

Being spun on WROB and getting invited to play in the Beanpot is like suddenly getting A-listed after years of trying to crash the party. Today we're giving a free concert in the middle of Copley Square, a gig we couldn't have dreamed of six months ago. It's a weekday, so it will mostly be a bunch of secretaries and sales clerks scarfing their lunches while we do our thing, but ROB is broadcasting us. *Live.* And not just to Boston, but to New Hampshire, Rhode Island, Worcester, the Cape. They've been running hourly ads for the concert with "Car Keys" churning away in the background, so we're already almost famous in three states. Or at least Will is.

We have to, *have to* be on time today since there's a deal with the city for the concert to end promptly at one. Chas has instructions to pick up Boone and break the door down if necessary. I hop on the subway, the Green Monster in tow. I can't very well claim I can't play it, since I strummed along on a few songs at Great Scott, but we've proven I don't *need* to play for our set to work. And not much Will can do if I whip it off halfway through – that's the beauty of a live broadcast.

Chas and Boone are in the Batcave when I get there, Chas

135

puffing a Marlboro and disassembling his set while Boone changes strings, open beer bottle beside him. Boone's always had a high tolerance for alcohol, and a tendency to bring six-packs to rehearsal, but it's ten thirty in the morning. Maybe my housemate Jan, with all her natural foods and homeopathic remedies, would straighten him out. Of course, she's been mopey and depressed since I've known her, so maybe they'd just bring out the worst in each other. Sid and Nancy, meet Boone and Jan.

When Chas is packed we start loading out. We've already agreed the second we sign with Double Eagle we're hiring a full-time roadie – we've been humping amp cases since tenth grade, and it's getting old fast, especially on my post-car-wreck wrist and neck. Will arrives per usual when we're about halfway through, so maybe we should pay the roadie out of his share.

Chas pulls the delivery truck up behind the stage that WROB's rented for the occasion. It's the greatest feeling just to leave the truck parked right there on the sidewalk and not have to scuffle for a parking spot. They have a crew that helps us unload, a stage manager, and two sound engineers, all talking to each other on walkie-talkies: *More bass in the monitor. Move the snare mic closer. Two Asian prostitutes to the band trailer, pronto.* We soundcheck with a new song, "Mercy Left Over," that's basically a rant about how frustrating all the wait-wait-waiting has been. I can understand why Tom Petty put his hand through a wall; maybe we should have signed each other's casts. But the worst should be over. And the biggest plus about ROB adding us is that Will's been more amenable to working on new material. He didn't even say he hated this one.

We stow our guitars then change in the trailer. Will's wearing a Red Sox jersey for the occasion, number 26, Wade Boggs, who's leading the league in hits in more ways than one. I'm wearing baggy light blue zoot suit pants and a hand-made T-shirt with a streak of blue latex across the front that I'd found at an art sale down by Fort Point Channel. Chas is in red satin parachute pants and a black muscle shirt. Boone tops us all, bright yellow stovepipe jeans and a yellow and black horizontal striped jersey – a six-foot five-inch bumble bee. Collectively, we'd look ridiculous anywhere *except* on stage, and I have second thoughts about looking like just another party band; maybe Khartoum's day-laborer outfits are the way to go. But before I can say anything, there's a knock on the trailer door. Showtime.

A stagehand leads us up the metal stairs and we get in position. The square is packed, and we haven't even started yet. Jesus, we better not suck. A jock from ROB tells the crowd to yell hello to the radio audience, and they do. Then he says, everybody at home, yell back! There's a moment of silence and people laugh. "Here they are, Shadowland!"

Chas starts thumping out "Next Big Thing." I'm wearing my new oversize green guitar and chord along as I sing. It sounds good in the monitors, solid but clear, but people are just sitting there. I work the second verse a little harder, try to put more soul into it. Still nothing. As Boone starts his solo I take one more look at the crowd, complacently eating their baloney sandwiches on the grass. Fuck it. I pull off my axe and lay it on the drum platform, run to the front of the stage. I put my hands over my head, start clapping along with Chas's snare hits, *one TWO three FOUR*. It's a generic rock star thing to do, but damn if it doesn't work: people start clapping along. Still clapping, I walk over to Boone, who puts a few hip thrusts into the end of his solo and we get a few cheers. I grab my mic stand for the last verse, John Lydon style, and sing from the edge of the stage. I conduct the final chord with an arm pull, and we get a pretty decent ovation for twelve-fifteen on a Wednesday afternoon.

I avoid Will's gaze as I wear my Gretsch intermittently for the next few songs. About halfway through the set some people get up and dance on the grass, and I wave them forward. Some others join them, so there're maybe twenty people dancing on the concrete right in front of the stage. Will shoots me a "don't you dare" glare during "Second Glance," but I take my shaker to the lip of the stage, then when he's not looking I jump down into the crowd, almost breaking a leg in the process. A circle of dancers, mostly young women, forms around me, and we take turns imitating each other's moves. Now *this* is what I call songwriting. I give a quick squeeze to the nearest typist and climb back up just in time for "Mercy Left Over." Will pops his bass like he's pissed as hell, but somehow recovers enough to sing "Car Keys" with his best McCartney smile in place. On the last chorus I go to the edge of the stage again and hold out the mic, and the audience shouts along with us: *I've got her CAR KEYS! She left her CAR KEYS! Look at her CAR KEYS!* Boone hits a last chord and Chas does a long rolling fill. Will signals the cut off with the neck of Rickenbacker, then we take a bow as the DJ sprints onstage to sign off.

There's a small crowd of well-wishers by the trailer, so I chat and chug Evian with some of the dancing typists. Kat's in school, but Jackie appears and gives Will a proprietary kiss. He seems like he's maybe a B-minus on the happy scale, probably because I got to bump with a few secretaries and he didn't. Too fucking bad – he got to sing the single.

I don't know if it's because we *are* better, or people *think* we are because we're on the radio, but either way I notice people are treating us differently, more deferentially, clapping longer and louder, giving us more respect. Almost like we really are rock stars. I could get *used* to this.

When I get home, there's a message from Wayne. Morocco Mole got a nibble. Hot fucking damn. Or as Chas would say, hot damn fucking.

### 30. *REWIND:* Brookline, August 1982

Will and Jackie are throwing a party at their new apartment. And not just any party. *This* party has a theme: it's a Bad Music party. Everyone is supposed to bring the absolute worst record in their collection, and play the absolute worst song off it. Those who survive the aesthetic poisoning get to vote on the worst of the worst, and the winner gets to keep, or possibly destroy, all the records.

It was Will's idea, of course. His senses honed by years of cutting school to watch daytime TV with his mother, he's been a lifelong connoisseur of bad – bad movies, bad TV shows, bad fashion statements. Will also has an unfair advantage: since he works in a record store, he has a vast pool of vinyl to make his final selection from. But it won't be a pushover: Chas has soft spot for mediocre thug rock (Kiss, the Dictators, Norman Nardini), Boone has an impressive collection of overly ambitious prog-rock

(Tull, Rush, early Genesis), and I used to have a radio show at a free-form station that never threw anything away. May the worst song win.

Chas and I ascend the narrow wooden stairway, clutching our entries and (Chas) a six-pack of Rolling Rock. Jackie answers the door wearing a white halter that shows off her doe-brown summer tan. Would that I could apply the lotion. Chas heads to the kitchen/bar, and I go say hi to Boone, easily findable since he's a head taller than the rest of the room.

Will's also invited Jay and Stevo from Rock Paper Scissors, good thing since Boone's been down about Annie. We'd done a show at the Grog in Newburyport, Boone's first as an official member of Shadowland, and afterwards we'd driven out to Plum Island to look at the stars. It had been beautiful: a silver streak of reflected moonlight reaching out to the horizon, waves gently breaking on the sand, a warm salt breeze caressing our faces. I'd thought of Maggie, back in LA, wondered if she was looking at her ocean the same time I was looking at mine. Jackie had gently asked Boone how he was doing, and he'd said Annie had moved down to DC that day. Then he'd picked up a piece of driftwood and heaved it into the surf like a javelin. Chas had called him over and they'd shared a consoling joint.

Now Will, wearing a spangly blue Uncle Sam top coat leftover from Jackie's dad's Fourth of July rug sale, calls the party to order and we gather in the living room. Their coffee table is actually an old wooden door, complete with knob, and we pile our entries on it, mostly LPs but a few 45s and cassettes, plus one beat up eight-track by Tony DeFranco and the DeFranco Family which we can only admire since there's nothing to play it on. Will's completely in his element as smarmy ringmaster/game-show-host MC, and he narrates as Chas does the needlework. ("That was 'Yummy Yummy Yummy,' courtesy of the Ohio Express. Air sickness bags are located in the seat pocket in front of you.") There's mawkish melodrama ("Run Joey Run"), sappy pop ("I Honestly Love You"), then some unlistenable (and interminable) twelve-tone fusion courtesy of Jay. Somebody else has brought an x-rated dance track that's basically an orgasm set to a thumping disco beat, and there's even a send-in-your-poem-and-we'll-set-it-to-music election anthem ("Jimmy Carter Says Yes!").

"Yes they're bad," Will intones in his best Bob Barker, "but are they bad *enough*?" We take an intermission, and Boone and Chas slip out to the porch, presumably to get stoned again. Considering the music I don't blame them. I go to the kitchen for a drink and see a woman, maybe a few years older than us and more elegantly dressed than my jeans and Converse, trying to extract the cork from a wine bottle. She has full lips and exotic green eye shadow, and I catch a trace of expensive-smelling perfume. Maggie's three thousand miles away, and Jill's off at school already, so why not be helpful? It's a challenge since there's no corkscrew, but together we manage to dig most of it out with a steak knife. I'm about to ask her name when Will calls us back to the living room.

Chas's eyes are red and he's lost some fine motor control, so I take over the turntable. Boone doesn't disappoint, with something called *A Space Opera*, then Chas hands me his, already out of its sleeve. I'm expecting music to drag your knuckles by, but when I put the stylus down a slow two-note organ riff begins.

Fuck. I know this. I've listened to it a million times. *Something warm is flowing down my fingers.* Then a line about a sheet across his chest. Shit. Ninth grade, the year I moved to Harding. I played it constantly on the little RCA stereo I'd inherited from my sister, sometimes five or six times in a row. Chas and I even jammed on it the first time we ever played together.

"Bloodrock," Boone says, impressed.

"'D.O.A.,'" Jay nods. "Pretty heavy."

"But is it heavy *enough*?" Will says in his unctuous tenor, and motions for me to lift the needle.

"Whatcha got, Zodzniak?" Stevo yells. Only two entries left, but I feel suddenly claustrophobic, like I'm drowning in hot air. Too many people. I hand my record to Stevo, start weaving my way through the crowd. "What song?" he asks.

"Side two, cut two," I say over my shoulder. Out on the porch, I clutch at the railing and let out a long slow breath. Inside I hear my selection starting. Serves 'em right.

In a minute I catch the same subtle perfume. "Mind if I join you? That song's truly offensive."

"But is it offensive *enough*?" I say, imitating Will.

"Absolutely. What is it?"

"Leonard Cohen. 'Don't Go Home with Your Hard-On.'"

"Jesus," she laughs. "Good advice, I guess. Mind if I smoke?"

Normally I'd say yes, or maybe move away, but I just shrug.

"You okay?" She lights a cigarette, blows her smoke over her shoulder away from me. "You left pretty quick."

"It just got crowded." I look out over the yard, with Jackie's little garden of tomato plants growing on stakes, see a lightning bug flicker. My sister and I would catch them, or at least try to, in rinsed-out Jiffy jars with holes poked in the lids. My sister had given me hell when I'd killed one, rubbing its glow-in-the-dark tail into the back of my hand so my skin would glow too. Sorry, little guy. I glance back at Ms. Corkscrew, see her cigarette glowing, orange though instead of yellow-green. "Plus I'm sort of questioning the whole concept."

"Of the song?"

I shake my head. "The party. I doubt anybody *sets out* to make bad music. So it feels kind of cruel to pick on them." I could take people not liking our tape, but not *laughing* at it. I nod back to the yard. "Like squishing a lightning bug."

She takes another drag, exhales thoughtfully. "I see what you mean." Then Leonard Cohen yowls a particularly out-of-tune high note through the curtain, to increased boos and groans, and she makes a face. "But *this* is pretty fuckin' awful." She turns toward me, putting one hand on each of my shoulders. "I hereby absolve you of feeling guilty."

"Thanks." If only it were that easy. She leaves her hands in place and I'm thinking about leaning in for a kiss when the record abruptly stops, replaced by a chorus of mock cheers.

Chas pokes his head through the curtain. "Mark! Will says you gotta hear this."

"Coming? I ask her, but she holds up her half-smoked cigarette. "Chicken."

Will's lowering the needle smugly. He needs a home run – "Hard-On" was easily the worst of the worst so far. The music starts.

When I say music, I mean it in the loosest possible sense. I recognize the sound of a guitar or two, both horribly out of tune, and a cheap toy drum set, but not played how anyone's ever played them. A girl's voice comes in, singing nursery rhyme lyrics to a choppy, sing-song melody. She's looking for her pal Foot-Foot ("Foot-Foot!"), and whenever she says Foot-Foot ("Foot-Foot!"), another girl echoes her in random, overlapping timing (timing!). Instead of playing their own parts, the guitars and drum attempt to play right with the melody, so the overall effect is like the first day of grade-school orchestra rehearsal, only not as polished. People in the room, once the initial shock wears off, are equally divided between those screaming to break the record and those who want to hear more. Will plays a few bars of a second song – "It's Halloween!" – just to prove the first wasn't a fluke, then mercifully lifts the needle.

"What the fuck was that?" Stevo asks.

Jackie whispers in Will's ear and he laughs. "She said it was Frank Zappa's daughter's Brownie troop."

"I could see that," Boone says gravely, chin resting on his beer bottle.

Actually, Will says, it's a band called the Shaggs. "The record came into the shop, and no one could believe it. The bio says it's three sisters from New Hampshire."

"Right next door," Boone says. "Maybe they could open for us."

"Awesome idea," Will agrees.

"No way," Chas says, just before I would have.

"You're right, of course. What was I thinking?" Boone hits his forehead, like he's in that new V8 commercial. "We should open for *them*."

We vote, but it's just a formality: "Hard-On" gets a few token nods, but the Shaggs sweep the First Annual Bad Music Awards. In fact, we agree there's no point having a Second Annual, or a Third, since they'd just keep winning.

Tina – Ms. Corkscrew – lives in a high-rise a couple blocks from me and Chas, so I offer to give her a ride home in my little Datsun. We park, and I walk her to the door of her building.

"You have amazing lips," I say. What the fuck – if Jill was my jailbait experience, maybe I'm due for an older woman to even things out.

"Thank you. You may kiss them."

I do. She tastes like wine and cigarettes, but her tongue knows its business. She invites me in, asks if I want to see her apartment. Not that I particularly care about furniture, other than possibly her bed. But once I see it, I'm impressed – the place is pristine, with polished hardwood floors and matching chrome and leather furnishings, about a dozen pay grades up from my and Chas's hovel. There's a Polaroid on the refrigerator of a naked woman in a Mardi Gras mask holding a flute of champagne. I assume it's Tina, but before I can ask she grabs my hand and says check this out. She turns out the lights to her bedroom. In the sudden dark I can see a thousand tiny fluorescent stars glowing on her ceiling, her own private Milky Way.

"Wow, very cool," I say, impressed. "Very Carl Sagan." I ask her if it's an effective seduction technique.

She says in fact it is. I feel my pulse quicken and a tightening in my jeans. Tina's definitely a *woman*, not a girl, and she's probably wearing expensive sleek silk underwear. Who knows what secrets she could pass on, what those lips are capable of. Part of me wonders if I'll be able to keep up. "I was kind of a nympho," she says, shaking her head. "But I'm reformed."

"How reformed?" It comes out like a whimper, like air escaping a balloon.

She laughs. "For the moment, very reformed." She clicks the lights back on, punctuating her point.

"Too bad." I can feel my jeans deflating, my pulse dropping out of warp. "How come?"

A cloud crosses her face, furrowing her eyebrows. Which on close inspection look plucked, then painted on. "Self-preservation, I guess," she sighs. She sinks down onto the bed in an un-seductive manner, all coyness gone. "It's not exactly like I set out to fuck every cock of the walk around, you know." She looks at me, shards of anger poking through her jaded exterior. "I would meet somebody, think he was nice, let him take me to bed. Why not? I'm liberated. We'd have this great time, then he'd disappear." She shrugs, digs out a cigarette, looking older and more tired by the minute. "I'd get lonely, then get laid again to prove I was desirable, repeat. It got me all fucked up inside." She lights her cigarette. "So I'm trying celibacy."

"How's that going?"

"Longest two weeks of my life." She exhales, smoke rising like mist toward the paper stars.

"I tried celibacy for eighteen years. It was miserable. You ever meet anybody you really liked?"

"That's the sucky part. I'd *think* it was somebody special, get all excited, make all these plans. We'd have this nice weekend, go to a museum, dinner, or a few nice weekends, and then I'd never hear from him again. And if I called *him*, he'd weasel out on me."

"Sorry," I say. "I would call."

She reaches up and pats my cheek. "That's what you say, dear boy. But you wouldn't. Or not for long, anyway."

She's right. I'd call once, to be polite. But she's not really my type. Which doesn't mean I wouldn't sleep with her. Which maybe qualifies me for her all-men-are-assholes list. "So here we are."

She nods ruefully, stubs out her cigarette. "You can stay if you want. Platonically. It's a big bed."

"Um, that's okay." But on second thought, what's the rush? Chas is probably in his underwear watching a *Hogan's Heroes* rerun on our little black and white, enjoying a nightcap of Rolling Rock and Cocoa Puffs. And Marlboros. "Well maybe for a minute."

"Wanna see the stars again?" she offers. I nod and she flips the switch. "Take off your shoes."

She kicks off hers, and we nestle against each other on the bed, looking up at her homemade galaxy. It's not bad, nice even in a lowered expectations kind of way, reminds me of me and my sister sleeping out in our backyard in Morristown. Stars and lightning bugs. Of course my sister wasn't wearing expensive musk and didn't have lips like an African princess. I'm wondering how to re-broach the whole celibacy question when I hear Tina, every so faintly, start to snore.

*Fuck.* I slide off the bed, slip on my sneakers. Guess Leonard Cohen isn't the only one going home with his hard-on.

## 31. *FAST FORWARD:* Chestnut Hill, May 1986

The *Bosstown Bean* runs teasers above its main headline, and the week after our Copley Square concert, above a story about a nuclear meltdown in the USSR that's supposedly worse than Three Mile Island, the music teaser is a picture of a guy with receding temples and clip-on sunglasses onstage at Copley, with the question *The future of Boston rock???* Inside is an uncropped version of the picture, with the full band. The first line of the column, an obvious spoof of Jon Landau's Springsteen write-up, reads:

> *I have seen the future of Boston rock 'n' roll and his name is...Mark Zodiac?*

The column goes onto say some okay things about the record and everybody's contributions to it, but the writer's basic point is to contrast the record (slick) with the Copley show (a little ragged but a whole lot more fun). The critic also seems like he's on a campaign to take rock back to about 1957, before overdubbing and gated reverbs and Steely Dan, and uses our show as a case in point, how, just like Elvis – the '50s rock 'n' roller, not the cracker-eating tow truck dog – every time things threatened to get boring, I *did* something. He also actually *liked* my singing, or at least the spirit behind it, and lumped Will's in with the "too slick for its own good" category.

I have possibly been compared to E. Costello, but this guy is talking *Presley.* Will is going to shit bricks, then kill the critic, then kill me. Kat's proud of me, but also a little worried about Will. The good thing, or bad thing, depending on your perspective, is that after this article it's going to be impossible to go back to being full time anonymous rhythm guitarist. I'm the fucking *future of Boston rock* (!). The publicity also can't hurt our chances of nailing down a record contract.

We're meeting Morocco Mole today to discuss the offer. On the phone he hadn't said which label. Capitol would be cool; it was the Beatles' label, at least until they formed Apple. Jules and the Polar Bears had been on Columbia, until Columbia refused to release their third album and basically broke up the band. What a nightmare. Sire, out of New York, is maybe the hippest label, but Epic's been sniffing around Talon and some other Boston bands. I don't care, as long as we get some kind of rider that says they have to release our records. Will and Chas have been speculating how big our advance will be – the Cars had a half dozen labels bidding for them, and Elektra ponied up a nice chunk of change. Maybe we'll build our own studio too.

As Hayek shakes our hands his eyes are as watery and darting as ever. "Ever hear of a, *ahem*, P & D deal?"

I glance around the wood-paneled room; none of us has. Wayne's off at a session, or maybe he's still avoiding me after our "Car Keys" dust up, so we're at Morocco Mole's mercy.

"Pressing and distribution," he continues. He's wearing a pin-stripe suit with a pink dress shirt, wide-striped tie and actual gold cufflinks. Mole of the people.

"Sounds like a dry cleaner," Chas says.

"What about the advance?" Will asks brusquely. As predicted, he's not exactly thrilled with my *Bean* write-up, but a big fat check might help his ego.

"It's not that kind of deal."

We all stare at Hayek.

"So what kind of deal is it?" I ask warily.

"Bad," Chas snorts, Will nodding in agreement.

"What label?" asks Boone, withholding judgment.

As Hayek explains, our wild dreams of avarice shrink like a muff-diving poodle in the rear view mirror. The label, 10,000 B.C., whose claim to near-obscurity is releasing a few crudely-recorded discs by some spiky-haired groups from DC and Minnesota, will license our existing record from A Hole in the Middle, press a few more thousand copies, and pay us the minimum royalty rate. Minus promos and returns, of course.

"But what about 'Car Keys'?" Will asks.

"What about it?"

"The single's not on the album."

Hayek looks confused. Maybe I shouldn't be surprised that our own lawyer hasn't actually listened to our record.

"He said 'existing record,' Will," I say. "That means the album version. Not some bootleg."

"Yeah, but maybe they heard *my* version –"

146

As Will and I squabble, Chas reaches over and takes the contract off Hayek's desk. After a minute he whistles us silent. "You're arguing about nothing. They're paying us *less* than it cost us to record the damn thing." He tosses the contract back down. "Deedee's gonna fuckin' kill me."

Will and I both grab for it, but Will gets there first. "Won't exactly buy Jackie her dream house." He holds it towards me. "So much for Mr. Future of Boston Rock."

I ignore him and scan it. "Is this the only offer?"

Hayek nods. "So far."

"Great, I'll be stuck driving a bread truck for the rest of my life," Chas groans, shaking his head.

"Guys," Boone says, "you're looking at it wrong. That's five times as many copies of the record as *we* made. I bet they'll send one to every college station in the country. So the royalty's just like free money."

Hayek clears his throat. "Not, *ahem*, exactly free. They'll expect you to tour."

"Of course," I agree. "That's what bands do."

"In *what*?" Chas asks. "My van's stolen and you totaled the rental."

"Tour bus," Will says. "Which they'll pay for, right?"

"Um, I can certainly ask," Hayek says, with complete lack of conviction.

"Plus we'll need a promo budget, for the video."

Will isn't getting it. The only 10,000 B.C. clips I've seen look like they were shot with a hand-held camera, possibly by a fan who was being pummeled in the mosh pit at the time. But Hayek doesn't dissuade him.

"This is just, *ahem*, a preliminary contract." He leans forward, tucking his tie into his belt as his eyes do a quick, watery lap around the room. "We'll send them our wish list – tour bus, video budget, advertising, etc. – then they'll send us their, *ahem*, counter-proposal, and so forth."

"Sounds like it could take months." Even if it's a sucky contract, I still want our record out there, and soon.

Morocco Mole shrugs. "That's the way the game is played."

"No deal unless we get a video," Will reiterates. "*And* tour support."

Chas still isn't impressed, his look saying it would still be a crummy deal. I know how he feels. Maybe Kat will have second thoughts and go back to Dr. Kildare.

"I promise to do my, *ahem*, level best," Hayek says, ushering us out.

I shake his clammy Mole hand again, wondering how level his best is, and we leave, grumbling. Only Boone seems happy with the offer. Maybe he never expected a better one.

But 10,000 B.C. sent their contract *before* the *Bean* write-up. Maybe even Morocco Mole can parlay that into a real deal, with an advance. On the subway ride to Pegasus I read our review one more time as Will stares pointedly out the window. *The future of Boston rock....* First thing they tell you is, never believe your own press clippings. Wonder what the second thing is.


## 32. *REWIND:* Kenmore Square, August 198*2*

Third week of rehearsal with Boone, and we're jamming away in our tiny cell at the Kenmore Complex. We're doing kind of a Rick James funk groove, and I'm doubling Will's bass riff on my Duo Jet while Boone does a jangly Byrds/Beatles thing on top. We coalesce into a set pattern, and I step to the mic. I'd jotted some words in my notebook after not spending the night with Ms. Corkscrew, and I try them out against the groove:

> *I've watched her cut and pasting paper stars*
> *They glimmer from her ceiling in the dark*
> *There's one for every man who's shared her bed*
> *Now she's got a galaxy above her head*

I lean over, twist the dial on the delay to multiple repeats:

> *Now would you like to take (take, take, take, take, take) a ride*
> *(ride, ride, ride, ride, ride)*
> *With a girl who's all fucked up (up, up, up, up, up) inside*
> *(side, side, side, side, side)*

Boone stomps a fuzz pedal and takes a dissonant solo, which is also picked up by delay. On the next chorus Will adds a harmony, also echoed, so both our voices pulse and swirl together with Boone's guitar for a thick, hazy effect. When it finally ends I say I think we have our song for Knife's compilation album.

"You realize," Will says, "no radio station will ever touch it."

"I don't know," I say. "I think it sounded pretty cool."

"Basic George Carlin, dickhead. The seven words you can't say on television."

"That's TV."

"Same dif."

"Maybe they could beep it out," Chas says.

"Maybe *we* could beep it out," says Boone. He plays the riff and sings, *with a girl who's all BEEPed up inside*, throwing his voice up an octave for the beep.

"Nice. One more time." Will circles his finger in the air, like a base coach sending a runner. When Boone gets to "fucked" Will chirps "beep beep!" like the Road Runner. And he does it on mic, through the delay, so it's more like beep beep! beep beep! beep beep!

All three of them are cracking up. Excellent, now instead of having two day-care students to control I have three. Three against one. Maybe Boone joining wasn't such a hot idea, especially if he's going to team up with Will for a cross-talk act. "Very witty, Wilde. Lots of songs have curse words. The Dead Kennedys, 'Too Drunk to Fuck.'"

"Yes, Mark, that was a *huge* hit. Right to the top of the *Billboard* charts." Will thumps a bass string for emphasis.

"Blondie, 'Rapture.' '...finger-fucking....'"

"Sure, but you can barely understand her."

"'Fight the Power' says 'bullshit,'" Chas says, tipping a stick towards Will.

"'God damn the pusherman,'" says Boone, playing the riff.

I say I'll call the FCC. Or maybe the ACLU. Or both.

I don't actually know the number of the FCC, but I figure it's a good excuse to call WROB and introduce myself to the local music director. I start a letter to Maggie, now back in California, saying I miss her but leaving out any mention of Jill or Ms. Corkscrew, then at midnight pick up the phone.

"Nigel All Nite, what's your request?"

"Can you say 'fuck' on the radio?"

"Hang on a second." In his radio voice he says, "That was Romeo Void, 'Never Say Never.' A fuckin' great track, don't you think? Here's Billy Idol." Regular voice. "Sorry, what was the question?"

I have the radio on low, so I know it went out on air. "Wow, I can't believe you said that."

"Said what? Who am I speaking to?"

"This is Mark, from the band Shadowland."

"Shadowland, Shadowland. You guys sent us a tape a few months ago."

"Right."

"You covered a Monkees track. Ska."

"That's us. 'Last Train—"

"—to Clarksville.' I know. I played it."

"On your show?"

"Absolutely. Vocal was a little rough, but it had a great vibe."

"Thanks. It was live in the studio, one take." I want to ask him what he thought of the ones I wrote, but I wimp out.

"So what can I do you for? I've got a segue coming up."

"We have a new song we're thinking about recording with 'fuck' in the hook."

"Can't play it. I'm on after the FCC goes to bed, but we could never put it on the daytime playlist."

"Fuck," I say. I hate it when Will's right.

"Sorry," he laughs. "If I were you I'd say 'funk.'"

"Funk?"

"You got it. Trust me, every time James Brown and Wilson Pickett say funk, they're really saying fuck. And every chick in the house knows it."

I say thanks and hang up. *Funk?* Tina's a girl who's all *funked* up inside? Is it stupid, blatant censorship, selling out? Yes, yes and yes. But would it get us on WROB? Maybe. Probably. Chuck Berry made a career singing about sex without ever saying the word, and he got on the radio, so why not us? Now *I'm* all funked up.

### 33. *FAST FORWARD:* Chestnut Hill, June 1986

Will says he got a call from Wayne. His TV friend could do a full-color, broadcast quality clip of us for just about what 10,000 B.C. would pay us to license the record.

I'm still wary, but it's a moot point because Will and Chas won't sign the contract. After three rounds of Federally Expressed back and forths (billable to us as an expense, no doubt), Morocco Mole's only succeeded in getting 10,000 B.C. to not deduct postage for the radio mailing from our royalties, and, under the heading of "tour support," to make a deluxe 11"x17" poster for us. No Winnebago with "Shadowland Across America '86 World Tour" stenciled on the side, no per diem, no video budget. But if we *do* manage to rent another van and drive to Seattle or Denver or wherever the gig is, at least there'll be a (black and white) poster of our album cover waiting to greet us, probably taped above the urinal in the men's room.

I'm telling all this to Kat while we're making dinner. Amazingly, we didn't have to wash any pots first – the newly single Jan has decided cleanliness is next to Gandhiness and even scrubbed the bathtub. Maybe we *should* turn her loose on Boone, who probably hasn't been to a laundromat since Annie left town.

"But they're not the only record company," Kat says. "I've seen your collection – there must be fifty different labels."

"So far, they've all passed," I say, stirring our powdered mashed potatoes, the cheapest meal on the planet. "That's why we should take the B.C. deal and develop a track record. Get the big fish interested."

"How long would your tour be?" She's slicing broccoli, which we've discovered cooks perfectly well in the same pot, floating in its own private Idaho, so to speak.

"Twenty dates on the East Coast, and another ten out West." I don't add that we'd almost certainly lose money, playing rooms like the Rat in towns that have never heard of us while paying mileage and gas on rented wheels.

"I would miss you." Kat looks genuinely sad, like Dorothy saying goodbye to the Scarecrow. Maybe she won't go back to David.

"I would miss you, too," I say, leaning over the pot to kiss her neck. I *would* miss her, I realize with something of a start. It's been kind of cozy having her to come home to. But that's no reason not to tour. Playing our songs every night, for new people, in a new town, is exactly what all this has been *for*. If only Will and Chas thought so, like Boone and I. I can see their point, though: touring is *supposed* to be opening thirty shows for, say, Cyndi Lauper to packed houses every night, then riding to the next city in a customized, air-conditioned land yacht with fold-down bunks and a built-in VCR to watch Monty Python movies on. Which is exactly what Wednesday Week, the band that won last year's Beanpot, are doing right now. They signed with Mercury, their album's not even out yet, and already they're on the road, being pampered like stars. And if I'm jealous, Will's downright chartreuse, since he worked stocking records for a year with the band's lead singer.

"I'm sorry Will and Chas won't go, though," Kat says, kissing me back. "So what are you going to do?"

Hire a new rhythm section, I don't say. "Hope we win the Beanpot, I guess," I sigh, dropping some Velveeta on top of the broccoli and spuds.

"Wouldn't a video help?"

I've told her about Double Eagle wanting us to do one for M77, the local music channel. "Maybe. If it's good." Of course, "good" is in the eye of the beholder – M77's current smash is of a guy in a rainbow fright wig leading a conga line through a beauty salon, a cocktail party and a mortuary.

Kat hands me a spoon, and we carry the pot to the kitchen table, placing it on a phone book so it doesn't melt the cheap plastic tablecloth. "You know, I've got some money saved. For tuition." She has a teaching degree, but wants to start taking courses toward her masters. "I won't need it 'til September."

I lower my spoon into the pot, inhaling steam. "Thanks, but it should really be the band. It's our problem." But as I take my first hit of Broccoli Surprise, inwardly I'm shaking my head: *Kat, Kat, Kat. Don't ever offer to loan money to a musician. We never say no.*

That night at rehearsal I mention Kat's largesse to the band. That is, Will and Chas, since Boone's late as usual. Probably what his tombstone will say.

Will's immediately psyched. "I'll call Wayne tomorrow, tell him it's a go."

"Not so fast," I say. "We haven't even voted yet."

"All in favor," Will says, raising his hand. "Chas?"

Chas is resting his chin on a drumstick, *Spin Magazine* open across his snare. "If it gets us an agent, so we start getting fucking paid, I'd do ten videos."

"Motion carries," says Will. "You were saying?"

"Boone hasn't –"

"Boone abstains."

"Will –"

"Mark, you know what he's going to say. We talked about this a month ago. You're just being a prude, when deep down you know we need to do it. Deep down you even *want* to do it. You want to be a rock star worse that *I* do."

"*I* just want to get our songs heard."

"*This* is how you get heard. Play your gui-tar on the M-7-7."

"That's how you get *seen*."

"Same dif."

"To you."

"To everybody. But you."

"So what song?" Chas interrupts, chin still balanced on his drumstick.

"Is that even a *question*?" Will asks incredulously. "ROB is playing 'Car Keys.' *That's* the video. End of story." He thunks the neck of his Rickenbacker against his mic stand to drive home the point.

I don't even bother to ask what *version* of "Car Keys." "Don't you think people are getting sick of it? It's not even our best song." I hit my vibrato pedal, play a G chord that wobbles like a drunk crossing a barroom at closing time. "What about 'Same Heart Twice'?"

"You *can't* be serious." "Same Heart" is the slow blues

ballad Will wanted off the record. Even Chas wrinkles his nose and says nah.

I start to make a case for *not* giving the world another mindless uptempo party clip when we hear the upstairs door slam. "Maybe Boone should come in halfway through."

"Sorry," says Boone, putting down his six-pack. "Halfway through what?"

"Our video," Will says smugly.

"We're doing one?"

"Not necessarily," I say. "You get a vote." I tell him about Kat's offer as he takes his Jaguar out of its case.

He pulls the scalloped body on over his head, ducking so he doesn't ram it against the low basement ceiling. "Hmm. Is the loan specifically for a video?"

I don't get what he means. "Well, she'd front the money, then we'd–"

He shakes his head. "No, I mean, does Kat care? What we spend it on?"

"Hookers and cocaine," Will says. "Plus a box of Tastycakes for Mark."

"Deedee would love that," Chas says. If she ever actually caught him *in flagrante delicto*, we'd have our boy soprano.

"What, Deedee likes Tastycakes?" Will deadpans.

Boone plays the J.J. Cale "Cocaine" riff. "Well think about it. Instead of a video, it could be a pretty decent tour bus, or a month's worth of motel rooms."

I get it. "We could be our own tour support. Take the 10,000 B.C. deal, do the tour, pay Kat back out of the royalties. No muss, no fuss."

"So where's the video?" Will asks.

My turn to look smug. "*What* video?"

"No fair!" Will whines, sounding about ten years old.

I shrug my shoulders.

"Wait a second," Will says, recovering. "We haven't *voted* yet. Chas?"

"I gotta talk to Deedee. And Daniel, about taking time off. When would we leave?"

"Day after the Beanpot," I say.

Boone says he has to talk to his boss too.

154

"I can't just pick up and go," Will says. "We're talking about six weeks at least. I have to ask Jack at Pegasus. You too," he says, flicking his chin at me.

"I'll quit," I say. "We all knew this day was coming."

Will slides his finger up a bass string. "We *still* haven't voted. I bet Wayne would vote for the video."

"Wayne's not in the band," I say. "Three to one."

"*If* the creek don't rise, and there ain't no meltdown," Boone says. "There's a lot of shit to work out."

"So let's work it out," I say, plugging in the Green Monster. Fuckin' A. Shadowland on tour.

## 34. *REWIND:* Allston, September 1982

Alexis from the band Red October is sitting on the beat-up couch in the Batcave, our new basement rehearsal space off Brighton Ave., which we've inherited from Rock Paper Scissors along with Boone. She's jotting notes as she listens to "Take a Ride" a second time, not smiling but nodding along with the beat. At the band's insistence I'm singing "funked up," which feels silly but Alexis isn't reacting adversely. Then again she never heard the real lyric.

Red October's a techno act we'd met back at the symposium, where Alexis had been the only woman on the producers' panel. Their records are very cool, icy almost, but with dramatic Bowie-esque vocals, and Will thinks that might be the right tone for "Take a Ride." I'd still rather have Ric Ocasek producing us, but when I'd worked up my nerve to drop off a cassette at the Cars' studio, the anorexically gorgeous receptionist said they'd be on tour for months, making it too late for the compilation LP. I'd left the tape just in case, and she dropped it in a mail crate that was already half full of band demos.

"Good, I like it a little slower," Alexis nods. She's wearing two-tone brow-line eyeglasses and a black turtleneck, so with her close-cropped hair she looks like an androgynous East German film star. "Hey bass man."

"Will." He's dropped "B. Fabulous," at least for now. We'll see when we get the satin tour jackets and monogrammed director's chairs.

"Right. That harmony sounds pretty good. Wanna try singing lead this time through?"

"Uh, sure."

"Um," I say. Will had done okay on "Just Like Where River Meets the Sea," but that was a demo tape. This is for a *record*. I also half wonder if Will put her up to it since he's the one who called her. I start to protest again when Alexis raises a palm, cutting me off.

"Just let him try it. If it doesn't work, we'll know."

I bite my lip and think about it. Ben Orr sings half of Ocasek's songs, and Roger Daltrey sings almost all of Townsend's. Maybe I should get over myself and let him try it, especially if it's gonna help get us signed. But with Boone playing lead, what does that leave me? I'll be Brian Wilson, digging in the sandbox while the rest of the Beach Boys go out on tour.

We play it again, and Will's smoother tone does seem to fit the feel. If only he wasn't so damn robotic. He fucks, er, funks up the bass line and apologizes. "Sorry, can't do both at the same time yet."

"Won't have to," Alexis says. "That's the magic of overdubbing." She says she'll program the drum sounds, and just have Chas play his cymbals live. Chas looks skeptical but Will nods, and I wonder what he's us getting into. We're usually the ones making fun of drum machines. She makes us promise to change strings before the session and tells Chas to polish his cymbals. When she's gone he bitches about the homework assignment.

"Polish my cymbals? What the fuck for?"

"Do not *question* your *orders*!" Will says in a B-movie German accent.

I say you want a little Nazi in a producer. At least maybe we'll stay on budget.

"What was the studio called again?" asks Boone. "The Vinyl Solution?"

The next night we're at Bunratty's in Allston, opening for Talon. Boone is excited; Rock Paper Scissors had been huge Talon fans. I'm excited too: it's our first show in town with Boone, and last year another opening act, World on Fire, had gotten signed by an A&R guy – who'd come to see Talon. Talon didn't get signed, which sucks for them, but all's fair in love and rock 'n' roll. And it would be cosmically right if we got our break tonight, since it's my birthday.

It's a Friday, so there's a good crowd in the medium-sized club, and most of our Massachusetts friends have made it out to wish me well. Daria, Maggie's organizer friend who saw us at the Rat, has brought her brother, who plays in the Corvettes. Jay and Stevo from RPS are here, and I wonder if it feels weird seeing Boone in a new band. When we soundcheck, Boone sets up on Chas's left, with me on the right and Will still smack in the middle. Not that I notice. I'm wearing my customary black and white ensemble, with brand new birthday Chuck Taylors. I also have a new, shorter haircut – the combination of stringy locks and wire rims was starting to make me look like young Ben Franklin. Chas has also trimmed his Frampton-esque curls into something more Flock of Seagulls-y. Will, who's recently discovered mousse, has a spiky Thomas Dolby-mad scientist look going. Boone, the veteran Boston rocker, is in a denim jacket and shades.

The soundman brings the house lights down as we plug in. Chas counts off "Next Big Thing" and Boone, Will and I hit the opening riff as the stage lights go nova. As I sing the first verse Boone plays the chords so I don't have to, then he takes Chas's harmony part, blending with Will on the *ooh, next big thing* for a stronger, hookier chorus. We divide up the guitar solo, then Chas pounds low toms while I get a little more pointed: *You've got the knack to act sincere, while making ads for your favorite beer....* We end with a mock symphonic "DUM dum DUM dum DUM" like *2001* and get our biggest ovation in Boston so far. Between the cheering crowd and our beefier stage sound, it feels like we're finally on our way. And only a year behind schedule.

Will starts the bass riff to "Visibly Shook." As I sing, I try to keep it eerie, describing the details – the black and white patrol cars parked outside the dorm, the twin stretchers, the ambulance pulling out slow. Boone makes feedback squeals in time to the beat, creating a dissonant, Velvet Underground edge. Then Will steps forward for "Take a Ride" as Chas taps sixteenth notes on his newly polished cymbals, which really do sound brighter. Next

Boone sings one he'd done with RPS. We really feel like a quartet now, even though I still write and sing most of the songs.

People have been listening more than dancing, but when we start "Clarksville" Jackie and her *Shape It!* gang take the floor like the Solid Gold Dancers and pretty soon the whole place is cutting loose. Leave it to the Pre-fab Four. Chas keeps the beat going, and I sing a verse of "Summertime Blues," then Will sings a bit of "I Saw Her Standing There," then Boone takes a free form solo that eventually segues back into "Clarksville." I'm waving goodnight to the crowd as Will shouts, on mic, four fateful words: "Party at Mark's place!"

Happy birthday, sucker.

## 35. *FAST FORWARD:* Newton, June 1986

Kat's invited Will and me to come play a few songs for her class. It's a pretty obvious ploy to try to get us talking again. We're actually talking, of course. Just not to each other.

What happened was this: our producer Wayne invited us to a cookout in his backyard. No big deal, some of the other bands he produced were coming, maybe some of his fellow ex-Triggers, we might jam but it was mostly just for fun, stuff our faces and watch his twin toddlers chase their cat across the lawn. All well and good. The weather was even nice.

Then Will started asking Wayne about touring. He got Wayne talking about the stint the Triggers had done opening for the Kinks, forty dates across the US and Canada. *Before* Ray Davies had gone on the wagon and cleaned up his act. Wayne, after some leading questions from Will, had given us the play-by-play of a particularly raunchy after-gig party at the Phoenix Hyatt, an all-night coke-and-Southern Comfort orgy featuring drunken nubile groupies and the Kinks' lingerie-wearing harmony singers all doing stripteases on tabletops before being led back to various bedrooms for unspeakable acts. And Ray himself drinking more than anyone and acting as ringmaster, directing who should do what to whom.

Wayne was clearly enjoying the attention, all his young

band charges hanging on every word. Only trouble was, Will made sure Deedee, Kat, and Jackie were hanging on every word, too, but with exactly the opposite reaction. So much for our tour. Deedee had promptly forbidden Chas to leave town, at least until she could come along and chaperone, and he and Will had officially declined to sign the 10,000 B.C. contract once and for all.

Then, as an encore, Will had Wayne hardsell Kat on a video – how the right three minute clip could make us stars, and nobody would come home with the clap. A bargain, relatively speaking.

I could have – should have – told Will to go fuck himself, but then where would we be? Deep down, I knew he was right – without a tour, a video is our best shot to make it, Beanpot or not.

Now Kat introduces us to her class. She's played them our record and passed around the album cover, so as far as the kids know we're as famous as Michael Jackson. Even so, only a couple of them applaud while the rest stare off into space.

Still not talking to each other, we do acoustic versions of a few of our songs plus a couple Beatle tunes. The kids seem to enjoy us, though most of them are too shy to look at us directly, with only the same two or three clapping after each song. Just like a club gig. A couple of the kids sing along, or at least make low-pitched humming sounds, and a few more rock back and forth in their chairs as we play. One boy in a plaid short-sleeve shirt waves his arms like he's conducting us. Of course others have their hands pressed over their ears, just like Will's mom used to do when coming down the basement stairs to make us turn down.

After the last song Kat asks if there are any questions. A hand goes up.

"What time do you go to bed?" It's Nathan, the chair straightener, one of the few who can stand eye contact for more than a second.

"Um, it depends." Kat had warned us the questions might not be what *Rolling Stone* would ask.

"On the day of the week? What about Monday? What about Tuesday? What about–"

Kat could tell him exactly when I go to bed, but instead she gently suggests the class ask questions about our music. I'm tempted to ask if they've ever seen the girl down the hall who takes off her clothes, but I don't think Kat would appreciate it.

"Do you play any songs by John Philip Sousa?" It's the plaid shirt boy, the one who'd conducted us.

"Nnno," Will answers tentatively. He glances over at me; even in our cover band days we hadn't fielded many Sousa requests. Too bad Chas isn't here in his marching band uniform.

"John Phillip Sousa wrote 'The Stars and Stripes Forever.'"

"Yyyes," Will agrees.

"And 'The Washington Post.' And 'The Minnesota March.' He was born in 1854 and died in 1932 and he wrote one hundred and thirty six marches!" The kid says all of this in one excited rush, without stopping to take a breath. He's also shaking his hands, and looking around the room quicker than Morocco Mole. Kat reminds him to slow down, stretching her arms out like she's pulling salt water taffy.

"You should learn some marches for next time," he concludes. I wonder what he'd think of Jimi's version of "The Star Spangled Banner."

"Thank you, Robbie," Kat says. "Anybody else?'

Another boy in the back has his hand up about an inch. Kat calls on him. He whispers something but I can't understand him.

"Can you ask louder?" Kat prompts sweetly.

This time he doesn't say anything, but points at my guitar, then turns his face away, embarrassed. Kat had mentioned some of the kids at school play instruments. She asks if I mind if Mitch tries my guitar. "It's up to you," she says.

I've brought my Ovation acoustic, the rounded back of which is made out of some kind of hardened fiberglass, like a hi-tech salad bowl, so he probably couldn't hurt it if he tried. I walk back to his chair and gently put it in his lap. I figure I can finger chords if he wants to strum.

He sits up straight and puts his left foot on the rung of the chair in front of him, shifting the guitar into perfect classical position. He closes his eyes and begins an etude by Villa-Lobos.

His technique is better than mine. Will's jaw is open, and Kat's smiling like a proud mom – *told you so*. The other kids, though, don't seem particularly impressed, and keep rocking in place or staring out the window. Maybe if he'd played a march. He finishes and Kat, Will and I applaud.

"That was wonderful, Mitch. How long have you been playing?"

Mitch mumbles something that sounds like "five," which could mean "five years" or "since I was five," or, just as likely, "five minutes" since that's how long the piece took.

"Well thank you for playing for us. Can you give Mark his guitar back now?"

Giving my guitar back isn't his first choice, but he eventually lets it go. We say goodbye as Kat lines up the kids and walks them down to their buses. Will and I are still sitting there, but Nathan straightens the chairs and turns out the lights just the same.

We sit there in the dark, listening to the wall clock tick. A full minute goes by.

"I think this was our best audience," Will finally says.

"Asshole."

When we drop him off Will tells Kat how amazingly patient she is with her class. "Must come in handy for living with Mark."

"Hey Kat," I say. "Think that Mitch kid can play bass?"

"You two sound like my brothers," Kat says. "Do you always have to insult each other?"

"Absolutely," Will answers. "It's the one thing we can agree on."

"That's where you're wrong," I say.

Back on Comm. Ave. Kat asks how old Will was.

"When we met? Um, fifteen I guess. Tenth grade."

"No. When his dad got sick and everything got...all complicated. Jackie was telling me about it."

I think I get where she's going. "You think Will's stuck then, emotionally ?" Makes sense. "He was, what, ten or eleven. Before my time."

"No, Mark, I'm just trying to understand him, that's all." She U-turns around a stuck Green Line train, then pulls into a quasi-legal spot next to a hydrant. "Must have been awful."

"Yeah, Will Sr. got pretty out-there." When I'd stay for dinner after an afternoon rehearsal, Will, his mom and I would huddle at the kitchen table while his dad blasted the news or *Sixty*

*Minutes* in the living room, yelling his latest conspiracy theory back at the set about how the Rockefellers had poisoned the water and cost him his bank job. Whereas over at my house things were so quiet you'd think we were the ones who had gone deaf. I'd always bring a book or a lyric sheet to the table for company.

"Poor Will," Kat sighs, shaking her head over the steering wheel. "His older siblings move out, and just when he finally gets his dad's attention…." She looks over at me. "Maybe you should be a little nicer to him."

Maybe I should be nicer to *Will*? "Kat, in case you didn't notice, he's the one who just fucked our tour. *And* our record deal. *And* stole our single." I climb out, grab my guitar. You'd think my own fucking girlfriend would take my side. "And *he's* been ripping into my songs since tenth grade." I start stalking towards the house, deliberately not waiting for her.

"And you make fun of his singing. And his acting. And his hair," Kat says, rushing to catch up. "Maybe you're both a little jealous."

I stop short on the porch stairs, almost knocking her over with my guitar case as I swivel to face her. "I'm jealous of *Will*? He's like…like…everything I hate in one portly package." I turn away and resume climbing.

"So why be in a band with him?"

I stop again, my hand on the doorknob. Why? Good question. Because. "Because we are," I shrug.

"Because you are."

"Right. It's like family, or fate." I picture it as I try to explain. "Because when I walked by the choir room that day at Harding High, it was Will I heard working on his Bowie imitation. Not Joe Blow, doing Lynyrd Skynyrd. Will, doing Bowie. And he was good. I knew the chords and started playing along. Everything else just kind of followed from that." I look back at Kat, interrupting the memory. "And I bet Will would say exactly the same thing."

"That's my point, Mark," she says gently. "You two have more in common than you think."

*Fuck no*, I think, twisting the doorknob. But as the heavy oak door swings open I know she's right, at least partially. With our decade-plus of shared history, Will and I may as well be fucking Siamese twins. Wonder how many Siamese twins end up murdering one another. I bet a lot. Cain and Abel, meet Mark and Will.

I set my guitar down in the empty walk-through. We don't have a show tonight, but we have an early call tomorrow. Here's hoping video *does* kill the radio star.


## 36. *REWIND:* **Brighton, September 198*2***

Day after my birthday I get a phone call.

"Hey." Nobody says "hey" long distance like Maggie: low and throaty, like Dusty Springfield getting up in the morning. "Happy belated. I tried yesterday but you weren't home."

"We had a show."

"How was it?"

"Long." It feels like early morning but it's probably late afternoon. I lie back down on my mattress and tell her about the party: after the gig, friends and strangers alike had followed us back from Bunratty's to Chas's and my apartment and basically made themselves at home. People were smoking, drinking, eating our food, talking, flirting, playing records, making out on the balcony, smoking pot in Chas's bedroom. I felt like I was back on safety patrol, quieting the crowd, gathering empties and providing ashtrays at the last possible second. It was dawn before they left, and I feel asleep, alone, still in my gig clothes.

"Sorry I missed it," Maggie says.

"Don't be." At one point somebody produced a Sucrets tin full of white crystalline powder and was laying out lines on our hallway table. I left and sat out on the front stoop and played guitar a while, one eye open for cops, but I wonder what Maggie would have done.

"Any good loot?" she asks.

"And you call yourself a socialist." It's a warm afternoon and I'm thirsty, so as we chat I get up and wander to the kitchen for some orange juice. Nada.

"Hey, until us workers control the means of production, Marx says grab all the shit you can."

There's a soggy half bagel floating in the backed-up sink, along with some lipsticked cigarette butts and a couple bobbing brown beer bottles. I think about rhyming "Marx and Hegel" with "lox and bagel" in a song but can't make it work. "Well, Boone got me the new Tom Verlaine."

"Cool." *Marquee Moon*, by Tom's old band Television, was our second favorite album at Antioch, right behind the Polar Bears' *Got No Breeding*. Both are kind of jittery, probably why Maggie likes them. "That it?"

I'm still parched so I stretch the phone cord towards the bathroom. "Well, Chas gave me a Shadowland baseball jersey he made back in his shirt factory days. And don't be surprised if you get a beret for Christmas."

"Will and Jackie?"

"Yup. They think I should wear it onstage to cover my bald spot." I glance in the mirror, arranging my hair with my free hand. From the front not too bad. Yet. "I tried it on but I felt like Camus the Killer Existentialist." I lean down, get a drink from the sink, then while I'm at it stick my head under the faucet.

"That's it? Nothing from Californ–"

"Relax, Maggie. I got it. Thanks." She'd sent me an LP by Stiv Bators' new band, with a cover of the Grass Roots' "Let's Live for Today," one of both of our first favorite records: *One two three-ee four-our!*

"Did you play it?"

"Um, not yet. Like I said, we had a show –"

"Play it."

"Now?"

"Why not? I'll wait."

"Um, okay." I put the phone down. I grab the album cover, hold it up slit side down to dump out the record. Along with the LP, out slides a – what?

"How cool, Maggie. Thanks."

"Welcome. It occurred to me I never exactly thanked you. For coming home when you did."

It's a home-made jigsaw puzzle, with a hand-drawn sketch of me and Maggie on it, posed like John and Yoko on the *Two Virgins* cover, and lines of song lyrics at various angles, quotes from my songs interwoven with Jules' and Lennon's. *Imagine there's no heaven. Reality's a shadow. Somewhere out there must be home.* Too cool. "It's really nice, Mags. It must have you taken forever."

"Time's not a problem. The funding for my position ran out."

"That sucks."

"Sucks worse for my clients."

"That's trickle-down for you." There are articles every day about somebody – veterans, mental patients, welfare mothers – being turned out on the street. "Maybe you should move to Boston."

"Thinking about it. Hate to leave my seniors, though."

"You just said there's no job."

"I know. But I feel like if I cared I would show up anyway. I mean, I can just pack up and drive away and they'll still be stuck here trying to figure out their Medicare forms."

"Maggie, you're an *artist*," I say, taking myself out to the balcony to air out. "It's not your responsibility to save everybody." We'd had this talk repeatedly at Antioch, where she'd gotten roped into serving on, and eventually running, student coalitions against apartheid, world hunger, CIA Recruitment, and M.A.D. – mutually assured destruction, *i.e.* thermonuclear war. The girl who couldn't say no. Luckily they all had the same office, and we'd done it on the couch more than once between meetings.

"I'm just saying it feels like a cop-out to leave."

"More time to paint. More distance from your mom. Art school if you want it. A free beret."

"There's that. If I come I wanna stop in New Mexico."

"Visit your *real* mom?" Maggie's adopted, and her paintings are heavily influenced by Georgia O'Keeffe.

"At least see where she painted." I could sing *hello cow skull in the sand* but I let it go. "If I like it there maybe I'll stay."

"Huuhh-uh," I whine, like a four-year-old having his favorite Tonka toy taken away. "I seem to recall you had a good time here last spring." A bulge develops along the zipper of my cargo pants as I recall the details.

"Yeah, but we never really talked," Maggie sighs.

"We were too busy f–, uh, making love."

"No, you were right the first time," she says. "Too busy

fucking. I enjoyed it, I admit it. But there's a difference."

"Maggie, I love you, you know that."

"Maybe you do, Mark, in your way. But I don't know that I know what that means."

Conversations like this make my head hurt. "You're still pissed about...."

"That's part of it."

"Just part?"

Maggie's quiet, a dangerous sign. When she's feeling strong, she's a fighter, apt to shout, scratch, throw things. Then she'll realize how ridiculous she's being, and start laughing and then crying right in the middle of the fight. Then we'll kiss, grope, fuck and she'll come intensely while she's still laughing and crying, and it's all incredible. Silence, on the other hand, means all those forces are turned inward. The anger's there, but it's buried, so there's no release, for either of us. And, worst case scenario, she might hurt herself again.

"Maggie, I said I was sorry. Repeatedly."

"You don't even know *why*..." she starts, then trails off again.

I have a pretty good idea. Back at Antioch there had been an English exchange student who looked and talked just like Malcolm McDowell in *If*, and worse, played piano and sang clever, sardonic songs, like a British Randy Newman. Maggie had developed a crush on him, like about half the girls on campus. She'd invited him to sing at an Oxfam fundraiser, then had come home late after (supposedly) getting a private concert in one of the school's practice rooms. I'd been jealous and suspicious, and in revenge I'd seduced the cute sophomore jazz singer I'd been playing campus coffeehouses with. Only problem was, Maggie hadn't actually had sex with Malcolm. No one had, since it turned out he was gay, which he didn't admit to 'til he was safely back in England. Even so, she'd given him her *attention*. Which was worse, especially since he reminded me of Will doing his fake English accent.

Maggie's still silent. I know from experience her pauses can last a minute or an hour, and then when she does start talking it can be hours until she's through.

"Can't we talk about this when you get here?" I ask.

She exhales audibly. "Sure, Mark, we can talk about whether or not I should move to Boston and what it means *after* I've already done it."

"Good."

"I was being *sarcastic*."

"I *know*. So was I. Just come, we'll work it out."

"I'll think about it."

"You can stay over at my parents'. See my sister's trophies again." When I'd taken Maggie home to Harding for school vacations, my mom had latched on like Velcro, clutching Maggie's arm, supposedly telling her stories about me but always ending up talking about my sister non-stop until Maggie had to gently detach herself.

Maggie doesn't say anything.

"Hey Mags," I say, changing tack. "The puzzle's really nice. I'm glad I came home when I did too."

"I said I'll think about it."

I glance down at my tumescence. *Patience, grasshopper.*

That night we're at Parallax for our session with Alexis from Red October. She and my bandmates are up in the glass-enclosed booth, staring down at me as I play. She's tracking us one at a time instead of as a unit, and it's my turn under the microscope.

"Again," she says sharply, and I hear the tape rewinding.

"Damn rhythm track keeps slowing down," I mutter, wiping sweat.

"Yeah, Z-man, that must be it," Will says into my headphones.

I hear the count-off, take a breath. I've been speeding up on the choruses, which is a perfectly human thing to do, except I'm not playing with Chas, but with a Linn drum machine that can't react to my cues. This time I pretend I'm Mr. Spock, all precision, no emotion. I must have done okay because she tells Boone to get ready for his solo. He nails his part on the first take, but Alexis thinks he can do better. After a couple more tries we wish he'd kept the first one, but eventually Alexis is satisfied.

"Hey bass man, you ready to sing?" She puts Will's mic in the middle of the big concrete room, no baffles, so there's some natural reverb in the sound. As if *Will* needs to sound more dramatic. I'm still pissed he's doing the vocal, but I stand in the booth with Alexis and we talk him through the lyrics, Alexis' bedside manner less frosty now that she's done dissecting guitarists. Maybe Will's paying her under the table, because she spends twice as much time on his vocal as on any of the other tracks, painstakingly piecing it together line by line from different takes. I still don't love his interp, which seems more Bryan Ferry cool than anything believable, but I have to admit he can hold the notes on the chorus longer than I could have.

Alexis nixes the repeating echo we'd used – my favorite part of the song – and instead adds some "ahs" to fill the space. Not to feel insecure, but instead of asking me and Boone and Chas to sing, she has Will overdub *all* the parts. Good thing I could play my guitar part in time.

With Will's tracks recorded I think we're done, but Alexis is just getting started. We call out for subs and eat in the booth as she adds and subtracts instruments from the mix, shaking her head no, then grinning fiendishly when she gets something she likes. A few hours of experimenting later, the song now starts with a backwards cymbal that sounds like the inhaling of a breath, and after the last verse everything cuts out except a lone guitar, joined by Will singing the hook from deep in a cave, then bam, the whole band's back in, with an extra blast of syn drums for a Phil Collins-meets-Phil Spector Wall of Sound effect. It's not exactly sterile anymore, just different, more mechanized, like a Berlin disco instead of an Allston basement. It's a brave new Shadowland, completely unrecognizable as us except for Will's voice. I wonder what the teased-hair rock 'n' rollers at Jumbo's will think.

Will and I drop a copy of the tape off at the local record company that's doing the new band sampler, and they say they'll get back to us. The office is beyond casual and reeks of cannabis, which doesn't exactly inspire confidence. If "Take a Ride" doesn't make the compilation, maybe we'll press it ourselves. We can make the B side the "fuck" version and get asked on tour by Prince.

## 37. *FAST FORWARD:* Chelsea, Mass., June 1986

"Action!"

We're set up, instruments and all, on the floor of an actual garage. There's a pile of tires behind Boone, a hydraulic lift behind me and Will, and a vintage Vargas pinup calendar on the wall next to Chas. We're dressed somewhere between Devo and the Bowery Boys, playing '50s auto mechanics complete with slicked back hair, blue Dickies work shirts, and high top Doc Martens. Wayne's TV director friend Dimitri lowers his finger and "Car Keys" comes blaring over the monitor system. We do our best to mime along with our parts, mouthing the lyrics as they rush by, feeling like the Monkees must have. Chas is really hitting his drums, though, and we can't hear the monitor and get out of sync.

"Cut!" yells Dimitri. Somebody tapes paper towels over Chas's drum heads and we try again. As we fake-play, a large mounted camera moves along a track in front of the band. We make it through the song, and a girl with a powder puff runs out to dust all our foreheads. Then we do it again. And again.

Dimitri, who has a thick black beard and is built like a Volga boatman, continually sucks iced coffee when he's not barking orders to his crew. He seems like he knows what he's doing, but I still wish it were Liz Polar Bear filming "Same Heart Twice" in the privacy of the Batcave. This feels like a full-scale movie shoot, with giant klieg lights and an army of tech people milling around off camera – lighting techs, hair and costume people, camera crew, even a guy who snaps a wooden clapboard at the beginning of each take. We've just started and it already feels out of control and *way* too slick. The techs all call us "the talent" and talk about us like we're not there. At least in the recording studio what we do matters; now we're not even making sound, just pretending. But if we're sinking Kat's life savings into a video, we may as fucking well make a good one. When Dimiti yells "Action!" again I pound the chords out on the Green Monster and try my best to look like I'm singing for every pent-up teen who's dyin' to find a party, dyin' to find a girl, dyin' to find some reason to *live*.

Of course *I'm* only singing the second verse. Typical Shadowland: we'd deadlocked on picking the song so Will had called in Wayne, who basically said we were idiots if we didn't do "Car Keys." Fuck integrity, *nothing* beats a hit. And Wayne should know – I'd heard through the grapevine that it was *his* band that had turned down "Pop Muzik." To mollify me (and by extension, Kat's bankroll), Wayne did a remix that's Will singing the first verse, me the second, both of us the third, though the current plan is for all four of us to each lip synch a line. Why not? The laws of logic do not apply in Videoland.

We finish another take, and someone comes around and gives us cups of water. I'm tempted to dump mine over my head, but all my layers of powder and hair gel would wash off. Dimitri wants a different angle, so they reposition the camera track, and we do a few more takes. I'm already exhausted, but Will is loving the camera, loving the attention, the hair and makeup girls fluttering over him just like in *Brigadoon* back in high school. One of Daniel's bakeries gave us bagels and cream cheese for the shoot, and Kat, Jackie and Deedee are making sandwiches for lunch so at least we're not starving.

Time for close-ups. Dimitri has me sing my verse a half dozen times, zooming in on my lime-green Gretsch as I strum, deftly avoiding my thinning hairline. At least my guitar will be famous. He gets shots of Boone soloing and Chas pounding his skins, but spends the most time on Will – Will singing, Will flirting with the camera, Will stripping naked and diving headfirst into a vat of potato salad. At one point Will flips his bass over and plays the backside, where there aren't even strings; so much for even the *illusion* of reality. Then a final shot of Chas hitting his snare drum, which Dimitri's poured glitter on, so on contact there's a small sparkling explosion of silver and gold. The crew's been here even longer than we have, and by now everybody, even Will, hates "Car Keys." Finally Dimitri says that's a wrap and we thank everybody and load out. When I get home I lie face down on Kat's bed and fall asleep before I even get my shoes off.

Maybe because I'm so tired and wound up my dream is especially vivid: I'm walking on clouds, kind of bouncing along an endless field of weightless white cotton balls. Ahead of me I see a figure sitting cross-legged on a mound of mist, quietly picking an acoustic guitar. It's John Lennon, playing "Julia," the first song he ever wrote for his dead mother. I walk closer, and I can hear him softly singing along with himself. I want to say hi, but I don't want to interrupt him, and I'm scared that if I do he'll give me hell for selling out and filming "Car Keys," like he'd cut into Paul for writing "Silly Love Songs." Lennon looks up and without stopping his fingers says, "It's all right, Mark. It's only me." I'm about to answer when I feel a presence at my shoulder. It's my sister, looking like she did before she got so skinny, no dialysis shunt, no thick cataract lenses. "John!" she shouts, in the same tone she and her girlfriends used to yell at the screen when the Beatles were bowing from the waist in unison on TV. She starts talking at Lennon a mile a minute and he stops playing, packs up his guitar, then retreats into the clouds. She's still talking at him when Kat's alarm goes off.

The next day's shoot is easier, with just a small crew and no special lighting. I'm still in my mechanic's outfit; the plot, not exactly *War and Peace*, has evolved so that a model/actress playing a garage customer drops off her sports car. We see her keys on the counter and can't resist a joy ride. As we're cruising around town we happen to pass a (mini-skirted, spike-heeled, long-legged) woman on the street and slow down to check her out, with Boone giving her the classic peek-over-the-mirror sunglasses appraisal. Surprise – it's her, the car's owner – so we're busted. But somehow she must forgive us, because the last shot is of her and Will riding off together in the vintage baby blue Mustang. Hey, it could happen.

Dimitri's normal gig is producing TV commercials, so I'm worried our clip is going to look like a J.C. Penney spot, or worse, like an ad for Will's new line of hair care products. The main thing is to get it edited so we can get on M77, sign with Double Eagle Talent, and pay Kat back before her tuition's due. Dimitri's working on "Car Keys" between his other jobs – and Will is helping him edit – so no sense holding our breath. But fuck the video – time to get ready for the Beanpot.

## 38. *REWIND:* Jamaica Plain, September 1982

"Don't look now," Boone says, "but guess who the waiter behind us is."

"Zeigleveit B. Schtoonk?" says Will.

"It's Roger."

"Roger who?" asks Boone's date, an efficient-looking girl named Carol.

I glance and see it's Roger Talon, the leader of the band we'd opened for at Bunratty's. "He's a waiter?"

"He's like a rock star," Chas says.

"He's a waiter *and* a rock star," says Will.

We're sitting in a bare-bones brick and beam restaurant on Green Street, in the run-down, south part of town where lots of creative types who can't afford the rent in Back Bay or Harvard Square are moving. We're celebrating our one year anniversary of relocating to Massachusetts, and "Take a Ride" making the *Dirty Water* compilation album. Not to mention Maggie's moving to Boston.

She'd done it with mixed feelings, but she'd done it: packed up the mini pick-up she'd bought with her counseling money and headed first to New Mexico, where she'd actually found Georgia O'Keeffe's cabin in Abiquiú but was too shy to knock on the door, then to Ohio, where she'd spent a night at my parents', then on to Boston. She insists she's not here because of me, but at least she's not *not* here because of me.

Right now Maggie's wedged in on the bench next to me, our thighs touching, and as we half-listen to the table conversation my right hand is between her legs, probing the denim crease for the soft spot. Carol, who works at Boone's office, is saying what a genius he is at programming. When he's there. Carol's pretty enough in a corporate kind of way, with short brown hair and a strand of small translucent pearls at her throat, but it's hard to imagine her having under-the-table sex at board meetings. Still, it's Boone's first post-Annie date, so Maggie and I nod politely at Carol as I apply more pressure through the denim.

Just as I'm about to undo the top button on Maggie's jeans, there's a high-pitched pealing sound from across the table. Will, tapping his spoon on his water glass. Good timing, doughboy.

When we're quiet he leans forward, like he's passing a stock tip in an E.F. Hutton commercial.

"From now on I'd like to be known as Loretta." This is Eric Idle from *Life of Brian*. Jackie elbows him. "Actually, we're engaged."

There's a moment of not-so-stunned silence before everybody says congratulations. I look over at Jackie, who's beaming and, sure enough, holding up a new ring on her finger, complete with small stone. And *I* thought we're supposed to be saving money for more recording. I glance back at Will, who's still looking extremely pleased with himself. Better him than me, despite Jackie's Garden of Earthly Delights. Maggie bites my ear, then puts her chin on my shoulder.

"Think Jackie's pregnant?" she whispers.

Fuck. If *that's* true, that changes everything. "Take a Ride" better catch on quick.

Will says the ceremony will be in Ohio over Christmas, and we're all invited. Chas says they should hire his dad's wedding-and-bar mitzvah band for the reception, which leads us to wonder if we should borrow Daniel's bread truck and bring our equipment.

"We could make it a tour," I say. "Play the Agora in Cleveland. The Alrosa in Columbus. Maybe Chicago, Detroit."

"I think Jackie was planning on a honeymoon," Will says skeptically.

"Jackie, you wouldn't mind, would you? Just a few quick gigs?"

She says something under her breath to Will and he cringes reflexively.

"Two words," he says through his grimace. "Testicle soup."

Boone immediately leans forward, extending his long neck over the table like a grazing giraffe. "Whatever you do, don't ask for a straw." Now it's Carol's turn to look disgusted.

Roger the rock star waiter notices us, puts down his tray and comes over. "Where do I know you from?"

"Shadowland. From Bunratty's." The night Will invited two hundred inebriated fans over for ice cream and cake.

"Shadowland, right," he nods. "I liked your stuff."

We say we liked Talon too, and I wonder if he feels

awkward, being outed as a waiter. After Will's dad had lost his hearing and gotten fired from his bank job, the only gig he could get was sweeping the halls at our high school, and it was always a little uncomfortable going by him, deciding whether to say hi or not, even for Will. Especially for Will. Roger, however, seems fine with it.

Boone says how much Rock Paper Scissors was influenced by Talon. "The World on Fire thing must feel weird." WOF – the band that got discovered opening for Talon – just released their album, and WROB is really pushing the single.

Roger shrugs. "I'm happy for them. We'll get our chance. Just keep doin' it if it's what you love." He says "gotta go" and heads back to the kitchen.

"Wow." Boone says Talon's been gigging steadily for six years, and that Roger had been in other bands before then.

*Six years.* I figure we'll be on our fifth album in six years. Chas says he better not still be driving a fuckin' delivery truck. Will says he plans to be on his third marriage by then, and Jackie kicks him.


## 39. *FAST FORWARD:* Back Bay, July 1986

"Look straight ahead. Keep your eye open. Keep it open. Okay, add another drop of saline and try again."

We're one week away from the Beanpot, and on Will's insistence I'm trying to de-geekify my image. I'm sitting at a counter at Eye Q on Newbury Street, attempting to put a soft contact lens into my right eye without blinking, so it can adhere before my eyelid sweeps it aside like so much trash. I'm on attempt number four, and so far it's gotten folded over twice, and once rolled up like a translucent taco. Supposedly the great thing about soft lenses is that you can keep them in longer. Of course you have to *get* them in first.

The contacts are a compromise. At rehearsal when we talked about our look for the show, Will brought up my bald spot and suggested the beret again, but I'd said no way. Then Chas said how about a wig, and Will said don't laugh, you'd be surprised who wears one. (Yes, Boone added, Nancy Reagan is *completely* bald. Even down there.) Then we'd had a group *vote* on me shaving my head. Shadowland is *not* skinhead music, I'd argued, at least not in the white supremacist-burning crosses-shitkicking sense. Corny as it fucking sounds, I'd like to think our music is about love. Looking for it, being skeptical of it, missing it, maybe even finding it. Plus I've spent the past six months trying to convince Kat I'm *not* some rock star freak who will flush her down the toilet the moment we make it big, and I'm supposed to meet her (Catholic, Midwestern, military) parents at her brother's wedding the week after the Beanpot:

> *Kat* (in her best Sunday dress, pink ribbon in her shiny red hair): Mom and Dad, this is Mark, the boy I've been telling you about.
> *Mom*: So nice to finally meet you.
> *Me* (head shaved, in black leather and shades): Fuck you all, I'll be in the bar snorting lines of coke off the cocktail waitress's midriff.
> *Dad* (in full dress uniform): Me too!

I put another drop of saline in the tiny clear bowl on the tip of my finger. I will my eyelids apart, then, despite flashing on the *Outer Limits* episode with the spike-loaded binoculars, jab the lens forward. *Fuck.* People, Will included, do this every day? This time, though, the lens sticks and doesn't fold when I blink. When I close my other eye, my vision clears, just like I was wearing my wire rims. The left eye takes a few less tries, and I walk out of the store *sans* glasses.

We have the night off – Chas is meeting *his* girlfriend's parents for the first time – and Kat's out babysitting for one of the kids in her school. Jan's out too, at some save-every-species-but-ours meeting, so I have the place to myself.

I still have the lenses in, and every so often I walk over and look in the mirror. I don't know that I like it – without my glasses my face looks narrow and weasely, and I can still see the red rim marks around my nose. But it definitely *feels* different, kind of daring.

I pick up my guitar, start noodling as I think about other

dares I've taken: jumping off the high dive at summer camp, starting a conversation out of the blue with a cool-looking woman on the Green Line, wearing my Che Guevara T-shirt in line with all the John Birch farmers at Elmer's Pantry back in Harding. Our whole life the past five years has been a dare: picking up lock, stock and barrel (well, guitar, amp and trap case) and moving to Boston. What if we hadn't done it? Would Chas still be working in the Whirlpool factory, Will selling wall-to-wall to support his mortgage and 2.5 kids, me giving guitar lessons in a tiny room behind Maumee Music? Would we still be playing "China Grove" in the American Legion hall every fucking Friday night? Would I have slit my wrists by now?

But we *did* do it. I strum harder, searching for a groove that feels bold, unexpected. I fall into a two-chord pattern, seventh chords, slow but funky, a little dangerous. I keep it going, try out a verse:

*Take a journey far from home*
*Where no one knows you and go alone*
*Betcha never done it*
*Too unknown*

I add a bass pulse that reminds me of "Heard It Through the Grapevine," picture the Andantes, Motown's background singers, dipping their shoulders in time to the groove. I stretch out the hook, add some *yeah yeah yeahs* to keep it soulful:

*Don't close your eyes for three days straight*
*Just to see what your mind will take*
*Betcha never done it, betcha never done it, yeah yeah yeah*
*Scared you'll break*

I segue into a straight rock feel for the bridge, then try thinking of other situations to match the first two. This could be fun. And just in time for the Beanpot.

I'm standing at the bathroom mirror trying to get my fucking contacts *out* when Kat gets back. I keep the nails on my right hand long for fingerpicking, and when I try to grab the lenses I keep stabbing myself in the retina. I switch to my left hand and I'm able to get the left lens out, but I can't get the right lens with my left hand. Kat tries too, but my reflexes clamp my eye shut whenever she gets close. I finally give up and go to bed, silently cursing out Will as Kat mouths her evening prayers.

I try again in the morning. By now I look like Rat Fink from one of those sixties drag race posters, all oversize bloodshot corneas with huge veins bulging out of them. I almost have it, but the lens curls up again, this time jamming beneath my upper eyelid so it scrapes every time I blink. Shit. I give up and Kat drives me back to the optometrist, who yanks the contact out with tiny tweezers while forcibly pinning my eyelid back. I say "thanks anyway," then order a new pair of glasses with thick Buddy Holly frames. *I'm Mark Zodzniak and I'm a nerd.* And Will can suck eggs.


## 40. *REWIND:* Comm. Ave., Boston, November 1982

The marquee on the Paradise says "*Love That Dirty Water* Record Release Party." We're on last in the first set, just like "Take a Ride" is the last cut on side one. It's only one song, but I'm excited: it's us, on vinyl. Finally. And from listening as it's been playing at the club, I'd say "Take a Ride" is one of the standout tracks, maybe *the* standout track. Not that I'm biased.

Even though it's early there are plenty of people milling around, lots of zippered black leather and too-cool attitude on display. Chas fits right in, but as usual I feel more like Clark Kent than Keith Richards, invisible in my gray hooded Antioch cross country sweatshirt. I'd take it off, but the club is freezing. Maybe I should borrow Chas's lighter, grab some of the busted bar stools that are piled backstage, and start a bonfire in the alley. Sing Clash songs around the campfire while we bond over Jack Daniels and s'mores.

There are ten bands playing tonight, so we're sharing equipment to save breakdown time. Good thing Drive Train's not on the bill. One of the bands is the Corvettes, Daria's brother's band, so Maggie and Daria catch up on lefty gossip, just like at

Antioch: Daria's pissed the prez has ordered an embargo on Nicaragua, while Maggie's bullshit he didn't extend the ERA deadline. "Three more states," she mutters, vulva aflame. Maybe I should write a song called "Viva Ortega (but Phyllis Schlafly Must Die)." Maybe not. Maggie also tells Daria about her new day job, at a non-profit called Peace Brigades, which she took after letting her art school deadline slide again. I'm looking too, since I'm freezing my 'nads off making bike deliveries and it's not even winter yet.

At least it's warming up in *here*. By now there's a real crowd, with all the band members and record label guests. We invited Alexis but Red October's gigging in Manhattan. I'd thought about inviting Tina – *aka* Ms. Corkscrew, whom the song's written about – but decided it might be awkward. Imagine Roxanne at a Police concert: *So the whole world knows I'm a whore, huh? Thanks a lot, you ass-wipes.* Plus with Maggie in town I have less incentive for updates on Tina's celibacy campaign.

There's a VIP buffet the bands supposedly aren't invited to, but Will gets admitted as an In Your Face employee, then we all hop the red velvet rope when the bouncer's back is turned. As VIP spreads go it's not much, but we stuff our faces with Ritz crackers, salami slices, and orange and purple wine-and-cheese spread. Real VIPs have gotten drink tickets, so there's no open bar, and I have to spring for my ginger ale. Maybe it's for the best, though, since it means Chas will be relatively sober during our set. And the last time Boone was here was the Rock Paper Scissors gig where he drowned out Annie, so I don't want him getting any flashbacks. We don't see Marlowe or Nigel All Nite, but we say hi to Knife, the college DJ, who tonight has a blonde streak down the middle of his jet black hair, making him look like a punk Pepe le Pew. His snack plate is so full I wonder if he's even on a meal plan.

The house lights go down, and there's a ripple of anticipation as people move towards the stage. The MC is a young female DJ from WQNC, the new alternative station south of town. Their playlist only goes back a couple years – no Zeppelin or Journey or even Aerosmith – and every time I tune in they seem to be playing Joy Division's "Love Will Tear Us Apart." Good for us, I think, because "Take a Ride" is a lot closer to that than to "Walk

This Way."

The WQNC jockette says a few words of welcome and then the music starts. Most of the bands are louder and cruder than us, sort of post-punk garage bands, but a couple are good. The Corvettes are fun in a surf-rock kind of way, and the Schematics, down from Portland, have a nice Byrds/Raspberries jangle. A metal band called Nantasket Sleighride blows everybody's ears out, then it's our turn.

Our soundcheck had been minimal, with the huge club dark and empty, so now when the DJ says our name and the lights come up across the big stage, it feels other worldly, it feels like being a *rock star*, a definite adrenaline rush that's almost sexual. *So this is what they mean.* The spotlight's so bright I can barely make out the audience beyond the front row, but as Chas counts off "Next Big Thing" I can feel them out there, feel the rising heat of bodies packed against each other. Sweatshirt off, guitar on, I'm not Clark Kent anymore, even if I'm still in my glasses. I belt out the lyric, try to make it count, and by Boone's solo there's a patina of sweat across my forehead. I come front as far as my guitar cord will let me, then dash back for the last chorus, slashing the final cadence in time with Chas's drums. We get a decent ovation and when it dies down I introduce Will, who's going to sing our song from the LP.

"Take a Ride" starts perfectly, the groove just right, and we can feel the audience begin to undulate back and forth with the beat. Will, in a frilly white shirt with oversize sleeves for the occasion, steps forward into the spotlight, his face posed in New Romantic seriousness. But when he opens his mouth to sing, nothing happens. He taps his mic with his finger, but still nothing. *Shit.* The mic is down, or dead. He tries to keep his cool as he waves to the soundbooth, but the mic never comes on. Biggest gig of our career, and the engineer has to use *our* song to call his fucking girlfriend. As we vamp it occurs to me it's *my* song, and I start walking towards my mic. Just before I start the verse Will bumps me out of the way and takes over. I'm tempted to bump him back, but onstage at the Paradise might not be the best time for us to play Martin and Lewis. Instead I saunter over to do the backgrounds with Boone, a challenge since he's six inches taller. So much for our flawless stage show.

We're supposed to close our mini-set with "Clarksville,"

the only cut we've had on the radio so far. But I can see the WQNC DJ standing just offstage, and I don't want to waste her attention on a cover. I turn around and hiss at Chas. "'Animal'!"

"Say what?" Chas and his song titles.

"The one that sounds like 'George of the Jungle.'"

"Owe me a beer," he says, starting the double time tom-tom beat.

Now Will whirls around and glares at Chas, who shrugs and flicks his chin at me. I mouth to Will, "We need to make it on *our* songs!" but who knows if he understood me. I turn to the audience, start my rhythm part. Boone, picking up the change, covers Will's bass riff an octave up. Will, shaking his ruffles, finally enters, deliberately overdoing his usual two-step shuffle. Despite the sarcasm the feel is infectious, the opposite of the glacial minimalism of "Take a Ride," and the crowd starts dancing for real. *Two panthers now that's you and me....* I can see the DJ in the corner of my eye, tapping her boot-laced toe in rhythm. *Good call, Zodiac.* Boone nails his solo and we get our best applause of the night.

During the break we notice Boone getting a drink at the bar. Maggie and I wander over to check on him.

"Where's Carol?" I ask, to keep his mind off Annie. Hard to tell if they're exactly an item, but aside from our anniversary dinner she's come to a couple shows, and he brought her along when we'd gone to see *The Great Rock and Roll Swindle* at Off the Wall.

"Connecticut. Home for the holiday."

I nod; it's the Saturday after Thanksgiving. With all the students gone I'd been worried the club would be empty, like at our Jonathan's show, but then we didn't have ten bands' worth of guests and free hors d'oeuvres. Even Will and Jackie had stayed in town, and Maggie, Chas and I had gone to their place for dinner, Maggie sticking to yams and green beans while the rest of us gorged on the Butterball special. Then we'd played board games (Colonel Mustard with the battleship on the triple word score!) and found a bad '50s sci-fi movie on TV for background. Boone, stuck at his parents' on the Cape, had called to say hi, so Will had him turn on the same movie, and we'd compared notes during commercials the rest of the way ("Solidified electricity? Isn't that a Rush album?"). It had been low key but nice, certainly more fun than watching my parents awkwardly attempt holiday small talk until Nowhere Man slipped off to his barstool at Dillon's. No wonder I stayed in my room and wrote depressing songs.

As Boone gets his drink I notice the WQNC DJ a few stools away. "I should go say hi," I say. "'Take a Ride' is right up their alley."

Maggie nods and turns her attention to Boone, already halfway through his drink. She'll probably have his whole life story by the time I get back.

Up close the DJ's attractive enough in a solid, Madonna-on-steroids kind of way, but her hair is curiously flat, like she'd been wearing a football helmet all afternoon. Maybe she moonlights for the Patriots when she's not on the air. She says she liked our set and promises to listen to our cut. Then she lowers her voice, leans toward me. She's either gonna tell me a secret or call the next play. I glance back at Maggie, but she's still engrossed with Boone.

"Is, um," the DJ starts, looking up at me sideways, "your, um, bass player seeing anybody?"

Fuck. So much for my rock star magnetism. I could say no, see if stringing her along gets us on the radio, but I don't really want to be pimping for Will, and it's curiously satisfying when I say "engaged." She nods stoically and starts scanning the room for other prospects.

Boone and Maggie are still having their heart-to-heart, so I join Will and Jackie and Chas at the little drinks table they're huddled around. Will, poofy sleeves dangling like he's Errol Flynn, is examining our copy of the *Dirty Water* LP in the dim light of the hanging lamp.

"Pretty cool, huh?" I say, nodding. The cover photo is of a diving board set up off the Mass. Ave. bridge.

"I'm looking at the credits," Will says. "It just says Zodiac."

"That's the song credit. Here's the track list." I point to our name.

"That's what I mean," Will says.

"What's what you mean?"

"The songwriting thing. It should say Shadowland."

"Will, I wrote the song. I wrote the lyrics and came up with the melody."

"Over our groove."

"Sure, but –"

"No but. You wouldn't have written it if we weren't jamming."

"Would, too. I already had the lyric in my pocket when I walked in." I look at Chas. "Remember Tina? The bad music party?"

"Chick with the lips?"

"That's her. I wrote it that night."

He laughs, draining his beer. "I would've been busy doin' her instead of just makin' up a fuckin' song about it." Probably true – the essential difference between drummers and songwriters. He lifts his empty bottle. "Hey, you owe me one, for 'Animal.'"

"Yeah, way to commandeer the set," Will says.

"Worked, didn't it?"

"Irrelevant." He waves the record cover to re-focus our attention. "The new Heads album says 'songs by Talking Heads.'"

"That's them. Besides, it says 'lyrics by Byrne, music by Talking Heads.'"

"Whatever. The point is –"

"Will, they're not gonna change the cover now."

"I'm not talking about the cover. I'm talking about the *royalties*."

Ah. Will the capitalist again. "Did you even read the contract? We'll be lucky to get a dime." We even had to agree to *buy* fifty copies just to be on the record. Guess what everyone's getting for Christmas.

"Then why be on it?" Chas scoffs, reaching for a between-beers Marlboro.

"Exposure," I say.

Jackie whispers something to Will, who laughs in spite of himself. "She said, 'Well, you can *die* of exposure.'"

Chas says fuck yes and high-fives her.

"And with our groove and my vocal, it might be a hit," Will says. "In which case they'll owe us royalties."

"Okay, okay," I say, holding up my hands. "If we ever get

paid, we'll share half the royalties for the music, and I'll take the other half for the lyrics. Deal?" I put out my hand to shake, but Will's wheels are still spinning.

"But I sing it, that should be worth –"

Fuck. Now I know why the Beatles broke up. And *we* haven't sold a single record yet. Now I'm definitely not telling him the QNC DJ asked about him. Maybe I'll just tell Jackie.


Later, lying in bed, after her earthquakes have subsided, Maggie says, "Did you know Boone was adopted?"

I pull myself back from Neverland, stifling a yawn. The thing I like best about sex is it makes your brain shut off. Unless of course somebody asks you a question right afterwards.

"Mark, are you awa–"

"I heard you," I mumble. I'm flat on my back, blanket half off me so the love sweat can dry in the chill air. "Aren't you *supposed* to say, gee Mark, that was amazing, I've never felt like such a complete woman before?"

"Arrogant sexist pig," she says, poking me. "Well, did you?"

"Know about Boone? I don't think he's ever mentioned it." I have a thought. "Wonder if his dad was a musician. Like Chas's." Chas's father was a doo-wop singer in Cleveland, was even on Alan Freed's radio show, and his mom was a sock hop groupie. Nothing like my parents, who were respectable and boring even before the gray cloud of grief descended. No wonder my sister seemed like such a beacon. Even Will's folks are at least entertaining, bickering like a *Honeymooners* re-run playing at full volume. I used to think, or at least hope, that I was adopted, but now that my bangs are going I can see generations of Zodzniaks in my bone structure. If biology is destiny I'm fucked.

"Might explain how private Boone is," Maggie says absently, like she's thinking out loud.

"That his dad played guitar?"

"That he's *adopted*."

"He told *you*." I turn my head to face her, but she's still on her back, staring at the ceiling.

"We sort of both guessed. It's like radar."

"Maybe you're brother and sister."

"Ha." Then, as if she's actually thought about it, she adds, "I doubt it." In a minute she scrunches toward me, rests her head on my bicep, pulls the cover up. Another minute. As I'm drifting off again she says, "So, did you sleep with her?"

I open my eyes. Apparently I'm not going to *sleep* with anyone tonight. "Who, the DJ? I just met her tonight. And besides, she has a thing for Will."

"Will? He just got *engaged*." Maggie rolls toward me, so she's on her side, up on one elbow. "Should Jackie be worried?"

"I doubt it." Will's had his share of flirtations since he's been with Jackie, but as far as I know has never actually done anything, beyond a few post-gig goodnight kisses. "Might get us some airplay, though."

"Excellent, Mark. That's a good reason to cheat on somebody. Almost as good as…" She doesn't finish, but she doesn't have to. "Besides, that's not who I meant."

"Then who?" Jill, my jailbait summer fling, hadn't come tonight, and I've never mentioned her to Maggie.

"The song." She lowers her voice pointedly. "I know you, Mark. You never make *anything* up."

"'Take a Ride'?" Now I roll towards her, so we're eye to eye in the dark, just faint outlines in the distant glow of the parking lot's lone Halogen. "It's just somebody I met at a party. We didn't even kiss." Oops, actually we had, but I don't correct myself.

"But you wanted to."

I wonder what this is about. We haven't discussed the rules of monogamy since Antioch, when I admittedly broke them. And besides, I *didn't* sleep with Tina. "That's not fair, Maggie. You were three thousand miles away –"

"Withdrawn," she says. I think she's done, but I'm wrong. "But you slept with *somebody*."

It's not a question. I feel her eyes on me in the dark, waiting for an answer. I don't want to lie, but I don't want to give her the play-by-play, so I just sigh and shrug. "Like I said, Mags, you were three thousand –

"I know," she says resignedly. I expect some retribution, some flare of temper, but it doesn't come. A thought occurs to me.

"You?" I ask.

She pauses, then nods too. So this is a *confession*. We're

silent for a minute, neither of us asking for details. Maggie's here now, so it couldn't have been earth-shattering. Still, I don't want to picture it, her astride some faceless male form, her head back, small breasts thrust forward, grinding her pelvis against him until... I suddenly feel tight across my chest, need a drink of water. Not that it matters, but I wonder how many times, and with who: her old high school boyfriend visiting back home, or maybe she'd gone to one of our Antioch friend Geoff's gigs and had too much to drink. Or maybe Malcolm McDowell hadn't been so gay after all. Like they say, never trust a musician.

"A year's a long time to be apart," she says finally.

"Yeah." I think back to all the stars pasted on Tina's ceiling. Maybe recreational sex is just a different form of loneliness.

"Nice about Will and Jackie, though," Maggie says.

Next morning Maggie gets a *Bosstown Bean* and starts circling housemate ads. I say she can stay, but Chas and my apartment really is too small, especially if we're not getting along. She makes a call and gets an appointment to see a place out in Newton. When I come back from rehearsal she's already packing.

"That was quick," I say, putting down my guitar case.

"Room's empty, and it's mine December first." Tomorrow. Fuck.

"I'll miss you."

"I'll be closer than LA."

"You know what I mean."

She nods, but doesn't stop folding the *US out of America!* T-shirt I'd given her for a birthday present, back when we were yar, to quote Maggie's favorite old movie.

"I don't just mean the sex, Mags. I like the sleeping part of sleeping with you, and just, you know, hanging out."

She shuts her suitcase, clicks the latches in place. "I think a little distance will be good for us. And I need room to paint."

I can't argue with that. We brush our teeth, get ready for bed in silence. We each have library books we're working on; she's got the new Marge Piercy, I've got Joan Didion's *The White Album.* Our last night together and we're spending it like some sexless middle-aged couple in a *New Yorker* cartoon.

*The White Album* doesn't seem to have much to do with the Beatles, but at least there's a surreal description of a Doors recording session (substitute Boone for Morrison and it could be us: "Sure wish *Boone* would get here. *Boone* would know which *Star Trek* episode that's from."). As I read I take my free hand and start rubbing the small of Maggie's back. After a few minutes she relaxes in spite of herself, and I let my hand wander farther down. I maneuver my palm between her thighs, and as I rub she starts arching herself against it. I reach down with my middle finger and feel her getting wet. After another minute she slams her book shut.

"You can be such a bastard."


## 41. *FAST FORWARD:* Allston, July 1986

"Humor me."

We're at rehearsal, four days before the Beanpot, and I want to play the band "Betcha Never Done It." I always tend to be a little bit in love with my latest progeny, so to speak, but I think this one could really help our set, its funk groove breaking up the "white-noise-from-white-boys" aesthetic of the rockers. Of course Will thinks I'm crazy to even think about adding something new this close to the show, but I've always thought our best song is the one we're most excited about, and for me right now that's "Betcha."

Boone says why not hear it, it'll take five minutes. Will turns to Chas for support. Great, it's gotten to the point I can't play my own band a new song without a vote being taken. I reach into my pocket and pull out a York peppermint patty, leftover from lunch at the Bee. I hold it up to Chas.

"*This* could be yours," I say in my best hypnotist voice. He waves it over and I flip it to him. I pass out the chord sheets I'd run off at Pegasus when no one was around.

I play them the tune. Halfway through Boone begins chording along, and Chas starts tapping his bass drum in time. The groove *is* infectious, and by the end even Will's playing along.

"One more time?" I say. Chas lays a tambourine over his hi hat so there's a little sizzle on every backbeat, and Will and Boone echo my *betcha never done its* like the Andantes would have. Boone takes a solo over the bridge, getting more dissonant as the chords ascend. Then we both drop out, so the last verse is just bass and drums, the tambourine ringing through on every two and four. Too cool.

"What do you think?" I ask.

"Doesn't suck," says Chas, earning his mint.

"Yeah, I like it," says Boone. "Nice changes on the B section."

"Your best work since 'Cold Turkey in Chillicothe,'" Will says, name-checking the fourth song I'd ever written, which was too embarrassing for us to play even in tenth grade. "Can't wait to work on it. Right after the Beanpot."

Arrrrgh. I have a performance idea for the last verse, but I don't want to say it now and ruin the surprise. But obviously if we don't perform the song it's a moot point. "Will, we need our *best set* if we're gonna win. Which we *need* to do, since the fucking video's still not done." It's been a month since the shoot, and Dimitri and Will haven't even let anyone see the raw footage.

"Editing takes time," Will says defensively. "We should have a rough cut soon."

"Summer's half over," I remind him. Meaning Kat's going to need her tuition.

"How long do we play?" Boone asks, deflecting us.

"Thirty minutes."

"That's six songs, maybe seven."

"Eight if nobody claps," Chas interjects.

"So what's our best six songs?" Boone shrugs.

"'Betcha Never Done It,' 'Same Heart Twice,' 'Dogtown Rain,'–"

"Mark, be real," Will interrupts. "First one's not even arranged, the other two are ballads."

Chas nods and Boone says, so what's our best set without "Betcha"? I get their point: it is going to be the most important thirty minutes of our career, so we may as well not fuck it up.

We run through "Betcha" one more time, recording a boom-box work tape for future reference, then try different permutations of the set, but it feels flat, no surprises.

"I know," I say, snapping my fingers. "What if we do

'Dogtown' acoustic, with Chas on bongos? Bet nobody else'll do that."

"Because it's *a stupid idea*," Will says. "We have thirty minutes to prove we're rock stars, and you want to sing 'Kum Bah Ya.'"

Chas pooh-poohs me too. What else?

"Hey Boone," I say. "What about the Horns?"

Wayne had recruited the New Orleans Horns, a local r&b band, to come into the studio for "Same Heart Twice." Boone knew the sax player from Berklee, even buying dope right out of his horn case.

"That could be cool," Chas say, bobbing his head.

"I can call Benny," Boone agrees. "See if they're free."

"Yeah, good to know if they're available," Will nods, "but that doesn't mean it's in the set."

Double arrrrgh. "You're so fucking…" Obstinate. Smug. Evil. Gutless. Predictable. "Maybe we should leave out 'Car Keys.' And 'Second Glance.'"

"Children, children," says Chas, which about covers it.

Usually just complaining to Kat about Will while she rubs my neck calms me down enough to fall asleep, but tonight I'm so worked up I say I'm going for a run.

"At 11:30?"

"Less traffic. I'll just do a lap around the reservoir."

"Watch out for the hermit."

I say I will. There's a little patch of woods at our end of the water, and a crazy homeless man lives there in a rock formation. Possibly the leader of Will's last band. On my way to the reservoir I jog past some BC students waiting at a train stop. They're goofing around, one guy holding up a set of keys out of reach of his girlfriend. He's singing, taunting her. Sounds familiar. *She left her car keys, look at her car keys, I got her car keys.* Fuckin' A.

## 42. *REWIND:* Harding, Ohio, December 1982

"I…do."

Will's in a gray tuxedo with black satin trim, hair blown dry to perfection, milking the moment for all it's worth. Jackie's in white lace, looking solemn but radiant, the gown accentuating her buxom figure. Jesus, lucky Will – if she stuck the ring down her cleavage they'll never find it. And if she's pregnant, the cinched waist certainly isn't showing it. Chas and I are in tuxes, too, though without as many buttons. It's the day after Christmas, and we're in the chapel at Harding College, where Will and Jackie had met their first day of freshman year. If life goes according to form, they'll die only having slept with each other. It's unnatural.

"You may kiss the bride."

"Not you, Chas," I whisper.

After the kiss, they walk down the center aisle, and Chas and I follow, each with one of Jackie's sisters on our arm. I can see Will's mom crying in the front row – giving away her baby. Maggie's in the third pew next to my mom, rattail hanging proudly down the back of her red-and-white polka dot dress, and I raise my eyebrow at her as I go by. I'm sure my mother thinks we're next.

Nowhere Man's in Taiwan for work, earning his name, so Maggie and I keep my mom company at the reception. It's low-key, just refreshments in the narthex: Chas's dad's wedding band would have been expensive, so Will and Jackie decided they'd rather blow the cash on a honeymoon. And Daniel, Chas's boss, wasn't crazy about us putting a thousand nonbillable miles on his bread truck, so the Midwest tour is off. Instead I brought Maggie and Chas in my tiny Datsun, which despite the cold boiled over on the New York Thruway, resulting in an indoor snowstorm. Maybe we'll hitch back.

Will's family is here in force: his dad dressed up for the occasion in one of his old bank manager suits, his hearing aids emitting their occasional high-frequency squawks, and all of Will's older brothers and sisters with their spouses and kids, like the Kennedys of Ohio, if the Kennedys were working class and into Lawrence Welk and *Hee Haw* instead of sailing and Irish tenors. Will has one too many glasses of champagne, but he keeps on his feet as he shakes hands and accepts hugs. Jackie's so effusive as we take our places in the receiving line that she actually kisses me on the lips. Sure, when Maggie and Will are both within ten feet. She just offers Chas her cheek, and he turns his attention to the

champagne and bridesmaids. A couple other high school friends
come, and we get updates on who else has gotten married and had
babies. Most of the advance placement kids I had classes with now
seem to be engineers of one sort or another, just like my dad. I'm
sure they all voted for Reagan.

We'd had Christmas with just the three of us, decorating
my parents' artificial tree with the macaroni-on-construction paper
ornaments my sister and I had made in grade school while Mitch
Miller played in the background. Nowhere Man had called, and
Maggie had wished him merry Christmas while I mentally thanked
him for the chromosome that's making all my hair fall out.

Maggie's technically in the guest room, with my sister's
pink-flowered bedroom set and hope chest full of straight-A report
cards, extra-credit book reports, and birthday and get well cards,
but that night after the wedding she sneaks back to my room, and
we lie in the dark beneath all my old band posters. No women,
Maggie had been quick to point out the first time she'd visited, just
the sounds of testosterone, so I'd tacked up a glossy of Suzi Quatro
in her skin-tight leather. Maggie hadn't been amused so I'd taken it
back down.

"Jackie looked happy," Maggie half-whispers, her body
pressed against mine for maximum warmth.

"Considering she was just marrying Will."

"Do you have to make a joke out of everything?"

"I…do."

"I'm just saying, she looked happy. It might not be for
everybody, but it's nice when it works."

"Yeah, but does it ever work? You're the one who quotes
Betty Friedan and Gloria Steinem." At Antioch she wore a *59¢*
button to show the difference between men's and women's wages.
Wonder what the original band versus real-job figure would be.

"I know," she says. "I'm not defending the institution."

"It starts when you sink in his arms, it ends with your arms
in the sink."

Maggie told me the day I met her that she never wants to
get married; as well as all the philosophical arguments, she told me
her father had died young and she'd watched her mother have to
raise two girls alone. I'd already sworn I'm never having kids, so
we're an un-marriage made in heaven.

"And look at Nowhere Man, leaving my mom alone again on Christmas." It doesn't occur to me to be *proud* of my father that his company wants to fly him halfway around the world to teach silicon plating to the Taiwanese, or even that he was the first Zodzniak to go to college. Instead I wonder if he agreed to go to China because he knew I was coming home for the wedding. He doesn't exactly dislike me, but I make him uncomfortable. Probably because he thinks I hate him.

"I wish you wouldn't call him that." Maggie knows the story: back in high school Will had noticed that whenever he came over to watch Python, my mother would stick around but my dad would always disappear, out to the garage or down to the basement to smoke or to Dillon's for a nightcap, and even if my dad *were* around he'd be so quiet as to be invisible, only opening his mouth to tell me I couldn't do something, wasn't allowed to go somewhere. So we'd nicknamed him Nowhere Man. Jeremy Hilary Boob. Of course Ringo had ultimately invited Jeremy to come along for the Yellow Submarine ride, whereas I'd been barely civil to my dad. Chicken or the egg. "Besides, Mark, your mom's not alone – we're here."

"Yeah, but he would have gone anyway."

"Maybe. Christmas is probably a tough time for him."

"For my mom too," I say.

"Of course. It's a tough time for my mom too. But women deal with that stuff better. It's confusing for men." She looks at me a minute in the dark. "You know you get to be sad too. You lost your sister."

"And you lost your dad. So we all get to be sad." I suddenly feel angry, like I want to brush it all away, clear the dinner dishes with my forearm.

"It's okay, Mark." She puts her arm across my chest. "We don't have to talk about it."

"Sorry." Maybe I need to do an album of primal scream therapy, like *Plastic Ono Band.* Or something. The only time I'd ever really talked about it, when a psych major at Antioch had interviewed me for a class project, I couldn't stop giggling, made joke after joke, talked about my sister being incognito. Maybe feeling irrationally angry is progress. "Let's go to sleep."

"Do you wanna…?" She lets the question hang. We haven't

done it since she moved out of my and Chas' apartment the week after our Paradise show, so maybe she's feeling sorry for me, or else is turned on in some weird feminist-backlash way by the wedding. But sex is sex.

We keep the sound effects to a minimum since my mom's right down the hall, and Maggie almost bumps her head a couple times on the low slanted ceiling. Afterwards I hold her until she's done quaking, then we roll over into our sleep position, my arm draped around her slender tomboy body. She snuggles back against me, and after a few minutes I hear her breathing deepen. This time I'm awake, though. It occurs to me that since we're in Ohio for the wedding, my mom and I didn't make it to the cemetery this year.

Some brother.

I think about stopping at the cemetery on our way back to Boston, but New Jersey's a major detour, and halfway back from Harding the oil light in my Datsun comes on. It needs a couple quarts, but we make it home in time for New Year's Eve. Good thing – The Cramps are in town.

We drop Maggie off at her new place in Newton, then Chas and I head home. Hovel, sweet hovel. At least the heat's on today.

A few hours later a freshened-up Maggie, in Cramps-appropriate vinyl mini-skirt, fishnet stockings and stiletto heels, rings our bell. She's brought her housemate Rima, who's pretty with dark curly hair but is more sedately dressed, and the four of us subway downtown. It's freezing, and Maggie's bare thighs flush crimson as the wind whips us over the Summer Street bridge. I lend her my hooded sweatshirt to tie around her waist, and the Southie townies drinking on the corner boo at the obstructed view.

Inside the Channel it's so warm and crowded that my glasses fog up. We've missed the opening acts, but we're in place by the time the lights come down and the C's hit the stage. I recognize the opening drum beat – "The Natives Are Restless" – and at the first chord from Ivy's guitar every stage light comes on full blast. Lux Interior is decked out in black matador pants and a pink tuxedo shirt, and as he sings you can see the arteries bulge on his neck. Maggie, one drink inside her and another halfway down, wants to dance, and we try to elbow out space on the floor. Rima seems a little overwhelmed by the crowd – Maggie said she studies classical piano, and a Cramps concert ain't exactly Symphony Hall – but Chas stands with her and they shout into each other's ears between songs.

After a particularly cacophonous rockabilly rave-up Lux strolls to the front of the stage and stabs a fist into the air. "Who thinks last year SUCKED?"

Everybody cheers.

"Well it's almost fuckin' OVER."

Another cheer. He looks at his watch.

"In about ten...nine...eight..."

We all join in. "Seven...six...five..."

Maggie and I instinctively reach for each other's hands.

"Four...three...two..."

"Happy fuckin' New Year, you drunken perverts!"

Maggie and I kiss as the band launches into a grungy, ear-splitting rendition of "Auld Lang Syne." We hold the kiss, and I can taste the champagne in her mouth. Lux is grabbing women out of the audience and giving them sloppy kisses, not to mention ass gropes, before shoving them back offstage. Chas and Rima kiss politely as well; he hasn't abandoned her to check out the local talent at the bar so maybe he likes her. Two hundred miles south, Will and Jackie are probably kissing in Times Square. Maybe they'll meet Dick Clark and get us on his next cavalcade.

The set goes on, and Maggie downs another champagne. Finally Lux and the band segue into an extended, doubletime version of "Tear It Up," then wave goodnight. It's so cold out we splurge on a cab to the subway, then huddle like Eskimos on the train, cringing as liquored-up revelers blow plastic horns inches from our ears. Bet they'll feel great tomorrow. Chas's and my stop is first, but we gallantly offer to see our dates home. I'm not sure Maggie will invite me to stay, but she leads me by the hand back to her room and closes the door behind us. That's one resolution down.

## 43. *FAST FORWARD:* Chestnut Hill, July 1986

Moving day at 1941 Comm. Ave.: we're carting all my stuff into the walk-through, so we can get a fourth housemate to replace Trav-Trav and keep splitting the rent four ways. The turning point in Jan's grief was a late night phone call from Costa Rica, in which a barely-English-speaking woman, possibly a prostitute, claimed Travis was the father of her unborn *niño*. Even though we explained Trav was gone, she asked if we wanted to adopt the baby anyway, and pretty much her as well. Kat was actually tempted, but Jan and I thought it might be a scam. As a compromise Kat wrote down the woman's address and asked her church to look into it.

I hand Jan a stack of albums. It's hot, and she's braless in a sleeveless cotton undershirt over faded denim cut-offs. Also, the humidity has made her frizzy hair into a full three-sixty.

"I had no idea you had so many records," she gasps, arms sagging. "Wonder how much they all weigh."

"Especially the heavy metal ones," says Kat, taking the stack and shelving them. She doesn't usually pun, so I glance over and she wrinkles her nose at me. *I can play too.* Kat's dressed more demurely, in a floral print top, but she's also in shorts, revealing long slender legs. Which are smooth and free of hair, unlike Jan's.

Jan says she needs a break and offers to make us tuna-friendly dolphin melts. We eat, all sitting on Kat's bed, which has become hang-out central.

Jan rubs her shoulder, rolls her neck. "All those bricks, too. I could use a back rub."

I look at Kat for permission and she shrugs. "They're my records, so I guess it's me."

Jan puts her plate down on the floor and splays herself across the bed. I kneel beside her, start to work on her almost-bare shoulders. "Ohh," Jan gasps.

"That okay?"

"It's fabulous. Don't stop." She wiggles, pulls down the shirt's spaghetti straps, so now her shoulders are *all* bare. I glance at Kat but keep working, moving down Jan's spine, earning periodic gasps and coos. I've had lovers who were less responsive. I brush Jan's hair aside and start on her neck. "Oooh."

"You guys are having too much fun." Kat puts her plate down, kneels across from me, and starts on Jan's lower back. Jan groans like a purring lioness.

"This is hea-ven," she sighs, extending the word on a cloud of tuna breath.

Kat and I are both leaning over her as we work. Our faces are close, almost touching. I move my cheek so it slides against Kat's, and when our mouths meet we start kissing. We're still rubbing Jan's back as we kiss, relying on Braille for hand placement. Jan moans again and we kiss harder, our tongues exploring deeper. I'm tempted to either lift my hand and put it on Kat's breast, or let it slide down to feel Jan's. Or both. But before I can do either Kat straightens up and pulls away.

"What are you guys doing up there?" Jan asks.

"Oh, nothing," Kat says. She lightly pats both hands up Jan's spine, brushing mine off. Backrub's over.

"That was fabulous," Jan says. "You guys want one?"

Kat shakes her head. "That's okay." Speak for yourself.

"Okay, just let me lie here a second until my bones reform."

I gather up the dishes and take them to the kitchen. I have a serious, serious erection.

That night after band rehearsal when Kat and I make love we're both more vocal than usual. If you don't count one ex-girlfriend's golden retriever who insisted on hogging the bed I've never had a *ménage à trois*. Maggie's way too hetero, and Ms. New Hampshire and I hadn't lasted long enough to get that far down the list. Kat's shyer that both of them put together, but I have to ask.

"What do you think would have happened?"

We're lying next to each other, barely touching in the summer heat, the faint ambient glow of Comm. Ave. hovering outside our window. Sometimes we see the outline of our Korean neighbor doing Tae Kwon Do in the dark in the next yard.

"What would have happened when?" Kat asks.

"Tonight. After dinner. On your bed."

"You mean Jan's backrub?"

"Um hum."

"Nothing. It was a backrub," she says with an air of finality.

"What if Jan had rolled over?"

"You don't get to rub her front. *That's* not a backrub."

"Okay. Dumb question." I lean over and kiss her neck by way of apology. "Sweet dreams."

"Are you attracted to her?"

"Jan? No." Unless of course she's already in bed and moaning. Then it's just, as Will would say, closing the deal.

"Then why bring it up?"

Good question. Obviously because I'm an idiot. "No reason. Go to sleep."

"Should I be jealous?"

"No, Kat. Remember, I was kissing you. Besides, they say never sleep with someone who has more problems than you do. Jan's kind of a mess."

Kat gets quiet, then pulls the sheet up and tucks herself in. I try to snuggle against her but she wiggles away. Damn.

"Kat, what? I was just joking, okay?"

"You're supposed to be in *love* with me, Mark. Doesn't that mean you're not supposed to *want* to sleep with other women? If Jan *didn't* have problems, would you be sneaking into her bedroom every night?"

"No. Of course not." But whether I'd *want* to is a different question. "I want to sleep with you." I lean over on my side, and motion down my body with my hand. "Here I am, sleeping with you. Okay?"

"Okay." She takes a breath, then says, in a little softer tone, "I'm new at this, remember?"

She *is* new at this, I remind myself, despite being almost engaged. One of her points against Dr. Kildare was he was always trying to get her to do things, go further, than she felt ready for. What was it Maggie had said? *Go slow, pay attention, tell the truth.* After she'd met Kat a few times at gigs Maggie had taken me aside and warned me that for somebody like Kat falling in love means something permanent, and that I shouldn't promise what I can't deliver. Maybe she should have warned Kat about *me*. Who knows, maybe she did.

I lean over and kiss Kat's forehead, then lie back down. We lie like that another few minutes, then I hear her breathing relax into sleep. I'm wide awake though: only three days 'til the Beanpot, and we still haven't even agreed on a set.

The next morning I'm in Dimitri's editing suite, watching the rough cut of "Car Keys." It's strange seeing myself on camera, my temples are now so far back I look more Brian Eno than Brian Jones. I'm also in my mechanic's uniform, so the effect is like watching a Vulcan Pep Boy. Will, however, is all smiles, loving the camera, making a song about pent-up longing seem like an outtake from *Spinout*. Maybe he's trying to take my Elvis crown back.

In fact the whole video's as oily as Elvis's pompadour, with special effects, rotating fade outs and quick cuts between band takes and gratuitous shots of the actress's long tanned legs and wiggling ass. I'm all for wiggling asses, but it's supposed to be a Shadowland video, not a soft-core porn flick. Then again, it looks exactly like every other MTV video, so maybe it *will* be a hit.

"Not *quite*," Will says. "I've got some more ideas."

I catch Dimitri rolling his eyes. Now he knows how it feels.

"Wrap it up," Wayne says. "We have to get this baby on the air while you guys are hot." Dimitri says they'll aim for next week.

By which time we'll know if we've survived the Beanpot's first round. I hardly slept at all, my brain cycling through different scenarios that could mess up our set: guitar strings snapping, amps blowing fuses, drum heads ripping, stage lights falling on my head. Chas and/or Boone getting one too many drink tickets, Boone tripping for old times' sake. Will using our set to announce his candidacy for Mayor of Munchkinland.

On the plus side, the debut album by last year's winner is out, and WROB is playing the shit out of the first single. Us in a year. *If* we win. Like Boone said, somebody's got to.


## 44. *REWIND:* Brighton, January 1983

We're gigging tonight at a new club in the Fenway called Jumpin' Jack Flash. It's the first leg of Shadowland's (two-date) '83 world tour – Jill had called from Amherst to say she'd also gotten us a gig at her college. Five hundred bucks, which will be our best

Massachusetts take so far. *And* her roommate goes home
weekends, nudge nudge wink wink. But that's tomorrow. Right
now the air inside J. J. Flash is so frigid I can see my breath. The
headliner is a band called Park Street, and while I'm at the bar
begging for the furnace to be turned on, their manager is there
doing the same. Only he's not begging – he's saying if they don't
turn the fuckin' heat on he's sending his band home. Andrew, Park
Street's manager, looks like an angry bear, with dark bushy hair
and a Fu Manchu moustache, and between the two of us the
bartender finally relents.

"Shadowland – you guys are on the *Dirty Water* album.
Nice track," Andrew says, calmer now that the thermostat's off
"Arctic."

I nod thanks, but say it's a bit more Euro-trash than our
usual sound, and that we're looking for a producer for our own
record. Andrew says he'll see if he gets any ideas during our set.
Once again my first choice is out of town: rumor has it The Cars
don't like the sound in their own studio, so Ocasek and the band
are moving to London for the year. Wish they'd left us the keys.

We're supposed to be on second, but the opening band
never shows, so we go on early and throw in a couple extras.
Luckily it's a Friday and there's a decent crowd, so between the
groaning furnace and the collective body heat at least peoples'
drinks don't freeze. We get an encore and do "Rock On" for the
first time in ages, with Boone and I both adding some atmospherics
behind Will's David Essex-clone vocal and Chas's sparse tom hits.

Park Street's good, with kind of an updated sixties sound,
like they'd been stranded on a desert island with nothing but a
stack of Tommy James and the Shondells 45s. Their singer, who's
even skinnier than Chas and with a lock of hair that's constantly
falling across his face, seems to attract women like flies, and I'm
conscious again of my receding temples. Maybe I should have kept
the beret. *Nah.* Maggie grabs me and Jackie grabs Will and the
four of us dance while Boone and Chas drink at the bar, and it's
fun, simple, uncomplicated. Then I remember I have a date with
Jill tomorrow night. Fuck. *Good one, Zodzniak.*

After the set Will and I find Andrew going over the
headcount with the doorman. That's what we need, somebody
aggressive and hairy making sure we get paid. When he's done

Will and I pull up stools. Will asks for some white wine, which the bartender dutifully pours. At least he didn't ask to smell the cork first.

"Nice set," Andrew says. "Good songs. And that cover of 'Rock On' was pretty cool." Andrew's got a glass mug of dark beer, and his mustache is tipped in foam.

We say thanks, and Will shoots me his "told you so" look.

"You the writer?" Andrew asks. I nod. He looks at Will. "And you're the sex symbol?" Will laughs. "It's a good combo."

"John and Paul," I say. "Well maybe Micky and Davy."

"I'm not that short," says Will. "And Dolenz had more hair."

I hold up my hand. "Any thoughts on a producer?"

Andrew takes another swig, wiping his mouth with the back of his hand, which is also hairy. "Actually you reminded me of a band in town. How long have you guys been here?"

"A year and a half, give or take."

"Might have just missed them. The Triggers. Good band, a little slick for me, had a deal with MCA that kind of stalled when they didn't hear a single. Guitar player's wife had twins and now he's getting into producing so he doesn't have to go on the road. They were poppy like you. Name's Wayne Bonaventure."

I ask if he's produced anybody yet.

"He did the Schematics' *Dirty Water* track. I can mention you to him if you want."

I liked the Schematics track, it's jangly but heavy, like early Cheap Trick, and sounds well mixed. *And* it's getting played on ROB, which beats the hell out of "Take a Ride." I say sure.

"Now let's get you guys paid."

Maybe the foam helps, because the doorman forks over our share without a fight.

Later the band's talking producers at IHOP. "Jimmy Miller," I say over my short stack. "He did *Beggars Banquet* up through *Exile*."

"Acid casualty," says Boone, who I guess would know.

"Brian Eno," counters Will, pointing a forkful of waffle at me. "Now there's a producer."

"Do we want to sound that spacey?" I ask. "His last album was ambient music for airports."

"*Bush of Ghosts* is pretty weird," Chas agrees, a string of melted omelette cheese trailing down his chin.

"I like him," Will says stubbornly. "His Bowie LPs are awesome."

"Okay. If you can get Brian Eno to produce us, I'll go along."

"Nick Lowe. He's a guitar guy," Boone proposes.

"Too retro," I say. "Todd Rundgren. He just produced Jules."

"Oh, so he's gotta be hip," Will chides.

"Bet he'd let me sing my own damn songs."

"I like him," Boone seconds. "*Something / Anything* is wicked cool."

"But how could we afford him?" asks Chas. "How can we afford *any* of them?"

"Get signed," I say. "Send the bill to E.M.I." That's how it was in *Eddie and the Cruisers,* the lame fake-Springsteen bio-pic that Will got us free tix to from In Your Face. My review: worth every penny. Will's co-worker, the blonde with the cheekbones, had even walked out halfway through.

"I could sell some paintings," Maggie offers. She never orders her own food, just picks at my plate. Which is fine, just as long as she's eating. "There's a gallery in Cambridge I might get into."

"That's great," I say. "Thanks." Since she moved out, there's more space in the apartment, but I'm not as up on her day-to-day. Which I kind of miss.

Jackie's been whispering something to Will, who chokes on his waffle laughing. "Okay, got it," he nods, leaning forward. "Tom Ruddgren."

"Tom Ruddgren? Who the fuck –"

"Chas, it's a joke," I say.

"It's not a joke. We produce ourselves, but on the back we say, produced by Tom Ruddgren. Say it fast, who'll know. Jackie just saved us twenty thousand dollars."

"Excellent, Will." I nod to Jackie, acknowledging her concept. "But since we don't know shit about producing, it's going to *sound* like shit. I think we should call this Bonaventure guy."

Boone and Chas nod, and eventually Will does too. As I

drain my coffee cup the waitress hands me the check. Sure, *now* I'm the bandleader.

On the way back to the rehearsal space we debate whether we should bother to unload Daniel's bread truck, since we have the Amherst gig tomorrow night. Then Chas reminds us about the band that had all their equipment stolen. Enough said.

Maggie comes back to my place, and I'm deciding how to nonchalantly un-invite her for our road trip when she says there's a human rights talk she should go to, is it okay if she doesn't come tomorrow? Back at Antioch I'd get pissed off if she missed a gig for one of her endless coalition meetings, but this time I'm relieved. I try to look disappointed as I tell her not to worry about it.

## 45. *FAST FORWARD:* Brookline, July 1986

Here's a scenario: *Will agrees to include "Betcha Never Done It" in the Beanpot set. If he can sing it.*

Here's another: *Mark demurs.*

Here's another: *Will challenges Mark to a sing-off. May the best interp win.*

Here's another: *Stupidly, Mark accepts. After all, it's his song.*

Here's another: *Will, the challenger, goes first. He's a little stiff at first, but he hits all the notes, and adds a little falsetto move that's out of Mark's range. Even the judge from East Germany sits up and takes notice.*

Here's another: *Mark, back to the wall, gives it all he has, channeling Joe Strummer channeling Iggy Pop channeling Wilson Pickett, oversinging the yeah yeah yeahs, forcing the bridge, shouting ad libs over the repeat chorus. Despite Will's offer to make Jackie's "Shape It!" crew available for sexual favors, Mark narrowly carries the judges, East Germany notwithstanding.*

And here's the best one: *Mark wakes up the next day with a full-blown case of laryngitis. Despite half a box of Cepacols and multiple squirts of Chloraseptic, he can barely whisper "fuckin' fuck face Will."*

"Hum."

I hum, barely.

"Don't speak. Don't whisper. Put your head under a towel with a kettle of steam and hum. Twice today and twice tomorrow. Once right before showtime."

Maybe we could cover "Paint It Black" and I could do the humming part. Kat and I are in the examining room of the same throat specialist Wayne sent me to last year when I'd creamed my cords recording "Car Keys." Wayne had said all the rockers in town use Dr. Houghman, and I'd even run into Steven Tyler here getting his weekly Rust-Oleum treatment. Today Houghman tells me what I *should* do is cancel the show, rest my voice, and come back in two weeks. He thinks all the Beanpot stress, combined with the over-singing, is what put me over the edge.

If only it were that easy. I'd asked Kat to call ROB to see if we could switch slots with another band, but they said all the publicity was already done, so it was either our assigned slot or nothing. And if we cancelled, they wouldn't guarantee us a spot next year. Not that we'll even *have* a next year, if Double Eagle doesn't come through. Houghman says good luck, shaking his head dubiously.

I spend the day in bed, Kat bringing me tea and boiling water for my steam treatments. She's exceedingly nice to me, which makes me feel like even more of an idiot, and offers to drive me to rehearsal so I don't have to take the train.

Practice is pretty subdued, with only a few Marcel Marceau jokes at my expense. Of course Will doesn't apologize either. On the assumption my cords will still be MIA, we draw up a set list of Will's greatest hits plus one of Boone's old Rock Paper Scissors tunes. Will tries a couple that I usually sing, and, rubbing salt, now insists on including "Betcha Never Done It." Chas, who hasn't sung a note since Boone joined, sets up his old boom stand to help out on backgrounds. We'll see how I feel tomorrow. Maybe my voice will be okay – and I'll break my hand again.

"Don't worry," says Will on our way up the rickety basement steps. "Got it covered. We'll be fine."

One nudge in that soft white belly and he'd be at the

bottom of the stairs in a pile of broken bones. It would almost be worth it.

## 46. *REWIND:* Brighton, February 1983

A couple of nights after our Amherst show Maggie has a Peace Brigades training – "The Twelve Warning Signs Your Government Is About to Be Toppled by a Coup" – and she stops in on her way home. She has mixed feelings about sending volunteers into conflict zones, and her Maggie-logic solution is maybe *she* should go.

"You're just the office manager," I say, shaking my head. "And you've been there what, six weeks? It's not your fight."

"I know  I just feel guilty that they're out there maybe getting shot at while I'm safe at home."

I'm all for saving the world, but I really don't want Maggie getting beat up, raped or disappeared in some Central American dictatorship. Besides, we'd helped out with day care for kids of migrant tomato pickers in Yellow Springs so I know firsthand her Spanish is lousy.

"Maybe you should learn to *habla español* first. And let me remind you you're a *painter*. That's your contribution." Since she moved out to Newton she's started a series of white on white canvases with barely visible shapes buried underneath, probably the effect of a New England winter on a native Californian. Working title: "Which One's *My* Car?"

She shrugs and says maybe she'll take a class. We start getting ready for bed, and I pull off my Peavey T-shirt and jump shoot it in my laundry bag. When I turn back around she's staring at her fingers. "*¿Las manos limpias?*" I ask. Hands clean?

"I'm looking at my fingernails. They're not that long." She looks up at me, a question on her face.

Oh shit. Back in her dorm room after the dance, Jailbait Jill had dug her nails into my back.

"Turn around," Maggie says.

"Maggie…"

"Turn around." Her voice has that cold, steely tone I hate.

I turn around.

"That's not me, is it." It's not a question.

No point lying now. "No. I was with somebody in Amherst."

"You just picked up some groupie and fucked her. Well I guess that's why you're in a band." She lets her hands fall.

"No, actually. It was the woman who booked us. I met her this summer. Before you moved here." Woman is maybe a stretch, but I think it might sound better that "eighteen-year-old voluptuous sexpot." "I kind of told you about her."

"So it was a date."

"It was a possibility." Maybe *some* point in lying. At least the time I hadn't come home at Antioch I could claim it was spontaneous.

"And you didn't think it was worth mentioning."

"I didn't know..."

"I mean now, after the fact. Like maybe it would matter to me the guy I was about to sleep with had just fucked somebody else."

"Okay. I'm sorry, I should have told you." I reach for a clean T-shirt, so the evidence isn't on display. "Back at school..."

"Back at school it was sort of obvious, since we were living together." She starts to put her clothes back on.

"You don't have to go."

"Yes I do." She slips on her hiking/snow boots and gathers up what she hasn't bothered to put on.

"Maggie."

"What?" She looks back icily, one hand on the doorknob.

"It didn't mean–"

"Save it, Mark." She steps through the door.

"Maggie," I start again.

"*What*?" She doesn't bother turning around this time.

"Don't go to El Salvador over this, okay?"

"Fuck you."

She slams the door, hard, and I can hear her stomping down the hall. One more door slam, then she's gone.

Fuck. I feel shaken, like I'm vibrating. I also feel seriously stupid – taking my shirt off in the light was basically advertising my tryst with Jill. Maybe that's why they call it indiscretion. I also may have really done some damage this time. I hope Maggie doesn't do anything stupid. Maybe I should ask Jackie to check on her.

Thing is, I was already feeling scummy, and not just about Jill. Last week Alexis from Red October had called for Chas, twice. Their drummer quit, and would Chas be able to fill in and play some gigs with them? He'd still been at work so I'd said I'd let him know. I didn't think he'd do it, especially after the cymbal-polishing incident. And even if he did, it didn't mean he'd quit Shadowland. But why take the chance? So I'd never told him. *Pretty good week, there, Zodzniak.* Maybe I will burn in hell.

## 47. *FAST FORWARD:* Lansdowne Street, July 1986

First night of the Beanpot. We're on last, which means I have a few more hours to rest my voice. Normally I would be tight, on edge, worrying about a hundred variables. Now I've only got one question – when I open my mouth will anything come out? Kind of freeing, in a *Zen and the Art of Rock Band Maintenance* kind of way.

We soundchecked first, which seems like weeks ago; I hadn't sung a note, just played my guitar parts while Will spent twenty minutes getting his monitor level exactly right. Then Kat took me home for more steam, rubbing my shoulders while I inhaled until my nose burnt. Now I'm in the loft at Spit, where I'd first met Marlowe from WROB at the Symposium. It's taken long enough, but we're here. Even in my diminished state, I'm conscious of a major jolt of pride. Too bad we're the fucking Willard Cole Project for the evening. Maybe me getting laryngitis was Will's plan all along.

Downstairs the club is elbow to elbow, concentrating the midsummer night's heat. Maybe for tonight they should call it Sweat. There are black lights on over the dance floor, so the dancers look like undulating neon signs. Not that there's room to dance – WROB must have bribed every fire marshal in town. I've only caught snatches of the other bands; nobody's wowed me, which is good, considering they're the competition, and one punk band, Combat Zone, sounds like they just learned to play their instruments this afternoon. The Corvettes, who were on the compilation with us, are on a different night, so maybe we'll go up against them in the next round. Also standing between us and the crown are the L Street Hammers, still in heavy rotation on ROB. But first we have to survive tonight.

Kat can tell I'm starting to get butterflies and lets me pace, occasionally saying soothing things in her teacher voice, pouring me more tea from the thermos she brought. Boone, doing scales, asks me if I've ever read *Dune*, then recites the Bene Gesserit Litany ("Fear is the mind-killer..."). I hope he hasn't ingested anything mind-altering for old times' sake. Chas is keyed up too, twirling his drumsticks like it's a halftime show as he talks to his girlfriend Deedee, who's carefully monitoring his beer intake. Will's sipping his room-temperature white wine as he does his makeup, gazing into a portable vanity mirror as Jackie gives him feedback. Everybody's in their own little world. I want to give a Knute Rockne pep talk, get us focused, but I don't have the voice for it.

Wayne ducks in with Padric, says hi to the rest of the band, and then flashes me hello in fake Helen Keller sign language. Ha fucking ha. He's dyed his hair extra red for the occasion, so with his Beatle boots and pale complexion he looks like a mod Foghorn Leghorn. "Tough break," he says, and I nod back. "Good thing you've got Will." Yeah, good thing.

Moment of truth: we huddle and Boone plays the opening chords for "Same Heart Twice" on his unplugged Jaguar. I clear my throat, try the first couple lines. It's pretty ragged, but there's some tiny semblance of voice. *Maybe.* Will shakes his head like it's a lost cause, and Wayne looks doubtful. But I'm not giving up that easy.

Spit has a stage with a real curtain, so when the next-to-last band finishes we wheel our amps into position behind it, plug in our guitars, check our tuning one last time.

I glance over at my bandmates: Boone in his yellow bumblebee stripes, Chas in his sleeveless muscle shirt and red parachute pants, Will, wind-up smile already in place, in patent leather shoes, moussed hair and a silver sharkskin suit. I'm in my blue zoot-suit pants and latex-stripe T, which is already sticking to the back of my guitar in the airless summer heat. Before I lost my voice I'd suggested dressing down, just wearing jeans and Chuck Taylors, but the idea hadn't gotten very far. I'd run it by Maggie for her visual input, and she'd pointed out that even the hippie bands had worn their bell bottoms and leather fringe as a statement, a sort of anti-uniform uniform.

Holding onto my guitar I don't feel as nervous, just keyed up, ready to rock, throat notwithstanding. Will gives me a nod and I nod to the stage manager, who talks into his walkie-talkie. In a few seconds the house music fades down, and the MC, who I recognize as the ROB lunchtime jock, steps out through the curtain.

"Tonight's final act... originally from Ohio... please welcome... A Hole in the Middle recording artists... Shadowland!"

Chas starts the martial snare beat for "Risking Your Life to Rescue a Dead Man" as the red velvet parts: DUM dum DUM dum DUM dum DUM. It's way too fast, like a racing pulse, but fuck it, too late now.

At the first guitar chord the stage lights kick in full blast. They're even brighter than at the Rat, but I'm ready with my darkest clip-on shades. It's still hot though, and I can feel the Green Monster's strings start to glow beneath my fingers. The monitors are loud and every bass drum hit thumps me in the middle of my chest. Boone and I dig out the circular riff as Will steps up to his mic and slowly surveys the crowd, like some bass-playing medieval lord about to address his subjects. *I am Arthur, king of the Britons.* As far back as I can see, people are packed together, and the ones up front are already bobbing their heads in time to Chas's blasts. Will takes a breath, leans in to start the vocal. *My* moment, by all rights, but "Dead Man" is a virtual scream and I wouldn't have made it through the first verse. I half wish Will's mic won't work again. But it does:

> *You read about these things in the paper every day*
> *The hero goes down while the drowning man gets clean*
> *away*
>
> *Well that looks like a bargain compared to how things*

*stand*
> *When you're risking your life to rescue a dead man*

It's eerie, Will's inflections are *exactly* like mine, only the vocal quality is different, McCartney instead of Lennon. It's a little stiff, but maybe in the circumstances I shouldn't complain.

Boone launches into his first solo of the night, screeching high up the neck of his Jaguar. I see Maggie in the front row standing next to Simon, and she gives me a "who me?" look. I wonder if boyfriend Simon knows what the song's about. I wonder if *Boone* knows; I've certainly never told him directly. I stab a couple chords in unison with Will's bass accents, bobbing my head with each hit as Boone climaxes. Too bad I don't still have the rock star bangs I had in high school. We bring it down and Will starts the last verse. I see Kat's copper hair shining in the white light; I find her eyes and she gives me a reassuring smile. Hope Boone never writes a song this fucked up about *us*:

> *You're twisting the knife in your flesh with your own hand*
> *Gasping for breath as you thrash on the cold sand*
> *Risking your life just to rescue a dead man*

We hit the last chord and a decent cheer goes up from the audience. I try not to worry if it's louder or softer than the other bands got. Chas counts off "Second Glance" and I play my one-handed synth part, shaking Chas's can o' nails with my other hand. Chas and Will get the reggae groove just right, and I can feel people start to sway. Everything I heard of the other bands was either straight ahead rock or power ballads; this is the first song with any breathing space or syncopation in it, and I hope it works to our favor. There's no way down off the stage so I don't go out into the crowd, but during Boone's solo I abandon the synth and play my shaker into Will's mic, both of us dancing in place, smiling like we're best of friends. Will's eating up the attention, why shouldn't he smile? Chas shifts the beat into double time for the last chorus and we get another cheer. I notice some of the front row are wearing Shadowland T-shirts; somebody – Maggie? Kat? Will's mom? – must have had them made without telling us.

Boone steps up for his song, and politely lets me do the

middle solo, which I play Keith Richards-style, even doing a little
Chuck Berry duckwalk. It's fine, people clap, but I feel like we're
too diffuse, no identity. I want to scream into the mic, take over the
show, but I know I don't have the chops for it. *Not my night.* Chas
starts "Take a Ride," which at least some people recognize as ours,
and I add some James Brown ninth chords to try to counteract
Will's jaded, lounge lizard vocal. Another medium response. Fuck
this. Time to set the night on fire.

I turn back to Chas and mouth "tambourine!"

He nods, *we're cool*, lays it over his hi-hat and starts the
pattern for "Betcha Never Done It." I ripple a few sustained chords
over Boone and Will's riff, then sling my guitar around my back,
Springsteen-style. I wave Will off, then approach my mic. Will's
shaking his head, but the spotlight's already on me, so he settles
for a "hope you know what the fuck you're doing" stare. I don't
even try to sing, just speak the words in rhythm. My voice is so
fried I sound like Tom Waits after his third pack of Luckies, but I
can feel people tuning in, wondering what's happening, what's
coming next. I glance at Will and he takes the bridge, then I'm
ready for the last verse:

*Hold a dollar bill up to a match*

As I talk I pull a dollar out of my pocket and hold it up in front of
me.

*Just to see if the flame'll catch*

With my other hand I grab the Bic cigarette lighter Chas loaned
me, and flick it, holding the flame to the bill.

*Betcha never done it, betcha never done it, yeah yeah yeah*

After a second it starts smoking, then bursts into flame. I see Will
looking over, eyes wide, and Boone watching from across the
stage. I hadn't told them what I was doing, so I hope they don't
lose the beat.

*Too attached*

The bill burns down almost to my fingers, so I let it go, and it drifts down to the stage still flickering. I stomp it out, since burning down the club would probably disqualify us. As Boone solos I find Kat in the front row and flash her a grin; I hadn't told her either. That gets us our best ovation of the night. And not that I'd actually *sung*, but my throat feels pretty good.

Will starts de-tuning his bass for the subsonic intro riff to "Rock On," but I shake my head. I catch Boone's eye and mouth "Same Heart!" as I pop a Cepacol for luck. Here goes nuthin'. Will mouths "what the fuck now" but Boone nods, then nods offstage. Boone starts the intro and the lights come down to a frosty blue, a nice break from the white light/white heat we've been enduring. I ditch my guitar in its stand and walk centerstage, pointedly avoiding Will's gaze. I know I'm taking a gamble, and I'm gonna feel worse than stupid if my voice gives out. But Will's already singing more than half the set, and I don't want five hundred people to go home thinking, Shadowland, right, the short guy in the Ricky Ricardo suit who sang that David Essex tune. If this is our moment I want to crash and burn on our own terms:

> *He's so pretty from a distance, and he always knows just what to say*

I try to sing it like I'm still humming, try to get that same vibration going through my head, my lips, my bones. It slurs the words, but people never understand Jagger, either.

> *And it's the path of least resistance to fall for him this way*

I have to punch each syllable harder than I should, but no turning back now. I slip the mic out of its stand, start prowling the edge of the stage. I turn it up half a notch, and I can feel the sting of air on my glottis:

> *But he won't be there to catch you, he'll be rollin' like tumblin' dice*
> *So tell me who's the fool if you let him...*

I think about the lyric as it goes by: it *should* hurt, it's a song about hurt. I breathe in as deep as I can, unleash a sustained "Oh!" as the New Orleans Horns come in out of nowhere and play a rising triad, lifting my wordless vocal with them. I hear a few gasps of surprise from the audience: the Horns had filed onstage in the dark, and their brass and silver instruments were only now catching the light.

I rasp the last verse, getting more ragged as I approach the finish line but what the hell. I go down on my knees for the last note, trying my best to hold it out with the horns 'til Boone conducts the cut-off with the neck of his guitar. There's a heartbeat's pause of silence, then the crowd, or at least the front row, goes crazy. I want to let myself collapse on the stage until the house doctor splashes water on my face, but I run back to grab the Green Monster as Chas clicks his sticks for "Car Keys" and the lights come up full again.

I'm done singing – am just the rhythm guitar – but I flash on Brian Jones in the early Stones clips I've seen, working the crowd, working the band, challenging Jagger for the spotlight. *This* performance, this song, this moment could be the difference between Shadowland's life and death, fame and obscurity. No time to let up. I strut over to Boone's side of the stage where we chug chords in tandem, then I join him at his mic for the chorus, even though I just mime the words. I scurry back to my side, do some Pete Townsend windmills, then dig out the chords as Boone solos. I downstroke so hard I draw blood on my strumming hand. No matter. I run to Will's mic for the last chorus, and this time I even croak along. Chas does one last fill, and Boone ends on a squeal of intentional feedback. I let my guitar feedback too, and Will, picking up on it, strikes a low E and lets it ring as he takes off his instrument. We wander offstage with the sound still caterwauling, the velvet closing behind us.

The stage manager says nice job and throws us towels. I gulp some water, feeling the burn in my throat as it goes down. Doesn't matter now: we did it. Even with my limited vocals, we got through the set. I'm drenched, hot and thirsty, but also hopeful: judging by the last three songs, anyway, we might even have a chance of staying alive.

"Pretty good set," says Boone, taking off his Jaguar.

"Yeah, not bad," Chas says, towel around his neck like he'd just won a swim meet. "If there's one thing Mark's good at, it's burning money. And the horns were awesome." I'd begged Boone to have them ready just in case, and I'd promised Benny and the other horn players each a fifth of Chivas Regal whether they played or not.

"Nice job," I whisper to Will. I mean it; he'd made it through "Dead Man" and the bridge of "Betcha" as well as his usual vocals, saving our butts in the process. *Maybe*. We'll see what the judges think. But *I* think we did it.

He nods. I'm sure he's pissed about "Rock On." But he'll get over it if we win. And if we don't, what does it matter?

Playing was the easy part. There's no rush to move our equipment like there had been for the other bands. Nothing to do but wait, kill time 'til time returns…. I come out through the stage door and find Kat and Jackie standing there expectantly. Jackie gives me a rare hug and says nice job, then goes backstage to find Will.

"You were so good!" Kat exclaims, squeezing me hard despite the sweat. "I was so worried. But you pulled it off!"

"Thanks," I whisper. "Went pretty well, considering."

Maggie and Simon come up to say hi, and I can see she's re-dyed the blue streak in her hair in our honor. She says we kicked ass and gives me a tight quick hug. I feel her familiar bird-like shape and register a pang of possessiveness, despite Kat standing five feet away. Maybe it's the effect of the Shadowland T-shirt.

"How are you feeling?" Maggie asks, concerned.

"Yeah, we noticed Will and Boone covering your parts," Simon adds.

I mouth "laryngitis" and point to my throat.

"Pretty tight set, though."

I nod thanks. Simon's a schooled musician, and pretty discriminating, so I tend to feel insecure around him. Luckily he's pretty tolerant of me and Maggie staying friends. He says we were the most *ambitious* band of the night, but doesn't say we were the best. Maybe there is some latent competition happening.

Kat asks if I want a drink. What I want is to dive head first into the Charles, but I whisper ginger ale.

"Mark!" I hear from behind me. A lot of fans are here, even more than at the record release, so it's a bit of a receiving line. I turn around.

Liz Polar Bear, in jeans tighter than Maggie's. Liz and Kat nod at each other, not especially warmly. Kat tells her I have a sore throat, but doesn't go get my drink. Sensing the standoff, Maggie tugs on Simon's arm and they slip away.

"I figured as much," Liz says. "So whatever happened with the video?"

I start to explain, whispering, and Kat takes over, telling Liz about Dimitri doing one, in Technicolor, for "Car Keys." "It's almost done," she finishes, and I nod. Will's promised us the absolutely final, final cut next week at the latest.

"Better hurry," says Liz, a little snarkily.

I widen my eyes at her, asking her what she means.

"You didn't hear about M77?"

I shake my head.

"They got bought. The Billy Graham Crusade. Next month they go all religious."

Holy fuck. "Really?" I manage to croak.

She raises three fingers, then pulls down the outside two. "Lapsed Girl Scout's honor."

I squeeze my eyes shut, in mock-but-real pain. I feel sick to my stomach: M77 had been our golden parachute. Now if we get eliminated we're splat on the ground from forty thousand feet. Maggie reappears, slides a ginger ale into my hand, disappears again. I take a gulp, then hold the cool glass against my forehead.

I want to get away from the crowd, so I lead Kat backstage and we sit down on a wooden speaker cabinet. Now that I'm sitting I feel exhausted, so I lean my dead weight against her shoulder. She rubs my neck, says again how good we were. *Maybe.* And if not, it was *my fucking fault*: Will may have fucked us delaying the record and the video, not to mention vetoing the tour, but my throat fucked us tonight. When it mattered most. *Good timing, Zodzniak.* I burrow my head a little deeper against Kat's neck, tasting salt as she ever-so-gently rocks me. I could almost start to fall asleep.

My eyes spring back open as I hear footsteps crossing the stage. I see the MC walk past, push his way through the curtain. Kat squeezes my good hand and I lift my head.

"Thanks for your patience. Lotta great bands tonight, the judges had a wicked tough decision. But tonight's winner…"

I squeeze her hand back, twice as hard.

"…is…"
"Abba!" I whisper.
But I'm wrong.

## 48. *REWIND:* Allston, February 198*3*

"I've got a new one," I say, shivering at rehearsal. After Maggie had stormed out of my apartment into the snow, I'd done what every shitheel rock star boyfriend does when he's been caught cheating: written a song about it. I'd meant it to be your basic plea for forgiveness, and it sounds like one of those Solomon Burke/Teddy Pendergrass testifyin' tearjerkers, but the lyric kept coming out backwards, like not only should Maggie not forgive me, she should run for her life.

"Lucky us," says Will from beneath multiple sweaters.

I glance his way, adjusting my glasses with my middle finger. "That *is* a comment."

I blow on my fingers, then start playing simple arpeggio chords through a Fender vibrato, like a slow "House of the Rising Sun." After a minute Will and Chas come in, adding minimal, classic backing, like James Brown's Flames *circa* 1963. I watch the smoke curling from Chas's cigarette, imagine us being in an unheated basement blues club in Chicago or DC as I sing the lift:

> *No sorry just isn't good enough*
> *When it's you who will pay the price*
> *Just walk away baby forget him*
> *Don't let him break the same heart twice*

Boone puts on his slide, starts gliding over the strings in slow motion, Duane Allman on codeine. We modulate up for the bridge. I don't even have words yet, just moan *oh*, the cry of a man realizing – too late of course – what he's lost, maybe for good this time. And the worst part is, he knows it serves him right.

We do a live fade out, getting softer and softer, 'til it's just Chas barely brushing his cymbal, then silence. I may be a jerk, but the song feels like a hit. Part of me can't wait to sing it for *Maggie*, like if I beat myself up enough then she won't have to. We try it again. It's sparse, slow but funky, and once the band settles in it feels almost like one of those early Al Green singles.

"Maybe we should forget Todd and call Willie Mitchell," I say.

"It's an okay song for a ballad," Will says, shaking his head, "but soul went out of style in what, '72?"

"Blame 'Disco Duck,'" says Chas, grinding his butt out on the concrete floor.

"You know what it reminds me of?" Boone asks. He has a wide wool scarf wrapped around his neck multiple times, so he looks like a slide-playing Dickens character.

"Very, I mean Barry, White?" Will quips.

"That new Culture Club single."

Chas makes choking sounds. He's not mad about the Boy. But Boone's right, take away some synths and "Do You Really Want to Hurt Me" is the same kind of blue-eyed soul.

"So are you saying it's so hip it's square, or so square it's square?" Will asks.

"Only time will tell," I say. "Let's get this Bonaventure guy over here and record it."

"Same problem," Chas says, pointing a drumstick at me. "How you planning to pay him?"

Good question. The five-Benjamin Amherst gig was a one-off; usually we're lucky if we cover our rehearsal space rent.

"What do corporations do for money?" asks Will, rubbing his hands together.

Any fucking thing they want, I think reflexively. Maggie had led the Nestle's boycott at Antioch, and the annual lampoon edition of the campus paper had featured a front page photo of the two of us snorting lines of powdered Quik with rolled-up dollar bills.

"Sell shares?" Boone asks.

"Bingo," Will says, touching his nose. "So why not sell shares in Shadowland?"

"Like stock?" Chas laughs. "Who'd buy stock in us?"

I think for a minute. "Hate to say it, but Will could be onto something." It might be a capitalist Ponzi scheme, but where else could we get the cash to record? "I bet Will's mom would buy shares. And Nowhere Man." Guilt can be a wonderful thing if applied correctly.

"That's two whole shares," Chas says. "Big whoop."

"Maybe my brothers," Will adds. "How about your boss Daniel? He's a businessman."

"Right," Chas says. "Meaning he's out to make money. So how do we pay him back?"

"Out of our advance," I say. "When we get signed."

"And if we don't?"

"We will." I hit a power chord for emphasis.

"But if –"

Will shrugs his shoulders. "All investment is risk."

"Daniel will love that."

"Or we pay them back out of record sales," I say. "The important thing is, we *make* a record."

"Could work," Boone says, nodding. "Annie was looking for investors when Rock Paper Scissors broke up."

Chas still looks skeptical, but he doesn't object anymore. Will and I make a date to meet at Mississippi's on his lunch hour and draft a fundraising letter. Welcome to Shadowland, Inc.

After rehearsal I call Maggie. Her housemate Rima answers and says she's out. I have the urge to call Jill, but that seems tacky even for me. I feel unsettled having Maggie mad at me, though maybe I should be used to it by now. I pick up the used copy of Greil Marcus's *Mystery Train* that I'd found on the sale rack at Bookworm, read about Robert Johnson, the itinerant blues singer who wrote "Cross Road Blues," "Love in Vain," and "Come On In My Kitchen." Supposedly he made a deal with the devil, recorded his masterpieces in the span of a year, and then died at twenty-seven, same age as Hendrix, Joplin and Morrison. Just three years older than me. But so far the devil hasn't come calling.

Or maybe he has. My mind keeps drifting to Maggie giving me her cold steely gaze, Jill and her impossibly smooth young body fucking my brains out. Worth it? To quote Jackie, ah, the eternal question. I put down the book and click on the radio for company. Instead of listening to Nigel All Night kick out the Nu Wave jams, I troll the college stations and find a midnight blues show, then slowly fall asleep to the scratchy wolf-howl of a lone harmonica and the slow thump of Delta guitar.

### 49. *FAST FORWARD:* Chesnut Hill, July 1986

Combat Zone. Combat Zone? *Combat Zone???* Are you fuckin' *kidding* me?

I'm lying in Kat's bed, staring at the ceiling, ears ringing, throat hurting, tapping out tempos on the mattress with my foot. Kat fidgets next to me, but she's been asleep for an hour. I'm replaying the night in my head, imagining our Beanpot set if I'd been in decent voice. If we'd rocked "Next Big Thing" instead of funking "Take a Ride," pounded "Mercy Left Over" instead of choogling Boone's outer-space boogie tune. If I'd driven home "Car Keys" instead of Will just taking it for a spin.

Would it have made a difference? Combat Zone weren't even from the same *planet* as us, they were like a *Cracked* magazine version of Khartoum, loud, crude and rude, played out of tune, screamed their vocals, sprayed the audience with beer between songs. Even Chas, who thought they were funny, didn't think they were very *good*. The only song I'd caught was a cover of "Smokin' in the Boys Room," which they'd updated to "Tokin'." They were a joke. And they won. *Our* fucking night.

Kat had given me a consolation hug when she heard the announcement – good thing, because I was so stunned I might have fallen over. Not that we'd *lost*; I'd given us up for dead the moment I woke up with laryngitis, and only let myself start hoping when our set began to click halfway through. I could see losing to Park Street or Wednesday Week or the Schematics. Or Khartoum, for that matter. But Combat Zone? I was *insulted* as well as despondent. If you're gonna get guillotined, you at least want a sharp blade. I hadn't said a word, just put my head back down on Kat's shoulder. As she slowly rocked me back and forth I felt a decade's worth of ambition seeping out of my bones. Leaving what? A limp, balding, throat-shredded, ex-future rock 'n' roll star? How pathetic is that?

"You deserved to win," she whispered, her bare arms still holding me like I was an orphaned orangutan. Maybe. Too bad they don't let your girlfriend be one of the judges. And no do-overs; you can only be in the Beanpot once.

Wayne had caught up with us at the van and said it was a pretty decent set considering, and not to sweat it, we'll get them with the video. I didn't have the heart to tell him about M77 getting bought. He also said keep your fingers crossed, and I asked what he meant.

"Wild card." Aside from each night's winner, the second place finisher with the highest score also advances to the next round. Since we'd finished second, we were technically still alive. We wouldn't know until after the last preliminary.

We *still* had a chance.

I rewind my brain to the beginning of the set as I see the first pale pink of dawn through Kat's window. What if we'd opened with "Next Big Thing"?

A few hours later I'm in the warehouse at Pegasus, still not talking above a whisper, when Will buzzes me – Dimitri's made the final video edits, and he's heading over for a look. I tell Daryl I'm taking a break and ride along. It's embarrassingly slick, with over-saturated colors and elaborate dissolves and freeze frames, but it's on par with the other clips M77 is playing. If we get it there today maybe we'll get a couple weeks' rotation before the Rapture.

Back at Pegasus we call M77. Will sits at my desk and does the talking, using all his salesman's smarmy charm, but no dice: they're not adding any more new videos.

"But what do you care what you play?" he says, his cool fading rapidly. "You just got bought. But it'd be a really big help to *us* –"

*Click.* Will slams down the phone. "Assholes."

Shit. We're screwed. Screwed, blued, *and* tattooed. The realization settles in the pit of my stomach like a hot anchor. "Speaking of which," I whisper, "you and Dimitri just blew Kat's tuition money on a five-thousand-dollar fucking home movie."

"Don't *you* start, Zodzniak."

But I can't help myself. Part of me just wants to hear him say, for once, *oops, sorry, guess I blew it. I, Willard Cole, fucked up.* "Even if you'd just edited it quicker, we would've been on the air weeks ago. Enough to get Double Eagle to bite."

"Don't put this on *me*." Will pushes himself to his full height, which puts him in the vicinity of my nose. "What have I said all along? We needed a *video*." His voice is rising in pitch, and I wonder if Daryl's in earshot, ready to call 911. "It was probably a mistake even *doing the record*." Will's right hand is balled in a fist, pressing against his thigh like he's squeezing Silly Putty. "If we'd done the video a year ago like I said we'd be *signed* by now. Have a *real* record out. Like Wednesday Week."

"You're revising history," I croak. "You've wanted to make a record since the day we met. Remember? So your mother could buy it?" I have a great view of his air-blown head, which is shaking like an angry bobble-head doll's.

"Yes, Mark. A-Hole Records, with me singing one crummy song. A fucking dream come true." His chubby cheeks are bright vermilion, and he's starting to spit his words. *Fight, fight, fight,* I can almost hear the sales staff chanting.

"Yes, *it is*," I say, taking a step back out of swinging range. "It's a start. We're still not out of the Beanpot. We have a single. And now we have a video." I can't even believe what I'm about to do. I pick up the phone's receiver. I've got the reach, could probably knock him cold. So tempting. Instead I dial information. "New York City. Could I get the number for MTV?"

Will nods, smiles, drops his guard, then hands me a pen. I jot down the number. Maybe I just should have let him deck me.


## 50. *REWIND:* Mattapan, Boston, February 198*3*

Before Maggie had moved out of my and Chas's apartment, she'd shown me an ad in the *Bean* for substitute teachers. She'd taken the Peace Brigades gig instead, but I'd kept the ad and after a few days of frozen slush in my face I'd quit Pedal Pushers and applied. Now I'm Mr. Z, have pencil will travel. It's actually fun; as long as the kids don't scream or jump out a window the schools pretty much leave me alone, and I'd learned from my Gloucester toughs how not to show fear.

Today I'm at Mattahunt Elementary, feeling especially Caucasian since all my students are black, Vietnamese, or

Hispanic. After six hours of playing hangman and Seven-Up when I should have been drilling multiplication tables, I borrow a school typewriter and peck out the investor letter Will and I had come up with. The school has a mimeograph but no Xerox machine – not surprising since they don't even have enough money for text books to go around – so I hop the Red Line to Central Square, then walk past dug-up Harvard Square to the copy shop where we do our band posters. I'm carless these days, since after limping back from Will and Jackie's wedding my poor ailing Datsun was diagnosed with a cracked engine block and is now just a two-foot square of scrap metal in a Waltham junkyard. And I had to pay *them* to take it.

At least I'm not fucking *biking*, I think, jamming all my fingers in my mouth and blowing out a lungful of steam. I trot down a flight of concrete stairs to the church basement where Peace Brigades and a dozen other lefty non-profits have their offices. Maggie's at a rickety folding table, stuffing envelopes with the latest fundraising appeal. I know how she feels. I slip off my coat, sit down across the table and start helping. She doesn't say hi, or even look at me, just takes my finished envelopes as if they'd magically stuffed themselves.

"How many?" I finally ask.

"What do you care? It's not your problem."

Maybe this wasn't such a good idea. "Maggie…"

"About two thousand," she says curtly.

"Whoa." Shadowland's donor list is more like two dozen, mostly relatives, plus a few camp counselor friends who are now orthodontists and ophthalmologists. "How many to go?"

"Like I said, not your problem."

She seems tired and skinny, with the overhead fluorescent lighting giving her drawn flesh a Frankenstein quality.

"You look like hell," I say.

"Thank you, Mark."

"I mean, are you hungry. Can I get you something?"

She doesn't answer, and we fold in silence another few minutes. Better to wait her out than to interrupt, I've learned. We each fold another dozen or so.

"Is it nice out?" she finally asks.

"Cold, but the sun's out."

"God, I haven't seen the sun in days." The basement office is windowless, and I imagine a race of translucent-skinned peace activists evolving, like the insects that live in caves, dragging sacks of rally flyers from catacomb to catacomb. "If we finish this pile, can we go to the veggie burger place?"

The light is fading by the time we get outside, so we run down to the JFK bridge for some unobstructed rays. There's snow on the ground and ice on the river, and the few spots still in the sun glow reddish orange as if lit from the inside. We stand by the railing as the last faint rays shine slowly disappear west south west.

We get our burgers. "I'm still mad, you know," Maggie says between mouthfuls.

"I know." We're in the booth behind the salad bar, as close to private as the tiny place gets. Probably generations of Harvard and Radcliffe herbivores have broken up here over their sprouts and Portobello pita pockets, the same Bruce Cockburn record playing tastefully in the background.

"I don't know *why*," she says caustically. "It's not like we ever said we were back together." She idly pushes her seitan patty back between the roll, done eating after three bites.

"I'm the one who said you should move here."

"I'm the one who did it. All you did was fuck a groupie."

"I told you, she wasn't.... Besides, I was on the road. You weren't there." I think about mentioning that she slept with somebody else too but I don't want to push it.

"Yes, Mark, you hadn't seen me for a whole *twelve hours*." A few students at adjoining tables look over, but she ignores them. "Back at Antioch you were getting even, or thought you were, I understand that. But I'm tired of keeping score. Tired of this." She shakes her head, which makes her braided rattail jump. "So I quit. You win." She stands up, pushing the molded plastic chair back in with a loud squeak.

"Maggie, you can't just quit. We're...best friends. We need each other."

She shrugs on her coat. "I have to finish a mailing."

"Let me walk you back." I scoot around the cramped table, hurry to catch up. We walk in silence to the basement steps. I go to pull the door open, but she's blocking the way.

"I guess you can help some more," she says finally, face

flushed from the wind. "At least 'til the volunteers come."

"Can't. Band rehearsal."

"Some fucking friend."


## 51. *FAST FORWARD:* Allston, July 1986

Will, Chas and I are waiting for Boone as usual, the miniature oscillating fan we'd suspended from the Batcave's ceiling barely moving the thick summer air. It's the week after our Beanpot show, and Will's lambasting our set as too much of a downer. I'm arguing back, but mostly via pantomime since I'm still trying to conserve my voice.

I'd wanted to go camping in New Hampshire to decompress, but the phone had rung and before I even knew who was on the line Kat had accepted an invitation from my mother for us to come to New Jersey for a family reunion. I'd spoken as little as possible, but Kat had talked up our record and video and gotten my cousins to agree to come if we ever play New York. I can just see my mom and her sister trying to get highballs at the bar at CBGB's. Nowhere Man had even made the trip to Morristown, sideburns more gray than I'd remembered, his limbs looking skinny and pale despite his Dillon's-acquired beer gut. He hadn't talked much either, other than commenting on the endless games of quoits my cousins tossed in the back yard.

The morning we left I'd taken Kat to the cemetery, just the two of us. We passed the obelisks and iron-runged plots of the local robber barons, the rows of soldiers' crosses with their Fourth of July flags, the bouquets of flowers wilting in the heat. There, partially shielded under a dogwood, next to two empty plots awaiting my parents, was the granite stone with my sister's name.

"So young," Kat had said, doing the math. She'd taken my good hand, given it a squeeze. "You must miss her so much."

It was hot and still, the only sounds some bees exploring the dead flowers and the constant faint whirr of the highway.

"Hard to say. It's been a long time. And she was sick half her life." I half laugh. "No wonder she won all our arguments, I wasn't *allowed* to fight back. And since she's been gone, her legend's only grown: The smart one. The ideas girl. Mark's lucky he can tie his fucking shoes." I see Kat flinch. "Sorry. It's not you."

"It's okay, Mark, let it out." My eyes are moist, hot. Kat puts her arms around me. "For the record, I think you're pretty talented. You can both be the smart one, okay?"

We stand there motionless, baking in the sun. Kat's tall enough to make me feel small. But it feels good, my face against her neck, strands of her copper hair tickling me in the hot breeze.

"We should go," I say. We walk back to Kat's car, open the doors to let the heat out. I start to climb in, then tell Kat to hold on. I walk back to my sister's grave, alone. I dig a hand in my pocket, pull out a guitar pick and lay it on the stone.

*Hope you're all right, wherever you are. Wish me luck down here.*

The morning after we got back to Boston I'd driven Kat to Logan, and she'd kissed me hard, a rarity in public. "I wish you were coming with me," she said and I'd nodded. I was skipping her brother's wedding, but I had a good excuse. If I really missed her, Kat said, maybe I'd write a song about her. I'd jotted down some lyrics for "Shy Girl" but it had come out pretty sappy. Elvis Costello would pick a fight with her just to get a song out of it – *got a black eye from a shy girl* – but I think Kat would just prefer the sappy lyrics:

> *She's a shy girl*
> *Takes a while to get to know her*
> *So if you've got something to show her*
> *Don't talk too loud or fast*
> *She's a shy girl*
> *She'll stop and look and listen*
> *'til she trusts her intuition*
> *That love is gonna last*

I can't imagine Will or Chas agreeing to play it in a million years. Chalk one up for the solo album.

Right now I can sense Chas bending under Will's barrage. We'd squeaked into the Beanpot semi-final by a hundredth of a point, and Will wants to front-load our set with more uptempo, poppier material. "I'd nix 'Betcha Never Done It,'" he says, caressing his latest chin fuzz professorially. "And definitely 'Same Heart.'"

Mere coincidence those were the two *I* sang. "Chas, you said the horns were awesome," I remind him. I'm still rasping, but I've got two more days to recuperate, and I want to make damn sure I get the chance to sing my own damn songs.

"Moot point," Boone says, ducking down the stairs, six pack in hand. "The Horns can't make it."

"What do you mean they can't make it?" I shoot back. "Their entrance in 'Heart' was the best moment in the show."

"They have a gig."

"Fuck 'em, this is important," I rasp.

"Fuck *you*, they have a gig."

Wow. That's uncharacteristically aggressive. I look at Boone closely; he seems flushed. "You okay?"

"Yeah, sorry. Weird day." Boone pops a beer. Who knows how many he's already had.

"That time of the month?" Will says.

"Sort of." He gets tangled up in his guitar strap trying to put it on, then finally slams his guitar back in its stand.

"Sure you're okay to rehearse?" Maybe he's on something. Speed? Angel dust? Neosporin?

"Yes! I'm fine!" he snaps back.

"So what about the set?" Chas asks, changing the subject. "Drop 'Same Heart' or do it without the horns?"

"Or hire other horn players," I say.

Will shakes his head. "Not worth it. Drop that puppy."

"Fuck *you*," I say, imitating Boone. "Seriously, I bet we could get Berklee students cheap."

"What about dropping 'Take a Ride," Chas asks. "That's kinda old."

"Then it would be *funk* you," Boone says. Phew, he's back.

We argue back and forth, and eventually come up with a list that nobody's very happy with. I take it easy on my voice as we run it down, but even so it feels flat, no excitement.

"Guys," I say. "It feels like we're just *auditioning*."

"Duh," says Will. "Beanpot. Contest. Judges. Prizes."

"Plus the Double Eagle guy," Chas adds, pointing a stick my way.

"Just what *is* a double eagle, anyway?" Boone asks, leaning back against the brick wall as he pops another Schlitz. "Some kind of trick golf shot?"

I shake my head. "Think about Combat Zone." I can't believe I'm using *them* as an example, since I'd rather rip my own face off than hear them again. "They didn't give a flying fuck what the judges thought. And they *won*."

"So we should spray beer on the audience, too?" Will says, motioning to Boone's tall boy. "Wait, you don't *drink* beer. Spray them with Yoo-hoo. Maybe pass out Animal Crackers."

"No, we just need to *play*. All out. Not be so damn *careful*."

"You're the one saving your voice."

"I won't be a couple nights from now."

"Lucky us."

He doesn't get it. "Will, we need to take some *chances*. Keep it interesting."

"Like what?" Chas asks.

"I dunno," I say. "I'll know it when I see it."

"Now you're *really* scaring me," Will says. "Besides, we got this far."

*This far ain't shit*, I think. But how to get us the rest of the way?

At the end of the night I ask Boone if he needs a ride home. The six-pack is long empty, but he says no. Chas takes off too so it's just Will and me.

"All bullshit aside," I say, "promise me something." The hanging bulb over Chas's drum set is already off, so in the shadows the little red light on my amplifier looks like a buoy light out on Boston harbor.

"Sorry, already spoken for." Will flips me off, but with his ring finger, complete with gold wedding band. So much for no bullshit.

"Seriously, Will. Whatever happens with the Beanpot, let's play New York."

"Feeling fatalistic?" He opens his bass case and lays his

Rickenbacker down on the plush velvet. It always reminds me of the inside of a casket, and I rub my arm, bracing for the usual flashback: my grandmother pulling me, telling me to look, look one last time, my parents just standing there in a fog. *Look how pretty, Mark. Don't you want to kiss her goodbye?*

"*No*," I say, shaking my head to break the spell. "I just think we've been too focused on Boston. It's not the whole world. Let's tour, 10,000 B.C. deal or not. We've got the record, we can just throw the amps in the truck and go."

"Jackie and Deedee'll love that. Not to mention Kat."

"They can come. Be our road crew."

"Sure, Mark. All seven of us can live like dwarves in the bread truck. Which we don't even own, if you remember." He laughs his gnome-like laugh. "Get real."

"I'm just saying, Boston's just one town. If we don't win, too bad, but so what. We could move again. San Francisco has a great scene."

"I'm *twenty-eight*," Will says, shaking his head. "I've got a wife and a job and a lease. Car payments. I'm not picking up and moving to play scummy new band nights somewhere *else*. If Jackie and I move anywhere it's...."

He doesn't finish, just shakes his head again, and I wonder if he was going to say "back to Ohio" or someplace entirely new, some plan he and Jackie have that I've never even heard of.

"Jackie wants a house," he resumes. "Kids."

I nod. She hadn't been pregnant at their wedding, but lately they've been elbowing each other when a stroller goes by, Will into it at least as much as Jackie. "I suppose you'll have to break down and do her. Or call Chas. Or me."

"Ha ha. And not someday, Mark. Soon." He picks up his instrument case, starts walking toward the stairs. "We don't hate life the way you do."

"What the fuck does that mean?"

"You don't want kids."

"There're too many around already. You saw Live Aid. Besides, I need to stay free –"

"Kat does," Will interrupts. "A whole bunch."

"Yeah, I know," I sigh. "You goddamn Catholics."

"So you gonna trash her too?"

I take a breath, exhale again. "Fuck, I don't know. We'll burn that bridge when we come to it." Thinking about the future really does make my head hurt.

"Good plan, Zodiac. Make her ditch her doctor boyfriend, waste her time for a few years, *then* trash her."

"I don't *know*," I say again. "Besides, it's actually none of your fucking business. And what the hell am I supposed to do? Cut off my dick, become the world's only atheist monk?" Back in high school when I'd sleep over at Will's and we'd stay up all hours talking about the future, it seemed so far away. Now it's *here*.

"The Atheist Monks," Will says, nodding appreciatively. "Good name for your next band."

"Hey, Shadowland's not done yet. We could even win this thing. Be signed in a week."

"I've heard that before."

"You sound like our drummer. And MTV could add 'Car Keys' any day now."

"*MTV* won't even take our calls. Face it, Mark, we'd be done *now* if it weren't for the wild card thing. Deedee's just waiting 'til we lose to lower the boom on Chas. We're on bonus time."

Bonus time. One of Jackie's. She'd had a close call as a little kid, wandering into the deep end of a pool before she could swim. Her dad had found her and pulled her out just in time, holding her up by her ankles and clapping her back while a gusher of water poured out of her mouth. She told Will she figures everything since then has been bonus time. Guess I'm on bonus time too. Maybe we all are.

"So if this is bonus time," I say, "might as well enjoy it. I have an idea for the beginning of the set...."

Next morning I'm back at Pegasus, humming scales to limber up my still-scratchy cords. As I'm picking orders Daryl yells my name and holds out the warehouse phone. I put down my armload of MIDI interfaces and grab it.

"Guess where I am?" Chas.

"Whorehouse?"

"Ha ha. The Brighton courthouse."

"Well it rhymes. What's up?" Day before our Beanpot

semi-final, we don't need more bad news.

"Boone got busted."

"Fuck, for what?"

"D.U.I."

"That's a surprise."

"Evidently he stopped at Bunratty's after rehearsal, got more buzzed and then tried to drive home."

"Did he hit anything?"

"Luckily no. Some cop saw him weaving and pulled him the fuck over."

"Might have done him a favor."

"Yeah, well. He sounded pretty pissed on the phone. Says he wasn't drunk."

"No comment."

"Anyway, I just posted his bail and I'm taking him home."

"Shit. Will he be okay to rehearse?"

"I guess."

"Ok, thanks for letting me know."

"Guess what else."

"Fuck, there's *more*?"

"His real name is Bartholomew."

I go over to the sales office to tell Will about Boone. For starters, we decide to enact a prohibition at rehearsal. Alcohol's pretty easy to detect, but I also wonder about drugs. Boone says weird shit all the time, so how would we know?

I go back to the warehouse and make another call.

"Peace Brigades." The voice isn't Maggie's, and sounds young.

"Is Maggie Preston available?"

"Sure, hold on."

Maggie picks up. "New recruit?" I ask.

"Yeah, she's taking over my job."

"Getting kicked upstairs?" Then I have another thought. "You're not volunteering?"

"God no, retiring. Simon thinks I work too hard and don't get paid enough."

"And you're listening to him? That's progress." Back at Antioch Maggie took everything to heart, like she'd failed personally if our little campus teach-in didn't actually stop the MX missile or the Trident sub. No wonder she'd crashed so spectacularly.

"Plus I'm celebrating. I sold a painting."

"That's great! Which one?" She's had a few pieces hanging in a tiny co-op gallery in Cambridgeport. The *other* work on display makes hers seem normal and reassuring.

"A new one."

"Not from the Mark-is-an-asshole series? Too bad, I was such great inspiration."

"No comment. Speaking of suffering, your throat sounds better."

"Getting there. But we might be down a guitar player." I tell her about Boone getting busted.

"Can't say I'm surprised," she sighs. "He's stupid to drive, though."

"He says he wasn't drunk."

"I think he's drunk a lot. It just feels normal to him. That's one reason I backed off."

"Probably smart," I say, though I don't recall *her* doing the backing off. Their whole affair only lasted for a few weeks before Boone did his usual disappearing act. And then Maggie cried on *my* shoulder, at least until she ended up with Simon, the last man standing. He may not be flashy – he collects odd instruments from around the world, and teaches oud, lute, and zither at a music school in Cambridge – but he seems completely reliable. Probably what Maggie needs, after me and Boone. Not to mention her dad. "You know, Boone seemed pretty weird at rehearsal last night. Maybe something's going on."

"Girlfriend trouble?"

"I wouldn't know. He's been pretty hush-hush about his women since the party."

Maggie laughs. "Poor guy, I don't blame him."

We'd attempted to throw Boone a surprise birthday party last year and invited the woman he was dating. Or rather, the woman we *thought* he was dating but in fact was avoiding, in favor of a new flame, who was also there. Boone had taken one look around the room, seen them both, then lowered his head into his lap, closing his eyes and rocking back and forth like one of Kat's special ed students. Old flame had stormed out of the house and sat crying at a bus stop while new flame proceeded to get rip roaring drunk. And *I* complain about getting a beret.

"We're supposed to rehearse tonight. I thought maybe you could check on Boone beforehand."

"Okay, I can stop his place by after work. But if you really want to get through to him, you might want to call Annie. He still talks about her a lot."

"Good idea."

I call Jay from Rock Paper Scissors for Annie's number down in D.C. He hits some computer keys and gives it to me.

"Tell her congratulations."

"How come?"

"She and Paul." Boone's college roommate. "Finally tying the Gordian knot."

"Boone know?"

"That's who told me."

Ah.

## 52. *REWIND:* Brighton, February 1983

I'm in a pissy mood. We'd invited Wayne Bonaventure over to our rehearsal space a few nights ago, played him the songs we're thinking about recording. He'd listened, made a few notes, then when we were done said "hmmm." Just "hmmm." I'd thought we were auditioning *him*; it hadn't occurred to me he was auditioning *us*. He finally said we had most of a record. But if we really wanted people to pay attention, really wanted to put ourselves on the map, we needed one more rocker, one more tune with a big beat and a killer hook. Fuck this moody English crap. This is America, and American kids wanna rock. Am I right or am I right?

He'd basically given me a homework assignment: write a hit single, then call him. So for the past few days I've been trying: copying down little phrases, picking up my guitar, trying to come up with something catchy, something memorable. *Used-to-be's don't make no honey. You can try and try, but love can't be denied. Stop! in the name of lust.* But I've never written to order, it's just something that happens, when I'm either playing guitar and something pops out, or I'm pent up about something and grab my axe. This feels like writing a term paper. And the band's great for jamming, but not for actual *writing*; Chas is basically non-verbal, Boone's lyrics are like sci-fi poems, and Will was always too busy acting to pick up a pencil. So it's me. Of course.

I strum a few chords on my Ovation acoustic. What to write *about*? Maggie and I are still on the outs, but I've already self-flagellated with "Same Heart Twice." Jill?

I know she's too young for me, isn't a soul mate the way Maggie is, but she's sensuous, almost innocent in her pursuit of pure pleasure. After the dance at Amherst she'd locked the door on her floor's bathroom and then filled the tub. We'd made love in the warm sudsy water by candlelight, and then again in her room, a stick of incense burning and something that sounded like Ravi Shankar on the stereo. Jill's like a night in the Garden of Eden, Eve before the apple. I start singing "Garden of Eden" over some open chords, but my heart's not in it; since Jill cost me Maggie I don't really feel up to writing a hippie anthem celebrating the joys of free love. I stick my guitar back in its case.

It's starting to get dark out. The apartment's quiet – Chas is at an early movie with Maggie's housemate Rima – and I'm feeling bored, out of sorts. It's snowing, and I can see kids sledding down Ringer Hill. Some cold air might wake me up, get the juices flowing. I lace up my boots, walk out into the gathering dusk.

The snow's already half a foot deep, and nobody's shoveled, so the path is just some footprints leading into the park. It's still, like being in the country, the falling flakes dampening the usual urban soundscape. I fire some snowballs at one of the backboards, but it's too cold and the snow doesn't stick. I watch the kids having fun for a few minutes, feeling left out. The wind comes up and starts blowing snow in my face so I turn around.

Now the apartment's all shadows, even when I turn the lights on. I could call Maggie, but it feels too soon, This one's gonna take some time. On the plus side, I'm officially a free man. I get the phone and dial.

"Thompson House."

"Jill Littlefield, please."

"Hold on, I'll buzz her." As I wait I hear the dorm lobby

sounds of passing conversations punctuated by door slams. "Sorry, wanna leave a message?"

I leave my name and number. I'm eating a leftover meatball sub and watching news footage of car pile-ups on Route 128 when the phone rings.

"Hey! Sorry I missed you earlier. I was out posing." Jill.

"Like for an art class?"

"Well, like for an artist."

"Nude?" Maggie had sketched live nudes at Antioch, and it's such a small town I could usually guess who the model was, which made going to the grocery store interesting.

Jill laughs. "Yes, actually."

"Lucky artist. I'd love to see the painting."

"Drawing. Charcoal."

"Nice. I'd still love to see it. Hey, want to come to Boston next weekend? Talking Heads are at the Orpheum."

"Sounds fun." She pauses half a beat. "But the artist is kind of my boyfriend."

"Wow." Damn. "That's new."

"Yeah, we just met this semester, and we were just getting to know each other when you came and played. He's a lot like you, funny and smart, you'd like him."

Fat chance. "Okay, um, congrats." Fucking artist, bedding his model. Just like Picasso. Then again, I have sex with the women I write songs about. Or maybe I write songs about the women I have sex with.

"Would it be weird if we both came?" Jill asks.

"It would be crowded. Unless your boyfriend wants to sleep in with Chas."

"Not likely. Some other time then, okay?"

"Okay." Damn, she's brushing me off.

"Hey Mark."

"Yeah?"

"I really liked you."

"I liked you too."

"But this is like...love."

"Good for you, Jill. I'm happy for you." Just bummed for me. "I know, maybe you could send me the drawing. Like a consolation prize."

She laughs, and we hang up.

Double fuck. So much for the Garden of Eden. A *MASH* rerun comes on but I'm not in the mood, so I pick up my guitar again. Jill's young and vivacious, of course she would fall in love. I'm lucky to have had my few nights with her. But I still feel pissed, however irrationally. I start playing the open chords again, but this time it's bittersweet.

> *I'm leavin' the Garden of Eden*
> *And I don't think I'm ever coming back*
> *I'm grievin' 'cause those nights in Eden*
> *Kept me warm when all was cold and black*

I slide up the neck for a higher inversion:

> *I hope she remembers*
> *The perfect love we made*
> *The way she made me shiver*
> *The way I made her quake*
> *But I guess heaven only lasts a little while*

The chords ring like a Dylan song, but if I dig in it jangles like the Byrds or REM, that new band out of Georgia that's all over the college stations. I pick up the phone again.

"Hey Boone, still have that twelve-string?"

"Yeah, somewhere."

"Can you bring it tomorrow night?"

"Inviting Roger McGuinn to sit in?"

"You never know." Could be just the sound for a hit single.

## 53. *FAST FORWARD:* Lansdowne Street, July 1986

The preliminary round of the Beanpot had been spread over six nights, and the prize was an invitation to do it all over again at the semi-finals. But tonight the stakes are *much* higher: the winner goes on to the two-band final, at the Orpheum Theatre downtown, playing in front of thousands, not hundreds. And per Wayne, since Wednesday Week has broken nationally, every major label will have a talent scout there. Don't even worry about winning, he'd said. Just get your ass to the final.

Which means winning *tonight.* And no wild card free pass, this time it's do or die. My voice is still rougher than usual, but I'll gut my way through if I have to, no more fuckin' Willard Cole Project. Of course now Boone's the question mark: he'd gotten visibly angry when we'd told him no more alcohol at rehearsal, said we were making something out of nothing. I probably hadn't helped any by saying then prove it, why not stop drinking, and drugging, for a day, a week, just to show you can do it. He'd left at the earliest possible moment, and I was scared they'd find his crumpled Chevette upside down in a ditch, him still at the wheel.

Now he's a few feet away changing strings, grim but apparently sober. We're playing at Metro tonight, Spit's big sister, but there's no backstage so we're again killing time upstairs in Spit's lounge. Only this time Kat's a thousand miles away in St. Louis, so there's nobody to hold my hand, pour me tea, make small talk with. Last night we were on the phone for an hour, her doing most of the talking while I saved my voice, neither of us wanting to hang up. She's promised to fly home early if we make the final.

There's a "shave-and-a-haircut" knock on the wall. I look up and see Jay from Rock Paper Scissors. With Annie, followed by her now-fiancé Paul. I look over at Boone, holding my breath. Yes, no, maybe?

He takes her in, takes a step back. Fuck. Then the corners of a grin start. Double phew.

"I'm so excited!" she says, flying around the room. "Are you excited?" Annie gives each of us a quick hug, then a longer one to Boone. Paul and Jay cluster around Boone too, and I wonder if he'll wilt from all the sudden attention.

I motion to Annie and we huddle in the corner, over my guitar. She's got her stage mascara on. Good girl.

As the wild card entry, we're low on the totem pole and kind of an afterthought; some of the other bands didn't even know we're playing. We're on first, the warm-up act, but that's okay: less time to get nervous, less time for Will to change his mind about the set, less time for Boone to fall off the wagon and/or decide to deck Paul. And *we* get to make the first impression on the judges, before their ears are blown by hours of relentless, high-volume pounding.

A tech with a clipboard comes by to say five minutes. Wayne appears with Padric, who's clutching his pipe as always. After sessions I suspect some hash got in there, which might explain why Chas and Boone hung around after Will and I went home. Wayne confirms that somebody from Double Eagle is here tonight – since M77 got bought they're having to look for talent again – but he tells us to just have fun and kick some musical ass. This reminds Will of La Pedomaine, a French vaudeville actor who performed songs by farting them. "That's your encore!" says Wayne.

"Sounds more like Combat Zone," I whisper, taking one last swig of warm ginger ale.

"Just be glad they're in the other semi-final," Wayne says. "Tonight I'd be worried about the Hammers."

I nod, frowning. Fucking L-Street Hammers, the band that kept the album version – *my* version – of "Car Keys" off WROB. Of course they'd fuck us tonight, if we let them.

"Love those guys," says Padric in his brogue. "Used t' live on L Street." He looks at us looking at him. "Rootin' for you, though." Nice recovery, Padric.

He and Wayne take off as Deedee and Jackie give Chas and Will final good luck kisses, Jackie being careful not to smudge Will's makeup. Will waves us over, then sticks out his hand, palm down.

"We're going to the top," he says in a bad Liverpool accent. He's wearing his sharkskin suit again, with a Salvador Dali tie of a melting woman's face staring out from between his lapels. If it weren't for the inverted V of close-cropped whiskers descending from his lower lip, he'd still look about seventeen.

"Which top?" I answer, as we lay our hands on Will's. I'm dressing down, for the heat, in a white mesh muscle shirt and baggy black khakis. I still have my lime green guitar for color, plus a teal silk scarf of Kat's wrapped around my still-scratchy throat.

"The very top," we all say, quoting the lame Fab Four biopic we'd watched together that first winter back in Rockport. Who knows, it might even be true.

On the stairway I pass Maggie, wearing a Shadowland T-shirt she's Magic Markered with guitars and daggers and then ripped half to shreds. Simon's right behind her, also in a Shadowland T.

"We were just heading up to wish you guys good luck." Maggie reaches out and smoothes my hair, like my sister used to do before our Ed Sullivan variety shows. She pulls me in close for a hug, whispers "go smash some glass, kiddo" in my ear. It gives me a glow, which partially dissipates when I see her reach up to hug Boone. But at least it hadn't been Will.

The clipboard tech leads us through a maze of cables and amp cases to a small hand-rail leading up to the stage. This, as they say, is it.

### 54. *REWIND:* Allston, March 198*3*

"Fuckin' slush!"

We're in the alley behind Bunratty's, loading in through an end-of-winter snow/rain/sleet shitstorm, and Chas has stepped in the same ankle-deep puddle I just waded through. It's worth it, though: the band we're opening for, Shay's Rebellion, is rumored to be under serious consideration by a major label, so there's a decent chance an A&R guy will be at the show. Make that almost worth it, as a rivulet of ice water runs down my back.

I want to try out "Garden of Eden" tonight, but Will's resistant. He hadn't loved it at rehearsal, saying it was too strummy-strummy-strum-strum to be a hit, but then we'd come up with a high harmony he could show off on, and Chas had punched up the rhythm track with some whack-a-mole jungle drums. It's still not the headbanger Wayne wants, especially with Boone chiming away on twelve-string, but I'm hoping it might be close enough.

Shay's Rebellion are taking forever to soundcheck, evidently trying to see how many decibels the room can stand before the windows shatter. Maybe it's over-compensation: Jon Shay, who's black, proving to us white guys he can rock. Which is backwards, since we're *all* playing black music, the same three chords, in the same order, that Chuck Berry played thirty years ago, Robert Johnson played fifty years ago, and generations of slaves played before them. Go figure.

I notice a slight, tomboy-esque figure dart in the club door and furiously shake the snow off her collar. *Maggie*. Looking pissed.

"God I hate winter," she yells at no one in particular. She starts to take her coat off, then decides to leave it on, rubbing her arms as she huddles at the bar.

"I'm surprised you came," I yell back. I haven't seen her since the day we stuffed envelopes in Harvard Square.

"Well, dancing to you guys is the only exercise I get out of bed," she shouts back. "And if I hear about one more kidnapped Central American labor leader I'll scream."

I wonder what exercise she's getting *in* bed, but I don't ask.

Shay's Rebellion finally finishes, so we're able to dial it down. "I have to go soundcheck. Jackie's in the dressing room if you want to say hi."

"Think I'll just sit at the bar." Uh oh.

Maggie had gotten very drunk and/or stoned at parties when I first met her, and when she noticed I didn't drink or smoke she asked me why. Instead of giving her my usual quip about needing my brain cells, I'd recounted how Nowhere Man had begun drinking after my sister died, and how my mom would send me to Dillon's to fetch him, and how lonely and pathetic he looked on his barstool, even among the other drunks, and how I'd sworn that would never, ever, *ever* be me.

Maggie had given me a long hug, followed by an even longer kiss, then told me that when she was little her dad would sometimes go drinking with his army buddies and then come home and yell at her mom and scare her, and maybe worse. Maggie had gradually toned down her act and now only drinks seriously when she's mad at me. Could be a rough night.

Boone tunes his twelve-string, and we run down "Garden of Eden." It's a little ragged, but we get some scattered applause, pretty good for a soundcheck. I look over at Will and he shrugs noncommittally.

We still have a few minutes before our set so I go check on Maggie. She has a drink in front of her, probably a rum and Tab, and probably not her first. She also has a cigarette going, which means she's doubly pissed.

"New song."

I say yeah.

"It was kind of like the Garden of Eden. I'd walk barefoot on the grass on the way to classes. Even in winter sometimes."

"Then you'd make me give you a piggyback ride."

She half giggles at the memory. "You were a pretty good boyfriend. Good kisser. Lotta sex." *Definitely* not her first drink.

"You were a pretty good girlfriend." This doesn't seem like the right time to tell Maggie "Garden of Eden" is not about us.

"Pretty good?"

"The best."

"The best," she agrees. "And yet," she waves dismissively, "here we are, freezing our asses off in New England slush, not even fucking to stay warm." Her "slush" has a few extra consonants. "Some Garden of Eden. And there's not even a snake to blame."

Phew. Maybe I'm getting off easy.

"Present company excluded."

Maybe not.

Before we go onstage I ask Jackie to keep an eye on her. Jackie kind of harrumphs, like she knows whose fault it is that Maggie's drunk. From the opening chords of "Next Big Thing" Maggie's up and dancing full tilt. Jackie gets up to join her, though at a more restrained pace. Every song or so, guys from the crowd attempt to join them on the dance floor or buy them drinks. Maggie seems more than happy to dance with anybody, and there's even a mini-altercation when a guy comes back with a round to find someone else dancing in his place. I feel like Keith Richards at the climax of *Gimme Shelter*, ready to jump into the crowd at a moment's notice.

The club's packed, and we're getting a pretty decent response. Halfway through the set we're supposed to do "Same Heart Twice," but I turn around and hiss "Garden of Eden!" Will rolls his eyes as I start the intro. At the moment I don't actually care about doing "Garden," I just don't want to do a slow one – guys would be all over Maggie like lamprey eels in heat, and who knows how she'd react.

Now Maggie's looking up at me with her big drunk eyes and I can't help but sing to her. And part of me hopes it'll come true:

> *Some night on the highway*
> *In a fierce and pouring rain*
> *Some face caught in a headlight*
> *Makes you look again*
> *You'll roll down your window and smile*
> *And I'll say Eve how's it goin', yeah it's been a while*

For that moment it's just her and me; everyone else in the club is irrelevant. Maybe it's *not* too late for us. Then Boone launches into his solo, another wobbly male hopeful asks Maggie to dance, and she's gone again.

After the set I find her back on her stool, cigarette in one hand, another rum and Tab in the other. The last guy she'd been dancing with, a big lug in husky jeans and a yellow-and-black Bobby Orr jersey, is chatting her up, and I squeeze in on her other side, ready to protect her honor. As I'm waiting for my drink, the guy abruptly moves off without a backward glance. Good thing, since he probably could have pounded me.

"What the hell did you say to him?" I ask.

Maggie tosses her head back, draining her glass. "I *said* if I want a pony ride, I'll go to Woolworth's." She signals for another. "That goes for you too, misther."

The dance floor's so crowded during Shay's Rebellion that no one can actually dance, and the volume's too high to just stand around and listen without going into sonic shock. I hide out in the dressing room while Jackie and Will take turns checking on Maggie. Chas comes in, hands over his ears.

"No Rima?" I ask. Even with the door closed, I have to raise my voice. If Maggie's housemate was here, she could help monitor Maggie's alcohol intake and ward off potential pony riders. Not that Maggie needs the help.

"Her mom's visiting," Chas yells back. "They're at the symphony." Rima's seriously studying piano, and unfortunately for Chas, transferring to Juilliard.

"Highbrow, eh?" Chas's favorite classical music is

Emerson, Lake and Palmer, but I recently caught him listening to something called "The Pines of Rome" by Respighi. Too bad Rima's leaving, maybe she could have gotten him to change socks more often. "Like these guys."

"Hey, they're okay. Just a little loud."

"Donnie's pretty confident they'll get signed," I say above the din. He's the club's manager, and also the band's. Pretty cozy; we could use someone who can have us headline his nightclub while he negotiates us a record deal. "But that's only the first step. People still have to *buy* the record."

"Maybe they should do the next *Rocky* theme," says Will, coming in. Survivor, who these guys sound like, just sold a million copies of "Eye of the Tiger" courtesy of Mr. Stallone. "Or we should."

"No way." I stick a finger down my throat. "Now *Rocky and Bullwinkle*, that's a theme I'd do."

"Which explains a lot," Will says. He rubs his latest chin shadow, which is still in its embryonic stage.

"Is that thing *painted* on?" Chas asks. "Swear it wasn't that dark earlier."

"I may have enhanced it a little," Will admits, producing an eyebrow pencil from his suit pocket. "Love your look or change it." He's quoting a Newbury Street salon ad, where for a small fortune they'll do anything short of a heart transplant. "Hey," he says, looking at me, "Maybe Victoria's does hair weaves."

It occurs to me as I flip him off that maybe Will's constant face dancing is a form of actor's insecurity. I might not be pretty, but at least I pretty much know who I am.

The door opens and Jackie walks in, slides an arm around Will's waist, pressing one V-neck-exposed breast against his side. So what's he got to be insecure about? I ask how Maggie's doing.

Jackie holds out a set of keys. Maggie's, by the little Navajo dreamcatcher dangling from the ring.

"At least we talked her out of driving home," Will says.

"Thanks," I say, taking the keys. "Maybe I should head down."

Will shrugs. "Last I saw, she was playing pool with Boone and some Berklee pal of his. Simon, I think." Jackie nods. Carol, Boone's coworker, hasn't made it again, or possibly hasn't been invited.

"Maybe we should get Boone's keys, too."

"He seems fine," Will says. "They're just hangin'."

It might occur to me that Maggie can be an affectionate drunk if she likes you, and that Boone's lost-puppy demeanor might appeal to her save-the-world tendencies. But Maggie hadn't been that thrilled with my company earlier, so I just pocket the key ring.

After Shay's Rebellion finishes we load out. Maggie's in no shape to even take the train home so she comes with us to unload. I suggest IHOP but have no takers. Chas and I offer her a ride to Newton in the bread truck but Boone says he'll give her a lift. See you at rehearsal.

Lying in bed my ears are ringing so loudly I can't sleep. I'm also starving, so I get up and pour a big bowl of Chas's Cocoa Puffs. *Then* I notice we're out of milk. I flick on our little portable TV but there's nothing on but a rebroadcast of the eleven o'clock news: *Celtics Top Bruins in Double Overtime Thriller!*

I look up and see Maggie's dreamcatcher on the hall table. Fuck, forgot to give her back her keys. Hopefully Rima got up to let her in. I picture Maggie passed out in her bed, naked in an alcohol-induced haze. She better not end up like Marilyn Monroe, just because she was pissed I had a two-night stand with an over-sexed teenager. I'd never forgive myself. Maybe I should go check on her. I've got her keys, I could go anywhere.

I *could* go anywhere, which is sort of interesting after being carless for the past few months. Maggie's probably dead asleep, but I'm feeling more awake by the minute. I still have Shay's Rebellion pounding in my head, and a line floats up to match the music:

*She dreams deep but I can't sleep*

What would still be open this late? IHOP, of course, with its bad coffee and beige-uniformed waitresses. Riley's Roast Beast, just down the block from Bunratty's, home of the 2 AM special. Buzzy's-even-worse-Roast-Beast, on Charles, home of the 3 AM horsemeat special. The Deli Haus. The strip clubs downtown. I visualize all the college kids out on Comm. Ave., thumbing rides between BC and BU now that the T's shut down. I know where Maggie's parked, I could go check on her, get some food, see what's happening around town. I could drive all the way to Amherst, surprise Jill and her new boyfriend.

*She dreams deep but I can't sleep*

I get out my Duo Jet, unplugged so it hardly makes a sound. I start playing steady eighth notes, all downstrokes:

*I see her car keys sitting on the table*
*I see her car keys just sitting on the table*

I keep it simple, try a verse:

*It's not that late I could still catch a show*
*Maybe run into someone I know*
*Maybe meet somebody, follow her home*
*I could be back before she knew I was gone*

It's winter now, but I imagine Hampton Beach in high season, kids making driftwood bonfires, getting drunk on smuggled six-packs then pairing off for first time sex:

*Ride to the ocean, walk down the beach*
*These warm nights there's always someone to meet*
*Pick up a hitcher and drive up the coast*
*End up at a party on a big private boat, yeah!*

I try adding different chords, and a verse about cruising the whores on Tremont Street, but it wants to be simple, straight ahead. I imagine Joey and Dee Dee Ramone, in their dyed bangs and black leather, saying don't mess it up, kid, leave it the fuck alone. Great, I've just written my first headbanger. And maybe gotten Wayne Bonaventure his hit. *Will* might even like this one. I play it again, and again, finally start getting drowsy as dawn starts breaking over Ringer Park. I fall asleep, the Gretsch still in my hands.
They say that Robert Johnson sold his soul to the devil to be king of the blues. If I hadn't forgotten to give Maggie her dreamcatcher

back I never would have written "Car Keys," and she never would have ended up spending the night at Boone's. At least that's what I'd like to think. And if I hadn't been with Jill in Amherst, Maggie wouldn't have gotten drunk the first place, wouldn't have had her lost weekend with Boone, wouldn't have, ultimately, maybe, probably, ended up with Simon, while I spent the next two and a half years lonely and adrift, fighting with Will while we made our record. Fair trade all around? Probably not, I think – unless of course "Car Keys" sells a million…

## 55. *FAST FORWARD:* Lansdowne Street, July 1986

The stage manager thought we were crazy when we'd had them open the Metro curtain on an empty, half-lit stage. But the one and only time I'd seen Jules and the Polar Bears, they'd done exactly that, wandering onstage one by one, fiddling with their instruments, gradually coalescing into a song while people wondered what the fuck was going on. Jules himself had wandered on last, picking up his microphone at the last possible second before his cue, and then *bam*, full tilt Polar Bear mayhem. Brilliant.

Will had wandered out first, picking up his bass and thumping out a sub-sonic heartbeat. Then Chas, pressing down on his drum heads to change their pitch as he tapped out counter-rhythms. Then Boone and me, to opposite sides of the stage, donning our axes and trading dinosaur roars, long sustained notes swooping in and out of focus. Will gradually added real notes to the low-end rumble, and he and Chas had locked into the stuttering riff of "Rock On" as the lights came up. Will went to his mic and started the vocal, and just when people were getting comfortable with the groove – *hey, I know this one* – we double timed it right into "Visibly Shook." Boone kept up his guitar noise and I did the best I could with the vocal while Will and Chas churned underneath. It felt *intense.*

We didn't wait for the crowd; as soon as "Shook" faded Chas clicked off "Next Big Thing," then on into "Second Glance," which Will sang with more grit than usual. There was no easy way down to the audience so I stayed onstage for my synth and shaker part, but the groove felt right, and the natural echo off Metro's distant walls became part of the sound, filling in the spaces.

Now for the fun part. I'd caved on "Same Heart Twice" since with all the Boone D.U.I. anxiety there hadn't been time to recruit a new horn section. This was my reward. "Please welcome Annie Branfman from the late, great Rock Paper Scissors."

There were a few whoops as Will and Chas started the intro for "Betcha Never Done It." I slipped my mic off its stand and stood guitarless as Annie, in white tights and a sleeveless turtleneck mini, positioned herself at Will's mic. On the *betcha never done it, yeah yeah yeah's* she and Will bobbed in true Andantes fashion, and then Boone laid down his hottest solo of the night. We kept it going, and I improv'd a couple of lines I've been thinking about since my and Will's last conversation in the Batcave, kind of the flipside of what Roger Talon had told us back at our anniversary dinner – keep doin' it if it's what you love – through the lens of Will's favorite hair care commercial:

*Love your life or change it*
*Don't suffer through all the same things*

Annie picked up on it, and she and Will started echoing me – *Change it!* – and pretty soon some of the front rows of the audience were shouting along as well. Boone slipped on his slide and started weaving an impossibly high harmony line over our vocals: *Change it!* (squeal!) Kind of ironic, our biggest crowd, our best show, our best *moment*, and I'm wondering, if Will and Chas really *don't* love it anymore, maybe it is time to change it. And even if we do get signed, do I really want another decade of Will's antagonism, Chas's apathy, Boone's chemical romance? I signaled the cut off and Chas immediately clicked his sticks for "Car Keys." Annie waved at the crowd and disappeared as I grabbed the Green Monster for our last song. Who knows, maybe ever. But fuck that misty-eyed nostalgia shit, we had a song to play.

You can tell when the audience really knows a song. The energy, the attention in the room just go way up. We'd felt it back in Ohio, hitting the riff of, say, Aerosmith's "Walk This Way" in a gym full of hormone-raging high school kids. But this time, it was our song. *My* song. WROB, WQNC, all the college stations playing it, we'd hit the threshold. People knew it, and they *liked* it.

Will took the verses, just as well since my voice was fried again. I ran around the stage, jumped on Chas's drum platform. I'd thought about crowd diving, but for better or worse it just wasn't in me. But they'd rigged a curtain for the show, with an awning that extended the first few rows over the audience. There was an exposed metal frame under the cloth. Could I?

I could. As Boone went into his solo, I jumped up and grabbed the pipe. It held, good thing since it would have been a little embarrassing bringing the whole stage down. I shimmied out over the crowd, hanging by my arms, my Gretsch still dangling around my neck. People got out of the way, but fuck, it was a long way down. I couldn't just shimmy back. What to do? I looked around and caught Jay and Simon's eye, and motioned them over, my arms getting more tired by the second. When they were beneath me I let go.

They mostly caught me, at least broke my fall, and eased me down. My guitar was still plugged in, barely, so I started chording along with the band, rocking back and forth to the chugging rhythm. Maggie and some other fans started dancing around me, forming a little circle in the crowd. A spotlight caught me, but this time there was a second one still focused onstage. I could hear Boone bending a couple extra frets' worth of range out of his Jaguar; time to get back up there. It was too high to climb so once again Jay and Simon did the honors, butt-shoving me back onto the platform. One last chorus and it was over. Way too soon.

It's four hours later and I'm pacing the alley between Metro and Spit, killing time while the final band – the dreaded Hammers – finishes their fucking set so we can hear the verdict and either pop champagne or go the fuck home. It's raining, but I don't care; without Kat to hold my hand and calm me down I'm feeling more and more pent up, like a Jet looking for a Shark, or maybe a Shamrock, to kick the shit out of. I keep having to clear my glasses every lap or so, so I finally take them off and slide them in my pocket, and now everything's out of focus, even the rats parachuting out of the overloaded dumpster each time I walk by.

Maybe you have to be Irish to love the L Streeters, but half of Boston *is* Irish, and sure enough people seem to be buying their shtick. *Their* hardcore fans have T-shirts that say "Kiss My F***in' Ass, I'm Irish" and I wouldn't place any bets if a rumble really did break out. They're pulling out all the stops – the song I walked out on even had a dozen kilted bag-pipers marching up and down the aisles. And I always thought bag-pipes were *Scottish*. And with my voice shot again, their singer and I sounded more alike than ever. Maybe they'll encore with "Car Keys."

On the plus side, we, Shadowland, did it. Give or take the extra sandpaper on my cords, I thought we played our asses off, so whatever the fuck happens won't be for lack of trying. Will had his moments, I had mine, Boone didn't implode, and Chas rocked throughout. Wayne had brought the Double Eagle guy backstage after the set, and he seemed reasonably impressed. His favorite tune was "Betcha Never Done It," even said we should think about adding a chick singer full time. Fat chance Deedee would allow that, having Chas stare at some other twitching, mini-skirted ass all night long. But it's a thought – if we make it.

One more round of applause from inside the club. More than we got? Hard to say. Last time, waiting for the verdict, I'd been able to bury my head in Kat's neck. Tonight I'd found myself looking for her copper hair in the crowd, scanning for her lanky body in the dancers down front, but she's still in St. Louis for her brother's wedding. She made me promise to call her tonight, no matter how late, and I might have called already from the pay phone in the lobby just for moral support, but she only would have heard a dull roar. Last night we'd talked long distance, me lying on the living room floor at 1941 Comm. Ave., just like during our first conversations. She'd told me about the wedding rehearsal, in the church she'd grown up in, and her voice had gotten quiet. I figured she was weighing our chances, but she faked me out.

"I wish you believed in God."

Pause. I could have asked her if she thought God believed in *me*, but instead I just said, "Kat, we talked about this."

"I know," she'd sighed. "But still."

We *had* talked about it, one of those very first nights. We were comparing childhoods, and she'd told me about getting dressed up for first communion, and the bishop coming, and having to kneel and kiss his ring, then how nervous she was going to first confession, the disembodied voice behind the window almost making her stain her dress. I'd jumped ahead a decade, to my hysterical mother screaming at our hapless minister why, why, *why*, if God was just going to take her anyway, did He put my sister through five years of hell first? What could the minister say? What could my father, or anybody, say? Nothing that helped, that's for sure. "Sorry."

"It's just...I'll miss you. In heaven."

Wow. What could *I* say? I'll miss you in oblivion? I just said don't go anytime soon. Say hi to my sister for me.

I'm about to head back inside when the exit door swings open and a tall, gangly form appears. Even without my glasses I can tell it's Boone, since his head is as oversized as the rest of him. He's still in his stage clothes, purple this time, shirt stained wine dark from sweat. "Hot in there," he says, lifting his face to the rain. After a minute he shakes his mane like he's a six-week old Labrador.

"What do you think?" I ask.

"I think I want about twenty-four beers. But every time I get near the bar, Annie, Paul and Jay watch me like a hawk."

"They, um, care about you." Boone's made a career out of avoiding confrontation, so it's awkward suddenly being his Twelve Step counselor.

"I wasn't even drunk. Well maybe just, legally."

11.9 steps to go. At least he proved he can *play* sober. "I meant, what did you think about our set?"

"Pretty good. Seemed short."

"Well that's good I guess." I flick my head toward the stage door. "We play as well as the Electric Leprechauns in there?"

He doesn't pick up on the sarcasm. "Hard to say," he says, leaning an arm against a wall. "I'm not sure it matters."

I straighten up, so we're almost eye to eye despite his extra height. "How could it *not matter*?" Boone's got to know we're running out of rope, that Will and Chas will bail if we don't get good news ASAP.

"Well think about it." Boone makes a fist, then extends his little finger. "These guys on now. Pub rock." He raises a second finger. "The Corvettes. Sixties garage. That synth band." He raises his middle digit.

"Cloud Chamber." They were a real party, with Sylvia Plath lyrics over ominous slow grooves. Wonder if they bought their software from Pegasus.

"Then us, jangly post-punk power pop." Boone straightens his index finger. "Four choices. If a judge likes techno, he'll vote A." He folds Cloud Chamber's finger down. "If he likes garage bands, he'll vote B. Et cetera. I don't know that it matters that our set was 97% correct, but the Corvettes were 98%." He shrugs. "Wasn't perfect, but it was fairly representative. And the 'Rock On' intro was pretty cool."

"Well I thought we were fucking *great*," I say, hands on my hips. "And any judge who doesn't think so is crazy. Or else on the take."

"Or both," says Will, stepping through the door into the mist. Despite hours in Metro's steam-room conditions, his hair is still perfect, like he'd coiffed it with Superglue. "Of course Mark thinks the Monkees shot JFK."

"Actually it was studio assassins," Boone nods sagely.

Will high-fives him – *good one* – but I'm too wound up to appreciate the joke. "I was just telling Boone –"

Will interrupts. "You know, Mark, I was wrong."

*That* stops me mid-sentence. Will, apologizing? I slide my neck back an inch, squinting expectantly.

"Losing the glasses?" He shakes his head. "Doesn't help."

I'm about to say "fuck you," but he flashes his "just kidding" smile so I let it go. "I was saying, I really think we did it. That set, those songs. We should win in a landslide."

"Maybe," Will shrugs. "But this is show biz. You've got to look at the big picture."

"What fucking big picture? *We* had the best songs, *we* played the best, *we* win."

"Who *looks* the best? Who's got the best radio voice? The best image? WROB wants a winner who can sell records. Like Wednesday Week."

"That's all bullshit. Our music's *real*."

"Real doesn't cut it, Zodzniak. That's why there's Hollywood."

"Said the glam whose make-up is running like Liza Minnelli on a crying jag. At least my *singing's* real."

"Real *ragged*. Every producer we've ever had –

"Guys –" Boone tries to interrupt the face-off, but it's a losing battle.

"Wayne picked *my* 'Car Keys' for the album," I yell.

"But who got the *single*?" Will taunts.

"Yeah, well good luck writing your next Fabulous hit."

"Good luck singing yours, frog-boy."

"Hair head –"

"*Guys*," Boone says again. "Same team."

Right. For the moment, anyway. I take a step back, exhaling into the mist. I glance at Will, who looks winded too.

"Had you going there," he says.

I shake my head. "Ass-wipe."

Just then the muffled thumping from inside the club stops, replaced by more applause. The door swings open and Chas sticks his head out. "They're done."

My smile vanishes. Time to ascend the scaffold.

Waiting.

Chas and Deedee are standing against the wall by the sound table with Will and Jackie. Chas is holding a beer bottle against his neck and Deedee's fanning herself impatiently with a *Dianetics* flier – evidently the lost lambs of Lansdowne Street are prime game for Mr. Hubbard. Not that Deedee needs any assertiveness training; she's informed Chas they'll announce their engagement once the Beanpot's over.

Jackie is saying something in Will's ear, he laughs, then stretches up to give her a proprietary kiss on the forehead. Maybe they will make it. She still looks damn good packed into a Shadowland T-shirt, her chestnut hair now clipped into a layered, moddish bob. Lucky, lucky Will. The impregnating weasel.

Boone's found Annie and Paul on the dance floor, I can see his head sticking above the crowd. Annie's gesturing, talking with her hands, probably telling Boone how great he was. Or at least how "fairly representative" he was. Maybe I shouldn't jump down Boone's throat, since he's spent the last three years playing my songs virtually for free, and we'd never even met before that first night at the Rat. At least I got Will and Chas out of Ohio, so we're sort of even for all the hours they've put in.

Now I *really* wish Kat were here, with her warm eyes and positive attitude, telling me not to worry, that we *are* as good as I think we are, that I'm just wound up from the show. I scan the crowd again, looking for company. I see my frizzy-haired housemate Jan. Not an option, especially since she's here with her new crush – our new fourth housemate, a Vermont girl with a buzz cut and a butterfly tattoo. The anti-Travis. I pick out Maggie, but she's at the bar with Simon, talking politics with Daria and her brother and the rest of the Corvettes.

I'm walking back up to the lounge when I hear a woman's voice say, "Hey rock star, can I get your autograph for my grandma?"

Liz Polar Bear, smiling like a fox. She's definitely not Kat – I can't imagine crying on Liz's shoulder if we lose – but she's female and she likes me and she's *here*. She's also wearing some kind of push up bra thing, and I can see red lace along the edge of her low-cut blouse. I can be Mr. Cynical Rock Star Guy for a while. "Sure. Next time bring Granny along. You can be our go-go dancers."

She laughs. "Nice work up there."

"Not too, you know, AOR?" Album-oriented rock, *i.e.* dinosaur bands.

She shrugs, which makes her breasts pop even more. "Just that last one."

"Yeah, not our best," I agree. I tell her we sent the video to MTV.

She wrinkles her nose like Samantha on *Bewitched*. "Good luck. It took Park Street a year just to get theirs on *Basement Tapes*."

"Fuck." Like we have a year to wait.

"Hey, some Museum School grads are doing an installation at the ICA, we're filming local bands, then projecting the images on doors and windows around the museum while their songs play. If you want I could do you guys."

"Sure, sounds cool." I lower my eyes, try to look vulnerable. "Even if we don't win tonight?"

"Are you kidding? We're the *hip de la hip*. Winning would just blow your credibility." She leans forward, giving me a view. "Bet the Velvets would have got bounced out of here in the first round."

I smile; she may be right. Lou Reed probably would have said, contest, fuck that, and then played a thirty-minute feedback loop of "Sister Ray" and cleared the room, like Khartoum did back at Jonathan's. As we talk I'm debating whether to invite Liz and her lace bra to IHOP. Like Will said one time giving me unsolicited advice on how to stay faithful: bright lights and crowded rooms. Add bad coffee and that's IHOP. And I *did* meet Liz first.

"I should go," she says, interrupting my good Goofy bad/Goofy moment. "*I* am on a date."

"Oh." I'm part relieved, part disappointed. "He a musician?"

"Of course." She brush kisses my cheek, then I watch her tight-denim-clad ass disappear into the crowd.

Maybe I should find that pay phone.

I get another ginger ale and wander over to where Will and Chas are. "Is it a good sign when the jury stays out a long time?"

"Good for the defense," Will says, downstroking tonight's chin-fuzz. *I'm not a lawyer, but I watch one on TV.*

"What are we?" Chas asks.

Will and I both say "offensive."

"Wow, an aardvark/aardvark moment," Jackie says. Since she became manager at *Shape It!* she's started speaking in her own voice, even when Will's around.

"That's Zimbabwe/Zimbabwe, you mean," he counters.

"Huh?" Deedee looks confused. She really does look like Chas, tall, blonde and bony, give or take the Jennifer Beals *Flashdance* outfit. Funny that after all his flesh-sampling he'd end up with a tomboy. We explain the aardvark/Zimbabwe exchange the night of Rock Paper Scissors' dust-up at the Paradise.

"Would have been a cool album title," says Will.

"Still could be," I say. "If we win."

"Right," Chas says. He knows even if we don't get Hammered tonight there's Combat Zone staring us in the face. "Hey, guess who's here?"

"Liz Polar Bear."

"Who else."

251

"Vicki Shehovic?" Will asks.

"Almost. Cindy and Jill."

"Whoa. How did they look?" I turn my head, scanning the crowd.

"Pretty fine." Deedee shoots Chas a warning glance so he doesn't elaborate. But just knowing Jill's in the building gives me a throbbing sensation, even more than Liz Polar Bear's lace bra did. Maybe we should have done "Garden of Eden."

My senses start racing faster than my mind can keep up with: the smooth weight of Jill straddling me, the wet warmth as she guides me inside her, the outline of her perfect breasts in the dim shadows. It's been a couple years, but I'm sure the chemistry would still be there. I could invite them, or at least Jill, to IHOP, see if she's still with her artist. Not likely, if she came here to see us. I've got Kat's car. Could I risk taking Jill back to 1941 Comm. Ave.? My room is the walk-through now. Do I have the nerve to fuck Jill in Kat's bed? Borrow the bread truck and go parking at Revere Beach again? Get a hotel room like real adults do?

Then I flash on Kat, at her parents' house in St. Louis, probably sitting in her summer nightgown rereading one of her old children's books, maybe *A Wrinkle in Time*, staying up waiting for the phone to ring, pile of pistachio shells at her feet. All of a sudden I have the same kind of shitheel feeling I did when, after a particularly pointless and dispiriting disarmament rally at Antioch (held as our new shoot-first president was doubling the defense budget), I'd blown off Maggie to go jam with my lithe young jazz singer, and then come home to find her locked in our bathroom: *Open the door, Maggie. Now. Okay, I'm breaking it down. Shit.* Not that Kat's Maggie. But still. First time I've ever felt guilty *before* cheating on somebody. Maybe I won't bring Jill to IHOP.

There's some commotion onstage, and a figure steps through the red velvet curtain. He's tall, skinny, and vampire pale: Nigel All Nite. He steps to the mic, envelope in hand.

I glance over at Boone, still standing with Annie and Paul and now Jay, a mini-Rock Paper Scissors reunion. Annie puts a hand on Boone's arm, waiting for the news. I know it's our night, not RPS's, but this is as close as she's gotten. Also, Maggie's right – Boone's obviously still in love with her. What can you do?

"We heard a lot of great music tonight," Nigel begins.

"How about giving it up for *all* the bands?" There's a polite round of impatient applause, with a few cheers and whistles thrown in. "We'd also like to thank our co-sponsors: *SCREAM!* The *Bosstown Bean.* In Your Face Records. Guitar City."

"WHO THE HELL WON?" somebody from the audience shouts.

"I was getting to that," Nigel says. "Tonight's winner goes on to the final, next week at the Orpheum. Hope to see you all there."

Will rolls his hand in the air front of him, like Michael Palin in the "gestures to indicate pausing" skit. Jackie puts her arm around his waist, gives an indulgent squeeze. She's only missed one show, Amherst, in the five years we've been here. Probably another reason Will's been so faithful.

Chas and Deedee have their arms interlocked as well. Wonder if she's silently chanting *lose lose lose.*

I'm standing alone, my back against a pole. No cigarette, no blindfold. Now I really, really wish Kat was here. Aside from the gig, it's Kat's birthday, and our six-month anniversary. I found her a copy of *Winterland '78* at In Your Face that's waiting back at the house, along with a cassette of me singing "Shy Girl." I've also started another new song, that's the sonic opposite, almost thrash metal, that I bet the band could really tear into. It's not about Kat, though; it's called "Good as You," and it's the first song I've ever tried writing about my sister. Who knows, maybe if she'd lived I'd be *her* bass player, her Will, vying for the spotlight. But thinking about her for the song made me feel, I don't know, kind of grateful I guess: in spite of all the crap, I *get* to do this. Win or lose, I *get* to bang my head against this wall, *get* to load out our equipment at 2 AM, *get* to trade bad puns at IHOP with my bandmates, *get* to call Kat to celebrate or commiserate with her. Even if it ends tonight, and we don't sell millions, I've *gotten* to do it, make a record, a video, have a band that plays *my* songs.

"So without any further ado…." Nigel tears open the envelope, like it's the fuckin' Academy Awards.

This is it. I straighten up to my full height, press my spine against the cool steel of the support pole.

"…tonight's winner is…"

I cross my fingers, close my eyes and hold my breath.

## Acknowledgments

The author wishes to thank:

Christian Bauman for the impetus;

The Cambridge Writes (Shelby Allen, John Amiard, Kitty Beer, Jackie Fenn, Jeanne Harnois, Marty Levin, David Rich),
The Chill Writers (especially Dom Capossela and Allen Converse),
The Boston Writers' Meetup (especially Kate Estrop and Sarah L. Hill)
for reading, critiquing, and then burning the earliest drafts;

Deirdre Bergeron, Ed Gaffney, Sarah Pinsker, Nancy Welch and Peggy Rothschild for reading early drafts and giving valuable feedback;

Tom Hauck for proofreading and editing the final draft;

David Henry Sterry for the rear jacket copy boot camp;

Brett Milano's *The Sound of Our Town: A History of Boston Rock & Roll* for augmenting my memory;

Cindy McKeown for feedback, encouragement and support;

and my former bandmates for years of great times and music. I'm sure if we got back together we'd be huge.

Purchase of this book entitles the reader to download the accompanying original soundtrack album. To download the soundtrack visit www.terrykitchen.com/nextbigthingsongs. The download key is Zodzniak1981. (Note the download key is case sensitive.)

Made in the USA
Charleston, SC
31 October 2013